Praise for *Things I Want My Daughters to Know*

'An emotional rollercoaster.'—*Now*

'Noble has a gift for tight plotting and rendering female friendships.'—*Entertainment Weekly*

'So fluid, the pages turn themselves.'—*Daily Mirror* (U.K.)

'A moving, poignant *tale*.'—*Bella* (U.K.)

'Her stories strike a genuine chord, with protagonists that are reassuringly "real," flawed, and oh-so-easy to empathize with … An irresistible comfort *read*.'—*Glamour*

'Superbly written and incredibly thought-provoking and poignant.'—*Sun* (U.K.)

'I cried, I laughed, I couldn't put it down.'—Penny Vincenzi

'Perfect stuff to chew on over a long night in.'—*Daily Mail* (U.K.)

'Noble hits her stride in her tearjerker fourth novel. Before Barbara Forbes, a mother of four, succumbs to terminal cancer, she leaves words of wisdom for her four daughters in the form of letters to each of them … [Barbara's] sharp wit and distinctive voice is a nice complement to the four nuanced stories of coping with death ... Noble's tender wit depicts the love between friends as steadfast and magical as any romance.'—*Publishers Weekly*

'This powerful tale packs an emotional punch.'—*Closer* (U.K.)

'[A] witty, affectionate, and unashamedly tearjerking look at female bonding.'—*Red* (U.K.)

'Noble is a mistress of the tearjerking message of love.' —*Express* (U.K.)

'A beyond-the-grave, mother/daughter heartstring-tugger, from the shrewd British novelist ... [*Things I Want My Daughters to Know*] is an unashamed tearjerker.'—*Kirkus Reviews*

'A compelling read, with characters you'll really take to your heart.'—*Heat* (U.K.)

PENGUIN CANADA

THINGS I WANT
MY DAUGHTERS TO KNOW

ELIZABETH NOBLE lives in New York with her
husband and two daughters. She is the inter-
nationally bestselling author of *The Reading
Group*, *The Tenko Club*, *The Friendship Test*,
and *Alphabet Weekends*. *The Girl Next Door* is
her most recent novel.

For more information about the author and
this novel, please visit
www.thingsiwantmydaughterstoknow.com.

Also by Elizabeth Noble

things i want my daughters to know

a novel

elizabeth noble

PENGUIN
CANADA

PENGUIN CANADA

Published by the Penguin Group

Penguin Group (Canada), 90 Eglinton Avenue East, Suite 700,
Toronto, Ontario, Canada M4P 2Y3 (a division of Pearson Canada Inc.)

Penguin Group (USA) Inc., 375 Hudson Street, New York, New York 10014, U.S.A.
Penguin Books Ltd, 80 Strand, London WC2R 0RL, England
Penguin Ireland, 25 St Stephen's Green, Dublin 2, Ireland
(a division of Penguin Books Ltd)
Penguin Group (Australia), 250 Camberwell Road, Camberwell, Victoria 3124, Australia
(a division of Pearson Australia Group Pty Ltd)
Penguin Books India Pvt Ltd, 11 Community Centre, Panchsheel Park,
New Delhi – 110 017, India
Penguin Group (NZ), 67 Apollo Drive, Rosedale, North Shore 0632, New Zealand
(a division of Pearson New Zealand Ltd)
Penguin Books (South Africa) (Pty) Ltd, 24 Sturdee Avenue, Rosebank,
Johannesburg 2196, South Africa

Penguin Books Ltd, Registered Offices: 80 Strand, London WC2R 0RL, England

First published in Penguin Canada paperback by Penguin Group (Canada),
a division of Pearson Canada Inc., 2008. Simultaneously published in the U.S.A.
by HarperCollins Publishers Ltd. and in the U.K. by Penguin Group.
Published in this edition, 2009.

1 2 3 4 5 6 7 8 9 10   (WEB)

Copyright © Elizabeth Noble, 2007

The excerpt from *Her Song* on pages 395–96 is reprinted by kind permission of
HarperCollins Publishers Ltd. © Brian Patten (1981).

Manufactured in Canada.

Library and Archives Canada Cataloguing in Publication data available
upon request to the publisher.

ISBN: 978-0-14-316880-5

Visit the Penguin Group (Canada) website at *www.penguin.ca*

Special and corporate bulk purchase rates available; please see
www.penguin.ca/corporatesales or call 1-800-810-3104, ext. 477 or 474

For my own daughters,
Tallulah Ellen Young
and
Ottilie Florence Young
With my love

Dear All of You,

Despite my controlling streak, there aren't too many rules, so far as the funeral goes. Do it as soon as you can, won't you? Good to get it over with. Lisa knows about the music, if you can bear to go with what I've chosen. We've talked about the committal — you know I only want you lot there, and you know which coffin, and which fabulous outfit. I'd like this poem — which, by the way, I love. Thank God for insomnia and the internet — I'd never have found it otherwise, and you'd be stuck reading something yucky. It should be read by whoever thinks they can do it without crying, because that is my biggest rule. No crying, please. If you can manage it. Oh, and no black. Wear the brightest thing you can find in your wardrobe. Both are clichés, I know, but better the colourful one than the sombre. And try and make the sun shine (although I recognize that this last one might be outside of your control). I'm not saying anything mushy in this letter — strictly business — but I daresay there will be other letters. I have other things to say, she says ominously — if I last long enough to write them ... (don't you just love terminal illness humour?).

I'm sorry you all have to do this; I really am.

So, never ever-ending love, as always ...

Mum

Do not stand at my grave and weep
I am not there, I do not sleep
I am a thousand winds that blow
I am the diamond light on snow
I am the sunlight on the ripened grain
I am the gently falling autumn rain

When you wake in the morning hush
I am the swift uplighting rush
Of quiet birds in circling flight
I am the soft starlight at night
Do not stand at my grave and cry
I am not there, I did not die.

(Isn't that perfect for a funeral in a field?!)

Lisa

Lisa lay back gingerly in her deep aromatherapy bubble bath and looked at the 8" x 10" picture she had taken from the top of the piano downstairs and brought up there with her. She'd propped it behind the taps so that she could see it clearly from where she lay in the steamy water, and now she was trying not to splash it. It was a black-and-white shot of her mother, Barbara and it was taken on her sister Jennifer's wedding day, eight years earlier. Mum looked desperately glamorous, with her salon-fresh hair and artfully artless outfit. No mother-of-the-bride peach suit with matching hat for her. Lisa remembered the hat – three feet wide, floppy brimmed espresso coloured straw. No one sitting in the four pews behind her saw a thing of the ceremony. You couldn't see why, and she no longer remembered, but Mum was laughing her big, loud laugh. Her head was thrown back, the ungainly hat long abandoned, the auburn waves of her hair blown messily across her face by the summer breeze. Her large, expressive mouth was open and wide, so that you could see a filling on the top row of her teeth, and her hazel eyes had almost disappeared into the crinkles of her face. It was an especially great picture of her mother, although Barbara had always been photo-genic. Lisa could almost hear it when she looked at the picture, deep and throaty, and so, so alive. It was Mum's raucous laugh she would miss the most – that, and the smell of Fracas.

She thought about the last big belly laugh they had

shared. It was the day Lisa had helped her mother plan her own funeral. She couldn't bear to do it with Mark, she had said. He would keep crying, and she so badly didn't want to cry. She was almost obsessed by not crying, towards the end. Hannah was too young, obviously. Amanda wasn't around. Off doing whatever Amanda was doing right now. And Jennifer ... well, Jenny Wren wasn't exactly the person that sprang to mind for the task, she said, making a stupid grimacing face and rolling her eyes. No, she wasn't – Lisa could see that. Part of her was horrified, and part flattered, of course.

She hadn't expected it to be hilarious, but now that she thought about it, she didn't know why not. The two of them had done a great deal of laughing together, through all of Lisa's life. Mum had been quite well that week. She was thin, and a bit of a funny colour – a sort of translucent pale lavender – but she was still mobile, and almost energetic. She'd had all these brochures and computer printouts spread across the dining-room table. Coffins, hearses, wreaths ... She always said life was a retail opportunity, but now, obviously, so was death. The last great party you got to go to, they said, if you planned it right. It was macabre and weird for about the first twenty minutes, and then they both just got silly, because that made it easier. Mum had even got prices for those horse-drawn affairs – but they decided that people weren't really ready for a purple crushed velvet, Kray-style East End send-off. She'd planned the clothes, though. She wanted to wear her Millennium Eve party dress, although it was a bit big for her right now. Which was a minor cause for celebration, and almost the justification for an open-coffin ceremony, since she'd eaten cabbage soup for a week and had one of those ridiculous

4

lymphatic wrap things in order to squeeze into it on December 31st, 1999, and it hadn't been near her since January 1st, 2000, when the wrap wore off and all the cellulite flooded back. Lisa remembered the dress – it was emerald green, lithe and silky, and her mum had looked amazing in it. The kind of good that almost makes adult daughters a little bit resentful. There'd been an underwear issue – she'd talked Mum into the first and last thong of her life, convincing her it was the only acceptable option under the dress bar going commando. Mum had rung, on New Year's Day, to say it was so uncomfortable she'd taken it off after about an hour and seen the New Year in knickerless – with a Magistrate and a headmaster at the table, if you please. More laughing.

'Isn't that a bit of a waste of a perfectly lovely Ben de Lisi? I was hoping I might have that,' she had joked. Actually joked. Jennifer would have been fulminating. 'Too bad,' said her mum, winking. 'There'll be a bit of money. Use it to buy one of your own.'

What really did them in was the music. Mum said she couldn't bear to have something miserable – no 'Abide With Me' ('no one can ever make the high notes – you can always hear the tear in their voice'); no 'Nearer My God to Thee' ('Too *Titanic*.') 'Lord of the Dance' was nixed because it reminded her of Michael Flatley, and who the hell wanted to think of that daft prancer as they were shuffling off their mortal coil? And 'He's Got the Whole World' was far too tambourine-y. She'd got a fondness for 'Jerusalem', which was more wedding than funeral, but who cared? And definitely, definitely 'Be Thou My Vision', although preferably the Van Morrison version, piped in, even if it sounded tinny in the high-ceilinged church. She had also surfed the net for a website recommending popular non-religious music choices, however, and it was this list that finally had them shedding tears of mirth. Frank Sinatra's 'My Way': 'As if dying at 60 would ever be *my* way!' Gloria Gaynor's 'Never Can Say Goodbye': 'Well, I suppose it's more appropriate than "I Will Survive,"' she spat out through the chortles, 'but who the hell *are* these people, and why have I never been invited to one of their funerals?' Imagining the coffin being carried out to the saccharine strains of Doris Day's 'Que Sera Sera' made their ribs hurt, and the idea of quietly listening to Vera Lynn's 'We'll Meet Again' sounded like the funniest thing ever to the pair of them. When they'd regained their breath and dried their wet faces, they'd settled on Louis Armstrong's 'Wonderful World'. But the moment her mum nodded decisively and wrote it down on the A4 pad in her round, girlish handwriting, Lisa heard it playing in her head, imagined the scene and had to turn her face away so her mum didn't identify the fresh tears she refused to see.

Now that day – the day they had meticulously planned, but that, somehow, found her so very unprepared, was here. Van Morrison and Louis Armstrong were lined up in the portable CD player and the organist had his sheet music open at 'Jerusalem'. Just that now it wasn't funny any more. Lisa sank down into the hot water so that it splashed around her nostrils and squeezed her eyes shut. If only, if only, if only Andy was here.

Jennifer

Stephen said he was parking the car, but he'd done that. The driveway was full: Mark's car, and Mum's Polo. Lisa's VW beetle – she'd said, when they'd spoken the previous morning, that she was going to stay the night. So he'd driven a little down the street and expertly parallel parked. She could see him, for God's sake. He'd switched off the ignition and wound the window down a little. Now he'd picked up his BlackBerry and was staring at it intently. Today was terribly inconvenient for him. She'd gotten that message. He had these clients, passing through London on some trip from somewhere. They'd only had today to see him; they were important. He'd made sure she understood that. Not more important than her, obviously, since he was here, and not there but it was close. And he hadn't been gracious about it. She hadn't needed to know, after all, anything about any clients, or meetings, or power lunches. She was burying her mother today. It shouldn't have mattered. He was her husband. Everything about his demeanour, all the way here, had been irritated. The reception got fuzzy on the radio. He'd switched if off viciously. The line for a coffee at the service station was too long. He'd sighed dramatically, and bought a Coke. And now it was too hot. He'd hung the jacket of his black suit on the hook of the back passenger door, unbuttoned the neck of his shirt and loosened the black knitted tie. She stood at the end of the driveway for a few minutes, realizing she was too embarrassed to go into the house without him. They should be together. He should *want* to be with her, shouldn't he, today of all days?

Stephen hated funerals. He'd confessed to her, once,

long ago, that coffins terrified him. He couldn't stop thinking about the body inside. Wondering how it looked, how it smelt, how it would feel to the touch. He remembered losing it completely, when he was about 8 years old, at his grandfather's funeral – having to be taken out of the crematorium, screaming.

He was right about the weather, at least. It was too sunny for this. It was what Mum would have wanted, but to Jennifer it seemed wrong. It was like the day those two planes flew into the World Trade Center. As they made their final descent into hell the sky behind them was too impossibly, perfectly blue. It wasn't the right backdrop. She wanted a slate-grey sky and drizzle; she wanted to shiver with the chill. Not this beautiful day, not today.

The door opened and Mark stood on the doorstep. 'Jen?' Jennifer shuffled from one foot to the other, feeling like she'd been caught out. She waved and gestured towards Stephen. 'We'll be there in a minute. Stephen's just . . .' but Mark was coming towards her. He wasn't dressed – not for the funeral. He had on a pair of linen shorts and a scruffy pink T-shirt, and he was barefoot. He didn't speak when he got to her, just opened his arms and drew her into a tight embrace. Jennifer felt herself stiffen momentarily, then relax and lean into the man who had been her stepfather for the last sixteen years. God knows she needed the hug.

When he drew back, he put his hands on either cheek and looked intently into her face. He smelt of soap and coffee. 'How are you doing?'

'I'm okay. You?'

'I'm trying.' He shrugged his shoulders. 'She got the weather she ordered, hey?' Jennifer nodded, and smiled weakly.

8

Mark looked behind her, at Stephen. 'He coming in?'

'He's just got to check a few things . . . There's a lot going on, you know, at work, and . . .'

Mark took her hand and the squeeze he gave it said 'Don't explain him, don't defend him.' Out loud, he just said, 'Don't worry, no hurry. Amanda's not here yet. Show doesn't start for a couple of hours. Come on in – I've got some coffee going, and muffins and croissants . . .' Jennifer gave the back of Stephen's head one more sad, reproachful glance, and went into the house with Mark.

Hannah

Hannah stared at her face in the mirror and wondered whether it was okay to wear mascara. She couldn't wear it to school, but she could at the weekends and on holidays. To Church? There'd never been a rule that she'd known of. Maybe if she wore it she wouldn't cry, because she'd know that then it would run. Maybe wearing it would help her not do it.

'No one was with her when she died.' That was a line from *Charlotte's Web*. It had been one of her favourite books when she was young. And that was one of her best bits, the line when Charlotte the spider had finished her web-making, egg-laying mission, and gently slipped away into oblivion. 'No one was with her when she died.' It was so deliciously sad. You could revel in it, in the small dry ache it caused at the back of your throat and the little sting in your ribs. When she was younger, Hannah liked to feel sad, so long as it was 'artificial' sad; that was what she called it when the sadness was about something that wasn't real. Like when Leonardo

DiCaprio slips beneath the icy waves at the end of *Titanic*, with Kate Winslet hoarsely whispering her promise never to forget him. Or when Charlotte died. Well, this was different. This sad was real; the ache wasn't fun. Trying not to cry was a huge effort, one she made all the time, all day, until she got into bed at night, and didn't have to try not to any more. Especially today. They'd all promised that they wouldn't. They'd promised Mum, although Hannah didn't think it was fair of her to ask for that. Still, none of it was fair, was it? She tried not to think about Charlotte anymore. Unhelpful bloody spider! There'd been loads of people around when Mum died, anyway. She'd died in a crowd scene. All of them there, around that horrible high hospital bed they'd brought in, so incongruous in the pretty room. Her sisters, Jen and Lisa . . . Dad. And the vicar, and the doctor – both more by accident than design, she thought. It made her think of a Philip Larkin poem she'd learnt at school – something about the priest and the doctor running across the fields in their long coats trying to figure out all the answers to all the questions. The doctor came every other day, checking up on Mum. The vicar came because Mum had asked for him, which was slightly odd, since Hannah only really ever remembered seeing him before this year on Christmas morning, once every three hundred and sixty-five days, belting out 'O Little Town of Bethlehem', the tip of his nose perpetually bright red and dripping with a winter cold. She told Dad she was hedging her bets. Not in front of the vicar, of course. And even more people downstairs, Mum's friends, in and out on a rota, making tea that no one wanted to drink and sandwiches no one wanted to eat and taking phone calls no one else wanted to answer.

She decided against the mascara, and picked up the

hairbrush, running it through her long auburn hair. Mum's hair. Dad's hair was silvery above the ears, and still pretty dark on the top. That would have been okay too – the dark, not the silver. But she had Mum's hair. When she'd finished, she sat on the end of her bed, with her hands folded in her lap, squeezed tight together. And waited.

Jennifer didn't want coffee, but she took a mug for something to do with her hands, and wandered across the large living room. The house was immaculate. It was a great house for the summer. Mark had built it. Not with his own hands – he was an architect, and he'd designed it for him and Mum the year they married, just before Hannah was born. They'd bought a hideous bungalow with peeling, custard-yellow paint, on a lovely three-acre plot, and immediately knocked it down, even as the neighbours watched, open-mouthed, muttering to each other about how the elderly couple who had sold it to them had bothered to remove every picture hook and filled every crack in the place. It had taken six months to build the new place, and they'd lived in a caravan on the site the summer it went up. Jennifer remembered her mother standing on the steps of the van, pregnant with Hannah, offering cups of tea made on a camping stove. She remembered how obscene it had looked to her then. Jennifer had been 22. She hadn't lived at home since she was 18, and she felt like she barely knew Mark. It was all wrong – her mother, 45 years old, with her vast, fertile baby-belly. Living in this temporary squalor with a man ten years younger than she was. Jennifer had been embarrassed for her then, or for herself.

Now she stood staring at the garden out of the tall glass doors that ran the entire length of the back of the house downstairs and wondered whether she'd just been jealous. She'd never lived here; she'd never really been a part of the family that happened here, the happy, laughing life they'd had before Mum got ill. Each corner showed her a different memory. Baby Hannah, with her smooth, round arms and legs kicking contentedly on a plaid blanket under that apple tree. Her mother, kneeling at her beloved herb garden, tending the fragrant plants. Mark flipping burgers on the barbeque; Mum, radiant with happiness and contentment. She'd always been just a visitor.

Stephen loved the house. He'd spent hours, the first time he'd come, wandering around with Mark, looking at details Jennifer had never really taken in. His questions, and examinations, had gone way beyond flattery, although Mark was always happy to show it off. She knew he wanted something like it for himself, one day. They couldn't afford it now, of course. Their flat was a good start – right area, high ceilings, great light. It was modern and fashionable, all dark wenge wood and stainless steel. But it was nothing like this, and it had nothing to do with money. It just didn't have the heart.

Mark came and stood by her, gazing into the garden. 'Needs a damn good water. Everything's dying.' He didn't seem to realize what he had said.

She smiled at him. 'You've been busy. Cut yourself some slack.'

'She'd be cross.'

'No, she wouldn't.'

Mark smiled his half-smile at her, and she smiled back. 'Okay, maybe a bit cross.'

Then, 'Where's Hannah?'

'Upstairs. Lisa was having a bath – I think Hannah's in her room.'

'No Andy?'

'No. Haven't asked her about it. She came last night. We had a curry and too much red wine. But she hasn't mentioned him.'

Jennifer nodded. She wondered if she ought to offer to go and see Hannah. She didn't want to. 'How is Hannah doing?'

'She's quiet. She's been quiet for days. No crap music blaring out of her room. She hasn't been on the phone much to her mates, and no one's been round. I expect they'd like to come, some of them, but I don't think she's spoken to any of them. I'm not even sure she's told them, although they must know by now. She hasn't even watched *Coronation Street*, which has me *really* worried.' He was trying to sound lighthearted, but he was failing.

'It's early days, Mark. She's lost her mum. She's only 15.'

'I know. It's . . . it's hard. I'm trying, but I don't have a lot of juice left in my tank, you know? I know she needs me. But I need . . . I need Barbara. I need her to help me. And she's not here.'

Upstairs, someone knocked gently on Hannah's door.

'C'mon in.'

It was Lisa, still damp from the bath, wrapped in a bath sheet.

'You got any make-up, Hannah? I forgot mine. Can you believe it? Can I come in?'

Hannah nodded, and pointed to her dressing table. 'Not much. Some – mascara and lip gloss and stuff. You can borrow whatever you want.'

'Cheers.' Lisa closed the door again behind her, and let the towel fall to the ground. She was wearing a strapless bra, and she had a thong on. They were beige, with lace, and they looked expensive, and nice. Hannah felt shy, and Lisa saw her glance away.

'Excuse the blatant semi-nudity but I'm so hot. That bath was boiling, and it must be 90 degrees out there already. I should have had a cold shower, really.' She was pretty red, and her legs were blotchy. 'I forget you're not really used to sisters running around naked. Me and Jen did it all the time when we were younger.' That didn't sound like Jennifer. 'It's fine, really.' Lisa caught her sister's glance. 'Okay . . . not Jennifer. Just me. I ran around naked all the time when we were younger. Jen just tolerated it.'

Lisa sat down in front of the dressing table and started applying make-up, although Hannah didn't think she really needed it. She was dead pretty. Lisa's hair was much lighter than her own – strawberry blonde, with really light bits in it. And she had all these freckles, tiny ones, across her nose and cheeks. But her lashes and eyebrows were surprisingly dark (maybe she did something to them?), above eyes that were more green than hazel most of the time, and almond shaped. Hannah didn't think Lisa had had spots when she was young – if she had, there was no photographic evidence in the albums Mum kept. She was slim and tall, with great skin and hair that just looked nice, without you spending ages on it – the kind you could just put up in a ponytail, and the ponytail didn't make you look like you hadn't had time to wash it – it looked pretty and natural. Hannah felt a stab of envy and misery. She wasn't spotty, or fat, or ugly, or anything. She knew that much, at least. She just didn't feel comfortable in her own skin like Lisa seemed to. She wasn't easy like her sister was. She'd rather die than have anyone see her in her bra and knickers.

'What are you wearing?' she asked Lisa.

'Well . . . Mum really did a number on me with her "brights and primaries only" thing. I'm more of a black and beige girl, myself; neutrals all the way. I found something in the summer sales. Don't you hate how they have those in July – it's like summer's over before it even starts, don't you think? It's bright yellow. A bit Jackie O, I thought. A sundress, thank God! I doubtless look like a giant banana in it. But it fits the bill. You?'

'I've got this pink dress from last summer. I wore it to a wedding – my friend Amy's sister got married and she was allowed to invite one friend, and she took me. Mum got it for me, so I think she liked it. It's a bit sparkly, is all . . .' Hannah's voice tailed off.

Lisa looked at her in the mirror, through narrowed eyes. 'She'd love that even more,' she said, as gently as she could. She swivelled around on the stool.

'Hannah?'

Hannah stood up. 'Don't be nice to me, Lisa. You'll make me cry. Please don't, okay? Let's just get it over with; I just want to get it over with. Doesn't matter what we're wearing, does it? It's a stupid, stupid rule.'

Lisa nodded, and when she spoke again, she made her tone jokey. 'Well, you and Jennifer have that opinion in common, at least. She was bitching about it the other night on the phone. Said that Stephen would refuse to wear anything but black; said she was thinking about it. I said she could compromise – black dress, red shoes, you know. God knows what she'll be wearing when she turns up.'

'What about Amanda?'

'God knows if *she'll* even turn up . . .'

They smiled hopefully at each other. That was how Amanda was – you wouldn't exactly count on her in a crisis, although neither of them really doubted that she would be here today.

'Is someone coming with you?'

'No.' Lisa looked at her quizzically. Hannah shrugged. 'Didn't ask anyone. I don't really want anyone to come. How about you? Andy isn't coming?'

'No, he's not.'

'How come?'

That was a good question . . .

The sound of a car stopping outside the house saved Lisa from further questions. The engine idled, doors were opened and closed again. Hannah ran to the window.

'It's Amanda.' Until she heard the words, and felt the relief, Lisa hadn't realized how much she needed to hear that her sister had arrived.

Amanda

Amanda paid the taxi driver and thanked him, as he heaved her rucksack out of the boot of his car.

'Blimey, girl, are you telling me that you lug this thing halfway around the world?'

'Someone has to!'

'What the hell have you got in it? Bricks?'

'No bricks, no. My entire life.'

'That explains it!' He doffed an imaginary cap at her, like Dick van Dyke in *Mary Poppins*, and opened the driver's door. 'Good luck to you, then, girl. And welcome home.'

'Thanks.'

Home.

She'd been 8 years old when they'd come to live here, in the house that Mark built. She'd lived here for eleven years. And then she'd left. Not permanently, of course. She'd been back. Sometimes for months at a time, sometimes just for the night. And she'd had other places to live. Flatshares, rented flats, rooms in houses, university halls . . . But this was still the place she thought of as home; still the address she wrote in the boxes on the forms.

This time she hadn't been back for nearly three months. She hadn't seen Mum when it was really bad, and she hadn't been here when she died. That was deliberate, and, at the time, she believed, or so she told herself, that Mum understood, and that it was okay. But now she didn't know whether or not she was glad that she had missed it. She looked back down the road to where the taxi was driving away, and felt a familiar flight impulse, and then she turned back to the house. With some effort she hoisted her backpack onto her shoulder and trudged up the path. Mark saw her and came to the front door. Behind him, she saw her three sisters. When she reached her stepfather, Amanda put the rucksack down beside her and almost fell into his arms, and the two of them stood there for a long time, without speaking, holding each other. After a minute, Hannah pushed past Jennifer and Lisa on the threshold, and wrapped her arms around her father and her sister. 'You're home!'

Stephen, presumably having finished whatever crucial business he had been conducting in the car, was coming up the path to the front door, adjusting his tie. He sidestepped the emotional scene and went into the welcome cool of the entrance hall. 'I see the Prodigal Daughter has returned,' he remarked wryly as he passed his wife. Jennifer threw him a withering look. 'Sssh!'

Behind him, a few other people were starting to arrive now. Mark's brother Vince and his wife Sophie were parking behind Stephen, and more cars behind them. These were the prime spaces – you could walk to the church from here. Mark remembered strolling back, flanked by friends and family, one beautiful May morning, after Hannah's christening, as she slept in his arms. Some of the same cast would be here today. Looking at them, he groaned quietly. 'Christ, should have got my trousers on earlier!' He released Amanda, and went out into the front to say hello, and be hugged, and answer inane questions about parking.

Hannah and Lisa took the rucksack between them and set it down at the bottom of the stairs.

'You cut that a bit bloody fine, didn't you?' Jennifer didn't mean it to sound as harsh as it did.

'Don't start on her,' Lisa chided. 'Not now.'

'I'm sorry.'

'No, *I'm* sorry. I didn't mean to make you worry.'

'You never do.' Jennifer said this quietly, and under her breath. Lisa was the only one who heard.

'Go and make her a cup of tea, or coffee, or something, will you?' Looking Amanda up and down, she asked, 'I assume you've come straight from somewhere, right?'

'From Stansted. Yes, please. I'm parched.' Jennifer sniffed into flared nostrils and went to the kitchen.

'Come upstairs. We've got to get out of these dressing gowns. Why the hell are people arriving early? It's not like you need a great seat – she's in a bloody basket! Is that what you're wearing? *Please* say it isn't. Hannah, can you manage the rucksack . . . ?'

'Where the *hell* have you been?'

They were in Hannah's room now, with the door closed behind the three of them. Lisa was climbing into her startlingly yellow dress, not looking straight at her.

'You sound like Jennifer. And I thought you'd rescued me from her wrath downstairs.'

'I did, but only so I could subject you to mine up here. And my wrath might be less frequent, but it's not less scary. Where the hell have you been, Mand? Mark's got to have been going nuts.'

'*Has* Mark been going nuts, Hannah?'

Amanda looked to her little sister for support. Hannah shrugged. 'He just said you'd be here if you could.'

Amanda looked at Lisa, who gesticulated in exasperation.

'That's not the point, Mand. *I've* been going nuts, okay. *I've* been going nuts.'

'I wrote, in that email, that I'd be here.'

'Almost a week ago.'

'And I'm here.'

'Just.'

'But I'm here.' Lisa threw her hands out in exasperation, then turned to the mirror, saw her big yellow self and snorted.

Amanda was rummaging in her rucksack. She had, of

19

course, been wearing what she thought might do for the church. She just didn't want to admit it.

'Bright, right?' she now asked Hannah.

'Bright.' Hannah shrugged. 'Mum's wishes.'

'Right . . . Bright.' She opened another flap, and started pulling creased clothes out of the pack's dark recesses. 'She'd be lucky to get clean, let alone bright. Even the stuff that started out life bright isn't so bright now . . .' Her voice cracked. Lisa softened. She put a hand on Amanda's back, as she bent over a pile of her stuff. 'Are you okay?'

Amanda's eyes had filled with tears. 'I'm fine.'

She wasn't fine. Of course she wasn't fine. Had it been a week? It could have been a month, or just two minutes. Time had stopped, there in the internet café. The world had gone weird. She'd sat, for ten minutes, looking at the screen. Mark's address . . . the red exclamation mark flashing urgency at her. The email was dated with yesterday's date; no heading – it didn't need one. She knew, before she pushed the button that opened the text and made it real: Mum was dead.

She hadn't gone far, this time. She'd been in Spain. Working at a beach bar on the Costa Calida, near Murcia. Staying with some friends of friends whose parents had a little villa out there near the sea. It wasn't somewhere she would normally have stayed for long. But she couldn't have gone further. She'd been waiting, waiting for this email.

When it finally came, she sent a one-line reply, saying she'd be home. And now she was. In the five days between, she had drunk too much tequila, taken long walks along the beach and resisted the urge to change her tickets home to somewhere else, *anywhere* else.

But it wasn't because of the trouble she would inevitably be in with her sisters. She found the idea of other people's grief far more frightening, far harder to cope with than her own. She had come home to immerse herself in it, and she was afraid it would feel like drowning. It wasn't going to be like some film – *Steel Magnolias* or *Terms of Endearment*, where the funeral marked the end of the really bad time, and the start of everyone getting better. It wasn't going to be like that at all: it was going to be the beginning.

Hannah took her hand. 'I'm glad you're here now. I don't really care where you've been.'

'Thanks, Hannah.' Amanda let herself be held. It wasn't something that happened often. Mum had always said she was a wriggly cuddler – unwilling to sit still and be embraced. Mum once said she'd almost enjoyed it when Amanda was poorly as a young child – it was the only time she allowed her to put her arms around her and stroke her hair.

Jennifer came in without knocking. Amanda readied herself for round two.

'Listen, Jen. I know you're mad at me, and you probably have every right. I'm sorry I took off and left it to all of you. I know it was selfish and cowardly, and all that. And I'm sorry if you thought I would be back sooner. I just needed a bit of time, that's all, to let it sort of sink in. I know – selfish again. That's me, hey? But I really am sorry. And I really am here now. Can we leave the flagellation out, just for today. Hey?'

'What's flagellation, anyway?' Hannah asked.

'Beating. Brought on by guilt.'

'No one wants to beat you up, Amanda.' Jennifer tried

to sound less like a teacher. 'I just thought we should be together for this. For *all* of this.'

She was biting back. Amanda was right. She *was* mad. It wasn't fair – she'd buggered off, and left it all to the rest of them. And now she was crying, damn her, and that just wasn't supposed to happen.

Hannah stepped between the two of them, facing her oldest sister. 'Please, Jennifer. Don't be angry at her, not today.' She held her gaze, and Jennifer was shocked, as she often had been in the last couple of years, at how grown up she looked and seemed. 'Today is about Mum: our mum.' And she was right.

Amanda and Jennifer joined hands on either side of Hannah's hips, and pulled her into a hug, which Lisa joined, her arms encompassing all three of them, and squeezing tight.

Like sisters throughout time, whatever battles raged between them, it was always, always, all four of them against the rest of the world. They emerged from Hannah's room a few minutes later, holding hands, Amanda dressed in something Hannah had found in her wardrobe, her hair pulled back from her face, her tears dried.

The church wasn't too bad. Amanda said they looked like extras from some cheesy musical, or a girl band scoring nil points at the Eurovision Song Contest, all dressed in their bright colours – Lisa in yellow, Hannah in pink, Amanda wrapped in orange and red – and even Jennifer, in a sky-blue shift dress. They stood ramrod straight in the front pew, flanked by Mark – now changed into a purple linen shirt – and Stephen, who remained resolutely and ostentatiously dressed in black, but at least he had left his BlackBerry in the car. They got there early, so they wouldn't have to watch everybody else file in, and they didn't turn around. They knew it would be full. Mum had a lot of friends; friends they would eventually have to talk to, they knew, at the wake. But not now.

It was the committal that made them break 'the big rule'. Barbara had chosen a humanist site, about three miles from the church where they held the service. She said she couldn't bear to be cremated, with that supermarket conveyor belt effect, and the vaguely comical curtain that opened and closed, and that she didn't want to be put in the ground in a churchyard. So she was going to decompose gently, in a biodegradable coffin, and go back to the earth. And eventually have a tree growing on top of her that they could come to, if they wanted to, and visit her. In an expanse of green with grass and butterflies, she said, instead of some depressing grey field of marble and granite. She said it would save them a fortune in flowers. Jennifer remembered the night she had told them that, remembered being jealous that she'd sorted everything out with Lisa. Why not her? Mark had squeezed Barbara's hand, all serious and po-faced. Then he'd whispered to her, 'Christ, you want flowers as well! Is there no end to the demands?'

Which was how the four of them, along with Mark and Stephen, came to be standing alone except for the officiant, on a hot August afternoon, with the heat haze shimmering all around them, in a field, in front of a strange and beautiful woven willow casket containing their mother, reputedly resplendent in emerald green Ben de Lisi, listening to Van Morrison sing 'In the Garden' on a tinny tape recorder. Where every one of them cried exactly as much and for as long as their broken hearts dictated.

'God, Mark, you're going to be eating Coronation Chicken for the rest of the month!' A bunch of Barbara's local friends had catered the wake, and cleaned up, storing leftovers in clear Tupperware containers. They'd done a beautiful job. It had looked for all the world like a party – a wedding, maybe, or some family reunion. There were trestle tables set out on the lawn, draped in yellow crêpe paper, and jugs and vases with roses cut from the garden dotted between the large bowls of rice and potato salads, French bread and heirloom tomatoes. There were trays of oatmeal biscuits, and small bowls of strawberries, with dishes of clotted cream, sweaty in the heat. People had drunk Pimms and real lemonade. It had all been beautiful. Instead of the low, respectful hum usually heard at funerals, there had been laughter, and stories, and a soundtrack from inside the house of Simon and Garfunkel and the Mamas and the Papas. The men were not shifting uncomfortably from foot to foot, hands in pockets; the women did not have red-rimmed eyes. It was exactly how she would have wanted it to be – good friends, good food, good weather. Just no good reason.

Barbara's friends had cleared up too, graciously and more cheerfully than they felt, and now they had gone and the family was alone, sat in the living room, staring at the vast Tupperware offerings on the kitchen counter.

'Looks that way.'

The music was switched off now. Lisa had kicked off her shoes, and was curled into the corner of the sofa, her legs beneath her. Hannah was almost dozing, her head on her sister's lap. Amanda was cross-legged on the floor, her back against a stool.

At the front door, Jennifer was being hugged goodbye by Stephen. Barely. His lips were dry against her cheek, and his arms had no squeeze in them as he held her. He'd tried to take her hand, walking back from the burial to their car, and she'd let him take it for a minute or two. She was irrationally angry with him about the black suit and tie, and the BlackBerry. And, of course, mostly about the one thing totally beyond his control. She knew that too; she knew work was busy at the moment. She knew he'd missed too much, really, in the weeks before Barbara's death. But she was still mad at him. When he put his arms around her, she held herself a little stiff, and wouldn't relax into the embrace.

'Are you sure that you want to stay?'

'Yeah. I haven't seen Amanda in a long time, Hannah is a mess and I don't want Mark to be by himself . . .'

'Aren't Amanda, Hannah and Lisa here to look after him?' His tone was almost sarcastic, almost amused. 'You look exhausted.'

'I just buried my mum, Stephen . . . How do you expect me to look?' She didn't want to go home with him, that was the truth of it. She wanted to stay here.

'I didn't mean that.' He knew it, whether she told him or not. He knew she'd rather be with all of them tonight. He tried not to let it hurt him.

'I know. Sorry.'

'I'm sorry.' God, this politeness.

'I'll be back tomorrow, by the time you get home from work. Lisa'll drop me off, I'm sure. Or maybe I'll take a train . . .'

Stephen raised his hands in a gesture of unnecessary surrender. 'Fine, fine . . . Seems to me, to be honest, like you haven't really needed me all day.'

'Is that what you want to feel – like I need you?'

He rubbed his eyes impatiently with one hand. 'You know what, Jen? It's fine that you stay; it's fine.' He kissed her again, the same dry lips skimming her skin. 'I'll see you tomorrow.'

She leant against the doorframe and watched him walk to the car, get in, drive away. He looked back at her, and called out that he loved her, not waiting for an answer. But once again, it felt as if they were on opposite sides of a big hole, a chasm they both made attempts to cross, just never at the same time.

When she got back to the others, Mark was making tea: the national pastime. She got the milk from the fridge and poured some into each mug. He put them on a tray and carried them back to the sofa.

'How mangled are you all feeling?'

Lisa laughed weakly. 'Scale of one to ten? A good nine.'

Hannah raised a limp hand from her reclining position. 'Eleven over here.'

'Why?' Jennifer asked.

'Because there's more,' replied Mark. 'Not the official stuff – we'll sort that out at the lawyers. This is your Mum. She did manage to write a few more letters, like she said. I have them. I was supposed to give them to you all after this was finished. I'd have waited until tomorrow, but Jen's not going to be here . . .'

'I am, actually. Stephen just left . . .'

Lisa raised an eyebrow quizzically at her sister.

'He's got an early start tomorrow. I just thought . . .'

Mark put a hand on her shoulder. 'I'm glad you're here. Your Mum would be pleased – to know that all her girls were here together.'

They didn't open them right away. It wasn't Christmas morning, after all. Each of them held their letter in their lap. Amanda tried to remember what her mum's hands looked like, imagining them holding the envelope. They chatted until they were too tired. Hannah fell asleep, and had to be gently shaken. They peeled off one by one, a subdued chorus of Waltonesque goodnights issuing forth on the upstairs landing, and went to bed, glad, at least, to have put the day behind them.

Lisa

The letter was stuck to the outside of a rectangular box, about one foot square. It was tied with a wide green ribbon. Just the packaging was a reminder – Barbara always wrapped things beautifully. An organza ribbon, or a wax seal, or plain brown paper with sprigs of lavender tied in utilitarian string. It was her signature. Lisa left the package there while she undressed and slipped naked underneath the duvet. She looked at it for a moment, almost afraid of it, and then slipped the letter out of its envelope, her hand faltering as she opened the page: Mum's writing, as familiar as her own, neat and rounded on the page.

My lovely Lisa,

We're the closest, you and me, in many ways. I think we're a lot alike. You're my firstborn child, and the

27

*person who first showed me the miracle of this love a
mother has for her child. You made every morning
Christmas morning. Thank you for that. There's lots of
things I don't even think I need to say to you because
I think you know them already. I love you. So much.
You're the strongest, I think. Too strong for your own
good, maybe. Ask Andy about that sometime. By the way,
I love him – did I ever tell you that? So to you, my
darling girl, a request, instead of a bequest. Look after
your sisters for me. Look after Mark. And let someone
look after you.*

Mum

*PS Re the contents of the box: you're right – it would
have been a waste. Wear it when you dance like no one's
watching.*

Inside the box, neatly folded and lain on white tissue
paper, was the emerald green Ben de Lisi dress.

Andy answered the phone on the second ring. Lisa's
voice sounded muffled and hoarse.
    'That was quick,' she said.
    'I thought it might be you.'
    'It's me.'
    'Hello, me.'
    'What you doing?'
    'Watching footie. You?'
    'Calling you.'
    'How was it?'
    'I'm sorry I asked you not to come.'
    'That's okay.'

'It's not okay, Andy. It was stupid. I don't know what I was thinking.'

'I don't think you really were thinking. I don't mean that to sound unkind – I just mean that it wasn't really about thinking, it was more about feeling. You wanted to do it without me, on your own.'

'Don't be so bloody reasonable with me!'

'Sorry.'

'And don't be bloody sorry!'

Silence.

'It's me who should be sorry.' She paused. 'I wish you had been here.'

'Me too.'

For just a while Lisa sat with the phone and listened to Andy breathing, which was almost as comforting as an embrace. Then she sighed.

'So I guess I'll see you tomorrow.'

'I'll be here.' He was being so careful of her.

'Goodnight.'

'Goodnight, Lisa.'

He'd heard a break in her voice when she said that last word, and that was all he needed. He hadn't been watching the football. He'd been sitting on the sofa in front of the football, but that wasn't the same thing. Now he stood up, grabbed his car keys from the stand by the front door and went where his mind and his heart had been all day.

As he drove, a little too fast via the M25, he listened to the radio, a little too loud, and wondered, not for the first time in the last two years, what the hell was going on in Lisa's head. She wasn't like any woman he'd ever known before. The highs were higher and the lows were lower. They'd been friends first, before they were lovers. They'd met at work; they'd both been with other people. Nothing serious, but it meant romance was off the agenda, and that they got to know each other pretty well before anything happened. He knew that she was clever and fierce, and stubborn and sharp, and that she didn't suffer fools gladly and that she sometimes took three sugars in her coffee when she was hungover, which was not infrequently. She was funny and sarcastic, but never cruel. She was good company – no, she was *great* company.

One day a friend of theirs was made redundant, out of the blue. A bunch of them went to the local wine bar to drown their collective sorrows and bitch about senior management. One by one the others had melted away or staggered off and it was the two of them, setting off to catch the night bus together. She was different drunk. In the office she was immaculate and stylish – to the point of almost seeming unapproachable. Now she looked ten years younger, and those barriers had obviously come way down. She'd taken off her vertiginous heels and climbed into a fountain, then stumbled and sat down squarely in the water, like a toddler, laughing and crying, and gasping. He'd gone in to fish her out, and she'd pulled him down beside her, and then they'd both been too wet and too giggly for the night bus, and they'd gone to the cashpoint for money and taken a black cab home. She gave the driver only one address.

At her flat, she pulled him into the hot shower the same way she'd reached for him in the cold fountain, and they'd undressed each other there, kissing with drunken abandon and then with something else . . .

He wouldn't have taken it any further. He knew she was completely inebriated, and he'd been to that awkward, short movie with other girls before and was determined not to again, but she looked at him through half-closed, only partly-glazed eyes, and told him exactly what she wanted. And then she'd shown him, pushing him back on the soft unmade bed and straddling him, lowering herself onto him gently, but determinedly. When he was buried deep inside her, revelling in how hot and moist and fantastic she felt, Lisa leant forward and whispered his name once, into his open mouth, as if to release him from responsibility, before she leant back, her soft round breasts arching upwards beautifully, to ease herself into a fast, powerful orgasm. And Andy couldn't believe his luck.

He couldn't believe it the next day, either, when she brought him coffee in bed. Three sugars in hers, obviously.

'How come you're so perky?' he groaned at her, rousing himself from a place far, far away, where he could have happily stayed all day.

'Great sex does that for me.'

'It was great sex?'

She slapped his thigh playfully.

'Don't fish for compliments! It *was* great sex, least it was for me. Think you got left a little behind.'

He shrugged sheepishly. To be honest, his memory of the night before wasn't all that detailed.

'But I'll make that up to you, if you like. Tonight?' She looked at her watch. 'Not quite enough time this morning, I don't think . . .'

He put his own mug down on the bedside table and took hers from her. Then he pulled her down next to him, and pushed the dressing gown she was wearing away from her shoulders.

'I suggest we *make* time . . .'

They'd both been very late for the sales meeting that morning.

And that was how it had been – the first six months had flown by in a blur of wine and sex and laughter. In the next six months they'd calmed down a bit. She said she knew when things got serious because they took to lingering in restaurants – eating dessert and drinking coffee, instead of rushing home after one course, desperate to tear each other's clothes off. She said she lost 10lb in the first half of their first year, with all the 'exercise', and put it all on again in the second half, eating pudding.

After a year, he wanted more. That summer, they went on holiday to the Greek Islands. He lay on his beach towel and watched her lovely lithe figure saunter down to the sea to paddle, and realized that he felt as happy as he had ever been. Emboldened by retsina, later that night, he took her hand, told her that he loved her – a sentence he had seldom volunteered – and asked her to move in with him. He wanted to see her every day, and every night. Maybe forever. It had taken her another few months, and several more requests, to agree. After Christmas she'd given up her flat and come to live with him.

On paper, he had what he wanted. He saw her every day and every night. But he didn't have her. He knew it and so did she. She was holding herself back from him. It frightened him. He believed himself in deeper than she was and that made him vulnerable. He wanted things to keep moving, but she was always putting the brakes on. He couldn't keep bringing it up with her. On the couple of occasions when he had tried to talk about what might come next, she withdrew a little, so that his two steps forward ending up feeling like three steps back.

So long as he didn't push, things were good. Things were really great. He worried that he was fooling himself, setting himself up for a fall. What he couldn't figure out – the 64 million dollar question that kept him awake at night – was whether she was holding back because of him, or because of her. And even if he knew the answer, he would keep on doing this because the thing was, he loved her. He couldn't walk away if he wanted to.

So when she said she wanted to do this whole funeral thing alone, he went along with it, and let her do it alone. And when her voice broke on the mobile, he dropped everything, and went to her. And when he parked and climbed out – the car door sounding incredibly loud in the dark, still silence – and caught the twitch of the curtains in the bedroom with the light still on, and waited for her to open the door, and picked her up, clutching her tightly and silently to him, he knew that it had all been the right thing to do. For both of them.

Hannah

Hannah was too sleepy – the night of the funeral – to read her letter. She was still enough of a child that even something like burying her parent couldn't interrupt the rhythm of her needs. She still felt hungry and she still felt tired, even when everyone around her had lost their appetite, and wandered around with the wide staring eyes of the exhausted sleepless. The next morning, when she woke up, a warm, unfamiliar presence was beside her in bed, and she sat up, confused. For just a second, she thought it was her mum. When she was younger, and poorly, Barbara had sometimes slept with her. She remembered nights of coughing and snuffling against her mum's chest, the aroma of Olbas oil wafting from both of them, feeling arms around her and hearing gentle words. 'There, there. Mummy's got you; Mummy's got you.' It wasn't her mum, of course. She hadn't done that for years, and she would never do it again. It was Amanda, curled with her smooth brown back to her, hair spread wildly across the pillow. She didn't mind; she quite liked it. It made her feel like she'd had something important to do, even if she hadn't known she was doing it. Amanda must have been lonely, or sad. Hannah lay back down, and tried to fall asleep again, but she couldn't. The letter was the first thing she saw when she opened her eyes again, lying propped against her alarm clock.

My Hannah,

This is probably hardest for you. I've gone far too soon for you, haven't I? There is still – however much you deny it! – growing up to do, and I'm going to miss it. You know, in all of this, that is the only thing that makes me mad. It makes me so fucking angry that I ... well, that I want to write 'fucking' in a letter to my daughter, who isn't allowed to say the word. Don't be cross with me, sweetheart. It isn't my choice.

You were my magical gift. That I should have been able to conceive you, carry you and give birth to you at 45, when I thought that part of my life was over, was a miracle to me. The funny thing was that I never realized you were missing from my family until they put you on my stomach and I looked into your face for the first time. You were red, and angry, and you had that amazing spiky hair sticking out all over your precious head, and I knew straight away that you'd always been meant to come. You were a present from your wonderful

34

father, and *proof of our love for each other.* (*Doubtless a gross thought right now, but if you keep the letter and read it again in a few years, you won't think so . . .)*

   You are turning into a confident, beautiful, accomplished, wonderful young woman, Hannah. I have to believe that you and I squeezed more than 15 years into our time together, and I want you to know that I have faith in your ability to carry on and to thrive and to be joyous, all without me. Not that you'll ever, ever be without me completely, sweetheart. I'll always be with you. Look after your Dad for me, honey. He's brave and strong on the outside, but you and I know what's going on inside, don't we? And keep talking to him. He'll listen to whatever you have to say, I know.

   I love you, baby girl,

Mum

When she'd finished reading, Hannah put the letter under her pillow. Something was making her feel panic; suddenly she couldn't take the really deep breath she wanted and her lungs felt tight. Tears ran down her face, dripping onto her arms, crossed firmly over her chest.

   Amanda awoke to the sound of her sister's crying. She felt empty. Last night, she'd lain in bed and cried until her head throbbed. The red numbers on the alarm clock projected the time onto the ceiling: 2.30am, 2.45am, 3.00am. She'd staggered to the bathroom, found paracetamol, and swallowed a couple with water from the tap. She sat on the stairs, her sore head against the wall, until her nose unblocked and her breathing had steadied. She didn't want to be by herself. Which was strange and new and a bit scary. She was very good at being by herself. She hesitated outside Hannah's door, and then opened it, very quietly. When Hannah didn't stir, she'd found herself climbing into bed beside her, holding herself tense and rigid under the duvet for a minute or two, until she was sure she hadn't woken her. There were no numbers on the ceiling in here, and after a while – she wasn't sure how long – the pills took hold, and Hannah's steady, gentle breathing calmed her, and she fell asleep.

Now Hannah was crying. There was no need to ask her why, and there was nothing she could say that would help. She pulled her sister down into her arms, and stroked her hair, feeling her vest get wet with tears and snot, and just held her.

All this pain, all this crying . . . It wasn't that she hadn't expected it; she had just underestimated it. It felt like a heavy, dark blanket that had been pulled across all of them. She hadn't known that it would make it difficult to breathe. She hadn't guessed that it would seem so enveloping, and so total, and so permanent.

Jennifer

Which was how Jennifer felt, sitting on the train a few hours later. She felt like she'd escaped. They'd all had breakfast together. Andy had been there, suddenly. No one really had the energy to ask why or how. He'd been sitting on the sofa when she came down, with Lisa's head on his lap. Someone had left muffins and croissants yesterday, and Mark had made cafetières of coffee. All week they'd had the funeral to talk about. Now there was nothing left to say. Last night she had wanted to stay. This morning she just wanted to go. There'd been a bit of a scene – Lisa wanted to drive her. Andy had come in his own car, so they had two – she could use the company, she'd said. Jennifer had wanted anything but. Everyone else seemed to think that sharing helped. She didn't.

It was probably a weird place to read a letter like this, but Jennifer felt safer in this environment, more in control. She couldn't exactly burst into tears on a crowded train, could she? You just didn't do that sort of thing. Anyone in the carriage watching her might have imagined her to be reading a business letter, or a chatty note from an old friend. She arranged her features into a pleasant, innocuous expression, and read.

Darling Jennifer,

You girls only knew me for a part of my life. Children don't ever seem to realize that. I had a life before you, you know. Hell, you never even met me before I had a stretchmark! The big problem with motherhood of girls, it seems to me, is that we're both women. And I know stuff – I've learnt things – been through some of the same things that I watch my girls go through. The trick is helping without interfering, guiding without pushing. I don't know if I've always been very good at that. Sometimes I've pushed too much, and sometimes stood back too far. And lately I think I've gotten it wrong with you. I've watched you, these last couple of years, get more and more unhappy, sweetheart. You're brittle and fragile and hard to reach. And we haven't been as close as I would have liked because of it. And I'm sorry for that. And if you're reading this, it's too late. But know, please, my lovely, complicated little girl, that I loved you, and I always will. You might be interested in this notebook. It's a diary, I suppose. But it's also about the things I know that I wish I could make you know — I suppose I would like to save you from some of what I've been through. Maybe that's a stupid idea. Anyway, read it, think of me, and know that I love you, darling. I've marked the bit I think you should read first. Let your sisters read it, too, when you've finished.

All my love, forever,

Mum

When she had finished reading, she folded the letter neatly, slipped it back inside the untouched folder that had come with it, put both into her handbag and picked up the copy of *The Times* that the previous incumbent of the seat had left behind.

Lisa

In the end Lisa left her own car, and went home in Andy's. She'd come back at the weekend, she said, and get it. She didn't want to be by herself. She'd slept heavily, at last, when he'd arrived. In the morning, early, she'd rolled towards him and started kissing him without opening her eyes and he'd responded to her touch before he was properly awake. They'd made love silently, and sadly. Affirming life, she supposed. Now she sat in the passenger seat with her bare feet up on the dashboard of his car.

'Thank you for coming.'

'You're welcome.'

'I'm sorry I said I could do it without you.'

He shrugged.

'I couldn't, not really. I missed you all day.'

'It doesn't matter.'

'It does; it was mean of me. I'm sorry.'

He reached over and squeezed her knee. 'Shut up, will you?'

She smiled, and put her own hand over his, squeezing back.

'Mum left letters for each of us, you know?'

'Did she?'

'Mmm.'

Andy didn't ask.

'She said she loved you.'

'That's nice.'

'She said I was too strong for my own good, and that I should ask you about that sometime.'

'She was a wise old bird, your mum.'

'So?'

'So what?'

'I'm asking you about it. Am I too strong for my own good?'

Andy considered for a moment.

'I don't think there's such a thing as too strong. Strong has to be good, right? Too independent? Probably. Definitely.' He smiled at her sideways.

'But I asked you to come.'

'And I came.'

'You came.' Lisa looked out of the window, squinting in the sunshine, and spoke almost to herself. 'You came. Lucky me.'

'What shall we do today?'

'Don't you have to work?'

'I called them this morning, told them I wasn't coming in ... Family concerns. *My* family. So – what shall we do?' Today seemed suddenly surreal to her. There was absolutely nothing that she needed to be doing; the craziness of God knows how long before this day had passed. The world looked to her now, from the car window, like a storm had passed. The air was so clear.

'Let's find a park, or a field, or a river. Somewhere no one else is. Let's lie on a blanket, and look at the sky, and hold hands and not talk. Can we do that?'

'We can do that.'

Mum's Thoughts

I've been reading all morning, so now I'm going to do some writing. I won't call it a diary. It won't be anything like that regular a commitment, if I know myself at all. Besides, the entries on lots and lots of days, including the day I started this particular dark chapter in my life, would just be line after line of expletives. All the rude, angry words I can think of; written repeatedly. Lucidity would, I feel, strike seldom. But a bit of writing.

Mark has taken Hannah to the cinema and out for pizza. I didn't ask him to, but he needs to do something. Men need to fix problems, and he can't fix this one, but he can take Hannah away and let me rest. Don't want to rest; can't rest, really, mind keeps rolling. Sometimes I get so scared, so stomach droppingly, skin scrawlingly scared that I can't keep still. I have to pace up and down. Or read. I have this teetering pile of books from a section of the bookshop I had never ventured into before. Actually, the bookshop is where I had my first taste of the new face the world was going to make at me. I've been going there for years – support your local independent shops, as they say. We lost the butcher and the greengrocer, but we've kept the bookshop, so far. I wouldn't mind if it went a bit Waterstones, mind you. A sofa would be great, a coffee bar – something like that. Or even just Saturday kids who know how to alphabetize. But I'm a loyal customer, even if I occasionally buy a beach read for £3.97 at Tescos – I always feel guilty when I do. I bought my Enid

41

Blytons there for you girls. Then the Penguin Classics, for O-levels, and the Letts Guides. Got my Teach Yourself language tapes there (money well spent – hear me order lunch in 10 different languages and marvel), and the Highway Code, of course, during what I now refer to as the Terror Years, when you lot were learning to drive. Crikey, Hannah – yours are still to come . . . I may be tearing my hair out before it falls out, ha ha! So they know me, and I know them. They knew when I got an Aga, for God's sake, and had to go in and get a Mary Berry cookbook because all I could manage to serve up was charcoal sausages.

They'd never seen me in the self-help section. And there I was, suddenly studying the shelves with intent and buying these books – in hardback, at great expense. Taking Control of Cancer, The Living with Cancer Cookbook, Challenge Cancer and Win!: The Independent Consumer's Guide to the Non-Toxic Treatment and Prevention of Cancer. And I'm just scratching the surface. There are mountains of them. I don't think I really expected that I would read them, or indeed, that if I did, they would help. It's a bit like when you join the gym. You convince yourself that just writing the first cheque and having your tour of the weights room is somehow going to make you fitter. Well, it doesn't. And this won't cure me, or at least if I am to be cured, it won't be by this. Anyhow, I wished I hadn't. Because they made the face. The oh-my-God-you've-got-cancer-you-poor-cow face. Hate that face, already, and I'm not even bald yet.

Hannah's obsessed with what I will look like without eyebrows and eyelashes. I'm kind of glad, for the first time in my life, to have a relatively sparse and spindly set of both. It would surely be much harder to part with thick, strong, lustrous ones. Someone said your hair can grow back differently – but I liked my hair. I'd like it back just the way it was. I wonder what kind of skull I have. There's such a thing as a good one and a bad one, when it comes to being bald. I don't know. I've had long hair all my life – long, good hair. Bugger! Look, there I go with the expletives. Told you. Why does this bit – the hair bit – matter so much?

Anyway, I digress. So, I bought the books, but I don't expect I'll read them. Haven't I got a teetering pile of unread must-reads by my bed already? I'm the only person in the world who still hasn't finished Captain Corelli's Mandolin. Okay, maybe the only person in the world who admits it. I reckon my mental attitude is doing okay at this point. I've got the full lexicon of warmongering words, and I'm not afraid to use them. Fight . . . Battle . . . Overcome . . . Determination . . . Courage . . . Win . . . I want to do all of those things; I'm ready to do all those things. I want to live – simple as that. We all do, don't we? It's instinctive. Besides, it's 2006. They cure cancer these days. They catch it early, they treat it 'aggressively', (that expression makes me think all the oncologists will charge around the ward looking like Mel Gibson in Braveheart, but I don't suppose that's what they mean. I'd settle for oncologists who look like Mel Gibson, though. Good-looking obstetricians I can live without, but oncologists aren't excavating around downstairs, as my mother would put it): they cure cancer. Success rates are higher than ever. The disease has bad PR, that's for sure. It makes people make the face. But they cure it, and they will cure me.

If I wrote a book (ha, ha), I know what picture I would put on the front cover. I have this fridge magnet – you bought it for me, Lisa, long time ago. I can't remember exactly what it says and I can't be bothered to go downstairs and see, but it's this black-and-white photo of some Edwardian-type women sitting at a table, and it says something about the ladies on the Titanic, who waved away the dessert cart. Makes me laugh every time I remember to notice it. I'd call my book something like Life's Short: Eat Pudding First. Could be a Christmas bestseller, that could.

You can't just do that when you get ill, girls. (Maternal lesson alert!) You have to do it all the time. Do it always. Life is short. Even if you don't get cancer, even if you die an old lady in your bed. It's still a blink and you miss it, ever increasing speed, white-knuckle ride.

I've been pretty good at that, but not always. I'm not perfect, but not bad. I've lived a life. Even had a Shirley Valentine moment, but if you think reading on will reveal the secrets of that to you, you're much mistaken – you don't need to know everything . . . ! (That's called a teaser.) If this goes the way I want it to, I will have died an old lady in my bed. I'm just covering myself in case.

But if you think I'm going to start drinking wheatgrass, you're very much mistaken. Make mine a G&T, ice and a slice . . .

October

'Happy Birthday, Hannah!' They were celebrating in a restaurant. Everyone was there except Stephen, who was working. They'd always done family birthdays at home, but this year the local bistro seemed safer. This was the first birthday. In her head, Hannah called it 'BD' and 'AD': Before Death and After. This was her first birthday AD. So far, so okay. She'd woken up, been to school, come home and changed to come here, and she still hadn't cried today.

'Sweet Sixteen and never been kissed.'

'What do you know about it?'

'I know the look, and I'm not seeing it.'

Hannah pressed her lips into a Marilynesque pout, blew a kiss at Lisa and grabbed her last unopened present. She knew it was Amanda's not so much by process of elimination, but because it wasn't actually wrapped, just shoved in a bag. An ethnic shop type of bag that smelled of sandalwood and still contained a receipt. No card. Occasionally, while she was travelling, Amanda would send a card in lieu of a present – always in a foreign language, always containing a joke no one understood, since it was in Croatian, or Malaysian. In attendance this year, she saw no need for a card to say in writing what she could very well say in person. Mum would have been terribly disapproving. Jennifer's gift had been a big bottle of Stella by Stella McCartney, wrapped in thick lilac paper to match the perfume bottle, and tied with a silver chiffon ribbon. Lisa had given her a Whistles voucher, with a card attached saying the condition was that she be present when it was spent. Mark had upgraded her far too childish shuffle to an iPod that played films and music videos. He'd had the back engraved with her name and even downloaded some concerts onto it. The presents made her feel quite grown up.

'I've got something for everyone now.' They'd finished dinner, and the waiters had brought a chocolate mousse cake with candles on it from the kitchen. All the diners, much to Hannah's excruciating embarrassment, had sung 'Happy Birthday' to her. They were drinking coffee. 'I hope Hannah doesn't mind me doing this here,' Jennifer was continuing, 'but we aren't all together all that often, and I wanted us to all be together for this . . .'

She's pregnant, Mark thought.
She's left Stephen, thought Lisa.

Jennifer pulled out a thick sheaf of papers from a tote bag she'd kept beside her at the table. The pages were all neatly bound with plastic edges. Amanda thought, not for the first time, what a good but scary teacher her sister would have made.

She's not pregnant.
She hasn't left Stephen.

Independently Mark and Lisa wondered whether their disappointment could be heard.
'Mum left us . . . left *me* something, when she died – she left me this.' She held up a colourful folder. 'It's a

46

journal, really. Things she wrote; things she wanted her daughters to know, when she was ill, and when she knew . . . when she knew she was dying. She left it for me first because . . .' she paused, not wanting to say why. '. . . because I'm the eldest, I suppose. But she obviously wanted the rest of you to read it too. I can't give it to everyone all at once, so I've made some copies . . .' She handed them around as though she were giving a seminar. 'I know it's not so personal as the actual thing, you know, the paper she wrote on. You can all have a turn with that – I'm not hogging it. I just thought . . . I just thought we should all have a copy we could keep . . .' Her voice trailed away a little.

The image of Jennifer standing by the photocopier at the office feeding bits of their mum's diary into a machine made Amanda want to laugh. It was so efficient, and *so* Jennifer. Mum would have loved it!

Hannah opened her copy, saw her mother's hand-writing and closed it again. Not tonight.

Lisa and Andy gave Jennifer a lift home. Amanda was staying the night. They put clean linen on the bed in the guest room, giggling as they both fought to be the fastest to pull the elasticated bottom sheet over the corners. Once they'd secured it, Amanda threw herself back onto the mattress, and Hannah lay down too, from the other side, so their heads met in the middle. They both stared at the ceiling.

'I've had too much to drink.'

'Disgusting!'

'I know, I'm a lush. Did you have a nice time, baby?'

'You're going to have to stop calling me baby soon. I'm 16 now. Besides, it's very *Dirty Dancing*.'

'Okay, no more baby. Did you have a nice time, HANNAH?' Amanda turned her head too fast to look at her sister.

'I did.'

Amanda was still looking at her, or squinting, in a sort of unfocused way.

'I *really* did. I mean, I was afraid, a bit, that I'd be all sad. But I was okay.'

'You were cool.'

That felt nice.

'And now I'm going to go to sleep.' Amanda closed her eyes.

'You're still dressed. And you haven't brushed your teeth.'

Amanda laughed, but she didn't open her eyes. 'What are you, the personal hygiene police?'

Downstairs, Mark was waiting for her.

'I've got something for you . . .'

'*More*? Even *I* think I'm spoilt now . . .'

He held out a card and a small, beautifully wrapped box. Hannah knew immediately.

'It's from Mum.'

Mark nodded. 'She told me to give it to you today.'

'Oh.'

She opened the box first. Inside it was a pair of very small, but nonetheless very sparkly diamond stud earrings. Hannah put the box down very carefully, leaving the lid open. The card wasn't really a birthday card. It was white, and it had big black letters on the front. GO CONFIDENTLY IN THE DIRECTION OF YOUR DREAMS, it said. She was still at it – issuing instructions from beyond the grave. Hannah smiled.

Inside, Barbara had written:

'No sadness today, my birthday girl. Some bling from me. Wear them and dazzle. Your first, and, I hope, your smallest diamonds! Love you, Mum.'

She'd signed it with crosses and hearts, like she always did.

Mid December

Hannah

Hannah had wanted *Now That's What I Call Christmas*, while Mark favoured *The King's College Choir*. So they had settled on *The Jackson Five Christmas Album*. Robin was currently rocking, well and truly. The tree had been chosen, netted, driven home and dragged inside, leaving a trail of needles that they would still be vacuuming up in March. It was huge. 'What the hell!' Mark had said. 'Let's get a whopper.' It nearly reached the ceiling.

Over a pizza the night before, they'd decided, the two of them, to buy new decorations. Neither was ready to get the big box up from the cellar. Full of handmade ornaments, and cherished mementoes, it was too much. They had both learnt, over the last few months, not to wallow. If they'd opened the box, they'd have been opening the door, and, for now, they chose to leave it closed. Instead, they'd driven into town on their way to get the tree and bought new lights, new glass balls and new tinsel for their new Christmas.

They decided a lot more together since . . . well, lately. Hannah liked it. Before, she'd been an add on. Important, but not . . . not at the centre of things. She ate dinner with her parents, of course, but no one ever said to her: 'What d'you fancy for supper tonight, Hannah?' She'd sat and watched TV with them, but no one ever asked her what *she* wanted to watch. If she didn't like the same thing as them, there was always the television in the study, or the one upstairs in the oak cupboard at the end of their big bed. Now, Dad consulted her about everything. It made her feel grown up. Hence the pizza, and the fabulously colourful tree, and The Jackson Five.

Dad was more interested in her – that was how it felt. He talked to her about the news; he watched the programmes she liked with her, and asked her to tell him about the characters and the plots. He'd never done that. She'd come home with all this careers stuff, and he'd read it with her, asking her lots of questions – about her A-levels, and UCAS forms, and universities. She sat in the front seat of the car now when they went somewhere.

Dad had always been the cook. Mum used to say that if there was a pill you could take that meant you got all the calories and nutrition you needed, she wouldn't bother to eat. Mind you, she used to eat what Dad produced. Hannah didn't think it was the actual eating so much as the shopping and preparing, and the cleaning up that Mum hadn't been so keen on. Dad was different – he loved it. When Mum was alive, in the evening she would sit, with a bulbous glass of red wine, on one of the stools at the breakfast bar and watch him slice and tenderize and whisk. She used to say she'd really won the lottery when she found him. Since she'd died – before that, really – since she'd been really ill, Hannah had helped him. He'd shown her how to cut vegetables, pivoting the knife up and down against the chopping board so that you could go really quickly, and how to mash garlic with the side of the blade, adding a little salt as you went, and how to make a smooth roux, too. They'd never talked about this shift of habit. One evening she had come to him and started to chop something, and he had silently tied one of the oversize denim aprons that hung on the kitchen door around her neck and waist, and then he quietly told her what he was doing.

Now they cooked together almost every night. They'd

started making desserts. And dips. Now when Hannah stood in front of the mirror in the bathroom and stared at her naked reflection her stomach was rounder. You could no longer see the hard muscles beneath the surface. Sideways, there was a curve. She quite liked it.

She wanted to get it pierced. Dad would never let her. She'd have stood more chance if Mum was alive. Mum would probably have said yes. She'd have said she should enjoy her flat stomach while she still had it. She'd have said piercing was better than tattooing, because you could always take a piercing out. She'd have said anywhere except the face. She especially hated those rods people had put through their chins and their eyebrows. But she'd have been okay about the tummy button. She could probably get away with it now, if she wanted to. She wouldn't have to tell Dad. They didn't do that naked thing anymore. He wouldn't see it until next summer. It would be too late then to throw a wobbly. Maybe she would do it . . .

Life's too short, after all, isn't it? Not to do the things you want, the things that make you happy. Hannah had been thinking that quite a lot lately. Mum had gotten really really thin. This new little belly felt like health, and like life. And the cooking, she knew, felt a little like therapy. Dad let her have a little glass of wine, too, sometimes. He once said that he felt better when there were two glasses.

Tonight they were making mince pies from scratch. They'd made the mincemeat a few weeks earlier when they'd made the cake and the Christmas pudding. That had been a real Martha Stewart day, and the kitchen had been full of the strange smells of candied peel and boozy currants. Now, in the glow of the Christmas tree, to the sound of The Jacksons singing 'Rockin' Robin', they were rolling pastry on the grey marble slab, cutting ivy leaves and stars out to top their pies.

Everyone was coming. Hannah had insisted. When they'd all been together for her birthday at the beginning of October, she'd made them commit, marking it off in their diaries. She'd told Amanda that she absolutely could not leave the country until January. Lisa was coming with Andy. Jennifer had agreed to see Stephen's parents the weekend before so that she could be there. Day to day, it was fine, it just being the two of them. Not all the days were the same, not all good. When one of them was having a bad one, that was okay. When it was both . . . well, those were the duvet days. And she wasn't going to risk a duvet day on Christmas Day. There would be music and mince pies, and Pictionary. Mum would have liked that.

Lisa

It was the perfect party. Okay – it was the office Christmas party, though the office (Andy's) had had a really good year and had splashed out on a pretty impressive venue. But it was perfect. Hers, the day before, had been at a ghastly Mexican down the road and a classic example of the wrong kind of clichéd office Christmas party. Where private parts were photocopied late at night and someone from Accounts woke up next to the post-room guy, who they didn't even speak to on the other 364 days of the year, unless they needed to FedEx their sister's birthday present on company funds. She'd left really early before the ladies' bathrooms had begun to run with tequila sick.

This was much better. The DJ was playing the perfect

music. They were with the perfect friends (also Andy's, she realized, but they were good party companions – not too drunk, nor too sober. Happy, festive). And she was wearing the perfect dress.

Lisa stood, resplendent – and only slightly wobbly, in her heels – in Barbara's green silk Ben de Lisi dress, at the top of the Cinderella staircase, and surveyed the scene. This wasn't her grand entrance – she was on her way back from the bathroom. And this wasn't the beginning of the night – dinner had long been cleared away, and she had drunk enough champagne to feel giddy and sentimental. The event space had been transformed as only light and flowers could manage: the ballroom had been made magical – dressed with sparkling white fairy lights and flickering gold candles, and about a million white poinsettias. Christmas, the classy way. Not an inflated Santa or a sprig of plastic mistletoe in sight.

Lisa didn't normally love big parties like this. Smaller things where she knew everyone were more her style. She was that noisy kind of shy. The worst kind, because no one knew that noisy could be shy. But it could, and she was. Places where she knew everyone were much easier for her. Plus, she was firmly in the 'getting ready is the best part of the night' camp when it came to big 'dos'. Luxuriating in a deep, fragrant bath, taking the time to paint on a smoother, prettier, more colourful version of your face; that first glass of decent wine, drunk alone – all that much better than getting hoarse, shouting to make yourself and your inanity heard above a crowd of noisy strangers, drinking cheap alcohol and feeling the balls of your feet throb with each step you took in the high heels the dress demanded, but your feet rejected wholesale.

But tonight was different. When she was dressed, earlier, before she left home, Lisa had sprayed perfume into the air in front of her and walked through its mist. Mum had taught her to do it that way. Only she called it scent. She'd walked through that fragrant piece of air, in Mum's dress, and in some weird way, that action had been like walking through the portal in some science fiction fantasy book – she'd wafted into a different mood entirely. The perfume felt more than a little like armour – a shield against . . . who knew . . . whatever stopped her from liking parties like this one. Or maybe it wasn't the perfume at all; maybe it was the dress itself.

Mum's dress. Mum loved big parties. She loved dressing up, and champagne bubbles tickling her nose, and dancing with her arms above her head, shoes thrown to the edge of the dance floor, and shouting inane happy things at people. Lisa remembered, when she was very small, the smell of Fracas on her goodnight kiss. Perhaps when the dry cleaner removed the small sweat patches from the armholes, and the dots of mud on the hem, after the last big party she wore it to, he didn't quite get the essence of her out of it. Lisa loved that idea.

And now she wondered whether her drink had been spiked, with some happy party drug. Or maybe it was just spirit – Christmas or otherwise. This was a great, great party. Below her, across the floor, she could see Andy. Her gaze went straight to him, as though he were standing under some beam of ownership. He looked handsome and happy. He was wearing a dinner jacket, but with a normal black silk tie, not a bow – he always said he felt ridiculous in one. He said the only people who should ever wear one were the people who were born to it – whose fathers had worn one. And he wasn't one of those people. He looked like one of the *Reservoir*

Dogs. He was talking animatedly with a friend – gesticulating expansively with one hand. The friend was laughing. He'd been like that all night; the proverbial life and soul. Funny and popular and . . . special. Why was it that, sometimes, you needed to see the people closest to you as others saw them to remember how fantastic they were? Why couldn't you always remember that? When it was just the two of you . . .

Behind him people were dancing. The music was a skilful mix of the songs that reminded them of their youth – in all its abandoned, gilded freedom, while convincing them that they still had it. Not so loud it forbade conversation, or so quiet that it permitted abstinence. Like everything else, it was perfect. She felt a wave of gratitude wash over her. She was *so* lucky.

Andy looked up and saw her in the dress. Something in him shifted. He'd wanted to ask her . . . for God knows how long. Sometimes he thought he'd known he would end up here from that first night, when he watched her sitting in the fountain. Known, or hoped. He knew it was more complicated for her. He knew she was certain of so much less – that for her life was shades, not stripes. But tonight . . . tonight she was different. How did the song have it go? Had it given him the girl, and the music and the moonlight? Was it leaving the rest to him?

Their eyes met, and they smiled at each other. One of those smiles with history and memory, and knowing in it. Andy put up one hand to stop her descent, and pointed to the top of the stairs, indicating that he would come up to her. He grabbed two glasses of champagne from a waiter's silver tray and weaved his way through the crowd towards her. As if he had ordered it himself, the song suddenly changed to something Motown slow

– rhythmic and romantic. His heart was racing. He'd only done this once before – ask a woman to marry him – and everything had been different then. *He* was different. He always thought he would never do it again, unless he was 100 per cent sure – of both the woman and the answer. Right now he wouldn't give you more than 60/40, and yet he knew that he had to ask her anyway.

When he got to her, she took one glass from him and sipped from it, her eyes never leaving his. She looked about 20. Tendrils of hair escaped from the pleat she wore, and curled across her ear and down her slender neck. She put her arm around his neck and pulled him towards her, her lips brushing his ear as she whispered, 'Have I told you lately that I love you?' He heard the emotion in her voice, and it gave him the courage he needed. Andy inhaled deeply, and whispered back: 'Marry me.' An instruction, not a question. She pulled back and her eyes searched his face. He nodded, smiling, and answered her unspoken request that he repeat what he had just said. 'Marry me, Lisa. I mean to say, *will* you marry me?' Then, 'Please?'

Maybe it was Smokey Robinson, maybe it was Moët & Chandon. Maybe it was the spirit of her mother, woven into the fibres of her dress. And maybe, just maybe, it was because, for a second, the clouds of doubt parted and she saw a future where she suddenly, shockingly could not conceive of not having him beside her. Lisa laughed. 'Yes, yes, yes!'

She awoke, the next morning, with the beginnings of a creeping headache stirring behind her ears. She knew that by lunchtime it would have taken up residence in her temple, and would be throbbing there through the afternoon, not really leaving until the next morning. Not so perfect. Her heart was beating fast, which, again, was due to champagne and not romance. For the first two minutes, as she lay with her head back against the pillow and closed her eyes again, she forgot the romance. Then she heard Andy, whistling in the kitchen. He was whistling the song from last night, and she remembered. Oh God, oh no!

She listened to the whistle come through the hall and into the bedroom. A beaming Andy entered with a tray bearing tea and toast.

'Morning gorgeous.'

'What time is it?'

'About 8.30.'

She groaned. 'Too early! No wonder I feel like death. What woke you up?'

He shrugged, setting the tray down on the chest of drawers, and pulling pillows from the warm tangle behind her head, propping her up as though she were a patient.

'Sit up, like a nice girl, and drink some tea. You'll feel better, I promise.'

'Don't make promises you can't keep.'

'If the tea doesn't do it, the toast will. I put extra marmalade on it.'

She smiled at him, grudgingly. 'Thank you. I don't deserve you.'

'Quite right. You must have been great in another life.'

She nodded, self pity momentarily overtaking her, and sipped at the hot tea. It helped a little. 'I think I was Mother Teresa.'

'You *can't* have been her! She would have to have died before you were born.'

'Okay, pedant. I was Florence Nightingale, or Marie Curie.' He laughed.

'Okay, Flo. Eat your toast. I'm going to get the papers.'

The green dress was on the back of the chair. She vaguely remembered putting it there before she and Andy made love last night. Normally she wouldn't have bothered – they were both pretty wound up, as she remembered, by the time they got back. But it was *the dress*. Suddenly she remembered a guy – a guy she hadn't thought about in years, who'd carefully folded his suit trousers along the crease and lay them reverently over a chair before climbing into bed with her. For the first and last time, given what a passionkiller that was. Lisa shot the dress a spiteful look. It was all its fault. Andy had asked her, and she had said yes, and now everything that was so clear last night was all cloudy again, and, between that and the headache, she felt utterly lousy. She pushed the tray aside, lay back and pulled a pillow across her face. Like that would help.

She was asleep again when she felt Andy slide into bed beside her. Despite herself, she leant back into his solid warmth. He put his arms around her, and lay his head against her neck.

'Did the tea help, my lovely?'

'A bit.'

He squeezed her tight. 'Brrr ... It's freezing out. You're all toasty, mmm ...' He lay one of his legs between hers, forcing her to turn towards him, and began to kiss her, his hands on her face. She pulled away, a little irritably.

'Blimey! Haven't even brushed my teeth yet. Can't imagine why you'd want to kiss me.'

'Can't imagine why I wouldn't.' But he brought her head down to his chest, stroking her hair. 'Aren't you the woman who agreed to marry me last night? Then brought me back here and did unspeakable things to

me? Because if you aren't, I was drunker than I thought!'
He ran his hands down her flanks, onto her bottom. 'No
. . . no . . . I'm sure it was you . . .'

Now, now was the time. If she just explained . . . she
was carried away. She wasn't sure, she wasn't ready, it
wasn't the right time . . . She'd had too much champagne,
it was the fairy lights and the song and that bloody dress
. . . Now was the time. Maybe, just maybe, if she did it
now, she could salvage this – she could make it okay.
Maybe he'd laugh it off, and they could go back to what
they'd been before last night.

So why wasn't she saying anything? Why was she
letting him kiss her? Letting him press himself against
her, stroking so gently, so insistently up and down her
back, letting the mood change to something more serious
and intense and sexy again. It felt good, of course – it
always did. But that wasn't it. This was . . . easier. And
so she didn't say anything. As he moved on top of her,
his breath hot and coffee flavoured against her ear,
she stared, wide-eyed, at the ceiling, fighting a ripple of
panic, or was it nausea, and the moment for honesty
passed.

She pushed him away, playfully at first, and then
seriously, with urgency. 'I'm serious, Andy. Get off me!'
He rolled off, and she ran, naked, to the bathroom, tea
and bile and champagne rising in her throat. She threw
up violently in the toilet, then sank to the tiles and lay
her head back against the wall. 'You okay?'

'Fine. Don't come in.'

But he was already in, passing her a hand towel to
wipe her mouth. 'I don't care about a bit of mess. I'm
good with bodily fluids of all types. Here . . .' He reached
down and helped her to her feet. 'Get back into bed . . .
If you're finished?' She nodded weakly. 'Think so.'

'I'll get you some water and let you sleep a bit more. You'll be fine in a bit. Pisshead!' He pulled the duvet over her, tucking it back, then kissed the top of her head.

She felt less queasy now, but her head still hurt. And that was before she remembered that Andy's daughter was coming for the day . . .

Amanda

'Bloody hell, it's cold!' Amanda opened the door to Starbucks, and held it as her flatmate Bex walked through, following her gratefully. There was a long queue, but at least it was warm in here. In theory, she objected completely to Starbucks. Today, though, she objected more to being frozen.

She pulled off her hat and shook out her hair. 'Remind me again why I'm here, and not on some beach somewhere like Goa?'

'For the love of temping?'

Amanda made a TV game show 'nah, nah' noise.

'For the love of living with me and Josh?'

'Are you having a laugh?' Amanda made balance scales with her hands. 'Beach hut in Goa, squalor in Earlsfield, beach hut in Goa, squalor in Earlsfield. Mmm, close . . .'

'Oy! I object to "squalor"! It's not *that* bad!'

Amanda threw her arms theatrically around Bex. 'Okay, I take back squalor. Mmm, you're warm!' She rubbed her face against Bex's.

Bex released herself, laughing. 'Get off!'

'Coffee is on me – to make up for being so rude about the home I should be grateful to have . . . What you having?'

Bex looked at the board behind the till. 'Eugh! Egg nog latte! *Gingerbread* latte! Eugh! Are they still doing a plain latte, or is it mandatory to have some sort of seasonal "eugh" syrup in it?'

'Oh bah humbug, Ebeneezer . . . Don't knock it till you've tried it. Go and get us a seat, as far away from the door as possible. I don't have to be at work for twenty minutes. Should be able to get some feeling back in my feet by then . . .'

Amanda looked at the customers already seated beside her. A couple of determined-looking Christmas shoppers, scribbling lists while they waited for the shops to open. That reminded her – she hadn't bought a thing yet . . . She'd been away last Christmas. A phone call home had been gift enough. Or so she'd told herself. This year she might need actual tangible gifts.

A mum fed her baby a croissant, pushing small bites of the flaky pastry into an eager little mouth while talking on a mobile phone wedged under her chin. A guy with a laptop caught her eye. He had red hair, teased and gelled into a fin, and he was wearing a sky-blue polo neck sweater. It made him look like Tintin. She was smiling to herself, wondering whether he knew he looked like Tintin, when she saw him look up from his newspaper – the *Guardian* – and follow someone with a long lascivious gaze, his mouth practically hanging open. The object of his undisguised desire was a tall, willowy blonde, wearing skin-tight black trousers and unfeasibly high-heeled dominatrix boots. Oh God, she thought. How obvious. As Miss Whiplash passed, and was gone, he looked back towards his paper, but his eyes lighted on her instead. He caught her amused disapproval, and almost squirmed with discomfort, colouring pink above the polo neck and giving a small shrug which admitted his guilt. Amanda raised a mock judgmental eyebrow at him, smiled and shook her head at him.

An hour later, she was reorganizing a filing system to which the last temp had clearly not been emotionally committed. Everything was filed under M for miscellaneous. Fired up by a double shot of espresso and a fervent desire not to be drawn into the office politics that simmered and occasionally boiled over around her, she attacked the task. Who could do this every day?

The Shop

I'm a bit sad today. We've just come back from the solicitor's office – I've signed all the right pieces of paper, and the shop is not mine anymore. I sold it to someone really nice. I'm pleased about that. I even turned down a slightly higher offer from some woman I just didn't think was going to be right for it. A husband-and-wife team – they have a new baby, and they're going to move a bit more towards toys and little handknits and things, but essentially keep it the same. You can see they are brimming over with ideas and schemes. Part of me wanted to talk to them about it – their excitement was contagious. But I didn't. I signed the papers and handed over the keys, and came home. It makes me sad. I remember when I felt that way about it.

Mark says we'll get another shop, when I'm better. Put the money away while I achieve that, let it grow a bit in a high interest account, and then get a better site, a bigger square footage. I got extra money for the stock and the goodwill . . . I was a bit surprised to see how much it was worth, when I remember what it cost me when I started it . . . He says maybe we'll put a little coffee bar in the back, with one of those shiny Barista machines, cater for the ladies who lunch. But I don't know if I ever will.

That shop was much more than a business to me. Which is not to say that it wasn't a good business, she says proudly! Wasn't I the original juggling single mother? That, and pioneering meditation techniques in labour. Did you girls know what a model for the modern woman your mother was?! I knew diddly squat when I got started. Thank God for all the fun Mum and Dad never had. They left it to me. It wasn't a fortune, but it was enough to get me started – the rent, stock, money to print flyers, and advertise in the local paper, and paint the front of the shop. I loved that colour. Sea foam, it's called. I remember being so proud and so excited and so bloody terrified, standing and watching the painter peel off the tape where he'd put the name of the shop. White letters, castellar typeface, on a sea-foam background. It looked so classy.

The bank manager and the accountant scared the **** out of me, and I didn't think I'd ever get the hang of that side of it. But I did. Studied my bookkeeping course and all the government small business handouts at night, when you lot were sleeping. Sometimes I ironed at the same time. Who knew you could? I was exhausted, most of the time. Made some pretty big errors in the early days, too, though none of them, thank God, big enough to put me out of business . . . but it was touch and go for the first few years.

I found a niche in the local market. More luck than judgment. It was never going to make us rich, but it made us independent, which was worth more than gold to me, after me and Donald split up. I've always tried to teach you girls that. Always be able to walk away and be on your own. Sounds defeatist, doesn't it, when you say it like that? But it's anything but, I think. There's such a joy, and such a satisfaction in it.

But, like I say, the shop was much more than that to me. It was my office, Amanda and Hannah's playroom, Jennifer and Lisa's homework space. Every corner of that shop had a memory of you four in it. I met Mark there. It saved my life. And I loved it. Every new delivery, every satisfied customer, every new friend made across the counter . . . I loved it.

And now I've sold it. Mark asked me if I'd ever hoped one of you would take it on. I'd never thought about it. I suppose it might have been nice. But it breaks my cardinal rule. Well, one of my cardinal rules. You four are not here to live out my dreams for me. I've had my dreams, and some of them have come true and some of them haven't. But they've been my dreams. You have to have your own. Have them, cherish them and never let go of them. Do something you love. Whoever was the fool who decided that we should work for six days and rest for one? But if you're doing something you love, you'll be okay.

Well, sorry Mum, but Amanda most certainly had not found the thing she loved to do. This was mental treading water, what she did for money. That was all. It was nearly time. Amanda knew this cycle of old. Every time she came back from a trip, she tried. Tried to put down some roots in an everyday ordinary life. It usually worked for a while. She would get a job, pay rent, spend as little as possible of whatever was left, and save the rest. She knew she was old enough now to be saving for a deposit on a flat, or even a car. But she only ever saved for plane tickets. She was always getting ready to leave. Not that she didn't have fun meanwhile. Amanda always had fun.

Bex was an old friend. They'd been at school together. She and Amanda had stayed in touch all these years via postcards, texts and the occasional drunken night in London together when Amanda was home. They weren't especially close – after all, Amanda wasn't especially close to anyone, but there was an empty room . . . Bex was a beautician at an upscale salon off Oxford Street, just up from the temping job. Probably the most indiscreet beautician in London with a hilarious line in disgusting stories about her wealthy clientele and their excess body hair. Their third, sourced from an ad in *Loot*, was Josh – a gay hairdresser who wore sunglasses in all weathers and worked in some cutting-edge place in Sloane Square. Apparently he even wore his sunglasses while cutting and pretending to be vaguely Italian, when, in fact, he was the son of a librarian and a dentist from Saxmundham. At home with them, Amanda always felt vaguely as though she was taking part in anarchic, hilarious dinner theatre. There was always loud music, and cocktails. And usually a walk-on cast of extras, since they were both fairly promiscuous. Sunday breakfast (served around lunchtime) was often a crowded affair. What they had in common, and what made this living arrangement okay, for now, was a total, dedicated lack of concern for the future. No pension, no career ladder, no ticking biological clocks, no great need to nest ... The flat was shambolic, none too clean and full of laughter.

Which was more than could be said for the office she had had the misfortune to be assigned to by the woman at the temping agency. Still, two weeks to go. Christmas, she'd stay. She'd promised Hannah. And then probably New Year's – there was some all-night rave in a warehouse in Lewisham that Josh had tickets to – but then ... then she'd be on her way.

She wanted to go to Australia. She'd saved enough for a ticket – if she waited until later in January, when all the long-lost relatives had finished toing and froing, and relative bargains could be had. Maybe via Bali, or back to Thailand. She'd been about four years ago, and loved it. She'd stayed in a beach hut in Kata Noi with a Kiwi she'd met on a train in Bangkok. Three weeks of swimming and lying in a hammock, eating amazing seafood from stalls near the beach for pennies and talking late into the night with the backpackers passing through. They all felt like they were extras in *The Beach* – they'd discovered Shangri La, and it was theirs. The beach hut with the narrow verandah, where she had hung her bikinis to dry, and sat to watch electrifying sunsets wouldn't be there any more. The Boxing Day tsunami would have swept it away. But still, she might go back. God knows, they needed the tourists.

Sometimes, like when she was filing, Amanda thought

about her addiction to being on the move. About whether she was running away or running towards. She loved the mystery of a plane landing somewhere new, of a train pulling into a station. She loved to stand in the middle of a market square, or a park, or a beach and take in the smells and the sounds of a world that was completely new to her. She loved being an anonymous extra in a crowd scene, like some real-life *Where's Wally?*, a tiny face, wide-eyed with wonder, in a vast, ever-changing picture. She didn't get frightened. Well, hardly ever. Once, in Malaysia, packed into a boat she knew was too full, asked to sleep for eight hours on a deck no more than four feet deep. And maybe a few times, on trains and in buses, feeling a thousand strange eyes on her and her belongings, fighting the overwhelming desire to sleep. But she was a smart girl – she didn't do stupid things, and she didn't take daft risks. Mum had insisted on at least one phone call a month, and she'd always made it – and, now of course, there was hotmail everywhere, and it was almost impossible to be lost. She supposed, briefly, that she'd call Mark now.

If she was running away, and not running – arms wide – towards the world, she was running away from responsibility and pressure and obligation. And she wondered why the whole world didn't have the sense to do the same thing. Surely, she was the sane one?

It was at least five degrees colder the next morning. Bex had a day off, and Josh had never even made it home, so Amanda went to work alone, stopping outside the tube station to pick up one of the free papers that had nothing interesting to say, so that, five stops in, the paper languished on the empty seat next to her, and she was almost back to sleep, her head leaning back against the bulk of the thick scarf around her neck. She was thinking about warm water lapping at her toes, splayed in white sand.

'Excuse me, is this yours?'

Her head sprang up with an awkward snap. It was Tintin. What were the odds?

He was holding out the free sheet. She shook her head, and he sat down. Winter coats made the seats too small, and his whole length made contact with hers. She shifted slightly, and sat up straighter. She wasn't sure he recognized her, or that if he did, he intended to acknowledge the fact, until he turned to her, and smiled the sheepish smile of yesterday again. She looked at their fellow passengers, establishing there were no obvious candidates for his equally obvious admiration in the carriage, and replicated his small shrug by way of reply, rolling her eyes.

'Sorry about that.' His voice was deeper than she was expecting. Tintin had quite a high-pitched voice. But Tintin was Belgian, as well, wasn't he? This guy was clearly British, although not very – British people didn't normally try and establish a conversation with you on an underground train at 8.15 in the morning.

That was another thing she loved about travelling. Donning Birkenstocks and a rucksack – a proper one – was like wearing a sign on your forehead that said 'Talk to me – I'm up for making friends with like-minded individuals.' Like a secret handshake, granting admission to a society where you pretty much liked everyone else who belonged . . .

'Hey,' she smiled. 'You're a guy, aren't you?'

The commuters around them started to listen, although they didn't look up from their newspapers, romance novels or County Court Summons. A couple who'd been hanging on to the central pole and facing the other way, staring into space, angled themselves so they could see who was talking. You might as well be on an orange box at Hyde Park Corner.

He smiled a broad, surprisingly sexy smile. The sheepishness had vanished.

'And you're a feminist, I gather?'

'Just a woman who's learnt that men are utterly predictable. More realist than feminist.'

'So young, yet so jaded.'

She laughed. This was a novelty. Normally conversations like this were limited to old episodes of *Dawson's Creek*, which she only knew about because Josh had a giant crush on Dawson and watched the show on Sunday afternoons while he recovered from the night before. In sunglasses. Personally, she'd far rather have Pacey, but that wasn't the point.

This was their stop, her stop. The Starbucks stop, at least. They stood up at the same time. He gestured with one arm for her to leave the carriage first, and then walked beside her. She was amused.

'I'm Ed.'

'I'm late.'

'You want to walk faster? We could walk faster.'

Instead she stopped. The commuters behind her tutted and walked around her. Lemming out of line alert. 'Look, is this strange – albeit novel – approach something you make a habit of?'

'No, not at all. Nor is gawping at obvious women in coffee shops, incidentally.'

His face was so open. She didn't know what to say.

'Can I buy you a coffee? Go back to the scene of the crime? Penance?'

'There's no need.' She couldn't decide whether she was intrigued or exasperated. Either way, she was still late. She looked at her watch.

'Tempted?'

'No, not tempted. Just wondering exactly how late I'm going to be.'

'Late for what? What do you do?'

'I'm temping.' Why was she even answering?

'They won't fire a temp, not this close to Christmas. Not because they're all heart, just because there isn't time to get anyone else.'

He wasn't like anyone else she'd met lately, and it was pretty obvious that he was being a pain in the arse because he liked her – liked the look of her, or liked the way she'd sized him up the day before, or something. And that was flattering, damn it. After all, she'd accepted stranger invitations, in weirder places. Sometimes, you wished you hadn't, and sometimes amazing things happened. And the filing was seriously, *seriously* dull . . . He sensed her waver.

'Come on, a coffee . . .'

'I don't like Starbucks.'

'Good, me neither. Evil, scary, like plastic bags and disposable nappies.' He shuddered theatrically. 'And that stuff you spray out of an aerosol to get the smell out of your curtains and stuff. Yuck!' He thrust his hands into his pockets. 'Bloody good coffee, though!'

Jennifer

Jennifer loved her husband's mother. It was her father-in-law she couldn't stand. Kathleen was warm and funny, and had always made her feel welcome. Brian was cool and sharp, and left her, each time she was with him, with the impression that he was disappointed by her. Actually, as the years passed and the feeling went from being un-comfortable, to upsetting, to habitual, she began to realize that Brian was disappointed by life, and not just by her.

This year he was disappointed by having to have his family Christmas celebration the week before Christmas. Which was her fault. She wanted to be with Hannah, and Mark, and the others. That felt like the right thing to do, and it would sure as hell be more fun, her poor dead mother notwithstanding. So her in-laws had brought the whole Christmas thing forward a week. No one had asked them to do that. Kathleen said she loved to see everyone together. Or, at least, that domestic disturbance was what Jennifer supposed might be the problem, as she stood in the doorframe between the kitchen – Kathleen's feminine, inclusive domain – and the living room, where Brian held court, sitting like an old man, wide-legged in his armchair, watching his grandchildren play on the rug.

Stephen's sisters Anna and Joanne were here. Their husbands were not, being, respectively, an ex and an estranged one. And Brian was, sure as hell, disappointed by that. Anna's husband had left his pregnant wife for his pregnant girlfriend three years before and Joanne's had walked out on her and their two children almost exactly two years later. Although Jennifer supposed that, in reality, this family simply reflected national statistics, it seemed like a singular failure to her. Two out of three of your children in a failed marriage. Mustn't that have had something to do with the parents, even if it was nominally the fault of the deserting husbands? What had it been like here when Stephen, Anna and Joanne were young?

Stephen was the middle child. Joanne was older by thirteen months and Anna younger by two years. Kathleen loved to talk about the time when she had three children under 5 – two of them in terry nappies. It was, clearly, when she had been happiest. Stephen himself remembered a tired mother, an absent father, but nothing, he said when she asked him, that made him any different from any of his mates. When Jennifer questioned him more closely, he'd shrugged and answered, 'They're still married, aren't they?' If that was Stephen's measure of success, it was no wonder that she couldn't get him to talk to her, to really talk to her. After all, the two of them were still married, weren't they? What more could she want?

Kathleen, Anna and Joanne were a long way down a bottle of white wine in the kitchen, huddled around the kitchen table, although it was after two in the afternoon and lunch was more than ready to serve. A little like a coven of witches, albeit more of the giggling than the cackling kind. Cursing man in general, and some men very specifically. Stephen was watching television with his father, bending over occasionally to ruffle the hair or tweak the nose of one of his three fatherless nieces and his nephew Jake, currently hunched over a Nintendo DS.

Jennifer wanted lunch to be served and to be over. She didn't want to be there. Her heels hurt, her head ached and she wished she was at home, in the flat, in a pair of sweats.

It hadn't always been this way. The first time she had been there for Christmas, she'd been high as a kite, head over heels in love with Stephen, and wanting more than anything to hasten the process by which she could become a part of this new family. Desperate to make a good impression, she'd carefully packed and prepared, bought thoughtful gifts and wrapped them with care.

Joanne's first child, Jake, was about 6 weeks old, and the whole Christmas revolved around him. He spent the day, somnolent on a bean bag, centre stage, dressed in an elf babygro with matching hat, the star player in a protracted Kodak moment. Everyone, even Stephen's dad, was doting and love-struck. Joanne had worn elastic clothing, breast pads and an expression of beatific exhaustion all day. It had felt contagious, so that by the end of the evening, they all reclined on chairs and sofas, gazing happily at Jake, and each other, and the Bond movie. That had been the first year. It had been pretty much downhill from there, until it reached the point where Jennifer started dreading it around Halloween.

She must have sighed for Stephen's mum stood up and came to her, a comforting arm snaking around her shoulders. 'You alright, love?'

She pursed her lips together in a non-smile and nodded.

'Thinking about your mum?'

They hadn't known each other well. Engagement party, wedding, the odd Sunday lunch . . . They'd had the peculiar, forced intimacy of in-laws, a stilted relationship. They weren't alike, and Jennifer doubted they would have been friends under different circumstances. The truth was, she wasn't thinking about Barbara now, not really. She was thinking about the things in her life that she *did* have some control over, not the ones she didn't. But it was easier to nod, and accept the sympathetic cluck and the hug, and then, from Joanne, the big glass of wine.

Given that she was condemned to eat two Christmas lunches, she was glad this one was first. Mark's lunch would be delicious – this one was dry, and flavourless. The turkey was overcooked to the point of sawdust, and the gravy was like dishwater, which made you glad there was barely enough in the gravy boat to moisten your bullet-like Brussels sprouts. No stuffing, no cranberry sauce, no chipolatas wrapped in bacon . . .

'For the sake of the children' there were crackers and hats and stupid jokes. But they had no interest in sitting at the table, anxious to escape back to their new toys and the afternoon film. Jennifer, studying the clock above her father-in-law's head, knew how they must be feeling. Anna and Joanne were talking in code about the CSA and their exes' new girlfriends. She was getting a headache from trying to keep up with their encrypted references. Several times Stephen's mum tried to change the subject, but new forays into Stephen's job, and their plans to holiday in Tunisia at Easter, and the new Italian that had opened down the road would inevitably peter out into semi-awkward silences that led right back to the bitching.

Jennifer sensed that she was the only one here who found the meal difficult. It felt as though the rest of them were inured to the mediocrity – of the food and the conversation and the happiness level. She guessed that maybe, apart from that first magical year, when she acknowledged that she was looking but not really seeing, Christmas here had always been like this . . .

When the children were finally excused to rampage in the next room, it grew even quieter. As though he'd been waiting for the perfect moment, Stephen's dad leant forward, elbows on the table on either side of his unfinished bowl of Christmas pudding, and looked first at her, and then at Stephen. She knew what was coming.

'So, how many more years are you two going to make me wait for grandchildren?' The stupid remark hung in the air like cigarette smoke. Jennifer felt tired. He may have been looking at Stephen, and referring to both of them, but he was talking to her, trying to light her touch paper. It seemed a malicious sport to her. She smiled as lightly as she could manage. Her voice carried a warning, but she doubted it would be heeded. 'You *have* grand-children, Brian – they're those adorable, noisy little people jumping on the sofa next door . . .'

'I mean *your* children – *Stephen's* children. A man wants to see his son produce a family.' He sounded like some idiotic Victorian.

'Brian, leave them be!'

Kathleen was trying to come to their rescue, but he was belligerent after a morning of drinking. His words were slightly slurred, and he didn't even look at his wife when she spoke.

'I'm only having fun with them, Kathleen. Besides, haven't I a right to know? They've been married for years.'

Jennifer looked to Stephen for help, or rescue, or even just for a shared moment of exasperation, but Stephen looked down at his place and swept away a few imaginary crumbs from the cloth. He wasn't going to say anything, and she didn't think she had ever felt more alone. Kath-leen's smile pleaded with her, while Joanne and Anna looked embarrassed and sympathetic, and perhaps the tiniest bit curious, but no one was going to tell him to shut up. She pushed her chair back – its legs squeaking unpleasantly against the floor – and stood up, forcing her voice to be calm and quiet, as she said, 'You know what, Brian? You don't have a right. You don't have any bloody right at all!' Then she turned and walked through into the kitchen. She grabbed her coat and handbag and opened the back door.

Kathleen loved her long, narrow garden and kept a bench on the patio right outside the door, on which she would sit and watch the birds at her birdbath. Jennifer sat down heavily and pulled her coat around her against the cold. Her breath came in clouds. She fumbled in her bag for a cigarette and lit it, taking a deep first drag. He could bloody well bugger off, the stupid, insensitive nosey sod! She was too angry to cry.

Kathleen followed her out, her coat around her shoulders, but her slippers still on. She sat down beside her.

'Can I have one of those?'

'You don't smoke.'

'Nor do you!'

'Bloody well need one now!' She'd bought the packet a few days ago. It was the first one she'd bought for months – since Mum, really, and this was the first one she'd lit. It wasn't really like her, and even as she drew deeply on the cigarette, she wondered what she was doing. Stephen would be cross. Maybe that was why she'd bought them . . .

'Well, me too.'

Jennifer half smiled at her, and passed the packet. Kathleen lit a cigarette with the shallow breath of the half-hearted smoker.

'You think you need a fag to get through a day with him, try a lifetime.'

It was the first time she'd ever said anything remotely like that and the statement hung in the air with their smoke and their cold breath, like smog.

For a moment, Jennifer stared at her in shock. Then Kathleen shrugged, nodded, took another pretend drag and burst out laughing.

*

They didn't talk much on the way home in the car. She was driving. Stephen had drunk several glasses of wine and port with his lunch, and his head was nodding before they'd gone five miles. She told him it was okay for him to sleep, and he'd reclined the passenger seat, balling up his sweater to make a pillow and fallen asleep. She listened to the radio for a while, but then switched over to CD. She wanted Norah Jones or Paul Simon. This was Stephen's car, though, and bore testament to his peculiar weakness for Heavy Metal; Megadeth and Metallica were not really what she was in the mood for. The roads were quiet this late in the afternoon the Sunday before Christmas, and the drive was an easy enough one – she'd been doing it for years.

She'd hugged her mother-in-law warmly at the door, but she'd refused to be conciliatory with her father-in-law. He could stew on it all week as far as she was concerned. She wasn't in the least sorry she'd stormed out in the middle of their Christmas dinner. Maybe it would make him think twice, the next time. The rest of the afternoon had had a sense of forced gaiety – they had all turned their attention to the children, while he slumped in his armchair, dozing to *Chitty Chitty Bang Bang*. She'd played endless games of Uno and Pictionary. Once, looking up, she'd seen Stephen looking at her strangely, but when his eyes met hers, he looked away.

Kathleen had never said one word about finding Brian difficult to live with before, not in the whole time she'd known her. It made her think. Who else had a marriage full of secrets, and things unsaid, and things ignored until you could bear it no longer? Not just her. Her mind went back to Mum's journal. She'd read it and reread it, and even when she didn't read it, she kept it by her bed, where she could see it, and it made Mum feel close by.

Stephen had asked to look at it, but she had said no, that it was personal, and only meant for her and her sisters. He had shrugged, and looked pained, as though her saying no was one more instance of her pushing him away as he tried to get closer. Which, of course, was exactly what it was.

The passage Mum had marked, the one she wanted her to read first, was one about Dad. And Jennifer knew why. She wanted Jen to know that she knew how it felt to be in a marriage that wasn't working. The journal entry was the conversation she knew Barbara had tried to start with her a dozen times; the one she had never let her start. Tonight, driving along the M40, with her husband asleep and snoring beside her, she missed her mum as much as she ever had.

He woke up as they pulled into the underground garage. At the door of their apartment, he put his hand on her arm.

'Take no notice of my Dad – he's a bugger. I'm sorry.'

'Sorry he's a bugger? Or sorry you didn't stand up for me in front of him?'

'I don't want to argue.'

'Apparently not.'

'No one takes any notice of him, anyway.'

But she had gone into the living room, and was switching on the television set, and didn't answer.

'Aren't you coming to bed? It's late.'

'I'll be there in a while.'

But she fell asleep in front of the late film and was still there, stiff and chilly, when he brought her a conciliatory mug of tea the next morning.

Lisa

Lisa and Andy were a small child's width apart on his sofa, watching *Miracle on 34th Street* – the remake, sadly, and not the original, with Cee Cee. Actually, they were pretending to watch. Andy had *The Sunday Times* on the seat beside him and Lisa was pushing back her cuticles with an orange stick, occasionally pushing at her temples with her thumbs, trying to edge the headache out. They'd watched the same film twice already in the last month. It was a current favourite.

Cecilia Joan Armstrong – 'Cee Cee' to everyone who knew her – was 6 years old, white blonde, brown-eyed, small for her age, with a lisp currently exacerbated by the absence of her two front teeth. She could read, and add units, tens and hundreds, and Google. She could not, apparently, flush a toilet, or digest a meal without ketchup. She liked ballet and rabbits, and she still slept with a piece of her receiving blanket wound around her left arm and pushed into her ear. She did not like big dogs, or radio where people were just talking to each other, with no music. When she was poorly, she liked to watch *Maisie* videos, even though she was too old really and had watched them all a thousand times anyway, and she liked to watch them lying on the sofa with her backside in the air. When she was well, she often watched TV upside down, hanging by her legs over the back of the sofa, her neck precariously twisting, although she was the right way up today.

Cee Cee loved Andy, her dad. She loved her mum too, of course, but her mum was less fun. She lived with her mum all the time, so her mum was the person who had to shout at her in the morning, when she was eating her Cheerios one at a time, and hadn't even brushed her hair yet. And who put her to bed when she wasn't finished watching her programme, and made her tidy her room. All of that stuff. Her dad was her hero because he didn't have to do any of those things. He was her every other weekend, half the school holidays, two weeks in the summer, and each second Christmas daddy.

But Cee Cee was no fool. She had already worked out what the older children of divorcing parents sometimes took much longer to figure: she had the 'two Christmases, two summer holidays' thing all taped up. She knew that Mum was happy with Steve, who was very, very tall and strong, and could fly her around the room, balanced on the palm of his hand, making airplane noises, and that Dad was happy with Lisa, who couldn't, and that this was a much better scenario – for them, and for her – than both of them being unhappy together. Which was what they had been, apparently, and why they decided not to live together any more. She didn't remember that, of course. She'd only been two when they split up. But she'd heard that, all her life. From Mum, and from Dad, and from her granny Joan, who was Mum's mum. She'd also heard, about ten times a day, how much they both loved her, and so, having never knowingly lived any other way, she believed them, and accepted it and was happy. She could be a little manipulative, but then, who wouldn't have learnt to be under those circumstances?

Lisa might not go so far as to say that she loved Cee Cee, but she had perhaps recognized that she might, one day. She liked her a lot, at least. They'd gone ice-skating together, the first time they'd ever met. Lisa – too keen to impress – had fallen so soon and so heavily on the ice that she'd been afraid her coccyx would come out through the top of her head. She'd cried fat tears of pain and humiliation. Cee Cee had cried too, and Andy had hugged them both to him, and laughed. He'd been so thrilled that day, watching them skate tentatively around the rink, hand in hand. She remembered his grin.

Cee Cee wasn't the problem. At least, not entirely. Although Lisa had been a little surprised, and even ashamed, the first time she realized that she was capable of being jealous of a 6-year-old child, it wasn't that. It was Cee Cee's mother, Karen – Andy's first wife. That was what Lisa just couldn't move past.

Andy's previous marriage had never been a secret. When they started working together, there was a picture of a baby Cee Cee on his desk. She'd known it before she got to know him, before the day that led to the night that led to the beginning of the two of them. Of course, it was a while after that when Lisa really started to care about Andy. At the beginning it was just fun, which was all she was ever really looking for. He'd managed to get himself under her skin, though, and within a couple of months the casual thing had become more serious – more serious than anything she'd been involved in before. For her birthday that first year he had surprised her with a weekend away. He'd booked a little bed and breakfast in the Cotswolds, in Bourton-on-the-Water, and not told her until the day before. They'd slept, and eaten, and read the papers, and laughed and walked. Driving back leisurely on the Sunday, unwilling to let the weekend go, they had parked and walked again, spread a blanket under the sunshine on a quiet hillside and made love. Afterwards, dressed again, and lying spent (a phrase she had often read, but believed she never fully understood until that day) – perpendicular to each other, her head on his stomach, she had asked him to tell her about

83

his marriage. He had taken a deep breath, and told her, answering all her questions – many, and detailed – with disarming honesty, and more than a little courage.

Karen and he had met the summer he'd graduated from university when he'd taken a job with a company that ran sailing holidays on the Turkish coast. He'd grown up on the water, in Norfolk, and boats were his passion. He taught novice sailors. Karen worked in the office at the resort. She'd just graduated, too, in hotel management. It was one of those long, glorious summers, where their responsibilities were straightforward and their free time was their own. In the evenings, and on their days off, he would sail them to a nearby cove and light a fire on the beach. They fell in love that summer, he said. Karen was light and funny and free.

She knew all of that already. A few months earlier, Andy had left her alone in his flat one night when he went to the off-licence. And she'd gone snooping. She wasn't a woman on a mission, but she was, by now, mildly curious about him. And he wasn't a man who seemed to have secrets but he was gone and *Coronation Street* had finished, and she was the sort of girl who snooped a little. She always opened people's medicine cabinets, too. She'd opened a stiff desk drawer and found a shoe box full of photographs. They'd been taken somewhere hot and sunny – now she knew where. The girl was tall and lean and white-blonde. She was topless (and how Lisa stared at those innocuous breasts), and golden, squinting against the sunshine, her hand pushing her hair back from her forehead. She looked exactly as Andy had described her, only he hadn't said anything about how sexy she was. That had jolted her. She'd heard his key in the lock, and pushed the drawer closed hurriedly so he wouldn't know what she'd been doing. Although pride and something like fear prevented her from asking questions, she couldn't stop thinking about the pretty girl in the photographs.

Now, though, she was free to ask him whatever she wanted to know. And she wanted to know everything. She thought that if she probed every detail, understood everything, then she wouldn't be able to imagine anything else. That knowing would enable her to put it away, that chapter of Andy's life, and not to worry about it. It hadn't exactly worked that way.

Karen had changed, Andy said, as soon as they left Turkey. Slowly, at first. He didn't notice until after they were married. He hadn't seen the ambition, the drive and the slight streak of ruthless selfishness. Maybe it hadn't been there on the beach, maybe she grew into it. He said he had almost admitted to himself that he wasn't in love with her anymore when she'd gotten pregnant with Cee Cee. It had been an accident. (Lisa didn't understand how that happened. She'd had a lot of sex, with a lot of guys, and she'd never come close to having 'an accident'. She never entirely believed intelligent people who said they did.) For a few weeks a sullen and sick Karen had talked about 'the pregnancy' and not 'the baby' and Andy suspected that if it were up to her she might not stay pregnant. He tried, he said, for Cee Cee. He said she did too, though Lisa found that harder to imagine.

Lisa never worried that Andy still had feelings for Karen. That wasn't it. She was just jealous of the feelings he had once had for her. Mum had once told her off about it. She'd said it was immature, that people were who they were and that included a part of all the people they'd loved before. And that you should be glad of someone's capacity to love and then love again, not jealous. That virgins – emotional and physical – had far less to offer in an adult relationship. Lisa remembered telling her mum she'd been watching too much *Oprah* on cable TV.

'Delicious. We did good!'

'No amount of chestnuts and bacon could ever make Brussels sprouts delicious.'

'And that's why we made you carrots.'

'With maple glaze, if you please. Taking the vegetable as near to being a sweetie as it can get. Just for your sweet tooth.'

'Now *they* were delicious!'

'Forgot the cranberry sauce, but other than that, pretty good.'

'I just wish it took as long to eat it as it took to wash up.'

Lisa was washing, Amanda drying. Jennifer was clearing, and Hannah was sitting on one of the bar stools, eating brandy butter straight from the bowl with her finger.

Jennifer pulled a face. 'That's disgusting! You'll be sick.'

Hannah smirked. 'It isn't Christmas Day until someone's been sick.'

'I wouldn't mind if you at least ate Christmas pudding with it.'

'But Christmas pudding *is* disgusting.'

'Philistine, spoilt philistine! When we were little, we weren't allowed brandy butter without it.'

'Fortunately for me, they'd chilled out by the time I came along.'

'They weren't chilled out, just knackered.'

'There have to be some perks to being the baby.'

'Some perks! The whole gig is one long perk! Try being the oldest,' Lisa shrieked.

'Forget that. Middlie, that's the tough position. Ask any shrink.' Jennifer was half serious.

Amanda snorted. 'But there are two of us in the middle – what does that mean?'

'It means in this family you don't even get the worst position in the family to yourself, that's what it means . . .'

'Shut up moaning – who wants another liqueur? If we're stuck in here while the huntergatherers roam free, we may as well have a drink . . .'

Mark was outside, with Andy and Stephen. Apparently they were chopping more logs for the fire. Actually they were smoking cigars and avoiding the dishes – a perfectly open secret, and the way it had always been. No one really wanted it to be any different. Lisa peeled off her Marigolds and grabbed the Baileys and the Amaretto, plus a few of the small glasses Amanda had just dried.

'Then Amanda can tell us what she's so smiley about.'

'What do you mean?' Amanda's question was playful. 'Aren't I always?'

'Not with so much twinkle . . .'

'Is it a guy?' Hannah asked, eyes wide.

'Of course, it's a guy,' said Lisa, winking at her little sister.

'Fantastic!' Jennifer sipped her drink. 'Dish, Mandy-Pandy – let's have a little bit of vicarious romance.'

Lisa caught the faint note of bitterness in her sister's voice, but Jennifer avoided her gaze. She turned back to Amanda, who was still wearing her paper hat, rakishly pushed back on her head. On her it looked good. 'So . . .'

'Blimey, it's like the Spanish inquisition,' Amanda

laughed, looking from one expectant face to the other. 'Okay, okay! There might be a guy.'

Expectant silence.

'There *is* a guy. I met him on the Underground. Well, actually, I'd seen him before, but it's a long story. I really first talked to him properly on the Underground.'

'That's not fair. The only people who ever talk to me on public transport are drunks and beggars!'

'He's neither. He's a student.'

'They're usually both, most of the time.'

'He's not. He's studying to be an architect, like Mark, actually, so as you know, that takes longer than, I don't know, being a doctor or a vet or something.'

'Oooh, clever boy!'

'And handsome boy?'

'Well, not in the conventional sense, I don't think. He's a redhead.'

'Ginger pubes!' Lisa nodded sympathetically.

'Gross!' groaned Hannah.

Amanda gave Lisa a playful shove. 'I wouldn't know – we're not all slappers.'

'Ah, those were the days.' Lisa shook her head in mock wistfulness.

'So are you two seeing each other?' Jennifer asked.

Amanda smiled shyly. 'I think so, yes, a bit. We only met a couple of weeks ago, so it's early days. And what with Christmas and stuff . . .'

'Is he at home, doing the family thing?'

'Yes, in Cornwall. He's from this huge family, apparently – you know, a million cousins.'

'Was *he* the call this morning?'

She nodded. 'He was. He gave me a present, the other day, before he left. He wanted to see if I'd opened it.'

'We didn't see it.'

'I opened it on my own, early.'

'And what was it?'

'Mind your own business!'

'You're leaving us with no choice but to assume it was, I don't know – Agent Provocateur knickers or something . . .'

'Assume what you want.'

'Leave her be,' Jennifer chided Lisa. 'A girl is allowed a secret.'

It had been a square box, wrapped so beautifully – so Mum-like – that she wondered if he could possibly have done it himself. Inside, nestled on gold tissue paper, was a CD with no markings. The note had said, 'I know this is obsolete technology, but I could hardly steal your iPod and load this, so it's the best I could do. I hope you have a CD player at home. You seem like the kind of girl who wakes up early and sneaks a peek at her presents. I'm the kind of boy who will be woken early by half a dozen hyperactive nephews, so listen to this before breakfast, and I'll be thinking about you . . .'

It was a mixed tape. She hadn't had anything like it since she was about 15 and mixed tapes were really tapes, and Paul Young was on all of them. It was a mixed tape full of the cheesiest, most saccharine laden, goofy love songs. Really. We're talking Cliff Richard's 'Miss You Nights', Phil Collins' 'Groovy Kind of Love'. A Top 10 of naff. She'd snuck into Hannah's room while she was in the shower and borrowed her boombox, which was, indeed, the only piece of compatible technology in the house, and she listened to it while she got dressed. She had laughed delightedly, and danced and sung along. The last song was Mariah Carey's 'All I Want For Christmas

Is You', which she belted out from atop her bed, hair-brush in hand, missing the falsettos by a mile. It was quite possibly the best present ever.

When he'd called, he hadn't said who he was, which normally drove her mad. She knew, of course. The caller ID on her phone announced Tintin was calling.

'So? What do you think?'

'What – no Paul Young?'

'Nope. "Wherever I Lay My Hat That's My Home" is about the inevitability of leaving someone. Not a happy, happy tune at all.'

'What – nothing recorded post 1990?'

'Listen, I have all that stuff. I could have done a Damien Rice, Green Day mixed tape. But where's the fun in that? All that angst . . .'

'It was perfect.'

'It was, wasn't it? I loaded it onto my nano – listened to it when I woke up, as promised.'

'You're crazy.'

'Crazy about you.'

'Ah ha – chat-up lines to match the music. Nice touch.'

'Just didn't want you to be in any doubt.'

'About what?'

'I've got it pretty bad.'

'*You've* got something pretty bad? That's true! But I'm sure you can get a lotion to clear it right up.'

'See you New Year's Eve?'

'Will there be music?'

'There's always music.'

'Then I'll have to think about it.'

'You think about it, I'll dream about it.'

'I'm hanging up, Monsieur Fromage.'

'Merry Christmas.'

'Tin?'

'Call me Ed.'

'Ed?'

'What?'

'Thank you.'

'You're welcome, Amanda.'

So that explained the grin.

'It must have been good. You're going to crack your face open.' Jennifer was watching her intently.

'It was nice. Now bugger off, you lot, and mind your own business!'

'I'll save you,' Lisa put her arm around Amanda. 'Allow me to deflect the attention . . .'

'What with?'

'Andy asked me to marry him.'

Amanda's jaw dropped. 'He *did*?'

'He did. At a party last week.'

'And . . .'

'And I said yes.'

Amanda threw her other arm around her sister. 'Yeah.'

Lisa backed away, her arms raised in protest.

'Not so fast. I shouldn't have said yes.'

'What do you mean?'

'I mean I didn't mean yes. I was a bit pissed, and a bit carried away . . .'

'You don't accidentally agree to marry someone, Lisa.'

'It wasn't an accident, it was just . . .'

'So that's why no announcement, no ring . . . You've told him, right? God, poor Andy!'

'No, I haven't told him.'

Hannah took a large fingerful of brandy butter. 'Even *I* know that's a really bad idea . . .'

Amanda shot her a filthy look. 'Shut up Hannah.'

New Year's Eve

Hannah

She'd said no, to the party invitation. Someone's parents had a barn, and they'd said their kids could have twenty friends each over, for New Year's. They were having a black-tie dinner in the house, so it would be supervised, but only sort of. There were four kids – and Hannah's friend Beth was the second youngest. So that would mean about eighty kids altogether, half of whom would be older, and presumably, since Beth's older siblings were brothers, male. Which made it pretty much the most exciting party invitation she'd ever had. She knew if she told Mark about it he'd make her go. He'd lecture her about drink and drugs and abstinence, and stuff, but he'd make her go. But that would mean leaving him alone on New Year's Eve, and she didn't want to do that.

She'd been out with her friends on the 27th. All day. They'd been to the sales, armed with the vouchers and wads of cash that Christmas had yielded, in a big giggling crowd of girls exhilarated at being freed from conversation with their grandparents and aged aunts. She'd been home much later than she'd said. When she opened the front door, there'd been all these boxes and bags lined up. Mark had cleaned out Mum's wardrobe. He said he'd been meaning to do it for months, and that now was as good a time as any – New Year, and all that. She'd known it needed to be done, and part of her was glad she'd missed it. But he looked so sad and so pale and so lonely, standing among the carrier bags, that she felt awful.

He'd turned down all his own invitations. Vince and Sophie had practically begged him to go there. There were the usual suspects – neighbours, colleagues, old friends . . . He said no to everyone. So she pretended the invitation she was turning down was the less-than-thrilling opportunity to waitress at the same friend's parents' dinner party, with free drinks thrown in after dessert was served. If he questioned her truthfulness it didn't show in his face. They rented DVDs of some of the films they hadn't made it to earlier in the year for obvious reasons and bought some extremely smart ready-made food from Marks and Spencer. Hannah told Mark she wouldn't let him cook on New Year's Eve, coming so soon after Christmas, and that she certainly didn't intend to wash up. They had King prawns with dipping sauce, and lobster, and imported strawberries. They ate in their pyjamas and dressing gowns in front of the fire and let the machine pick up all their calls.

At 12.15am, Dad woke her up, very gently, and they both went to bed. She'd missed it. Once she'd climbed the stairs and slid between the sheets, cool on her skin after an evening in front of the fire, she felt very awake again. The party would be in full swing now, everyone laughing and dancing and shouting to each other over the thump of the music, and the house was so quiet.

Lisa

Lisa and Andy toasted the New Year at 7.30pm. Cee Cee insisted. She also insisted they do it because it was already New Year for her mummy, sailing in the Caribbean, and no amount of cajoling would persuade her that the Caribbean was five hours behind and not five hours ahead. They had picked her up from Karen's on Boxing Day, and she'd been dictating the content and timing of their meals all week, as well as waking them up at 6.30 every morning. She'd heard noises from their bedroom a couple of nights ago, and came in while they were making love. Andy had grabbed the duvet and covered them, and she'd climbed up between them. He'd told her Lisa was having a bad dream. It was certainly a nightmare, Lisa smiled to herself, lying there high and dry, but not the one he described. Almost at once Cee Cee had gone back to sleep there and they thought she might have forgotten, but the next day in Pizza Express she described the scenario in no small detail to the waitress, who blushed knowingly.

New Year's Eve was no different. She was up before 7, demanding pancakes and *Charlie and Lola*. And to be honest, the absence of any kind of a lie-in all week meant that neither was inclined to argue with her any more. They opened champagne, Cee Cee drinking hers from an eggcup, lit sparklers and attempted a linked-arm 'Auld Lang Syne', which was largely unsuccessful. Andy had bought a single-fuse firework box, which he'd lit at the end of the garden, so they had a damp and somewhat unimpressive two-minute firework display at 7.35, and by 7.45 the brouhaha was largely over. They'd argued a little, earlier. Andy thought tonight would be a good night to tell Cee Cee they were engaged, but Lisa had stumbled on the perfect excuse and convinced him, forcibly, that it would be wrong to tell her before they'd had a chance to tell Karen, in case of trauma. Truth was, of course, that she did not want Cee Cee to know. Definitely there was a trauma factor, but it was all her own. Not that Cee Cee needed any encouragement in this area. After all this time, she had apparently decided that she approved of Lisa and all week her line of questioning had run along such happy families' lines that Lisa might have suspected Andy had already told her, if she didn't know him to be so scrupulously honest and straightforward. Putting Cee Cee to bed at 8 provided her with some relief from the questioning about the likelihood of a new brother or sister for next New Year's Eve.

When she got back downstairs, Andy had poured the rest of the bottle into her glass. She drank it, settling back into the crook of his arm to watch *The Mask of Zorro*, and they had both woken up at 12.40, having slept through the whole thing.

Jennifer

Jennifer wasn't hungry, although it was after 10pm and she hadn't had anything to eat since lunchtime. She pushed her Fettucine Alfredo around the plate, and sipped at her prosecco. It was noisy and smoky. Most people were already on the way to being drunk, although there was still an hour until midnight. Revellers passed by on the street, occasionally leering unsteadily through the window where they were sitting. She wished she was at home; she wasn't in the mood for all this good-naturedness. She spoke when spoken to, as animatedly as she could, and kept a smile frozen on her face. When left alone, her mind wandered somewhere else.

It was New Year's Eve three years ago when they had first tried for a baby. It had felt like an appropriately adventurous thing to do, to celebrate the New Year by creating a new life. When she was a child, Jennifer used to like to see the front of the local paper the first week in January – it always carried a photograph of a smiling mother clutching the first baby of the year, born at the local hospital at two minutes past midnight on New Year's Day. Mum used to look over her shoulder, clicking her tongue and exclaiming that being in labour was no way to spend New Year's Eve, but she would always admire the baby, nonetheless. 'You forget how small they are!'

They'd been in New York three years ago. The pound was strong against the dollar, and seats were cheap, so they'd found a little hotel off Times Square that had a good rate. They'd flown on December 28th, and packed all the touristy things into a few days. The city was crowded with bargain hunters – Fifth Avenue was a jungle. It was bitterly cold – the wind whistled up the island like a thousand tiny knives, and many, many hot chocolate stops were required.

Stephen bought them earmuffs from a street vendor. They'd been up the Empire State Building in bright sunshine, marvelling at the urban tapestry laid out before them, danced cacophonously on the giant piano in FAO Schwartz, taken a ride round Central Park in a horse-drawn carriage, and skated – (badly, and painfully) – at the Rockefeller Rink in the shadow of the biggest Christmas tree either of them had ever seen. Skating, it appeared, was the one sport Stephen was destined to fail at. He flailed and slid like a cartoon, landing on the hard ice from every angle, over and over. Jennifer and Lisa had begged their mum to take them skating at the rink in Queensway practically every weekend for about two years when they were about 14 and 15. Although she hadn't done it since, the memory of how to skate came flooding back when she stepped onto the ice and let go of the sides.

'You can go backwards!' Stephen's tone was incredulous, but admiring. 'You never said.'

'I'd forgotten. We used to go when we were kids.'

'You're pretty good. You can do that one foot to the other glide thing.'

'I know!' She'd hunched her shoulders with delight, and sped up, no longer watching her feet. Lapping him, she came up from behind, shouting, 'Feels good to be better at something than you are, for a change. This, mate, is how it feels for me when we're skiing.'

Stephen made the grave error of turning to look at her, a smart retort on the tip of his tongue, and fell, hard, on the ice. He actually felt sick at the impact. When she skated over, contrite and sympathetic, to help him stand up, he grinned sheepishly at her. 'Except snow isn't this bloody hard!'

By December 31st, they had ticked all the tourist boxes except the Circle Line cruise around the island, which only a raving idiot would attempt at those temperatures. They spent the afternoon in Macy's, buying cheap Levis and Calvin Klein underpants. The crowds gathering to watch the famous crystal ball drop in Times Square on New Year's Eve started to thicken in earnest at around 6pm. Police herded them like sheep through an elaborate system of fences towards their target. It was freezing cold. Even wearing hats, gloves, scarfs and their thickest coats, and even in the midst of a pressing, eager crowd, Jennifer was so cold that her face hurt, and her feet felt like they might shatter. At 9pm, by mutual agreement, they abandoned their plan to wait for midnight and went back to the hotel, while they could still extricate themselves from the crowd. Stephen had run her a hot bath, and ordered a cheeseburger and chips for them both from room service. She was luxuriating in the bath, enjoying sensation returning to her feet, while he gazed out of the window at the ever-increasing crowd milling around below.

'They must be crazy. All to watch some ball drop.'

'But it was exciting out there – the atmosphere and everything. Bet it's great when the music starts.'

'Bet it's not that great. There's hardly any room to stand upright, let alone dance.'

'I'd like to have seen when they drop all the confetti and stuff.'

'Yeah, well, I'd rather watch it from up here.'

'You're getting middle-aged.'

'Watch it!'

He appeared at the bathroom door, clutching two miniature bottles of champagne he'd procured from the mini bar.

'They're not that cold, but there's that ice machine out on the landing. I'll be back in a minute.'

'Don't they cost more than a full bottle bought outside the hotel?'

'Oh give it a rest, Ebenezer. It's New Year's Eve!'

Back with the ice, bottles plunged into it to chill, Stephen pulled his sweater over his head.

'Shift over, I'm coming in. Bags you get the tap end. You've already been soaking for half an hour . . .'

Jennifer smiled, and turned around in the water, laying her head to the left of the taps. He climbed in, but the bath wasn't really big enough for both of them, and he sat, with his knees clasped to his chest, looking uncomfortable, for a moment until she laughed and climbed out, bubbles running down her legs onto the bath mat.

'Here, you have a go on your own.'

She put on a dressing gown and went to the window, towelling her hair. She loved the city. It throbbed with life, twenty-four hours a day. Mum and Mark had had a honeymoon of sorts here – just a weekend. Mum said it was her favourite place on earth. Jennifer could see why – it would suit her mum.

Stephen was calling again, from the bath.

'You know what we should do?'

She walked over to the doorway, and leant against the frame, watching him and hoping this new plan of his didn't involve getting dressed up and heading out into the cold night again.

'What should we do?'

'We should make a baby.'

'Right now?'

'Well, not *right now*, obviously – there are burgers on their way. Tonight. A New Year's Eve, New York baby. Can you get a US passport if you're conceived here?'

'Don't think so.'

'No matter. You'd still have been conceived here. Great place to get made.'

'Are you serious?'

'Perfectly.'

She shook her head, smiling, and not quite certain how in earnest he was.

'Think about it. A baby conceived tonight would be born in, what, September? Don't you remember what an easy ride the September kids had at school? They were always the oldest ones in the year.'

'You've really been thinking about this, haven't you?'

'Not really.' He grinned. 'But why not?'

'Are you bored of just having me?'

'What an odd thing to say. Bored with you?' He looked puzzled. 'Of course not. What a weird way to see it. It's what people do, Jennifer. They fall in love, they get married, they have babies. We've been married, babies are the next bit.'

There was a knock at the door.

'Shut up a minute, will you?'

Jennifer shut Stephen into the bathroom and, checking how she looked in the mirror, answered the door to room service. She fumbled in Stephen's jeans pocket for a couple of dollars while the man set up trays at the table near the window and smiled at him. 'Happy New Year.'

'Happy New Year, ma'am.'

'Great, I'm starving.'

Stephen had wrapped himself in a towel and went to grab a chip from his plate. Water dripped onto the tablecloth and Jennifer picked up the hand towel she'd been using to dry her hair and ran it along his arm and shoulder. The touch was proprietary. He pulled on his jeans and a T-shirt, kissed the top of her head and sat down to eat in earnest.

'So, what do you think? Of Plan Baby . . .'

'You've sort of sprung it on me . . .'

'Okay, so I've sprung it on you. Tell me your thoughts, oh careful, ponderous, non spontaneous one . . .' His tone was affectionate, not cruel, but she felt just a little irritated. You couldn't spontaneously decide to have a baby, could you?

'I thought we'd wait a bit more . . .'

'Why should we? We're not that young. I'm making good money – you'd take maternity leave, go back when you wanted to . . . We'd have to tighten our belts a bit, if you didn't want to or something, but we'd manage – millions do.'

Jennifer felt slightly railroaded. Of course they'd talked about kids. In the abstract, starry-eyed way you did when they were still some way off. And now Stephen had jumped tracks onto the express. She felt almost breathless.

'You are serious, aren't you?'

'Absolutely.'

'You really want this? It's not some elaborate sort of foreplay?'

'Elaborate, and not, so far, terribly effective! I think I'd have done better with a couple of compliments and some ear nibbling, don't you?! 'Course I want this. I love you.' He made it all sound so simple.

That was better. She took a large bite from her burger and made him wait for a response until she'd finished the mouthful.

'I'm on the pill. You can't get pregnant until you've stopped for a few months.'

'Party pooper.'

'Realist.'

'If you got pregnant straight away after that, we could still tell him he was conceived in New York on New Year's Eve, couldn't we?'

'Only if you're planning to raise a kid – sorry, a son, clearly. Very "my boy Bill" of you, by the way, who can't count and never gets past a rudimentary understanding of biology.'

'Okay, wise arse. You don't half know how to piss on a man's bonfire. But there's nothing to stop us practising, right? Doing it like we mean it . . .'

She laughed. 'No, we can do it like we mean it. I thought we usually did.'

He stood up and went to sit on the bed, patting the mattress beside him.

'Come on, then . . .'

'You'll get indigestion.'

'It'll be worth it . . .'

'Don't I even get my midnight champagne?'

'Honey, it's 10.30! You know me. You can have your champagne at 10.40. Now get over here . . .'

So they'd been laughing together, back when it all began. She remembered them laughing such a lot. That's what had been so wonderful, after John. He'd been so bloody serious about everything, so earnest and so thoughtful. Stephen was his polar opposite. The sex had been light-hearted and fun and good, although she was right about the indigestion, and he'd needed antacid before the ball dropped on Times Square. And she was on the pill, so even though she'd agreed, or at least stopped disagreeing in principle, she knew they weren't really trying for a baby that night. But that was when it had started. It had all seemed wonderfully simple. He'd always been able to spin things that way in those days.

He'd waved her packet of pills at her a few days later, back in England.

'Shall I get rid of these?'

'I suppose you'd better.'

'More practising?'

'Get lost! I've got laundry to do, and you said you'd go and see your parents when we got back . . .'

He winked, kissed her on the cheek and headed in the direction of the front door. 'Okay then, but just you let me know where and when . . . I'm always ready.'

For six months, they carried on like they had been, just without chemical intervention. And for six months they didn't worry. They laughed, and they made love, and often both at the same time. For the next six months, she paid a little more attention to the right time to conceive. She made little doodles in her diary, counting fourteen days forward from a period. She even turned down the odd invitation from friends, when it fell on a likely night, although she never told Stephen that she had. For the six months after that, she used an ovulation prediction kit from the chemist. Stephen called her 'the Professor'. When nothing had happened for eighteen months, at Stephen's request, she went to the doctor.

At every stage, when she knew any normal woman would have been increasingly anxious and worried, Jennifer grew more and more ambiguous about the whole thing. Stephen was certainly doing well at work. She didn't really understand much of what he told her about what he did, but it appeared that he did it well. He had a couple of promotions, got a company car and started going to more and more overnight sales conferences. He got a BlackBerry and was never off it. It came on holidays with them, demanding constant attention, and slept in the bed beside them. Often she woke – far too early – to the clicking of his fingers on the miniature keyboard. She told a friend at work they didn't need a baby – they had a BlackBerry, and that was enough. He was preoccupied; he wasn't listening to her so much.

Worse than that was the subtle, inexorable change in his attitude towards their conceiving of a child. At the beginning, it was both of them, and it was fun. Both of them trying, both of them failing. Then she knew the focus had shifted. Something in him needed to believe that it was more to do with her than with him, some ancient, buried machismo, an unwillingness to admit defeat. When she was unwilling to go to the doctor – claiming that with a young, healthy couple, the system wouldn't be interested until they'd tried on their own for a long time – he gave vent to the insinuation that had been there, unspoken, for a while. He was less kind to her, less patient. They stopped laughing so much, and all the time, she became less and less certain that getting pregnant was what she really wanted.

Had things changed so much in three New Year's Eves? They'd been so happy, young and in love and at one in New York. It was as if something had happened, as if one of them had had an affair, only no one had. It was what hadn't happened, what apparently *couldn't* happen, that had caused this. She sometimes wondered whether she had simply fallen out of love with him, like she had with John. Maybe there was a time limit on her ability to love another person but still there were moments between them when she knew it wasn't that. You couldn't explain it, could you? It was a million tiny things that made things change.

And so they went out, of course, this year, as they did most years. They were all about making it look as if everything was fine. They met friends, in this noisy Italian restaurant, ate, drank and danced. You would have to be watching very closely to see what was missing between them. They were not the kind of people who would ever fight in public, or make anyone else feel uncomfortable, or show their vulnerability. That was something they still had in common – this ridiculous, dumb pride. But that just made her feel more isolated. If only Mum was alive. She'd give up, she'd talk to her. Maybe she only told herself that because Mum was dead, and it couldn't happen. No, she would. She was desperate; she'd listen to what she had to say. As the clock chimed midnight, and everyone was falling into each other's arms, kissing and whooping, she was thinking of her mum, and how she'd missed her chance.

When Stephen found her in the crowd, he put his arms around her and held her close. 'Let's make this one a better one, hey,' he whispered. It was a request, and a promise, and a plea. He was just as sad, just as unhappy as she was. She didn't know how he interpreted the tears in her eyes, but she nodded yes, and held him right back, praying that it would be.

Amanda

Amanda had imagined Ed was taking her to a party. He'd arranged to meet her at the Underground station at 8pm. She was excited. She'd met a few of his friends, people he was at college with, before Christmas, at the pub, and they were fun. She'd dressed carefully – in a dress, which was rare – this dress being pretty much the only one she had; also heels, which was even rarer. Normally she didn't wear make-up, but tonight she'd put on mascara and lipgloss. It was really cold, and she knew her nose and cheeks were pink.

It was crazy, really, being so excited. She barely knew him. They'd been out, what, five times. Three of those had been in a big crowd, where conversation was almost impossible. One coffee, and one curry. A few kisses – standing up variety. One brilliant Christmas present, and a few phone calls while she'd been home. He wasn't her type, he wasn't in her plan and she didn't, for the life of her, know why she was having palpitations standing here in the freezing cold. She should be with her wacky flatmates and a thousand drunken idiots at a rave in Lewisham.

But the palpitations just sped up when she saw him walking towards her. He didn't say hello, he just pulled her towards her and kissed her, more seriously than he had done before, his hand was on the back of her head, holding her, close and insistent. 'I missed you.'

'There are a couple of parties we could go to. Or there's the big crowd in Trafalgar Square. I know a good pub near there, full of Canadians. We could go there. Or . . .'

'Or?'

'Or we could go back to my place.'

'Who's there?'

'No one. I'm the only one who's in London for New Year.' He looked sheepish. 'It would just be us. But . . . I mean . . . we don't have to . . .'

'That sounds good.' It did. She realized she didn't want to be in a crowd; she wanted him all to herself. Somewhere it wasn't so cold that you felt like your feet might shatter if you took one more step.

He paused, putting the key in the lock. 'I don't want

you to think ... I mean, just because ... I'm not expecting...'

She pulled him through the open door and slammed it closed behind them. 'Shut up, Ed.' She kissed him, hard. '*I'm* expecting...'

Like everything else about this new relationship, this was not really her style. There had been a handful of lovers before Ed. She supposed, if she were ever itemizing them, that they represented an average amount for someone her age. She always knew them really well; she always thought long and hard about moving to the next level with someone. She was circumspect with herself. Her sexual practice was slightly at odds with her free spirit, she knew. Sometimes she wished she were a little more like Lisa, who had slept with, she imagined, and it always sounded like, dozens of guys before Andy. Lisa treated sex a bit like a sport – a highly aerobic, heavy-contact sport requiring no specialist equipment. Although, knowing Lisa, specialist equipment was almost certainly involved at some point. It was fun, it was healthy, it was good for you, and so long as you were careful, both with your health and your feelings, it was okay to do it with anyone you fancied who fancied you back.. On paper, Amanda believed there was nothing wrong with that. It just wasn't how she felt about it. So far as she knew, Jennifer had only ever slept with Stephen, and the boyfriend she had before him, the university one. So she was somewhere in the middle of the two on the morality ladder.

But right now, she didn't want to think about it, and she didn't want to wait. She wanted to do what she never normally did, and just go to bed with this guy. She wasn't pretending this was love – it couldn't possibly be, could it? Maybe it was just lust, and she was going to give into it, and maybe there was nothing wrong with that. And then there was the CD . . . Still, the point was, she wasn't going to analyse it. She was just going to do it . . . Twice . . . Before midnight. And once more, while the distant symbolic noise of fireworks still sounded.

Thank you very much. Hip, hip, hooray for impulsive, reckless behaviour! And a happy, happy . . . *happy* New Year!

It was the best sex she'd ever had. If that was what spontaneity got you, she was suddenly all for it – a converted zealot. Ed was much more domineering in bed than he appeared to be out of it, and if she was momentarily curious about where all this imaginative expertise came from, she quickly put it aside and was grateful that it had come from somewhere. He was like some Fabian-esque hero in an airport novel; he knew exactly what to do, where, when . . . how to move her body all around his own like she was the proverbial putty in his hands. Blimey, yummy! Good night.

She slept for about ten hours. It was almost lunchtime by the time she surfaced. Arguably, if he hadn't kissed her awake, she may have pushed on through to teatime. She protested, pushing his face away. 'Mmm, morning mouth! I haven't brushed my teeth.'

'Don't care – you're gorgeous.' He was undeterred. He nuzzled her armpit. 'You haven't washed yet either, but you smell fantastic.'

'You're a randy sod.'

'Not until I met you.' He winked, looking for all the world like a member of Fagin's gang.

'Yeah, you had the tentative approach of a virgin,

I felt.' She pinched the delicate skin under his arm. *So* not the case.

'Just practising for you, my lovely. Just practising.'

'Charming! All those girls would be thrilled to hear you say so.'

'Must you say "all those girls", like it's been the cast of *Ben Hur*?' He pretended to look hurt.

'It's either a long and varied list, or you spent your formative years in a brothel.'

'Is that your way of telling me you enjoyed yourself last night, Amanda?' Now his face was mock serious, but the twinkle never left his eye.

'Can't remember much about it, matter of fact.'

He climbed on top of her, pinning her down with his powerful legs.

'Then I'd better remind you, I think . . .'

'Again?!'

'Oh yes, again.'

So teatime it was, then. New Year's Day was already New Year's Almost Night by the time they did brush their teeth, wash and emerge from Ed's apartment, hand in hand, in search of food and drink, neither of which had been partaken of since the previous afternoon. He'd lent her some jeans that one of his flatmates had left on the drying rack in the kitchen, and a pair of her boots, assuring Amanda she wouldn't mind, and an old rugby shirt of his that smelt of Persil. You wouldn't run a marathon without loading on the carbs, and they were both a little light-headed and woozy. Thankfully the pub at the end of the road was serving Cumberland sausages with mash and onion gravy, and within minutes they were wolfing down giant portions and sipping Whisky Macs by a suitably roaring fire.

Unsurprisingly, given what they had just spent almost twenty-four hours doing, Amanda felt incredibly close to him. She was as happy as she could remember being. She felt as if she had a neon sign on her forehead, flashing 'Satisfied' at the world. For twenty minutes or so, they just ate. They sat so close that their thighs touched, all the way down.

Hunger assuaged, they started to talk. They were still talking when the landlord called time, reminding them gruffly that there had been a lock-in the night before, and that now he was tired and wanted to go upstairs and watch telly. In many ways it was a typical getting-to-know-you conversation. One she'd had around the world, a thousand times. But in other ways it was more, as if in taking their clothes off back at his place they'd peeled away a few layers of the social onion already. This wasn't an exchange of facts; this was more real.

Ed told her about his Christmas in Cornwall. His dad was much older than his mum – twenty-five years, in fact. He was 75 now, and he'd seemed frail to Ed this visit, suddenly older. He was still sharp as a tack, though. Evidently they were incredibly close – he'd retired from the law firm where he was a founding partner when Ed was still relatively young – at primary school – and the two of them had spent far more time together than most fathers managed. He'd been married before – had four children with his first wife, who was rich, and thin and bitter – Ed said they all called her 'The Duchess', as in Windsor, until she died a few years earlier. His half brothers and sisters were all weird, he said, poisoned against his father by too many years of listening to the Duchess deride and castigate him, although it was she who left the marriage. He didn't see much of them or their children. He told Amanda he thought his dad's relationship with his four older children had a lot to do with why he was so close to the three more he had had with Ed's mum, Nancy.

'It's like he knew he'd played a part in losing them, even though what happened wasn't really his fault. It made him determined to be really close to me and my brothers.' Amanda nodded.

'And I was the youngest, which helped. Tom and Dan were at senior school when Dad retired, and always busy with sports and girls and stuff. I had him to myself a lot. We used to go flyfishing, and tinker with engines and things.'

'Sounds pretty idyllic,' Amanda smiled.

'You know, it sort of was. He and Mum have always been really, really happy together. That filters down, you know.'

She nodded. 'My mum was happily married too.'

'To your dad?'

'*No!*' She laughed. 'Sounds a bit like your dad, actually. My father – he's dead now – he went off with someone, before I was born. I've got two big sisters – Jennifer and Lisa – they're quite a bit older than me. I suppose I must have been the Elastoplast baby, or an accident – one of those; didn't work. He scarpered when Mum was about four months pregnant, I think. Bugger! But they were not happy together. That's what Mum always said. And I don't think Jennifer and Lisa have many happy family memories from before. It wasn't a big shock, or anything, I don't think. Probably he just had the opportunity first.'

'Were you and he close?'

She snorted. 'Barely! I didn't see much of him, to be honest. He lived a long way away and he started a new family. Died of a massive coronary about five years ago.

I didn't go to his funeral; didn't especially want to. He wasn't especially missed, so far as I ever knew. Mum went, and my sisters. But then they'd lived with him, and I never did.'

Ed shook his head. 'Families.'

'Don't know one without a sniff of trouble.'

'Not possible, I think. My mum's lot, maybe ... They're pretty straightforward.' He shrugged. 'So – your mum married again?'

'She did. Mark. The architect – remember, I told you?' Ed nodded. 'They married about sixteen years ago, when I was pretty young. Had Hannah, my kid sister, who's fifteen now.'

'Christ – four girls!'

'Christ – three boys! What about your brothers?'

'Tom's a lawyer, like Dad. Works at the old family firm in Cornwall. He's in training to be just like the old man. He married a girl called Ginny and they've got a couple of sprogs, who'll no doubt grow up to be lawyers and work at the old family firm. Tom and Ginny live in Mum and Dad's old house. Beautiful place, with five or six acres. Mum and Dad moved to the sea, to a smaller place, when Tom got married. We have Christmas at their place because there are lots of us – Mum's relatives descend en masse – and that's the only place where there's room for us all. Dan's a captain in the Tank Regiment. Went to Sandhurst, the full Monty. Career soldier ... We're lucky, really, we've all gone in very different directions, so there's no competition, you know – no one treads on anyone's toes. That helps.' He stopped talking and kissed her on the mouth, pulling back and smiling. It acknowledged how good this felt. 'Tell me about your sisters.'

'Lisa is the oldest. She's most like me, I suppose, if

I'm like any of them. She's meant to be marrying this great bloke, Andy, but I think she's collateral damage from Mum and Dad's divorce – commitment phobe, that sort of thing. Then there's Jennifer. Neat freak. Shoes always match the outfit, if you know what I mean . . . She's married to Stephen, who is a bit of an enigma. No children – think that might be a bit of an issue, but she's not a great communicator, our Jen. Hannah's just a kid, really . . . ridiculously good-looking and a weeny bit spoilt. I'm the definite black sheep, the one with the itchy feet . . .'

'And the matriarch of all this?' Amanda had forgotten that he didn't know.

'My mum died. Last summer.'

'Fuck!'

Amanda laughed. That was an honest response. She hated the people whose eyes glazed over with pity as they immediately started apologizing, as though her mother's death were in some way connected to them. What could you say to that?

'Fuck indeed! She had cancer, of course. She was 60 years old.'

'What was she like?' She loved him, *really* loved him then, for an instant. This, this was easier.

'She was . . . she was amazing. She was larger than life, you know. Lots of people say that about lots of people, but it's true of relatively few, I find. It *was* true of her. She was loud and funny and irreverent and wicked, and contagiously happy, and the most loving person you could ever know, and she was fierce about us, passionate about us . . . and . . . and . . .' Amanda wasn't, for once, horrified at her own tears. It was okay. 'And I miss her. I wasn't there when she died, because I'm cowardly and stubborn and selfish, and I should have been, I should have been there, with her and with all the others. It's really come back and bitten me in the arse, you know, since. I wish I had been there.'

'To say goodbye?'

She nodded, tears rolling now, down her cheeks and into the plate in front of her. Ed had a handkerchief. How old fashioned and wonderful of him. He pulled it out of his pocket and pressed it into her hand, and she dabbed at her face with it.

'To say goodbye.'

For a while, he just held her, which was all she wanted. When she had composed herself a little, she sat back and blew her nose. 'Sorry. 'Spose you don't particularly want that back now?' He winked and shook his head. She crumpled the handkerchief and shoved it into her pocket.

'She left a kind of journal, things she'd been writing, on and off, from the time she was first diagnosed. Thoughts, and stories and stuff. Things she wanted us to know, I suppose. And we all got these letters; she left these letters for each of us.'

'What did yours say?' From anyone else, that might have been an intrusive question. From Ed, it didn't seem to be.

'I haven't read mine.'

'Why not?'

She shrugged. He was the only person in the world who knew she hadn't opened it. She carried it everywhere – it was with her right now, in her bag, tucked into the front of her diary. 'I'm afraid to.'

'Why?'

'I'm afraid that she was angry with me, at the end.'

'Because you weren't there?'

She nodded slowly.

Ed leant forward, propping his elbows on the table. When he spoke, his voice was gentle and slow.

'I didn't know your mother, of course. Sounds like I missed out there. But I very much doubt that some-one – someone's mother – would go to all the trouble of writing a deathbed letter simply to give someone a bollocking from beyond the grave, particularly the mother you just described, to the daughter I'm just beginning to get to know.'

Amanda smiled at him, grateful as a child being told that of course there's a Santa Claus.

'You think?'

He nodded. 'I think.'

The bell rang, and the landlord was looking specifically at them since the pub was empty . . .

'I also think we should leave now . . .'

The street outside was deserted. It was still cold, and their faces, which had turned red and hot from the fire, were stung by it. Ed put his arm around her and pulled her towards him.

'Will you stay tonight?'

She was a little taken aback. She realized she hadn't for a moment considered doing anything else. A tiny seed of doubt sprang up in her head. Did he want her to stay?

'Is that okay?'

He kissed her, hard. 'That is *so* much more than okay. I don't think I'd let you leave, matter of fact. I may *never* let you leave . . .'

It was probably just talk, but it felt really good.

*

That second night was less Judith Krantz, more Danielle Steele. His eyes almost never left hers, never closed, never stopped telling her how much he felt. She loved believing him.

On the second morning, the milk, a relic from before Christmas, smelt bad and the bread had a pale green hue that was distinctly unappetizing. Ed went out for supplies. He banned her from dressing, saying he would be back in ten minutes and he wanted to find her naked and warm under his quilt. She lay back, her arms and legs splayed like a child's, and made a bed angel of happiness, the duvet tucked obediently in her armpits. Everything about this, right now, felt right. That didn't happen every day. It felt like the start of something. The fact that she'd gone from 0–60 even felt right – strange, but right. But if he thought she was going to miss the opportunity to tart herself up while he was gone, he didn't know women as well as he thought he did. She went to the bathroom and looked at her wanton self in the mirror. Her bed head of shag tangles was a fright. She brushed her teeth and showered quickly, wondering whether you could borrow the razor of a man you'd only just met, and deciding that if you'd let him do some of the things she'd let Ed do to her last night, the razor seemed a strange place to draw the line . . .

Clean again, and wrapped in a towel, she pulled her handbag onto the bed, into her lap. She'd been incommunicado for thirty-six hours now and she should check her phone. She switched it on, and waited to see who might want her. No messages. Charming. But no more than nomads could expect. She put the phone back in her bag, and was about to put it back down on the floor so she could lie back and luxuriate in imagining Ed's hands moving all over her, which, if she was lucky, they were about to do all over again, when she saw her diary. She pulled it out, her fingers stroking the worn brown leather, pale now, in places. She opened it, and took out her Mum's letter, her own name written in a familiar round hand, in Barbara's trademark turquoise ink: *Amanda.*

She was sitting up in bed, hugging her knees, with the letter balanced on top of them, when Ed got back.

'What you got?'

'My mum's letter.'

'You going to read it?'

'Thinking about it.'

'Do you want me to get lost for a bit?'

'I'd rather you stayed with me.'

Ed didn't answer. Amanda surfaced from her reverie and peered at his face. Had she frightened him? Was this all a bit much?

He nodded slowly. 'Right.'

'Right.'

'I'm going to get into bed, next to you, and just lie there and not say anything for a while. Does that seem right?'

She smiled weakly. 'That seems right.'

He lay down beside her, with one arm around her back, resting on the mattress, gently stroking her hip. She took a deep breath and opened the letter.

Darling Amanda,

So brave, so fearless. My adventurer. You've given me more sleepless nights than all the others, you know that? One day, you'll know the worry of a mum waiting for a fortnightly call from somewhere, wanting to know that your baby is okay and safe and happy. I wouldn't have stopped you, even if I could. I envy you your spirit.

Blimey, this letter's the toughest so I've put it off until the last, and now I'm tired, so tired you can't imagine. And just the tiniest bit afraid that I'm not making complete sense any more – you take enough pills and you start to question everything.

I remember the day you were born. When Lisa came, I was young and ridiculously overexcited, and she was the baby I had for Donald, and for the family, and for everyone else. I was still in the baby fog when Jennifer came, bless her, and whole months passed in a blur. And still, there were people around all the time – Donald, his mum, other mums with babies and toddlers the same age. But it was different with you. It was just us, the two of us. Your sisters had gone to stay with their cousins in Yorkshire for the week and I was supposed to be getting a room ready for you. I'd painted the walls, and I was just about to get up a ladder and start hanging this frieze – Winnie the Pooh and friends – when my waters broke and stopped me. I guess you had artistic sensibilities even then! Never did get to hang that frieze ... You were a few weeks early – it was like you couldn't wait to see me. Fast too; in a hurry, like you've always been. And it was just you and me and the midwife – and she slipped out and left us alone. It was so quiet. You didn't even cry. No fussing, no noise, and no interference. No one else wanting to hold you. You were mine, Amanda, all mine. And I loved you so much.

People were gossiping about me in the ward. I could see them behind their banks of tasteless flowers and helium balloons, and relatives bearing down with

Chelsea strips and baskets of grapes. The single mother with no visitors. I didn't give a damn.

You mustn't blame Donald. Okay, you can blame him for being an inadequate human being because he pretty much always was. But it was me who held him at arm's-length when you came. We'd been living apart almost the whole time I was pregnant. The decree nisi was through, and we were waiting for the absolute. He'd already met Marissa, hadn't he, and started his new life. I know he wanted to do the right thing, or at least that he wanted to be seen to be doing the right thing. He was always a stickler for appearances. But I couldn't see the point.

Have you guessed, my darling girl? Have you wondered and thought and imagined, lying in the couchettes and hammocks and tents and beach huts of your long journeys? Have you already hated me for my dishonesty, or does that start here? Will you listen to my excuses and my justifications, or stop hearing at the first words? Because, of course, and now isn't it so obvious? Of course Donald isn't your father.

I've known I would tell you this since they told me I was dying. No one else knows, and I couldn't let it die with me. But I have played the conversation and written the letters over and over in my head, and never been sure until this moment whether I would tell you who the man was. I can't call him your father because he isn't – he hasn't been. Neither was Donald. Mark – wonderful Mark – he's been the best I could do for you, and he's been pretty bloody terrific.

And so I won't tell you. It doesn't matter. We had an affair. My own marriage was even more in tatters than I thought it was. I don't know about his. I don't even know if I was the only lover he had. He was, for me. But it wasn't a wonderful thing. It was a tacky, sort of sordid thing. It didn't last long. I'm a lousy liar. God, are you reading that and thinking what a stinking irony that is? I'm not lying about this. A few weeks, that's all.

He didn't even know I was pregnant. There was no point. I wish I could say I'd stopped because I didn't want people to get hurt. In lots of ways I wish I could tell you I'd done that — made the ultimate, noble sacrifice and given up someone who was the love of my life because it was the right thing to do.

I did give him up because I didn't love him. That was why. I was flattered and excited but I didn't love him. I don't think he loved me either. We were slightly pathetic, actually, the pair of us. Acting like teenagers when we were far too old. And actually, I didn't know for sure that you were his. After the first time I went home and went to bed with my husband. Pretty grim, when you think about it. Believe me, Amanda, nothing about that time in my life makes me especially proud of myself, but I was frightened so I couldn't be sure.

Of course, you didn't look a thing like Donald when you were born. And I knew then. By then they'd moved away; he was spooked as hell by my being pregnant. My belly was his scarlet letter. Not that he ever asked me, the coward. And I didn't want him to anyway. He got himself transferred, and they sold their house and moved away. And I honestly never saw him again.

I've always wondered whether I would have stayed with your father — with Donald, I mean, if he hadn't left me. I'd like to think not, but maybe I'm lying to myself — maybe I never was that brave.

So here we are, and I'm a coward again. I'm writing this down when I should be telling you face to face. And I can honestly say, as I lie here waiting to die, that how you feel about this letter is the biggest thing I have to worry about. I should have told you the last time you were home. We both knew you weren't coming back until it was all over. I should have told you then. I made excuses – you seemed happy and excited about the trip – there were people around all the time, but they were all just excuses. The truth was that I was frightened and I let fear make me fail you as a mother. And I will die (I guess I have, if you're reading this) with that guilt.

Maybe, if things had been different, you would never have needed to know. You weren't close to Donald, I know. I gave you a happy childhood, I think. No, I know. Whatever else I have to feel bad about, that I don't. I was the best mum I knew how to be, and when Mark came along, whatever problems Jennifer and Lisa might have had with him, he was great for you. I remember watching the two of you together and thinking that I had gotten so bloody lucky. And even when Hannah came along, he still loved you the same, I know he has. We made a family, and we were happy. He was the miracle of all of our lives.

But there is a thing in you, my lovely. The thing that keeps you travelling, the thing that makes you hold yourself a little apart from people. My girl with a thousand mates around the world but no best friend. The beautiful woman who slays men with her smile and her wiggle, but has never been in love. The thing that took you away from me, let you walk away or made you walk away, knowing that you would never see me again. I feel like there is something inside you that I need to solve and I wonder if this is a piece in your puzzle, Amanda.

I hope that knowing doesn't make more questions than it answers. I'm sorry I'm not here to answer them. I should be, I know. I hope it helps. And most of all, I hope that it doesn't make you hate me because I have always loved you so, *my beautiful child. Not more than I have loved your sisters, but differently. Because you were always just mine to love.*

Mum.

Amanda was still for a long while. The letter lay beside her on the bed. After a few minutes, Ed stroked her and asked, 'Okay?'

'My dad wasn't my dad.'

'*What* did you say?'

'My dad – the man I thought was Dad – the man Mum was married to when she got pregnant with me – he wasn't my dad.'

'Christ! That's what's in the letter?'

'Yep.'

'And that's the first you've heard of it?'

'Yep.'

'Bloody hell, Amanda!'

She smiled at him, tight-lipped.

'Yep.'

'Does anyone else know?'

Her voice was quiet and controlled. 'Apparently not. She's only telling me now so that "her secret doesn't die with her" ... I think that was the expression she used.'

'That's a pretty big lie to carry around with you for twenty-odd years.'

She snorted, and raised an eyebrow. 'Mark doesn't know.' She was talking more to herself than to him now.

'Mark?'

'My stepdad. I can't believe she wouldn't have told him.'

'So he's not your dad either?'

'"Course not! I told you – I was, like, 8 or something, when they got together.'

She knew she sounded irritated, which was unfair – they'd only talked about family once, last night, and he'd hardly expected to have to fill in a timeline the following morning. But she couldn't help the shortness in her voice.

'Sorry.'

She tried to remember that she liked this guy, she *really*, really liked him. This was nothing to do with him. 'No, *I'm* sorry . . . how should you know?'

He was struggling to find things to say. Ed was a little frightened. Amanda still hadn't moved and, apart from that first small smile she hadn't even looked at him. He felt the enormity of this news, but he knew he was ill-equipped to deal with it. Whatever he felt for her – and what he felt, he'd just contemplated, while paying for milk and bread in the corner shop, was a bit of a revelation to him – he hardly knew her. He didn't know what she wanted.

'So does she say in the letter who your dad is?'

'No, she says I don't need to know. Apparently I'm the product of some sordid little affair she had when she was married to my dad, to Donald. It's not worth me knowing.'

Ed thought he might agree, though he didn't dare say it out loud. What was that aphorism he'd seen written on fridge magnets, or mouse mats or somewhere? Any man could be a father, but it took somebody special to be a dad? Wasn't that it?

Amanda got out of bed in a sudden movement. She started to pull on clothes – hers, this time, and not his flatmate's borrowed ones.

'Are you okay?'

'Of course I'm not okay.' There was a new edge to her voice that he hadn't heard before. 'I just read – in a *letter* – that my mother, my perfect bloody dead bloody mother has been lying to me my entire bloody life!'

She pulled the New Year's Eve dress roughly over her head and her new voice was muffled.

'I can't believe it, I can't bloody believe it! All these months, I've been blaming myself for not coming to see her – feeling really shitty that I wasn't around, that I wasn't there for her, when everyone else was. I've been carrying this letter around like some talisman, waiting and waiting for the right moment, for the right feeling to come so that I could open it and read it. And now I have and I get . . . I get . . . I get this!' She was shouting now.

'And I want to ring her up and just yell at her, really shout. How *dare* she? Coward? Coward isn't the word. I mean, this is my life; this is *my life*. And I've been living it without even knowing the fundamental, basic things about myself. Like who my own father is. And I still don't, I still don't. And I never bloody will, because that secret is lying with her, rotting away in some stupid bloody field! Can you believe it?'

Clearly, Ed couldn't. This wasn't how he had hoped this morning would go. Amanda was a dervish now, pulling her coat on. It felt to him as if she could only wind up a little further before she would have to spin out and out and out of control, and be reduced almost to nothingness. His plan was to be still and be quiet until that happened, and then, maybe, hold her. If he was allowed . . .

Her hand was on the bedroom door.

'I've got to go.'

'Go where?'

'I don't know. Go home, go to work.'

'It's Saturday.'

'Just go. Go and see Mark . . . I don't know.'

She turned and looked at him. He was standing in the middle of the room, wearing underpants and a T-shirt, and a startled expression. Even his unstyled Tintin hair looked shocked. She remembered where she was.

'You didn't sign up for this.'

He moved towards her very, very slowly and gently.

'I don't think you should go anywhere just yet. Not until you've calmed down a bit.' He reached out a hand.

'Have I scared you to death?'

He smiled ruefully. 'A bit.'

'Not your average one-night stand?' She was looking at the ground, deflated now.

He took two steps nearer to her and tentatively put a hand on her shoulder.

'Two nights.'

When she didn't shrug it off, he stood right in front of her, and raised his other hand to rest on her other shoulder.

'And there was nothing remotely average about it.' He put one hand under her chin, and pulled her face up until her eyes met his. 'I just don't want you to go until you've had a think. We don't have to talk.'

For a moment he thought he had her. She let him pull her into a hug, and stood there, his arms around her, for a couple of minutes. He could feel her heart beating. It slowed and became even again. Her breathing grew less ragged. He thought she might cry. He hoped she would; he knew where he was with tears, but she didn't.

She pulled away gently.

'Look, Ed. I *am* going to go. This … this is a big thing, you know? I *can't* just pretend I don't know, that I didn't read it. I wish I hadn't, but I did. And I need to be by myself. It's nothing to do with you.' He hated that line, even though, in this case, he knew it was true. Something stopped him from asking when he would see her again.

He nodded. 'Okay, I understand.'

She kissed him once, on the lips. It was warm, but chaste, and brief. 'Thank you. I'll see you.'

'I'll see you.'

But Ed wondered if he would. Amanda let herself out, and he watched her walk away from the upstairs window until she turned the corner and disappeared from view.

The purposeful walk she had adopted, striding away from Ed's house, suspecting that he was watching her, evaporated when she got around the corner. She didn't know where to go. Now she slowed to a meander, and that pace took her, within a few minutes, into a warm café, where she realized that she looked ridiculous and inappropriate, but no longer cared. She kept her coat buttoned over the party dress, smoothed her bedhead hair behind each ear, and ordered tea and toasted tea-cakes. No one took much notice of her, to her relief, but the tea came quickly and she drank it down, though it burnt her throat.

She didn't know what to think about first. She tried to concentrate on her childhood, as if thinking back to the familiar might throw up clues to something she ought to have been looking for all along. But it didn't, of course. Who would think about something like that? It was totally bizarre. She ruled out calling Mark. He didn't know, and she couldn't tell him. She pulled out her phone and called Lisa instead.

Her sister answered on the third ring.

'Lisa?'

'Mand? Happy New Year!'

'You too.'

'You okay?'

'Not really.'

'What's wrong?' She heard the alarm in Lisa's voice.

'No . . . Nothing . . . Much . . . I'm okay, I just . . .'

'What?'

'I wondered if you were free, today, this morning, some-time . . . to meet up . . . for a coffee or something . . .'

'You sound weird. What's wrong?'

'Nothing.'

'Stop saying nothing, you idiot! Did something happen with that guy? Are you okay? Where are you?'

She hadn't meant to frighten Lisa, and for a moment, she wished she hadn't called. She couldn't tell her over the phone. She wasn't even sure she could tell her face to face.

'Nothing happened. Listen, Lisa, please. Calm down, I'm fine. I promise. I'm in London. I just wanted to see you – for a chat. Honest, I'm fine.'

Lisa sounded reassured. 'Okay, okay. So . . . today . . .'

'If you're free.'

'We've got Cee Cee. We were going to take her to a film, but . . .'

'I don't want to interrupt . . .'

'Glad of the chance to get out of happy families, to tell you the truth. Tell me where and when . . .'

Amanda looked down at the dress, sticking out beneath her coat. She needed to go home, take a shower . . . think what the hell to say . . . 'How about lunch? Covent Garden? One o'clock?'

'Long as we can hit the sales afterwards.'

'You're on.' She made her tone light.

'And you're sure you're okay? How did the date go?'

'The date went great. I'll fill you in when I see you, okay?'

'See you later.'

The hot shower felt good. She stood for long minutes under it, the bathroom filling with steam. She'd been glad to discover that neither of her flatmates was home, so there'd been no need to explain the dress, or, for that matter, her absence. Nor was there any need to share the shower, so she stood there, motionless, until her skin was red and the hot water ran to lukewarm. She wrapped herself in a towel, turning another into a turban, and stared at her blurry face in the wet mirror. 'Whose daughter are you?' she asked her reflection. She thought she heard her mum answer: 'You're mine, all mine.'

She dried the mirror off and looked at her body. Under the shower redness she blushed as she remembered Ed, remembered his hands on her, all over her. And her responses, and his eyes, boring into hers. She went back into her bedroom, and found her phone in her bag then dialled his number.

When the computer generated voice answered, asking her to leave a message, she glanced at her watch. She'd only left him an hour ago. He had to be there still. Maybe he was still there, at home, and he had his phone in his hand. Perhaps he was looking at it, seeing who it was that was calling and he was choosing not to speak to her. She must have been that terrifying. He didn't want to talk to her. She lost her nerve, and hung up.

She dialled again and got the same recorded message. Took a deep breath, and spoke.

'Ed? It's me. I just ... wanted to say that I'm sorry for going psycho on you this morning. It was a stupid thing to do, opening the letter then. I'm sorry. And I wanted ... I wanted to say thank you for the last couple of days. I had a great time, a really great time. I'm sorry ... that I ... if I ruined it. Sorry. So ... that's what I wanted to say. Take care. Call me ... if you want ... It's Amanda ...'Bye, then.'

For five minutes she sat in the chair, in her towel, with her phone in her hand. He didn't call her back. She shivered with cold, then, and got dressed.

Covent Garden was heaving with sales shoppers, and Lisa, scanning the crowd for her sister, didn't see Amanda until she was right next to her. They hugged, briefly, and then Lisa thrust her arm through Amanda's and pulled her in the direction of a restaurant they'd eaten at before.

'Thank God I called and made a reservation – the world and his wife are out today!'

They were shown to a small, round table in the corner, where they sank gratefully into their chairs and ordered two big glasses of red wine. Lisa leaned forward conspiratorially, and grinned.

'So, sis, dish ... how was it?'

'It was fine.'

'*Fine*?! You went off from Mark's on top of the world ...'

She didn't want to talk about Ed. Maybe there was no Ed to talk about anyway.

'Lisa, I read Mum's letter.'

'What do you mean?' Lisa looked confused.

'You know the letters we got when Mum died?'

'Yes, of course.'

'Well, I hadn't read mine.'

'Why on earth not?'

'I don't know. I couldn't bring myself to – I felt bad, not being there, I suppose. I wasn't sure what it would say . . . I don't know. Anyway . . .' She shook her head. 'I didn't read it at the time, and I hadn't read it . . . until this morning.'

'And?'

'And this morning I read it.'

Lisa realized that Amanda was looking pale, shocked. And she'd been crying. She could see it now – her eyes were red-rimmed.

'What did it say?' When Amanda didn't answer, she felt awkward. 'I mean, not that it's any of my business, not really, what it said . . .'

'That's why I called you . . .'

'Okay.' Lisa sat, looking at her sister, for long moments, her hands folded in her lap, her mind racing.

Amanda couldn't move the conversation forward. She couldn't get the words out.

Her sister felt a flash of anxiety.

'Come on, you're freaking me out now, Mand. What did it say?'

Amanda smiled weakly, and shrugged her shoulders, trying to sort her words into some sort of sense. 'Sorry, I'm making a real hash of this, aren't I? It's just not that easy to say.'

Lisa leant forward and put her hand over her sister's.

'Just *say* it, come on! This is *me* you're talking to. I don't need things sugar-coated.'

'Okay.' Amanda took a deep breath and looked straight at her. What was holding her up, she realized, was knowing how to describe the man she was talking about. 'Donald isn't my dad.'

'What?'

'Donald ... Dad ... He isn't ... he wasn't ... my biological father. He wasn't my dad.'

'Shit!' They sat in a stunned silence for a few seconds.

Amanda narrowed her eyes in an examination of Lisa's face. 'So you're surprised?'

'Of course I'm surprised! You thought I knew?'

'You were close, the two of you. Closer than the rest of us. I thought she might have confided in you.'

'Not *that* close, apparently! I had no idea.' She shook her head incredulously. 'Bloody hell, Mand!'

Amanda was almost comforted by Lisa's incredulity. She didn't think she would have liked it, if it had turned out that Lisa had known all along. And, in a funny way, it helped that her sister was just as shocked as she was. Well, almost. She still knew who her dad was.

Lisa's eyes were screwed up now, as she thought. 'Do you think Mark knows?'

'She says he doesn't, in the letter. She says no one did.'

'Bloody hell, Mand!'

Amanda pulled the letter out of her bag and handed it to Lisa. It was easier to let her read it for herself. Lisa's lips moved as she slowly digested its contents. Amanda stared out of the window at the manic sales shoppers.

*

132

When Lisa had finished, she put the letter down on the table. The top corner of it lay on a small spill of wine, and red spread like a stain across the thin paper. Amanda picked it up, and dried the corner on her napkin. Lisa looked at her face and saw she had tears in her eyes.

'I'm sorry, Mand.'

Amanda shrugged.

'I don't know what to say, really.'

'I know.'

'What does it make you feel?'

Amanda blew her nose noisily.

'Fucking angry!'

'Angry?'

'How dare she tell me something like that in a letter! That's what I feel. I've spent the last six months – the last year, practically, feeling like shit; like I was a coward for running away. I felt so guilty I couldn't even open the damn letter she left me. And when I finally do, I get this.'

'Would you rather not know?'

'I don't know. I'd rather never had known if the alternative was not being able to talk to her about it. Not being able to find out who he was, what happened.'

'She tells you what happened.'

'She tells me whatever the hell she wants me to believe; sticks it in an envelope and waits to die so she's not around when I read it! She could say anything she wanted in a letter like that. She knew she wasn't going to be around to answer my questions.'

'It sounds true to me – what she says and the way she says it, for what it's worth . . .'

Amanda looked as though she might laugh. She sat back against her chair and folded her arms. 'I should have known you'd defend her.'

'I'm *not* defending her.'

Amanda didn't respond.

'Listen, Amanda, honestly, I'm not. I think it's a rotten thing to do. You're right, she knew she wouldn't have to answer to it. That's inexcusable. I'm not defending it. I'm just saying – I read it, and I believed it. You did, too. You're just too upset to realize it. You know Mum wasn't a liar.'

'I thought I knew she wasn't. I thought she was brave too.'

Lisa thought about Barbara dying, about a face pinched with pain that was rarely mentioned. About a woman so tired she couldn't walk upstairs unaided, but who didn't moan about it. About a mother who listened to Hannah blathering on about some pop song, or some homework assignment or some boy even though you could see in her eyes that all she craved was silence. About all the things Amanda hadn't seen because she hadn't been there to see them.

'She was brave, Amanda.' She tried to make herself sound gentle. When she replied, Amanda's voice was just as soft and quiet.

'Not about this.'

'No, not about this.'

It wasn't easy to watch Amanda's pain, nor was it easy to know how to ease it.

'You should talk to Mark.'

Amanda's eyes flamed. 'No, I don't want him to know. I don't want anyone to know. Promise me you won't tell the others?'

'Why not?'

'I don't want them to know.'

Lisa obviously didn't look convinced.

'It's up to me, isn't it?'

She supposed it was. 'Why did you tell me?'

Now Amanda didn't know why she had. It was a lapse, a crack in her shell, an impulse, but an essentially pointless one. Lisa couldn't fix it anymore than she or anyone else could.

'Promise.'

Lisa put her hands up in a gesture of surrender. 'I promise.' Amanda nodded emphatically, obviously underlining the end of the conversation, and signalled to the waitress. 'You want another glass? I'm having one.'

January

Hannah

Hannah lay on her stomach across her bed, with her mother's journal spread out on the duvet. She'd been reading and rereading it. It had been hard to read, last year, when Jennifer had first given her a copy. She'd read it once, and put it away in the fabric-covered box she kept in her wardrobe, the one with the ballet certificates and the sports day medals. This year she could read it more easily. She wanted to. She'd read some bits of it over and over again. It was comforting now, not painful, hearing Mum's voice in her head. Some of it made her laugh; some of it made her realize that her mum was even cooler than she'd thought – and she'd always thought she was pretty damn cool. All that stuff about setting up on her own after she broke up with the others' dad. How she got the shop started, brought them up herself, that was amazing. She hoped she was half as strong. It was weird, thinking about Mum when she wasn't Mum.

Dad hadn't asked her about it. He knew Jennifer had brought it down for her before Christmas. She supposed he could have snuck into her room while she was at school or something and read it, but that wasn't really his style. She guessed he thought it was private, between Mum and them. Anyway, she was going to give it to Lisa when she came down next – she'd hogged it long enough. She liked the folder. It was just a cheap one, from W H Smith, but she'd chosen the most colourful one, of course. It was turquoise and hot pink, with a pattern of palm trees and flamingos on the front. The pages inside were all different. Some of it was written on hotel notepaper, some on lined pages that looked like they were from one of Hannah's A4 pads; some was on white Basildon Bond. Mum's handwriting was consistent, although she occasionally used a pencil. They had a pot that they kept by the phone, and it was supposed to be full of pens, but however often she filled it up with cheap Bic biros, it was emptied. People took them to write something and then wandered off with them, tucked them behind their ears or into their back pockets, and they were never returned. Hannah could hear Mum huffing and puffing to herself, complaining about the absence of a pen, before resorting to a pencil.

Mum screamed out of all of it, she supposed, and that was why it was so precious.

She stood up, and switched off her stereo. The part she was bringing downstairs now was written on lined paper. She wanted her dad to read it; she wanted him to remember how much Mum had loved him.

Mark was sitting on the deck, bundled up in a coat and hat, and watching the sun set, a glass of red wine in his hand. When Hannah touched his shoulder and he turned to her, she saw there were tears in his eyes, but she said nothing. He had the right to sit on the deck and shed a private tear for his wife, didn't he? Talking about it wouldn't help. She'd grown used to tiptoeing around his grief. These moments were getting rarer. Last summer, and in the autumn, it had happened all the time – she would come in from school, or down from the shower, and find her dad in tears. Sometimes he pretended he hadn't been doing it, but she knew the signs. Sometimes he didn't even try to cover it up. Now he pinched the bridge of his nose between his thumb and forefinger and sniffed hard.

'Hiya, gorgeous. What you got there?'

'Part of the journal. It's about you. I thought you might like to read it.'

He put his wine glass down and took the paper from her.

'Thanks, Hannah.'

How I Met Mark

*So, picture the scene. I'm divorced; I've been on my own
with my daughters for almost eight years. Things ended
pretty badly with Donald, so his involvement has been
sketchy. He pays; he pays every month. But he doesn't
come around at all, and there is certainly no every-
other-weekend or two-weeks-in-the-summer-holidays
arrangement going on. (That's another story, not for
today . . .) So I'm doing it all by myself. The house, you
girls, the job . . . Lisa, the oldest, she's nearly 22 now,
which makes me feel incredibly old – she's practically the
age I was when I had her. She doesn't live at home, of
course – she shares a flat with some girlfriends – but she
comes home at the weekends, loaded with laundry and
hungry for home cooking. Jennifer, she's at university. She
just left. I try not to mind that she chose St Andrews, in
Scotland. Of course, it was the best course, but it's so far
away. It feels like rejection. Amanda is the only one who
still lives at home permanently. She was 8 a couple of
months ago. Sometimes I worry that she's lonely without
a sister or a brother around, but she's great company.
She has that adult way about her that only children –
which is what she virtually is, given her position in the
family – sometimes have.*

*I love being a mother, always did. I'm bloody good at
it, too, I think, and I'd defy anyone to tell me the girls
lacked anything in their lives. I made sure they had
plenty of adult male, role-model type of company. And
I worked hard to make a good home for them.*

I own this gift shop. I love that, too. It's never going

to make me rich, but I wake up every morning and want to go in, and I know plenty of people who can't say that about what they do. And it's all mine, and, let's face it, I know that I like to be in charge.

There haven't been any men, not since the divorce. As far as that part of myself goes, it isn't so much that I was unhappy, more like cryogenically frozen. When I was first divorced, there just wasn't the time. I had three girls at home, one a small baby. The shop was in its infancy, too. I would work all day in the shop and all evening in the house, washing and ironing and tidying, and fall into bed, exhausted, barely an hour after my daughters. It was pride and determination, and, probably, obsession.

Now that Lisa and Jennifer were gone, and Amanda was at school and becoming a little grown up, maybe there was more time. But now there was no inclination. I just assumed the time had passed. I knew 44 wasn't exactly old, not anymore. I knew I looked alright, if you didn't mind a bit of gravity and a few fine lines . . . But anyway, where were these men you might choose to go out with, fall in love with, or into bed with? Every magazine you bought was full of articles about the lack of available men. Anyone would have thought the First World War had just ended and all the bachelors had been killed off.

When Donald and I first divorced, I'd allowed myself to think, maybe, just maybe, I'd find someone else who'd had the same thing happen to them, maybe someone with kids, and that maybe we'd lick our wounds together and have a little happiness. A bit like the Brady Bunch, with darker undertones, and better fashion. That hadn't happened either. And it was okay. I didn't lie in bed at night weeping with frustrated longing or empty loneliness. I was buggered if I'd give in to that sort of self pity. Most of the time, I just didn't think about it . . .

And then he wandered into the shop one day and turned everything upside down. Of course I noticed that he was handsome. I said I was resigned, not dead! He was Harrison Ford – circa Raiders of the Lost Ark – without the earring. Stubbly, which wasn't a look I normally went for, but it suited him. He looked a little like he'd dressed in the dark, but in a wardrobe full of good stuff, if you can picture that. So, of course I noticed. But he was young, far too young.

So far, so not that unusual. I asked him if I could help. He said he was looking for something for his mother. I showed him the shawls. They were beautiful, Indian, embroidered shawls in exquisite jewelled colours. I was impressed when he knew his mother's eyes were hazel, and even more so when he chose the three colours that would go best with hazel eyes. And then I felt him look right at me, and that was when this average day changed. Doesn't that sound ridiculous? But it did. He looked right at me, and said that her eyes and her hair were a similar colour to mine – although he himself was much darker – and asked if I would model a scarf for him. When I did, I realized my breathing had quickened, just from him looking at me. Which made me blush, because it was so silly, and teenage, and then he noticed me blushing, and I couldn't turn away because I was modelling the scarf. And then he blushed, because he'd made me blush, and then, thank God, or damn them to Hell – I wasn't sure which – the door opened and two pregnant women came in to ask for birth announcement cards, and the spell broke as quickly as it had been woven.

141

But he bought two, and said he'd let his mother choose her favourite, and I knew that he would come back with the one she rejected. And I wondered, that evening, as I cooked frittata for myself and Amanda – God, I even remember what I cooked! – whether he had done that on purpose. (Much later he told me he had. His mum had wanted to keep them both, and he felt bad telling her she couldn't because he needed one as an excuse to come back.)

He came back five minutes before closing on a damp Thursday evening. This time there were no pregnant women lurking and waiting to interrupt. This time I blushed even as I was processing the return. He was smarter than the last time he'd come in, but he didn't say anything out of the ordinary. He just thanked me politely, and went to the door.

When his hand touched the knob, he seemed to change his mind. He turned back towards me and, coming no closer, so that he seemed like he might run away at any time, he asked, 'Have you got a policy about going out with customers?'

I laughed. It was such a peculiar thing to say. 'What? Like doctors and patients?'

'Sort of.'

My heart was racing. 'I haven't needed one in the past.'

'And if you needed one now?'

'Do I need one now?'

'I think you might do.'

He was so cute, so young, and so cute.

'Then I think I'd have to think about it.'

And I did. I thought about it on and off all night. Changed my mind, changed it back, delighted at feeling girlish. Then castigated myself for being ridiculous. It had been so so long. Years, decades . . . I was more than out of practice. By dawn I'd made up my mind. If he came back the next day, I'd say yes. When I looked at my face in the mirror, peering over the top of Amanda's head as she brushed her teeth, I thought he'd change his mind the minute he saw me. You couldn't get away with a sleepless night when you were my age. My whole face looked ravaged.

He came back, he asked again, he took me out for lunch. Turned out he was ten years younger than I was – although that day, and many since, I've thought it looked like more. He was an architect. He was called Mark Forbes. And there you go – I was alone, without love, for eight years. And it took me about twenty minutes – over a cappuccino and an egg salad sandwich – to fall in love with him.

Mark remembered it exactly that way. He'd felt it too, that electrical, involuntary thing, when she'd put the scarf on for him and he'd looked at her, properly looked at her, for the first time. Maybe for him it was a bit more lusty than for her. She had a great figure – he remembered the edge of the scarf against the creamy skin of her cleavage – and the impulse he had to stare down her sweater when she was wrapping his purchases. But it was something. Something that made the walk from his office to her shop the next day, and the day after, magical and compelling.

And he remembered how nervous she was at that lunch. She'd blurted out, before they'd even ordered, that she was divorced, that she had three daughters, that she was too old for him, carrying too much baggage . . . Then she'd realized she was getting way ahead of herself, and blushed that delicious blush. He'd wanted to kiss every bit of skin that turned pink.

It hadn't frightened him, that first time. All that information. He wasn't a fool, he knew she was older. It didn't take a genius to figure out that there would be baggage. He'd been naïve – three daughters, two of them adults – it should probably have sent him screaming for the hills. There were times after that, certainly, when bolting seemed like a great option. He was no saint, but somehow he'd known, from really, really early on, that she was worth it. He remembered the froth from the cappuccino on her lip and the dangly silver earrings she wore that shook when she laughed, and the scent from her.

She'd told him, many times, that she'd known she was going to love him from the very start. She'd told him, lying in his arms. She'd told him and all the guests at their wedding eleven months later. He'd heard her tell Hannah, murmuring the story over her infant head during a night feed when he'd woken up and missed them both and crept downstairs to find them. He'd just never read it written down. And for just a moment, sitting framed by the setting sun, on the deck he'd built for them, he didn't feel sad. He felt lucky.

Lisa

The January sales had reached the stage where you understood exactly why every garment was left on the rack: because it was unflattering in shape, cut or colour for every shape and skintone known to woman. And even 75 per cent off was not going to make it speak to someone.

It was depressing, shopping at this time of year. Lisa longed for them to sweep the unwanted clothes away and bring in their ludicrously early ranges of sandals and sundresses, summer colours to give you something to look forward to. In fact, everything was a little depressing this time of year. Christmas was over. You knew you had 5 lb to lose, but the fridge was still full of mince pies and that most aspirational of cheeses, Stilton, which everyone seemed to buy in vast rounds in December, but no one ever seemed to really want to eat more than a sliver of. There were still three long months of winter to endure, of flaky grey skin and centrally heated hair and crap TV, and you couldn't even lift the malaise with retail therapy.

It was Jennifer who had suggested they meet in John Lewis – the temple. Lisa opted to join the lengthening queue at the coffee shop and risk an executive decision on whether Jennifer would prefer the coffee or the carrot cake, a latte or a camomile tea. She had chosen a table by the window and was about to plunge her fork into one or other of the cakes when Jennifer arrived. She obviously didn't feel the same way about the sales – she had several large carrier bags with her already.

'What you been buying?'

'Bedlinen, towels. Oh, and a KitchenAid blender. It's a funny colour, which obviously no one wants, so there was £50 off . . .'

'And you don't mind the colour?'

'I don't much like it, but I'm not wearing it, am I? I'm blending in it. And you know we don't actually keep stuff like that out on the counter, so who cares?'

Quite! You could actually perform an appendectomy on Lisa and Stephen's granite worktops without any fear or extra precaution.

'What about you? Bagged any bargains?'

'Just the cake.'

'Yum!'

Jennifer sat down gratefully and took a sip from her tea. Lisa took her cue and picked up the coffee.

'So, how are you?'

'I'm okay.'

'How's Andy?'

'Fine.'

'Fine, as in I've told him I don't actually want to marry him and he took it pretty well, or fine as in I haven't said a word and he still thinks I'll be a June bride?'

'Bloody hell, Jen! Cut to the chase, why don't you?'

'Sorry, it's just that I've been feeling incredibly sorry for him ever since you told us at Christmas . . .'

'I know, I know. No, I haven't told him I don't want to marry him.'

'Oh.'

'Don't say it like that. God, you can get so much disapproval packed into a single-syllable word, Jen.'

'I don't mean to. Sorry.' Jennifer smiled.

'We had Cee Cee from Boxing Day, didn't we? Karen went sailing on some yacht in the Caribbean, as you do for a whole week. I could hardly have that conversation with him with her and her big flappy ears in the house, could I?'

'Poor Cee Cee!'

'Poor Andy, poor Cee Cee. What about me?'

'Poor you.'

'Thank you!'

Lisa laughed a little. 'You're right, I'm an absolute coward. Cee Cee goes to bed at 7pm – there were vast tranches of day when I could have told him, I know. Do you know why I haven't?'

'No.'

'Because he'll ask me why, and I don't even think I can tell him. I don't think I can give him a good reason – at least not a good enough one. I can't even give myself a good enough reason, for Christ's sake! And do you know what worries me, I mean, *really* worries me?'

'Again, that would be a no.'

'It's that this will be the final straw for him. I think he'll break up with me, if I say no.'

'And you know you don't want that to happen.'

'I think so, yes.'

'Well, that's something, isn't it? You know you want to be with him.'

'That's not enough though, is it?'

'Not for him, obviously.'

Lisa ate a large forkful of cake. Crumbs fell from her mouth and she pressed them on the back of her fork. Jennifer nursed her mug between her hands, unconsciously drumming her fingers against the porcelain.

'You've got to talk to him, Lisa. Talking to him might make it clearer, to both of you.'

'Says you – you're hardly a Master of Communication! You and Stephen were barely speaking to each other at Christmas.'

'We were!'

'You know what I mean. You weren't . . . you weren't close . . . you weren't quite normal with each other. You *know* you weren't.'

'You're right.' Jennifer shook her head.

'Bloody hell, so we're both in a mess!' She smiled wryly. 'What would Mum say? D'you often ask yourself that since she died? What would she say?'

'More than I did before she died. Stupid, huh? All that good free advice I could have had, and I never wanted it. Now I might, I can't have it.'

'Hmm . . . Speaking of Mum, think I've got something to tell you about her that will explain some of where we get our ostrich-like attitude towards confrontation and communication . . .'

Jennifer sat forward. '*What?*' That didn't sound like Mum.

'Amanda made me swear not to tell anybody.'

'*Amanda?*'

'Yes, I said I wouldn't. But I think I have to tell you. D'you promise not to say anything?'

'Okay, say anything about what?'

'You know the letters Mum left us?'

'Yes . . .'

'Amanda didn't read hers at first.'

'Why not?'

'I don't know – weird reasons. You know Amanda! Anyway, she carried it around with her for six months, waiting for the right time to read it. That was, apparently, in bed with a bloke she barely knew, but that's beside the point . . .'

'At New Year's?'

'Exactly.'

'And . . . what did it say? Did she show you?'

'Yeah, she showed me. She rang me, sounding all weird, like she was fighting to come across as normal, you know, and ending up sounding anything but. I was really worried. I thought . . . maybe this guy . . . well, I don't know what I thought, but she didn't sound right. She got me to meet her – this was on January second, I think.'

'You're freaking me out now. What did the letter say?'

Lisa paused for a second. There was no easy way to say this. She remembered how shocked she had been when Amanda said it to her, but there was no other way.

'Amanda wasn't Dad's.'

'I don't get it.' Jennifer looked a little clueless. 'What do you mean?'

'I mean . . .' Lisa tried to sound patient. 'Dad wasn't Amanda's father.'

'Biologically?'

'Or any other way, come to think of it.'

Jennifer picked up her fork again, and jabbed at her cake, obviously with no intention of eating any.

'I don't get it.'

'Mum had an affair. Dad clearly knew about it – at least, I suppose he must have done. But no one else ever has. Not Amanda, not Mark, no one.'

'She wouldn't do that.'

'I wouldn't have believed it either. But she did. Which bit don't you think she'd have done?'

'Any of it. Had an affair, had a baby, not told anyone, not even Mark ... It just doesn't seem possible – it's not who she was, it's not how she was ...'

'But it obviously *was*.' Lisa understood Jennifer's desire to make their mother out to be perfect, but she wasn't. No one was.

'God – poor Amanda. How was she?'

'Pissed off, mainly.'

'Not upset?'

'That too. But I got the feeling that mostly she was cross that Mum had been waiting to tell her.'

'It can't be an easy thing to tell.'

'No, but if she'd known, if she'd known before Mum died – or before Dad died, for that matter – she could have asked them stuff about it, and now she can't. She just gets to know what Mum chose to tell her, in the letter. It isn't in the journals.'

'I suppose she was making it Amanda's story to tell.' Jennifer shook her head, but she was remembering the bit about Dad hitting Mum, just once. Mum said she'd provoked him. That ought to do it. 'What did she choose to tell her, exactly?'

'Well, not much. That she had an affair, that it wasn't serious or long-lasting; that she wasn't in love with the guy.'

'Did she say who he was? Did he know she was pregnant?'

'She didn't say who he was. She said, Amanda says, that it was a sordid affair she wasn't proud of, that she didn't love the guy – he was some sort of family friend, I think.'

'God! It gets worse ...'

'Or better. You wouldn't want it to have been some decade-long great passion, would you?'

'I don't know!' Jennifer sounded exasperated. 'I want it to have been Dad's baby, that's what I want. She's our Mum; I don't want her to have had an affair in the first place. How did she know it wasn't, anyway? They were still together, weren't they, when she was pregnant?'

'Yes, but think about it . . . Amanda's got Mum's hair, but facially, and in body type, she's nothing like you and me. And we're like Dad's side of the family.'

Lisa watched Jennifer considering what she said. She knew her sister would struggle with this. She had her own reasons for understanding what Mum had done.

'I suppose you're right. I just never thought about it before.'

'Why would you have done?'

'Quite.' Jennifer looked, Lisa realized, very shocked; almost more so than Amanda had done.

'And the truth is, she didn't *know*. It wasn't *Dynasty* – no one was demanding a DNA test or anything. She just figured. I guess she knew more about the timings of stuff . . .'

Jennifer wrinkled her nose with distaste, as though this were detail and information she didn't want to think about. Her mind went back through the story. 'What about the guy, the real father?'

'Like I said, she doesn't name him. She said Amanda didn't need to know. Said he knew she was pregnant, chose not to get involved and that he and his family moved away soon afterwards.'

Jennifer gazed out of the window, thinking, for a minute or two. Lisa finished her cake and coffee, contemplating another cup, but the queue had grown longer and snaked around the corner, out of sight.

'The Heywoods,' Jennifer said it quietly, almost to herself.

'*What*?'

'The Heywoods. We were always hanging out with them, remember? Heather Heywood was in my class at school. They lived down the road.'

'Don't remember.'

'Yes you do. Come on, the Heywoods.' She said this as though mere repetition of their name should make Lisa remember. 'They had rabbits, when we really, really wanted them; with that big run, in their back garden.'

Lisa had a vague recollection, then, of Heather Heywood, with her fat, brown pigtail and her fat, brown bunnies. She wasn't yet sure why it was relevant. Jennifer was warming to her theme. 'We used to see the Heywoods a lot. Mum and Dad were in Round Table and Ladies Circle with their mum and dad. You remember . . . And the Heywoods moved away before Amanda was born. I remember it especially because she took one of my Sindy dolls, even though Mum said I'd probably just lost it, and wouldn't let me ring them up and ask for it back. I knew she'd taken it, because it was one she didn't have, and she was always jealous about it.' She shook herself out of the diversion. 'Anyway, the point is, they moved away that summer before Amanda was born. It must have been him . . .'

'Calm down, Jennifer – that's a bit of a wild leap, don't you think?'

'Think about it, the timing fits.'

'So what?'

'What do you mean, so what? This guy could be Amanda's dad!'

'Yeah, and he might not be. Besides, what's the relevance of that? It's a quarter century later.'

'What's the relevance of *that*?'

Jennifer's voice was getting shriller and louder. Lisa wanted to calm the situation down.

'Listen, Jen. It's not like Amanda was close to Dad. They barely even knew each other, really. If she's ever considered a man to be her father, it's Mark, and this changes nothing. I can't see what good it could do, raking up the past and naming names, especially when you've no idea what you're talking about . . .'

'I wasn't naming names. I was just saying . . .'

'I know, I'm sorry.' Now she looked resentful and somehow hurt. Lisa was glad she had decided to tell her, rather than leave it to Amanda – if Amanda was planning on telling anyone at all apart from her. Jennifer could be so brittle.

'What do you think about it?' she was asking Lisa now. 'I mean, about Mum. Leave this guy out of it . . .'

'About Mum?' Lisa was a little sideswiped by the question. She wasn't sure how to answer it, being reasonably certain that her moral skew would be different to Jennifer's. She took a deep breath. 'I think Mum and Dad were unhappy for a long time. We know they were, in fact – we were there. Dad cheated on Mum. I suppose I think good for her, to be truthful. I hope it granted her a bit of happiness and restored a bit of self-confidence, to tell you the truth. I think it was colossally stupid of her to get pregnant, and if she were here I'd tell her so myself. And I think it was a bit cowardly, keeping it to herself all these years. It meant we all carried on being nasty to Dad, thinking he was the real villain. All it proves about Mum is that she was human and capable of making mistakes. I wish she'd trusted us enough to tell us, at some point because I wouldn't have judged her and I'd have felt a bit kinder towards Dad, and

Amanda would know who she was, and she'd have the chance to ask questions, and now she can't. But if you're asking me whether I think less of Mum now I know this, the answer is no. She was a person, Jen, and people aren't perfect, and she wasn't perfect. And that's okay. It all happened a very, very long time ago. I can live with it.'

But Jennifer didn't respond.

'Can you?'

'I don't know, I don't know . . .'

After they'd gone their separate ways, Lisa realized Jennifer hadn't said any more about Stephen. She was very good at that; being evasive. She didn't know what was wrong between the two of them and she guessed Jennifer didn't want her to know.

Not that she had time to worry about Jennifer as well as everything else. You were supposed to start the New Year with a clear, fresh head, weren't you? But she felt as if the sky was getting lower and lower, coming down on her. She wasn't sleeping well, waking at about 3am every day, unable to doze off again, her brain already fast forwarding, and that hardly ever happened. Amanda had gone a bit quiet on her since the text saying she was going away for a bit. That was vintage Amanda. She didn't know how her mum hadn't gone crazy, wondering where she was, and how she was, and in the same breath pondered why she now felt somehow compelled to take on the mantle of worry about her sister, when no one had asked her to. Oldest sibling syndrome, the curse of the firstborn perhaps.

Andy, Andy. She realized she was wandering around aimlessly now. A noncommittal shopper at the best of times, she was lost in a sea of glassware, cutlery and table linens. She didn't want any of this stuff. She felt in the back of her pocket for her car parking ticket and made for the nearest lift that would get her out of there. Safe and alone in her car, she rested her head against the back of the seat and closed her eyes so she couldn't see the impatient drivers, their cars filing past at 2 miles per hour, waiting for her to create an empty space.

For the first time in ages she let herself really think about what she'd done to Andy. It was always in the wings, on the periphery of her thoughts these days, but mostly she kept it away, refused to confront it head on. Now, talking about Mum, she couldn't prevent it. She had had an affair herself, of course and she was amazed no one had guessed. In her mind, the scarlet letter had been neon and flashing. How else could she have become so practised at the justification, and the excuses and the mitigation, if she hadn't spent months talking herself through the same things? The mantra of the unfaithful.

It was over, *so* over, but it had happened. No one knew, except for the two of them. She had gotten away with it. She was supposed to do the justification thing and move on, forget about it. Mum had clearly tried to do just that. But Lisa guessed that Amanda's letter proved what she was beginning to believe must be true: that you could never forget about it, or ever really forgive yourself. However great the justification, however much time might pass . . .

His name was Christopher Absalom. He had been managing a new development of townhouses and apartments, out in the part of the East End of London that was being gentrified. Her firm had won the contract to decorate the show apartments and she'd met him when she went out there for a site visit. He had made her wish, the first time she laid eyes on him, that she wasn't wearing a hard hat.

It had been purely physical. What did that mean? She'd asked herself that question, confessing out loud to herself alone in the car. She didn't want anything from him, apart from what he gave her in bed, apart from the sensations of his hands and his mouth and his body on hers. She didn't want him to really like her, or to get to know her; or even to introduce her to his mother. She just wanted him to want to fuck her. Purely physical. As if that made it better. For Andy, it would probably make it worse. Chris had had that twinkle in his eye that always worked for her. He'd worn jeans fashionably low on his hips and she'd glimpsed a muscled, tanned stomach beneath his T-shirt when he raised his arm, pointing at something above their heads.

The whole thing had smelt of her youth. A meeting moved to the pub, others had melted away, an invitation had been extended, and accepted. She'd put in a call to the machine at home, from the ladies': the meeting was overrunning, Andy should eat dinner without her, she didn't know what time she'd be back . . . She was surprised at how easily the lie came out of her mouth. She'd gone back to Chris's place. He lived in an old warehouse in Shoreditch. Just the space itself was sexy – high ceilings, brick walls; it was anonymous. He had almost no furniture. A couple of worn leather armchairs, an almost empty bookcase, a vast white bed, unmade and vaguely grubby.

The development took four months to complete. It was last summer. Lisa had sex with Chris regularly, once or twice a week all that time. She never fell asleep with him, she never stayed the night and she never left a single thing that belonged to her in his home. They never ate dinner in a restaurant, or watched a film together. She never met a friend of his, or heard about one. By September, she understood him no better than she had in June. She knew how every inch of him looked and tasted and felt. But she didn't know what the last book he'd read was, and she didn't know where he grew up. He didn't know, while they were fucking each other (and that was the only way she could ever describe it, even in her own mind), in the big leather armchairs, and the freestanding bath and on the big white bed, that she lived with a guy. Or that her mother was ill. If he'd known, the time that she'd shown up, naked beneath a thin white cotton dress, and made him touch her, pulling at his jeans before they'd even got out of the lift, that her mother had died two days before, he might have thought she was messed up. Maybe she was.

There was no discussion about the affair coming to an end, as there had been no discussion about it beginning. She finished the apartments, and she stopped showing up.

She didn't even understand it herself. The behavioural pattern was familiar. Before Andy, there'd been a lot of guys at university, at work. She liked men, she liked sex, she liked to have fun, but she hadn't ever been unfaithful to Andy. Until the first time, with Chris, she didn't think she was capable of it. But it wasn't just once. She had kept on doing it.

She couldn't tell herself it was just lust. It wasn't that simple. The sex was good, that was undeniable. She liked that he didn't really want to talk to her; she liked that he was happy to keep it on one level, that he saw no need for their emotional relationship to evolve as their physical one did. But she knew it wasn't about Chris at all. It was all so straightforward and simple, empty and clean. When he was inside her, his eyes bored into hers, but they saw nothing because they weren't looking for any of that. He did it because it was sexy, because he wanted to gauge her physical reaction to his touches, his tempo, his rhythm. He didn't care to see anything beyond that so it had been okay to stare back.

It was about Andy. It was about Andy loving her; it was about Andy wanting to marry her, and make a life with her. It was almost as if, by sleeping with Chris, she was trying to prove herself unworthy. Not good enough. Or trying to hold him at arm's length . . .

She'd rehearsed telling him but decided against it. It had ended, and she'd gotten away with it. He hadn't caught her, no one knew – he never needed to know. But it hadn't gone away. Guilt gnawed. It was always in the way; it probably always would be.

She'd nearly told her mum one day. She'd come to visit after work one day, not long after it had started with Chris. Barbara was in the garden when she arrived, sitting on one of the Adirondack chairs with her back to Lisa. She'd had a plaid blanket on her knees and the blanket, with all its connotations, made Lisa want to cry. As if she knew, Barbara pulled it off when she saw her daughter. 'If you haven't got anything nice to say about anyone, come sit by me . . .' Lisa had kissed her cool cheek, caught the scent of Fracas and something else, unfamiliar and medical, and sat on the grass at her mother's feet, Barbara's hand grasping hers at the side of her neck. She nearly told her then but the 'not nice' was about her, and she couldn't do it. And Barbara had died before it ended. If she'd known – about Amanda – she might have said something, and it might have helped.

Amanda

'How are you doing, kid?'

'I'm alright. How are *you* doing?'

Amanda had come to visit after work, on the train. Mark had picked her up at the station when he'd finished at the office and now they were driving home. It was a wet, cold, hibernating sort of a night, and he felt a father's relief and gratitude that two of his daughters would be under his roof tonight. Rain pelted against the car windows and on the soft top. It was good to see her.

Mark shrugged. 'It does get easier. I knew it would. Time passes, doesn't it?'

'I'm glad.'

'So am I, most of the time. Sometimes I resent it.'

'What do you mean?'

'Sounds daft, I know, but getting easier means she's getting farther away from me. Does that make sense?'

It did. Amanda held her step-father's hand for a moment and he squeezed her fingers.

'So, enough of the wallowing. Tell me about you? You're still in England, for a start. Must be some sort of record. What's that all about?'

'Ah . . .'

'This bloke, I presume . . .'

Amanda raised her eyebrows at him.

'Sorry – hope you don't mind. Hannah told me.'

'Bigmouth! I don't mind, no. It wasn't a secret. God knows, I went on about him to the others when we were all home, like an idiot. But, no, it isn't a bloke. That's over, I think.'

'I'm sorry – touchy subject?'

'Not really.' She tried to sound breezy. 'Just a bit of

fun. Actually, I'am thinking of going away again.' That, at least, was true.

'That's more like it! Where? When? Details, please. Let me have a little vicarious globetrot on this truly foul night.'

Amanda laughed. 'You make it sound like you don't have your own passport! Actually, when did you last have a holiday?' She looked at his face, lit by streetlights. 'Now that I think of it, you haven't been away for ages. Not since Mum . . .'

'This is true. Explains my pallor, at least.'

'And those baggy eyes.'

'Charming!'

'Hey, I don't do soft soap. But why don't you go away, the two of you?'

'I've got work, Hannah's got school . . .'

'Pah! You get holidays, she gets holidays. You *should* get away.'

'You're right, we should.' Mark realized he hadn't thought about a holiday, which was odd. They'd always had holidays before Barbara was ill. She'd been leisure director, of course. Planned everything, booked everything, packed, put Factor 30 on everyone's shoulders . . .

'I guess your mum just always took care of all that.'

'Well, you know what, she isn't going to anymore. Does that mean you're never going on a holiday again?'

'No, of course not. What's this – tough love?!'

'If you like. So, that's sorted. I'll help you. We'll go online at home and find you a fortnight in Torremolinos . . .'

Mark laughed. 'Okay, okay, you win! So long as you promise it won't be Torremolinos. I'll talk to your sister.'

*

Hannah was excited by the prospect. She insisted on hot weather, a white sandy beach and turquoise sea.

'Can't you come with us, Mand? Otherwise I'll be stuck with Dad.'

'Oi! You make me sound like sunstroke.'

'Come on, Dad. Just the two of us?' She grimaced at him from the computer, where she was happily googling luxury resorts in the Seychelles, but he knew she wasn't serious, not completely serious, at least, he hoped.

But Amanda was engrossed in the photo albums that lined one of the study walls opposite the desk. This archiving of their lives was, and had always been, Mark's department. Mum would never have been organized enough. She was absolute rubbish at stuff like that, gloriously chaotic. Mark was Ying to her Yang. There was one album for every year of their marriage. They were large, navy-blue albums, with the pictures neatly stuck down on real paper. Occasional pencil notations of dates, and places and names led you through the years of their lives together. Each album had its year embossed on the front in gold lettering and they were, of course, in the right order on the shelves. Amanda knew Mum had envied Mark his organizational abilities, but she did it grudgingly, gently mocking him for his neatness, always threatening to go into the study and rearrange things in his absence – 'That'll get him!' Amanda was flicking through them now:

1993: Amanda wheeling Hannah's pushchair along the pier in Brighton

1995: All the girls standing by a hire car in France. She remembered that trip. She'd discovered her first period at a service station somewhere near Limoges.

1997: On a beach in Crete, Mark's nose sunburnt
2000: Disneyworld, Hannah in Minnie Ears, Amanda in the stance of a petulant teenager.

Mark left Hannah and came to sit beside her. For a few minutes, they looked at pictures together in silence. Then Amanda looked up.

'The pictures from before she met you, of me and Lisa and Jen, and my dad? Did you keep them?'

'Of course.' Mark looked at her, surprised and mildly disgruntled at the question. 'I wouldn't throw those away. There are loads. Not in albums, though. Do you want to see them?'

'Can I?'

'Course you can. They're upstairs . . .'

They were in a large box, dusty at the top of a wardrobe in the guest room, stamped with a moving company's logo – in, of course, spectacular disarray. Bloody hell, Mum! Amanda thought, as she sat cross-legged on the floor, leaning against the bed, and began sifting through them. There were people she didn't recognize, places she didn't remember.

Mark leant in the doorframe, his arms folded. 'I should do something with them, really. She always meant to sort them out . . .' His voice drifted away for a moment, but Amanda seemed barely aware he was still with her. 'Are you looking for something specific?'

'Clues, I'm looking for clues . . .' She didn't look up and she didn't elaborate. She said it so quietly that he wasn't entirely sure whether she was answering his question or just talking to herself. After a minute or two, he left her to it. God knows, it did strange things to you, missing her.

Amanda lifted a large handful of pictures out of the

box and dropped them into her lap, flicking through them as they fell. They told a thousand stories, didn't they? The pictures of your life. But they left a lot out too.

She found a picture of Mum at her first wedding, young and slim, in a dress with a cinched waist and a big puffy skirt. She didn't know who the bridesmaids were. Why had she never noticed, never asked? Now, she supposed, she would never know. Lisa's christening, Jennifer's first birthday party . . . All the earliest pictures were special occasion shots. You didn't use a camera all the time in those days. Not like today, where parents spent years watching their children grow up through the lens of a camera or a video, capturing hours' worth for posterity. She didn't really know what she was hoping to discover. He just disappeared – Donald. Suddenly. He was in the pictures, and then he wasn't. There was no shot of him with a pregnant Barbara and two small girls around her. He wasn't at her christening, he wasn't at her first birthday party . . .

Amanda stared at her mother's face in all the pictures. She couldn't see what was going on behind her eyes and her smile. She didn't look any different after he'd gone. Why would she have done? She thought about what Mark had said, about Mum moving further away from them as time passed. It was weird. You looked at a picture of her, and it just looked weird. Like when they show a photo of someone dead on the news, like you fooled yourself into thinking you could see some kind of aura or something, some foretelling of their fate in an ordinary photograph.

'Did you find what you were looking for?' Mark asked, when she emerged from the spare room some long while later. Hannah was sprawled on the sofa, watching television, and Mark was reading the paper and drinking a glass of wine. He poured her a glass when she came in and pulled out the chair next to his.

'Not really.'

'Can I help?' He was watching her face; he looked concerned. For a moment, she thought about telling him. Trouble was, she believed her mum when she'd written that he had no clue, and she didn't want to be the one who told him. She loved him. Lisa was right – he was, by a very wide margin, the best father of the three of them. She pushed the urge back into her throat and smiled at him.

'You can give me a hug.'

Today is a bloody awful day. I don't know whether I should write for you on days like today. It won't make easy reading. Still . . .

Today I feel sick and tired in every sense of the words. I've thrown up so many times my diaphragm aches. There's been nothing to get rid of for hours, but it doesn't stop convulsing me. And tired . . . ? So tired. I saw my reflection in the mirror (note to self – get Mark to cover all the mirrors) – and it's just possible my hair is having a worse day than I am (what's left of it, but that's a whole other story). But, do you know, I can hardly bear to lift one hand above my head to brush it. Don't suppose I'd win any prizes for penmanship, either . . . Do you have any idea how debilitating it is to be this exhausted? The main problem is that I haven't the energy to drag myself out of this mood. This terrible, black, desperate mood. I'm so bloody sad. I said I wouldn't do this, but I can't help it. I don't want to die, I'm not ready, I'm not finished. You're not finished, nothing is over. I don't want to die.

It's like the world is suddenly all new and wondrous and exciting again. Like I've been wearing blinkers, or something, all these years. Never lay back and watched clouds changing shapes. Or raindrops hit leaves. Or saw just how perfectly smooth a baby's skin is. Never really listened to children laughing or choirs sing, or how beautiful an oboe sounds. All at once, the world – the same one I used to view with indifference – is the most perfect, fascinating, amazing place that I cannot bear to leave. And you, my girls. I don't want to leave you, I haven't finished. I haven't told you often enough how much I love you and how amazing you are; I haven't helped you enough, confronted you enough, listened to you enough, seen you enough.

Every minute you already had that I wasn't with you feels like a waste, a missed opportunity. I should have homeschooled you, I should never have left you with a babysitter because I thought I'd scream if I didn't have an hour without you. Why did I ever think that anyway? I sound like a crazy person, I know. I just never knew I didn't have that long. I never heard the tick-tock.

If we all knew — if there was some fortune cookie you could open and find out what your allotted time was — would we all live entirely different lives? Would we waste less time? 'Carpe' the 'diem' more. Really? I daresay I'd still have felt like I was going to strangle you if I didn't get away for an hour. I wouldn't have homeschooled you. (God knows, you wouldn't have a maths qualification between you if I had've done!) But I'd have played in the playground more. Swung, climbed, hung, instead of hogging the bench and reading the paper. Could I have loved you better? Maybe. If that's true, then I'm sorry. Could I have loved you more? I don't think it's possible.

Jennifer

Home alone. Jennifer was home early. These days she was clockwatching, switching off the computer on the dot of 5.30, leaving the calls she would once have returned until tomorrow. Work wasn't as much fun as it had been. She used to think she had the dream job. She organized perfect upmarket holidays for people who weren't counting the cost. Trips for men to propose, honeymoons, tenth wedding anniversary holidays, five-star suites in European cities, impeccable ski lodges in Whistler, luxury safaris, the kind where you could watch hippos bathe from your own private horizon pool . . . The Orient Express, hot-air balloons, First Class . . . She loved the minutiae of the details. Nicolas Feuillette, not Moët & Chandon. Evian, not Perrier. Teak loungers, never plastic. Fantasy, not reality. That's what it was. She let people pretend, for a while, that everything in the entire world and their own tiny lives was absolutely perfect. That was what she had fallen in love with, and that was what bothered her now so damn much.

She opened the linen cupboard to put away her new towels and observed, with irritation, that her neat piles had been disturbed. Stephen must have been in here, looking for something. Sighing, she pulled a whole shelf's worth out onto the floor, and began refolding and restacking. Completely unnecessary, but for her, always therapeutic. Some people thought while they ran – Jennifer thought best while she was tidying. She thought, for the first time in a long time, about how she and Stephen had met. She knew that if she'd been writing it down, instead of thinking it, it might have had that same tone: of exuberance, and thrill and thrall. Not right away, maybe, but she had felt it. Wasn't there some statistic somewhere she'd read about where most people meet their spouse, that claimed weddings were the third most popular place, after university and the workplace? She was sure she had read that. Something to do with all that romantic optimism in the air, and too much good champagne, no doubt. This wedding, the one where she met Stephen, was nothing like that.

She'd gone with John. Sensible, solid, reliable John. The boyfriend she'd had since university; the boy she'd always assumed she would spend the rest of her life with. They'd met really early on, when they'd both still been terrified of the whole new experience. Discovering a mutual love of their subject, and vegetarian food, as well as a mutual antipathy towards some of the more normal student pursuits, they clung to each other from the start, telling themselves they had found a soulmate. John was serious and studious, and wore bookish round spectacles. Jennifer thought he made her a better person. They worked in the library on Saturday evenings and cooked dahl.

After university, when maybe they might have parted, they had a relationship renaissance based on how scary this next new world was and carried on clinging. Lately – well, more like the last three or four years – Jennifer knew her own grip had loosened, but she didn't think John's had. It had all started to feel a bit suffocating. There were things she wanted to do, and eat a bacon sandwich was just at the top of the list. She began to realize that the girl she had been at university was a phase. The John that John had been was the real thing.

A few months earlier, a girlfriend had told her she

was bound to fall for someone else, that this catalyst would finally release her from the promises she had made to herself and to John a million years ago, when she was a different person. And she had half-believed her. She hadn't wanted to go with him to the wedding. By the time the invitation arrived, she had accepted that she and John were on their last legs, acting out the last pathetic steps in the dance of their relationship. A quiet, difficult, sad tragedy that would surely play out better – and faster – in private. But wasn't that the problem? After all those years together, so many of their friends all knew each other; she wasn't thinking about extricating herself from one relationship, she was thinking about walking away from dozens. And that made it so much harder. Just lately, though, she felt like the beggar in the Dickensian tale – all the windows she peered through seemed full of promise and excitement and adventure denied to her.

That John's presence at this wedding was required at all seemed a mystery. Peter was a friend of his from sixth form. He'd gone to university in America – his mum was from New York, apparently – and only just finished graduate school. They'd never met, and Peter had barely seen John since A-levels. The wedding was in Yorkshire – he was marrying some girl he'd known forever – at her parents' house, but under his mother's obvious influence there were touches of Americana about the proceedings. They'd received a 'save the date' card about six months earlier (she remembered wondering as she read it whether she would still be John's plus one by then, and being surprised at wondering), and then an elaborate invitation to what appeared to be an entire weekend of nuptial celebrations beginning on the Friday night with a 'rehearsal dinner' and finishing on Sunday afternoon with a 'survivors' brunch'. The wedding appeared almost incidental. John was to be one of five ushers, each to be accompanied down the aisle by a bridesmaid.

She felt disloyal wondering if the groom really knew what he was letting himself in for, in choosing John. He was hardly the type to put a friend on the sleeper to Edinburgh, or shave off eyebrows. Maybe he'd been chosen for his sobriety. As it turned out, John had been away working and missed the stag weekend in Istanbul altogether. Some months earlier he had been despatched for his morning-dress fitting and returned with a swatch of fabric for his waistcoat. This, presumably, was so that his guest would do her best not to clash with the wedding colours and ruin the photographs. Jennifer felt a mischievous impulse to wear black – wasn't she in mourning for the death of love?

This was clearly to be a circus, the likes of which Ilkley had never seen. And she felt like one of the performers. She and John hadn't had sex in about two months and now when one stayed over with the other, since they had never actually gotten a place together, they lay on opposite sides of the bed, sheets tucked primly under their arms, concentrating on their novels. When the lights went out, they fell asleep without touching at all, bar a dry, sad little kiss. It was as though if either of them opened their mouth, everything would come out. They talked about it, joked weakly about how tired they both were, idly wondered about a weekend away at some point in the future, but they were lying.

Earlier Jennifer had had an hour to kill while John and the others took part in the rehearsal. They were staying in a nice, country hotel, which neither of them could really afford, but it had been the cheapest option on the list that arrived with the invitation. It was chintzy and frilly, and she swore the matronly woman who registered them at the desk sniffed when she saw that they weren't married, but it had a beautiful view of open countryside.

She used the time to take a run. She'd started running a year or so earlier, and discovered – much like bacon sandwiches, which she had taken to eating in secret at about the same time – that she loved it. It made her feel powerful and free. Head down, headphones on, she ran hard for half an hour, trying not to think about John or what the hell she was doing here, at this wedding of people she didn't know and didn't care about; with a man she was no longer in love with, losing herself in the song lyrics on her CD walkman and the stunning scenery.

She met Stephen at the rehearsal dinner, to which she did wear black, having compromised and bought an entirely suitable coat dress and shift in an utterly appropriate soft green for the next day. Evidently he was an usher from university years, although he was English – they'd met doing an internship at a London bank three summers earlier. John sat at the other end of the table, beside the blonde bridesmaid he would accompany down the aisle the next day. He looked miserable. Which was actually, she realized, his normal face. Which was, actually, she then realized, why he was so exhausting to live with.

They stood obediently behind their marked places, waiting for the main bridal party to take their seats.

'You look great with your clothes on.'

Jesus! Was this weekend not hard enough? She turned

to see who was speaking. The man on her left was tall and blond, with broad shoulders and a narrow waist. Not at all her normal type, he looked uncomplicated and too healthy, with bright eyes and slightly ruddy cheeks. Typical Jock.

'What?'

'I mean to say, you scrub up well, if you'll excuse the phrase.'

She still had no idea what he meant.

'How could any woman in her right mind possibly excuse that phrase?'

He shrugged nonchalantly and beamed at her.

'Have we met?' She was bored already.

'Not exactly. I was watching you this afternoon, running.'

'Right.' That explained the appalling opening gambit, from which, she felt, the chances of recovery were bleak.

She looked pointedly at the place name of the man on her right, hoping the idiot would leave her alone, but he was already talking animatedly to the woman next to him. She was stranded. The tall blond held out his hand and smiled, and this time it was sheepish.

'Stephen. Sorry, I'm not a dickhead, I promise.'

She shrugged and smiled weakly. This could be a long night.

Only it turned out, he wasn't a dickhead. And it wasn't a long night. He was funny and far more clever than his earlier remarks had made him seem. And incredibly straightforward. He was a stockbroker, but he didn't want to do that forever. He wanted to work for himself. He lived in London, alone, in a flat he'd bought a couple of years ago and done up in the evenings and at weekends. He had a lot of mates, played rugby at the weekends, as she had suspected, but had no girlfriend, at least not one permanent enough or important enough to bring to this wedding.

'So how come you're here, Jennifer?'

'My . . . my boyfriend, John. He's the guy over there, at the end of the table. He was at school with Peter.'

Stephen glanced briefly at John, who didn't notice he was being discussed, and nodded. She thought she saw incredulity cross his face. 'How long you two been together?'

'Forever.' Or did she mean too long?

'How long is forever?' His eyes were laughing at her. 'You're not much into straight answers, are you?'

'We met at university. First week, first term, that sort of thing.' She pulled a face and he raised an eyebrow.

'Ah,' he nodded sagely, 'one of *those* couples.'

She laughed, indignant denial seeming suddenly pointless. ''Fraid so. Do you have to make it sound quite so ghastly?'

'But it *was* ghastly. Think of all the things you missed . . .'

She fell silent, and stared intently at her fingers, entwined in front of her on the table.

'So that would make it . . . how many years?'

He was like a dog with a bone.

'Well, I was 18, and I'm 27, so I guess nine years.'

'And you're not married?'

'Not married, no.' She waved her ringless left hand nervously in front of her.

'Why not?'

No one had asked her that before. People joked about it. Mum danced around the subject at family gatherings when she'd had a couple of glasses of wine. And Hannah made no secret of her burning desire to be a bridesmaid, for anyone at all who might ask her . . . But no one had

173

just come out and asked her. And here was this stranger, looking right at her, asking her straight out.

Jennifer looked at her hands, folded in her lap. When she answered, she was almost surprised to hear the words come quietly from her mouth.

'We don't love each other anymore.'

So this would be the point at which he'd cough, embarrassed, and change the subject. Invent the need to visit the bathroom, or the bar. She looked up, and he was staring at her intently.

'I'm sorry to hear that.' But he didn't look all that sorry.

The next morning she slipped into a pew near the back of the church. The elderly couple next to her nodded and smiled politely, and then they all listened to the organist. John had to accompany 'his' bridesmaid, Peter's younger sister, down the aisle. She'd wondered how she would feel about watching him come down the aisle with another woman. Turned out, she felt sorry for him. He looked awkward and uncomfortable, and the pair of them couldn't get their walk right, so it almost looked as if he was being dragged up the aisle by a 12-stone puff of burgundy taffeta. No irony there, then, she almost smiled. He smiled weakly at her as he passed. Stephen was two ushers behind him. They should have given him the hippo bridesmaid. He looked confident and amused, and – she was surprised to realize – a bit handsome. She saw him scan the aisles – for her? When he spotted her, he fixed her with a broad smile. She felt a ridiculous rush of warmth in the pit of her stomach. What the hell was going on?

She could see the back of John's head. His wedding haircut was too short and his neck was red. For the first time, she really listened to the vicar, to the words of the marriage service. They were profound and serious. It seemed to her, sitting in the back of a church full of strangers, watching two people she neither knew, nor cared for take lifelong vows, that the priest was talking directly to her. Except he wasn't a priest anymore; he was a scientist, this his lab and his words the litmus test of her feelings for John. The evidence was inescapable. Each vow forced from her heart a resounding no. By the time he got to kissing the bride, her relationship was as dead as theirs was born again, and when her eyes filled with tears watching them pass by, triumphant, on the way to be photographed in the churchyard, not one person, save maybe John, knew what those tears meant.

After that, of course, the day was an agony without end. John and the other ushers held the prone bride in their arms for photographs, stood on the endless receiving line, sat at the top table for the interminable schmaltzy speeches, waltzed bridesmaids around the floor to the strains of Celine Dion, and grew quietly and determinedly drunker. She saw Stephen up close just once more before she made her escape. She was waiting by the door for John, who'd returned to the fray for one more goodbye, or thank you, or something. Shifting from aching foot to aching foot, her back was to the room. She knew he was behind her before he spoke.

'Are you okay?'

She didn't look at him.

'Not remotely.'

He touched her arm, lightly, but long enough to make her turn and meet his gaze.

'You *will* be, Jennifer. You will be.'

*

It was three months after that before she talked to him again. He called her at work one Friday morning. Though it had been weeks, and though it wasn't a voice she knew well, she recognized him at once. Which was strange, since she didn't think she'd given him a single – well, not many – thought since that miserable day. And, actually, exciting.

'You're not easy to get a number for, d'you know?'

She laughed. 'I can't begin to imagine how you went about it.'

'Means fair and foul.'

'Is that why it took so long?'

'Nope. I've had it for a few weeks. Couple of months, in fact.'

'Taken this long to work up the courage?'

She was flirting. She didn't even know she knew how . . .

'Bah! You wish. You weren't that frosty . . .'

'And I was trying so hard . . .'

'Can't fool me.' She felt, then, listening to his voice at the end of the line, that maybe she couldn't.

'Why so tardy then?'

'Wanted to give you time . . .'

'To forget you entirely?'

'No, to get out of your situation.'

She let the line go quiet.

'And you have, I hope?'

She had. Almost as soon as their return from Yorkshire. Not because of Stephen – that would have been ridiculous, on the strength of two short conversations. And Jennifer was never ridiculous. Because it was the right thing to do, and because it had suddenly become clear to her, sitting in that church, and because once she'd made up her mind to do it, she couldn't wait.

It had been strangely easy to extricate him from her life. She was so glad they'd never formalized their relationship or moved in together. Two cardboard boxes (hurrah, the gluten-free pasta and the earnest biographies!) was all it took to eradicate all evidence of him from her flat, and there was even less for him to do. Telling him had been hard, of course. But not so hard as the sympathetic phone calls, and consolation cards and notes the postman delivered – and which made her feel like a fraud. Once the boxes were gone and she didn't have to look at his hurt face, she felt good, really good. Like when she was running. Free.

She'd gone home to tell Mum, who had hugged her, hard, and then, pulling back and searching her face, had given a small triumphant cry and said, 'Thank God!'

'I have,' she said now, to Stephen.

'Good. Then we can go out. What are you doing on Friday night?'

Just like that.

When Stephen arrived home that night, it wasn't the smell of something good cooking on the stove top, or the open bottle of wine or the soft music playing in the living room that surprised him. It was that Jennifer came to the door when she heard his key turn in the lock; that she put her arms round his neck and hugged him tight before he had even closed it behind him. And that she seemed so pleased to see him.

My Mum

I've been writing about being your mum, so I thought I probably ought to write a bit about being my mum's daughter. It's all related, isn't it? Are we the mothers we had ourselves, or do we make a choice to be different? What kind of mothers will you be?

We're on holiday. A long weekend in Bath. We're staying in a hotel on Great Pulteney Street – that lovely wide Regency street the BBC always uses in Jane Austen adaptations. We've got a bedroom at the front, and I'm sitting in an armchair with a great view of the comings and goings. Mark's gone to watch rugby. It's bloody cold, but the sun is streaming in through the window. We've had tea at the Pump Rooms, and sat on deckchairs in the gardens by the river, and toured the Spa (maybe I should have taken the waters – couldn't have hurt!) and done a bit of shopping. Great shops, here. We've bought Mark some lovely new suits and ties. Can't really get interested in shopping for myself. Bath is full of Americans. They come here from Salisbury and Stonehenge. They think everything is adorable.

We've had a lovely time. Isn't it funny how sometimes a couple of days away can feel like a two-week holiday?

Hannah is on the school ski trip. A week in the French Alps. We spoke to her last night. They had fresh snow the day before they arrived – by coach, poor things – and the skiing is apparently amazing. She's beyond blues now, she claims, and happiest on the reds. How terrifying! Gets that from her father . . . Nothing to do with her French ski instructor, she says. She sounds really happy and quite mad. God knows how the teachers who accompany them cope. (Note to Hannah: you said you didn't want to go. You didn't want to leave me, you said. In case something happened . . . I made you go, and I'm fine.)

So . . . my mum. I think only children are a really bad idea. I mean, I know that for some people it's okay. Some people can only have one child, and one is better than none. But I don't think it was a great thing for me. For one thing, most women, if they are only going to have one child, would want that child to be a daughter. Not my mum — she wanted me to be a boy; she always said so. She'd had brothers. Her brothers were younger, and she had had a hand in raising them. She said boys were nicer than girls. More straightforward and simple, less devious. You knew where you were with boys, she said. Often. From when I was young. I once, as a teenager, suggested that perhaps she shouldn't have said it to me so often when I was younger. She was clearly mystified that it should have bothered me. Another stranger to the self-help section of the bookshop, clearly, my mum. Didn't quite catch that groundbreaking work on bolstering your daughter's self-esteem.

I never quite knew why I was an only child. I would never have asked. Not that I recall ever seeing a single gesture of affection between my parents. What kept them together — if anything actually did, bar habit and necessity — was conducted behind closed doors. There wasn't a lot of cuddling for me either. They never hit me, or were cruel. It was just that home was a sort of dry place. What it gave me most strongly was a determination that my home, when I had one, would be

179

the exact opposite. My dad used to look at me like I was a stranger over the top of his newspaper. He clearly could not understood how a child with spirit and an easy laugh and that perpetual smile – the one that made people think I was simple – could have resulted from a union between him and my mother. They were both lean and spare, too, and I was curvy from the start. I was pink where they were greyish. My curly auburn hair apparently sprang from nowhere, too, although my dad was largely bald by the time I was born. They were both older than all my friends' parents – in years, and in outlook.

They'd both lost a fiancé in the War. Mum's childhood sweetheart was an auxiliary watchkeeper in the Royal Navy, who had been killed when the Germans sank the HMS Hood in the Denmark Strait in 1941. Dad's fiancée was already dead by then – killed in September 1940, in the early days of the Blitz. Her family had evacuated to relatives in Hove when war broke out the previous September, but, like many others, she had come back when the threatened bombings hadn't materialized. Twenty people died, including her entire family, during a night time raid. I only found out about them – Arthur and Margaret, they were called – by snooping and questioning. Dad didn't have a picture of Margaret, but there was one of my mum and Arthur taken just before he left, proud and formal in his uniform. I found it once, in the back of a book; it had a tear in it and bent corners. But she'd kept it.

If it sounds romantic, the two of them finding each other after all that heartache, I'm not sure it was. Maybe Arthur and Margaret had really been the loves of their lives, and anything else they fell into afterwards was destined to disappoint. I don't really believe that.

I'm not sure either of them had a great capacity for love, that was all. It's funny – mine feels bottomless! I never saw them kiss, and I never saw either of them naked. We had a lot of closed doors in our house. It sometimes felt like the three of us were living separate lives in the same space. We didn't talk about things. Not really. I remember my mum trying to talk to me about sex, the night before I married Donald. It was obvious she found it excruciating. It was also, by the way, completely unnecessary. I may not have 'done it', but I bet I knew more about it than she did! She said it was messy; she said I would need towels.

Do you remember when I told you, Lisa and Jennifer? I had all my props: A book, a box of Tampax, a pack of condoms, a carefully rehearsed speech . . . It was all going very well until Lisa asked me if I had to stand on my head for Daddy to get his willy in, and Jennifer ran screaming from the room. Probably not a much better job than Mum did, but I think I caught you both before you knew enough to think I was an idiot! At least I better have done . . . Anyway, I think Mum must have been the original 'lie-back-and-think-of-England girl', with towels. Maybe I've been doing it all wrong all these years, but I still haven't done anything that needed towels to clear it up . . . Answers on a postcard . . .

I like to think that maybe she made me a better mother, by showing me how I didn't want to do it. It's a cliché, I know. I never closed a door in our house. (Okay, except the bedroom . . . but that's a bit different.) I never wanted you to stop talking to me. I wanted us to laugh, and play and have fun. And we did, didn't we girls? We did. I hope you remember it like I do. The sun is putting me to sleep. It's lovely here.

Simple pleasures have become so much more significant. Having this illness makes everything in the world look and feel different. I don't think Mark will be back for another hour or so . . . So I'm going to act like an old lady, and take a nap. Sad, hey?!
Love you, girls,

Mum

Lisa

Lisa tried to avoid coming face to face with Karen, but this week it couldn't be helped. Andy was working late on something that needed finishing, and she was home. So it was Lisa who opened the door to Cee Cee and her mother. Cee Cee, her 'Hello Kitty' rucksack strapped on her back, dolls in each hand, ran down the hall towards the television, throwing a vague greeting over her shoulder towards Lisa. Karen was following with a wheelie suitcase, its handle too short for her in her 3" heels. Not many women looked good in pinstripe suits, but Karen did. This one had a pencil skirt. She wore it with a crisp white blouse, unbuttoned possibly one button too far. But hey, she had great tits! Lisa had seen them, hadn't she, in the photographs? She was still tanned from her child-free New Year shag fest with Steve in the Turks and Caicos. She'd had highlights, Lisa noticed. Her hair looked freshly washed and bouncy: it always did.

The laughing, good-time girl Andy had described from their summer romance a million years ago had more than grown up; she'd grown kind of mean. But today she was smiling. That meant she wanted something. She only tried to pretend that she and Lisa were friends when Cee Cee was around and she was playing Disney Channel single mum, or when she wanted to change visitation. Today she lunged in for the air kiss. She must want something big.

'Lisa, how are you?'

'Great, Karen. You? Still sporting the January tan, I see.'

Karen laughed, tossing her big hair back and showing her throat so that more bronzed flesh was on display.

'I'm great! The island was *amazing*! You have to get there.'

'I'll put it on the list.'

'Do. The most amazing food, and really, really nice people.'

Ho hum!

But then she saw it. It was hard to miss. In case it wasn't obvious, Karen ran her left hand through her hair, smoothing her cuticles quite unnecessarily. They'd never dare to be rough. The rings glinted in the wintry sunshine. Lisa would have much preferred to ignore it, but Karen wasn't about to let that happen.

'Oh,' she began, as though answering a question that hadn't actually been posed. 'Yes, Steve proposed. We got married over there.'

Bloody hell! Was there something in the water? Out loud, she managed a spluttering 'Congratulations, that's great news. Wow! That was fast.'

'Not really.' Obviously not the right thing to say. 'I mean, we've known for ages that it would happen. Couldn't decide how to do it. I mean, it's a bit silly, isn't it, having a big thing, when it's the second time? I mean, it wouldn't be, for you, of course, since it would be the first time for you. Only the second time for Andy . . .' *Got that, Karen! Yes, you had him first. Thanks.* 'Still, we wanted it to be special. It was Steve's idea – doing it out there – he's so romantic.'

'Well, yes. Sounds wonderful.'

'You'll tell Andy for me?' *Coward!*

'Sure, he'll be chuffed for you.'

'The only thing is Cee Cee. She was really fed up with me when we got back and told her.' Now there's a shocker, Lisa thought. You buggered off and got married without telling your 6-year-old daughter that was what

184

you had planned, and she had the audacity to be pissed off with you. Kids!

'She wanted to be a bridesmaid.'

Of course she did, you silly cow! She's 6! It's the nearest thing to being a bride she can aspire to for, like, the next 10–15 years, and aren't we all just obsessed with being one of those? They must send us subliminal messages in utero. What Lisa managed out loud was a less judgmental 'Aah,' her hands pushed into the pockets of her jeans.

It was cold out there on the doorstep, but she really couldn't bear to ask Karen in. She might expect to stay for a cup of tea. Lisa wished she'd get to her point.

'Still, I daresay it'll be your turn soon. You and Andy,' she added, as though it needed qualifying. 'So hopefully she'll get her chance . . .'

Was that her point? Were she and Andy supposed to get married so that Karen could make up to Cee Cee for not having her as a bridesmaid?

'I mean, you'll be doing it here, won't you? Not Andy's style, whisking a girl away.'

Now Lisa quite wanted to slap her.

'But I know how serious he is about you. He's told me.'

Or throttle her.

'And Cee Cee just adores you . . .'

Turns out, Lisa didn't need to tell Andy. Cee Cee told him. Over breakfast the next morning, between dips of her toast soldiers into her boiled eggs.

'Mummy and Steve got married on the Turkeys and Cocoas, so *he's* my new daddy. When you get married with Lisa, *she'll* be my new mummy, and my old mummy says *that's* when I'll get to wear a bridesmaid's dress and I want a pink one.' Lisa, pretending to get something from the fridge so she wouldn't have to meet Andy's gaze, rolled her eyes at the cranberry juice. There was a bloody conspiracy.

Jennifer

Jennifer took a chance on Kathleen being home alone. She was out of the office – she'd told her colleagues she was doing reconnaissance at a new boutique hotel in the country, but she hadn't been anywhere near the place. She'd needed space. Once she got into the car and out of the city, she just drove. Driving up here hadn't been a conscious decision; she'd just realized that she was heading towards her parents-in-law. Her need to talk was threatening to consume her.

Brian played bowls and drank beer afterwards at the bowls club. These days, it was where most of his mates were. He'd worked at a warehouse a few miles away for many years, starting on the floor and working his way up to manager – with forty or fifty lads reporting to him. He'd retired a few years back, the recipient of a decent pension and the ubiquitous gold watch.

She parked her car on the street, and walked up the path to the front door. Kathleen opened it before she had the chance to knock.

'Hello, dear. I saw you through the window. This is a nice surprise.' Kathleen hugged her and pulled her into the house.

'I was almost passing!' She felt foolish. What would Kathleen think of her, showing up in the middle of the day when she should have been at work? 'I thought I might scrounge a cuppa, if you weren't doing anything. I can go if you're busy . . .'

'How lovely! What would I be doing, love, that meant

I couldn't see you?' She said it as though she never did anything, and accepted her daughter-in-law's arrival as if she might have been expecting it. 'Come on in. I was just going to take a break myself. I've been ironing. Never stops, does it?'

The board was set up in the living room and *Murder She Wrote* was on the television. There was a pile of bed linen in the basket and several of Brian's shirts neatly finished on hangers on the French doors. The house was immaculate. Christmas, with its itinerant chaos, must be a struggle for Kathleen, by nature as neat as a pin. That much, at least, Stephen had inherited from her. She remembered, very early on in their courtship, watching him fold boxers into four when they came out of the tumble dryer. The sad thing was, she almost laughed, that had only added to his attraction as far as she was concerned.

Photographs crowded nearly every surface in the room – grandchildren in school uniform, their hairstyles and teeth marking the passing of the years.

'I'll just put the kettle on, and I'll get rid of this mess.' Kathleen reached for the remote control and turned Angela Lansbury off.

'Don't worry, no need. You'll only have to get it out again. Leave it, please. Let's sit in the kitchen.'

Kathleen held her arms up in surrender and they walked through to the back of the house.

'Brian not about?'

She winked. 'You're safe. You know Brian, he's down the bowls club. He won't be back until he wants his tea. About six usually. God knows they can't be playing – it's freezing cold out there today.'

In the kitchen, she busied herself making tea. Jennifer noticed a solitary plate and knife waiting to be washed up by the sink. Her mother-in-law had lunched alone as well.

'Is he gone all day?'

'Sometimes. I'm glad to have him out from under my feet, to be honest. Truth is, I never really got used to him being retired and around all day.'

'It must be different.'

'I hadn't realized what a misery guts he was, dear.'

Jennifer laughed.

'I mean, when he was working, he'd come home and be like that, but you told yourself he was tired, work might have been stressful. I mean, it wasn't all that high-powered a job, not like you lot, but it had its problems, believe me. So you made excuses for him being so grumpy. Trouble was, when he retired, I ran out of excuses. Had to admit I was just married to an old curmudgeon. He can't moan about work any more, 'cos he doesn't go. So he sits there, in front of the telly with his paper, moaning about the telly – what's on it – and the paper – what's in it – and Tony Blair, and Abdul bleeding Hammzer, or whatever his name is, and his people carrier. And that weather forecaster – the one with the huge mouth, Sian something or other. He never shuts up; he's like white noise.'

She looked a little surprised at her own outburst.

'Now listen to me prattling on. You haven't come all this way to hear me moaning, have you, love?'

She filled the pot with boiling water and carried it over to the kitchen table with a couple of mugs and a bottle of milk from the fridge.

'How are you?'

'I'm fine.'

Kathleen poured the tea and pushed a mug Jennifer's way.

'And your stepdad, your sisters? How are they doing?'

'Mark's okay, I think. He's thrown himself into work, as the expression goes, keeping himself busy. Hannah's better than the rest of us, I reckon. She misses Mum a lot, obviously, but she lived with her and I think we all underestimated maybe how difficult that was for her, for all those months. She is definitely a bit relieved, too, and I don't blame her for that. Those last bits were pretty ghastly. They're looking after each other – it's nice to see. They're very close. Lisa's around a lot lately. Mand is in and out of our lives, like she always was, but she seems okay. We're all okay. You have to be, don't you?'

Kathleen peered at her closely. 'You're not, and you don't have to be. I was nearly 45 years old when my mum died, practically middle-aged myself. I had my three kids, my own home. Hadn't lived with her for more than twenty years. I cried like a baby for months, every chance I got, when she died. Mad, isn't it? Took me a long time to stop missing her. I still do. I used to tell her everything. Even when we didn't see each other, we'd still talk on the phone. Brian would make such a stink about the phone bill. But I told him talking to her was my only hobby and that if he didn't like it, we could get her to move in, so I could talk to her in person. Funnily enough, he stopped going on about the bill after that! Brian, the kids, work, money – I'd talk to her about everything. Then all of a sudden I couldn't do it any more. She never lost her marbles or anything, you see; she wasn't even that old. Sixty-eight – that's nothing these days, is it? It was a major stroke that killed her. Just like that. She was sharp as a tack until the very last and the next day she was gone.'

She put her hand across Jennifer's on the table. 'At least, with your mum, ghastly though it was, you had the chance to say what you wanted to say to her, you know, before it was too late.'

Barbara had been in and out of consciousness for the last four or five days before she died. The morphine pump was keeping her pain under control, but it was also making her sleep. Someone sat with her all the time during the day, holding her hand, and at night, Mark shut the door on them all and climbed into bed beside her. No one ever knew, nor should they, what passed between husband and wife on those long nights. Mark looked exhausted. His hair was too long, and he shaved only when he appeared to remember, which was not daily. His eyes were sunken into dark patches, and they were washed red – the sure sign of a person who cried when they were on their own. The windows were open, and the curtains stirred in the breeze. You could hear life outside. By mutual agreement they kept the radio on in the room, all the time – very quietly. She liked it, she said. It marked the passage of time. Mostly it was Radio 4, with *Woman's Hour* and *The Archers* and *Loose Ends*. Some-times they changed it to Radio 2 so she could hear Terry Wogan's breakfast show, if she was still listening. It reminded Jennifer of her childhood, sat at the kitchen table eating Rice Krispies. Was he really still doing it after all these years?

The last time Jennifer spoke to her mum was about thirty-six hours before she died. She was taking the early-morning shift. Hannah was at school and Mark was returning some calls in the study downstairs. The Macmillan nurse was about somewhere but they'd been on their own.

The conversation hadn't been profound or long-lasting. Barbara had opened her eyes and seen Jennifer sitting there. She'd smiled. Radio 2 was playing Haircut 100's 'Fantastic Day'. Because it was – for everyone else out there listening, it was 70 degrees already, cloudless and perfect. They'd been playing happy summer songs all morning. Jennifer had asked if she wanted some water and her mum had given a slight shake of her head. She turned towards the breeze, letting it play across her face. Gesturing to the radio with her hand, she'd smiled again and said, 'Ironic, huh?' Then she'd put her hand back down on the blanket and Jennifer had covered it with her own. She'd said, 'I love you' and acknowledged her daughter saying it back with the merest nod effort allowed. Then she'd closed her eyes and drifted off again.

That had been it.

Jennifer had gone home that afternoon for some clean clothes. The nurse said she didn't think it was going to happen then, although she thought it would be soon. She'd come back that night and slept next door in the guest room with Lisa. Mark had kept Hannah home from school the next morning when she got up. He must have had a feeling. They were all there, except Amanda. Mum had died at lunchtime the next day, her breathing shifting slightly, catching in her throat once, and then gently stopping. They hadn't even been sure, until the nurse said, that it was finally over. It didn't seem possible you could die so quietly. The nurse said it was often that way. Mark finally switched off the radio.

Jennifer had cried then, and she started to cry now. She couldn't hold it in. Her eyes filled with tears and her shoulders began to shake, racking her with huge, desperate sobs. She knew Kathleen had never seen her cry before, nothing more than a little misting around the eyes, brought on by something on TV, and was afraid she would be discomfited. This was ugly, uncontrolled crying. But Kathleen threw her arms around her daughter-in-law, murmuring words of comfort as though she were a child, and let her cry for long minutes against her body, stroking her hair and telling her it would be alright.

'You poor, poor girl,' she said at last, when Jennifer's sobs had quietened and she was blowing her nose, rubbing at her eyes.

'I'm so sorry.'

'Don't be daft. You have to cry on someone.'

'I shouldn't be in this state. She's been dead for months. I shouldn't still be falling apart over it, like some kid who never grew up and grew away. I'm supposed to be stronger than this.'

'Do you know, that's half your trouble, if you ask me, Jen.' Her voice was gentle. 'You make these rules for yourself, and they're ... they're just impossible. You spend the whole time beating yourself up for not being perfect. And you don't realize how great you are. Crying for your mum doesn't mean you're not strong; it doesn't mean you're not coping. And anyway, who put a time limit on grief? Did you expect to wake up one morning and be over it? That isn't going to happen, honey. That's not how it works. Loving someone, and losing them – it isn't neat.'

'It's just that I'm so unhappy, Kathleen.'

'About your mum?'

She paused. 'About everything.'

'About Stephen?' She didn't sound shocked.

'Yes, about Stephen. And I need to talk to someone about it, and I needed to talk to my mum. And she tried, she tried to get me to talk to her, but I wouldn't. And I don't have anyone else. I don't talk to my friends about stuff like this; I never have, it's not who I am. I have my sisters, but I can't . . . I can't talk to them. They all think I'm the one who's got it all sussed, I'm the one who's happily married.'

She was as much wailing as talking. Kathleen fetched a box of tissues from the windowsill and handed her a couple. Jennifer blew her nose.

'And would it be the end of the world if you told them you hadn't got it all worked out? That you weren't always happy? Are they such a resounding success?'

'I don't know.'

'Because it seems to me, unless they're blind and dumb, they must already know.'

'What do you mean?'

'I mean, it's pretty obvious to me, that the two of you are having your problems.'

'It *is*?' Jennifer's voice rose with incredulity.

Kathleen smiled sympathetically. '*Of course* it is! Do you think the rest of us are blind? You can cut the air with a knife around here when the two of you are together. I didn't see you touch one another once when you were here before Christmas. I was ashamed of him when he let his dad lay into you like that at the table without standing up for you.'

'You never said anything.'

'What could I say? People don't want you sticking your nose in. You wait until people come to you.'

'Has Stephen come to you?'

'No, Stephen hasn't said a word. Stupid boy. But you have.'

Jennifer thought she might cry again.

'I don't know what to do. We're just not getting on at all.'

She explained then, to her mother-in-law, as best as she could what had been happening: the deterioration, the distance. A couple of times she was afraid she'd said too much – Stephen *was* Kathleen's son – but she held her hand up and told her she knew he could be a swine. 'I'm not blind to his faults, any more than I am to his father's,' she said. The more she talked, the more hopeless she felt. There were so many things, so many instances; they added up to a bleak picture. When she'd finished, she sat at the table, ashamed, and waited for Kathleen's verdict. Waited for help, or rescue.

'I don't have answers, my love. I can't tell you what to do. Sounds to me like you've got yourselves into a real mess.'

She stood up and put the kettle on again. Jennifer knew she was buying herself time, thinking of the right thing to say. She stared out of the window and hoped Brian wouldn't come home early. It was bad enough that she'd broken down this way in front of Kathleen. She couldn't bear Brian to see her like this.

When Kathleen sat down again, with fresh mugs of tea, she seemed to have decided. She lay both her hands on the table and spread the fingers wide apart, and then looked at them while she talked.

'I can only think of three things to tell you, Jennifer. The first is that I love you, like you were my own daughter. That's by the by, but I wanted to let you know that. You can come to me, now or at any time in the future, whatever happens, and I will still feel that way. Okay?' Jennifer smiled gratefully. 'The second thing is that I truly believe my son loves you. I remember the day he came home from that wedding, the one where he met you. He came in through the door, whistling like a madman, and he looked so bloody pleased with himself.

And he said, "I've met the girl I'm going to marry." I don't know what you wore, or what you said, or how you did it, but you cast a spell on him that first time the two of you met, and I don't think it's worn off. He loves you. I never saw him half so keen on anyone else, and I can't imagine him being again. Why in God's name he's let himself reach the point where he won't tell you, or show you, or make you feel it, I haven't a clue. I'd like to shake him, believe me I would.

'But the third thing is this, and I'm not being disloyal saying this: it's what I truly believe. I settled for his dad. I settled for him the day I married him, and I've been settling for him all these years since. My marriage has been at best satisfactory, and at worst, a sentence. I can count the days of pure happiness we've had together on the fingers of one hand. I haven't been unhappy so much as just not very happy, and allowing that to happen has been the biggest mistake and is the greatest regret of my life.

'Your mum got out of a bad marriage. I've stayed in mine, because it wasn't bad enough – and look what she got! She got Mark and your sister; she got a new life. And from everything I ever saw of her, it was a bloody marvellous one. Look at me, I've got Brian. It's too late for me. I've built a life around him. It largely excludes him, to be honest. I'm not tearing my hair out with misery, that's not what I'm saying. We're okay. I've got my kids, and my grandchildren, and my health and my home. I'm better off than most. But there are days when I think I've been a fool. I think what a waste it's been.

'Don't be like that, Jennifer. If there are things you can change, that you two can fix to make it like it was before – or better – then do it, do it fast. Life is too short, my darling, to live that way. And if you can't see a way to fix them, then move on. He's my son, and I love him, but this applies to both of you. You'd be better off apart, with new chances to be happy, than together with none. I didn't know your mum all that well, more's the pity, but I'm pretty sure she'd have been telling you the same thing, if you'd given her the chance – I truly am.'

This one is called . . . The Days That You Were Born

It's a few months since I started doing this. Told you I'd be sketchy, at best. I read the last bit and took my own advice – I've been sucking it dry. Yes, there's been the treatment, but I'm not going to, not ever, write about that. Bad enough having to do it without reliving it in print. In between the treatments (enough said) there's been holidays to take, friends to drink wine with, daughters to lie in the garden with, swinging on the seat, Mark to love . . . But I'm back now, I have more stuff to tell you . . .

I know we used to talk about this all the time when you were small, but we stopped when you grew up, and I don't know if you all remember the stories so I'm writing them down. They're part of your blueprint and I want you to have them. Do you remember the Mother Goose *nursery rhyme about birthdays? I always felt like she (was she a she? Who wrote* Mother Goose? *Who the hell knows! And I've better things to Google) got it so right for you lot. Lisa was my Sunday baby – bonny and blithe, good and gay. Of course, she's not gay, and I don't really know what being blithe entails, but she's definitely good and bonny. (Note: bonny does NOT mean chubby, Lisa, although the baby pictures tell their own story. My fault, I thought if I kept on feeding you, you'd be bound to sleep through the night. You were like a fois gras goose until you were about 10 months old. Sorry about that!) Jennifer – who came on Saturday during the football (an early indicator of both your loathing of team sports and your uncanny ability to wind your dad up) – works hard for a living. She works hard for everything. (And, by the way, always dresses immaculately. Did I ever tell you how much I admired that about you? You look like a magazine article – always.) Lo and behold, Amanda came on a Thursday, with far to go. (Have you got there yet, my lovely?) It got to the point where I was terrified Hannah would come on a Wednesday – her due date, incidentally, making her full of woe, but thank God she came two weeks early, helped along by my slightly elevated blood pressure, a sympathetic doctor and an intravenous wee dram of syntometrine, on a Monday. And was, of course, fair of face as you all were (apart from those little milk spots, which it nearly killed me not to squeeze). I was the Wednesday baby in the family. So that figures! Although the woe didn't really kick in until much later. My mother reports that I was an agreeable, happy baby; in no hurry to walk or talk, which, coupled with the inane grin I apparently always wore, made people think I was simple. Thanks, Mum! No photographic evidence exists of this phase, fortunately.*

I'm writing this in the hospital, by the way. I'm having a 'course' today. Mark drops me off, but I get him to leave me here. This is not a spectator sport. He buys me a vast stack of magazines in the hospital shop. As though Jude Law and Sienna Miller are a suitable distraction! Bless him. And sometimes a helium balloon, which he ties to this high-backed plastic, upholstered hospital chair I'm confined to. He thinks it makes it jollier. I think it makes the nurses nervous, especially the times the only balloon they have in stock says CONGRATULATIONS! I'm definitely full of woe today – I hate this. I get it, but I hate it. Never went to hospital for myself, except to have babies, before the C word stuff. These wards are not so much fun. Never had a broken bone, or a bad infection, or a rash that couldn't be explained, or a weird thing that needed to be cut off. Just had babies.

I would have liked the chance to be with one of you, while you had a baby of your own. Presumptuous, I know. You might not have liked it – the fathers of these babies might have been horrified at the notion of having their mother-in-law (get me, old-fashioned – their partner's mother, should I say?) muscling in. But I would have asked. I think it would have been amazing. And now, unless one of you (please, not Hannah) gets busy very soon – I'm afraid I won't get the chance, even to ask. I do hope you have babies. I'm not interfering, honest, I'm just saying. It was, without doubt, the very, very best thing that ever happened to me. I know women can exist happily without children, and I know society shouldn't pressure them – blah, blah, blah – and I get all of that, really I do – I'm quite modern, for an old girl. I just want my girls to have babies, that's all. So they know what I know.

Lisa came on a Sunday, like I said. She was a week and a half late, which felt like a year and a half. I was the size of a small cow. It was hot, and it had got so my thighs rubbed together and got sore when I walked, so I tried to avoid that. I couldn't get cool and I couldn't get comfortable. And I couldn't get you out, Lisa. Even drank castor oil, which I don't recommend. When my waters went – rather theatrically, really late on Saturday night – I was half-asleep on the sofa. Thought I'd wet myself, I was so excited. Because I was going to get to see my baby, of course – and don't forget, we didn't have scans and things like that, so we didn't

know whether you would be a girl (although I
desperately wanted you to be one. I never said, because
it seemed disloyal to a boy, that at night I used to lie in
bed and imagine a girl, and dream of a girl) – but also
because I figured I was finally going to get some sleep. I
know, idiotic notion. But I was young and naïve. We
didn't have a car so your dad called a taxi, and off we
went. I had one of those hard-sided round suitcases. I'd
had it to go on honeymoon. It was red. I'd been knitting
matinée jackets – all yellow and green, of course – all
summer; I could have clothed the entire maternity ward.
Off we went, and it was like I was heading for the
Omaha landings. I'd spent nine months imagining
this was going to be the worst, the very worst, most
agonizing pain a person could go through. For the
woman in the bed next to me, it clearly was. I told
myself I was a cabbage, and I just lay there, saying in
my head, 'You're a cabbage, you're a cabbage.' Who
knew I was an early practitioner of meditation
techniques in labour? A pioneer. Thing was, I kept
waiting for it to get really bad, waiting for death to seem
like a good option, and it just never did. I remember
this midwife – she was Welsh, and about 5'2" – I could
barely see the top of her head when she was down at the
foot of the bed, coming to do a check on me and asking
her whether she thought my baby would come today.
She'd laughed, and said she thought my baby would
come within the hour, and that they needed to get me
down to the delivery ward right away. I couldn't believe
it! I'd just sent your dad to the pub down the road for a
sandwich and a beer. It was all over by the time he got
back. Not that he'd have been there if he'd been there, if
you know what I mean. Really was the old days! Suited
me fine. They let me tell him you were a little girl after

I'd got into a clean nightie and they'd cleaned you up. None of this demand feeding stuff – you were promptly wheeled off to the night nursery.

You had the longest fingers. Everyone kept saying you'd make a great pianist. I loved them. You waved them around in front of your face and they were so graceful and expressive. They said you were overcooked – your nails were long and your skin was dry – but I thought you were perfect. I felt like the only woman alive who had ever done this. We stayed in for a week, in those days. Your dad took the bus up to the hospital every day after work and held you. I had a white knitted bed jacket. I remember my friend Maria bought me in some knitting needles and some pink wool – she had boys. We were all so delighted that you were a girl, who we were going to get to dress up and make pretty, and wheel around in the big Mary Poppins pram.

I was sure Jennifer would be a boy. I carried her differently – much neater and all out in front, so everyone else said so too. It was winter, so I wasn't so uncomfortable, and I didn't get nearly so big. I could still button up my winter coat until almost the end, probably chasing after Lisa did that. She was just walking – I swear all that endless leaning over her as she toddled everywhere got that labour going. I wasn't nervous at all. Whatever discomfort I'd felt last time had receded in my memory, and I thought I was an old pro. Jennifer was much more difficult, though. We should have known we were in trouble when she started during a crucial Man United game. Maria had Lisa for us, but we had the car by then. I remember not wanting to sit down in the front seat, so I ended up sprawled on the back seat.

It was all going along like it should and then

everything sort of stopped. The contractions were still strong, but they were much further apart and I was tired. You were stuck, they said. Forceps. Which, when you are lying flat on your back and see them wielded above your nether regions, are particularly terrifying pieces of equipment. You were literally dragged into the world. I remember watching the doctor leaning back and pulling on them. After Lisa I felt exultant and triumphant; after Jennifer I just felt like I'd been hit by a lorry! I barely looked at you when they wheeled you away to the nursery, barely registered surprise that you were a girl. You were a tiny, wrinkled face in a huge white blanket. They were having to stitch me up, and I was sore and exhausted, and probably a bit fed up. Then they gave me a cup of tea and a piece of toast, and I felt dreadful I'd taken so little interest in you and insisted they bring you back to me. I cried, I think. I was like a lioness then.

You had Lisa's fingers, too, but way more hair, curling on your neck. The forceps had left little indentations in your forehead, little bruises, and I remember kissing them and telling you how sorry I was that you'd had such a difficult journey. You'd had a tough day, too; you barely cried. You just stared up at me, and your eyes were practically black and unblinking. The midwife called you an old soul. She said some babies just looked like it wasn't their first time around and that you were one of them. Your dad whispered to me that she was talking rubbish, but I knew what she meant.

It seemed so neat, two girls so close together. The perfect little family. You had a little present for Lisa when your dad brought her in the next day to see you. It was a dolly – you remember Doll Baby? – and we put it in your crib so that she thought you gave it to her.

She was so uninterested in that doll, the first day. She just wanted to get to you – a real baby was much more fun. She adored you, until you were about 3 and you started arguing with her. But when you were new, she adored you. You and Doll Baby used to lie together on a towel on our bed. Her baby and my baby, being washed and dried and powdered, and talked to.

I wasn't with Dad any more when Amanda was born. I know it sounds selfish, but I enjoyed you being all mine. Not having to share you with anyone, even though I clearly caused a stir in the maternity ward. You were absolutely the standard seven-hour labour – straightforward, painful, but pretty quick. This time I really felt like I understood the process. I'd perfected the cabbage thing, and I got the rhythm of it. Each contraction brought you closer to me (I know, that sounds like new age bollocks, but trust me, if you think of it that way, it really helps). I also seem to remember there was quite a lot of gas and air involved. The woman in the next bed kept screaming, asking the doctors if they'd found her coil yet, and the gas and air made me think that was hilarious. I had these visions of the wretched thing being implanted in the scalp of her poor unwanted babe, like a satellite receiver. We'd moved by then, so I didn't have Maria any more. And the times had moved, too, so you didn't get to stay in hospital for very long. One night, two at the most. It was tougher – going home on my own, with a baby. Your big sisters were ridiculously excited and a great help during the day – it seemed like I never had to change a nappy – but I remember the nights feeling quite long. I think I was in a light coma for about twelve months. You sat up early, you crawled early, you were mountaineering on the sofa early. We had those stairs with the open tread (I know, very 80s), and you used to skid about on them in tights. I was convinced you'd never make it to your first birthday, but by then you were running around. Always in a hurry, Amanda. Matter of fact, you could hold your head up almost as soon as you were born. I know all mothers like to exaggerate about their own children, to make them sound just a little bit more special than other people's – I used to hate that, in the playground – but you really were strong, even then. The midwife said so. It was like you wanted to look around and see what you were missing. When I watched you, I remembered Jennifer's staring, quiet eyes, and I thought then that you must be going to grow up into very different people. And you did, didn't you?

Now, Hannah. They call you an 'elderly mother' when you have a baby over the age of 40. Depressing, or what? They like to fill you up with doom and gloom talk, and do nuchal scans and explain your increased risk of Down's Syndrome, and the need for amnio tests. Actually it starts before that, when you make the foolish mistake of going to the doctor to talk about even the possibility of having another baby. They want to tell you to think about how tired you'll be; how your body isn't capable of doing what it used to; how your fertility will have fallen away to such an extent that it may already be impossible anyhow. I came out of the GP's feeling like a dessicated old prune, I tell you. Forty-four years old. Forty-four and a half, to be precise. I didn't feel old. You never do, I don't think. Even now, in my head I feel 18 years old, despite major evidence to the contrary. Your brain doesn't age at the same pace. And your dad – my toy boy – had made me feel younger in that first year together than I had done . . . well, for ages.

Younger and more fun, and more alive and sexier (sorry!). And he wanted you so badly.

Turned out that GP was an idiot and I got pregnant the second month we tried, so that was that and you were on your way. Your dad took incredible care of me. We were living in a caravan while the house was being built. He flogged himself – and the poor Polish builders – to get it finished before you came, but made me take it easy the whole time. He would cook dinner, bring me tea in bed. Kept offering to get me coal, or pickles, or ice cream in the middle of the night. He also read 'the book', and became an expert. I refused point-blank to go to the childbirth classes with him on the basis that I would almost certainly be old enough to be the grandmother of most of the other babies, so instead he would read things out to me every night – visualization exercises, breathing techniques, the need for a birth plan . . . It was hard not to laugh at him, knowing what I knew. I tried hard not to remind him all the time that this wasn't new to me because it was so new and so exciting to him. I tried to explain the cabbage technique, but it wasn't in 'the book'. He bought wooden letters spelling out our boy and girl names, and said I should bring them to hospital and line them up on the windowsill while I laboured. Right! Do you know what your name would have been, Hannah, if you'd been a boy? James. That's why Amanda had a guinea pig named James. And that's why James's cage had his name on it.

What I remember mostly about the labour – which they induced a bit early – was that I couldn't keep him away from the business end! You've got to remember I'd had three babies without a man in attendance, and it wasn't exactly how I wanted to be seen. I'd started having my babies in the Frank Spencer era, for goodness sake, where fathers paced in corridors. But he was fascinated, totally unsqueamish and determined to cut the cord. About halfway through, I felt utterly tired, and I made up my mind before you were born that this would definitely be the last time – I'd had enough. They had scans by then, although not quite as sophisticated as they are today, maybe, and I was all for finding out what you were. But your dad wanted a surprise. I suppose I knew by then that I was destined to have girls. Funny thing was, that was what he wanted too. And you were completely different from Amanda – I couldn't get a look in. You've never seen a man fall so instantly and so deeply in love! You were jaundiced, thank God – that meant a night in hospital to recover, rather than being sent home the same day. You looked like you'd just flown in from the Caribbean, all sun-tanned. The one time I could have done with ten days in the cottage hospital, they wanted to give me two paracetamol and the number of a cab firm! Don't think I could have walked outside to the car if I'd wanted to. The GP had a point about age, after all. But I'm sounding flippant, and I didn't feel it: you were supposed to be born.

So that is roughly it: the four very best days of my life, the four very best things about my life, my four works of art. I have tips for you – what mother wouldn't? Actually, my mother, your grandmother, did a real number on me. She said it was hard work. Mentioned nothing about the indignity and the pain. Well, I'm here to tell you, it is painful, and it is undignified. Forewarned is forearmed. If they offer you drugs, take them. Drugs are good. Gas and air is like gin and tonic. Check the circumference of a man's head before you agree to have a child with him. None of this *big hands, big feet nonsense. It's all about big skulls. You'll thank me. If possible, lie down for all of the nine months because for the next nine months you'll be lucky if you get the chance to lie down at all. Don't knit yellow and green matinée jackets (as if – you girls can't even sew on a button – I blame the mother!) because once you have a flavour, pink or blue, that's the only thing you'll dress them in. Don't bother with a birth plan. I never met a woman who got the birth she requested. The ones who claim they did obviously had too much pethidine. And most importantly, make like a cabbage. Trust me, it works.*

Disposable nappies are fine. If you've ever had to rinse diarrhoea out of a terry napkin liner, you'll worry less about landfill, believe me. Tell yourself you're raising scientists who'll grow up to solve the problems you're creating. Breast may very well be best, but mastitis is a bitch, and if you can tell me which one of you lot is a formula baby, I'll give you a prize. (Answer: you, Hannah. I didn't feel gravity needed any encouragement.) Don't beat yourself up about it, any of it. Your kids will do that for you when they're old enough. Oh, and about stretchmarks. I have them, so the chances are you will, too. Can't help, but I apologise for the genetic cock-up. My advice is to wear bikinis now. You too, Jennifer.

Time's up. Come in #9 – we've finished dripping poison into you through this hole in your arm and we're ready for the next victim. Sorry, patient. We need the chair. Time to go home and wait to start throwing up. It's been nice, girls, reminiscing about the happier hospital times.

Mum

Amanda

Amanda was in line at Trailfinders, waiting for her turn to find a trail. She'd decided last night, while watching a particularly dark and depressing episode of *EastEnders*, that she wasn't going to waste any more time hanging around. She'd got a week or so left to run on her current temping job, and then she was off. Thailand, like she'd planned, if the flights were cheap. Somewhere else, maybe. It had been too long. At this point, she wasn't sure she cared where, so long as it was far away from here. And sunny. She'd had enough of this weather. She wanted to wear a bikini and feel the sun on her skin. This was her lunch hour, and everyone else's, though, so there was a long line. The freezing rain that had been falling without a break for three days must have driven everyone else to the same conclusion.

She was standing as patiently as she could manage, patience never having been her strong point, reading Sarah Dunant and completely absorbed by *The Birth of Venus* when her mobile rang. Tintin. His name flashed up insistently on the screen and she was almost surprised that she had kept it in the address book.

Ed. Now. Picking at the scab that was starting to heal over. Why did guys do that? Too little, too late. She wasn't interested. She pressed the red button vehemently and made him go away.

Three paragraphs of medieval Italy later he rang again. And she pressed again. By the third call, people in the queue were gazing at her inquisitively. She pressed the green button and held the phone to her ear, thinking that if the phone had video capacity he'd be bloody terrified by her scowl.

The scowl was a fake, though. It wasn't how she felt. She felt foolish, and embarrassed, and confused by her apparent ability to get something so wrong. When it had felt so right. She should never have slept with him. She'd been on the money when she identified that as Lisa's modus operandi, not hers. She didn't have the right emotional constitution. She'd segued straight in to behaviour you could only get away with when someone really cared for you, however entitled to that behaviour she might have been ... That was what messed it up. By sleeping with him before they'd even got to know each other, she'd put herself in the category of girls who weren't entitled to throw emotional wobblers, the same category as girls who didn't need to be called afterwards. It wasn't really his fault. Calling now was, though.

'Amanda?'

'Yes.' She sounded as haughty as possible, which wasn't very haughty. He sounded a little panicky.

'Don't hang up on me again. Please.'

She didn't speak, but she didn't hang up either.

'Amanda?'

'I'm here.' Her queue-mates were openly listening now, killing time, grateful for the one-sided mini drama sideshow.

'Thank God! I've been trying; I mean, I've been wanting to try to get in touch ...'

'What do you want, Ed?' She heard the hardness in her own voice.

'It's not what you think, Amanda. At least it's not what *I* think you think, if that makes sense ...'

It did, to her. She thought she'd scared him off, going off on one that morning, after they'd just spent two days blissfully happy in bed together. She thought he hadn't bothered to call her for – for what? – for two weeks since then. She thought she was crazy to be talking to him now, come to think of it.

'You don't have to explain anything to me, Ed.'

Which was true. She'd have been scared off too. It was shaming even to be reminded of it.

She'd left that message almost as soon as she'd got home, which he'd ignored. Then two weeks had passed. She'd been distracted – all this Mum stuff. She'd been jittery and anxious, then sad, then resentful, and now she was trying to forget about him. And about Mum. About everything. And, right now, in fact, to buy tickets to fly somewhere far away from him. She didn't really want to be having this conversation with him now.

'I want to; I need to. My dad . . . he had an accident – a heart attack and an accident, actually.'

'God, Ed!' As excuses went, this was a pretty good one.

'That's why I haven't spoken to you.'

That didn't immediately make sense. He could have called her at any point, couldn't he, and let her know what was going on? If he wanted her to know.

'They called – my mum called me – practically the second you left that morning. I was still watching you out the window. I had to take the train back down, straightaway. I was in such a rush – it sounded like they didn't know if he was going to live – and such a panic . . . I didn't take my mobile phone.'

Two weeks, Ed. It was like he could hear what she was thinking.

'And I know it's been two weeks. Christ, it's all so ridiculous . . . I feel like such an idiot. But my flatmates were away – do you remember, they went skiing? I told you – so no one's been at home, and no one has keys, of course, because that would be too bloody sensible, and you never told me who you lived with, not their surnames, and I didn't know your step-father's last name either, because, for God's sake, we only just met . . . and I had to wait. I had to wait until my stupid flatmates got back, which they did last night, and they didn't answer the phone at the flat until lunchtime because they were so tired – there were these huge delays at Geneva – so they slept late, and, and I've only just got hold of them, and got them to get my phone, and find your number . . .'

He was breathless. No one could make up a story that implausible.

'God, Ed. How's your dad?'

She heard him sigh with relief at not being more closely interrogated.

'He's better. Not much, but some. He's been in Intensive Care. They've moved him to High Dependency – they think he's going to be okay.'

'What happened?'

'He only had a mild heart attack, but he was driving, and on his own. He lost control of the car and ploughed into a tree. Near home. Knocked himself out; hurt himself pretty badly. They didn't find him for a couple of hours. No one was home, so no one missed him . . .'

'Poor man.'

The line was silent for a moment. Amanda thought about Donald. His heart attack had killed him instantly. A massive coronary. All over in minutes, before an ambulance had even been called. Ed spoke again, and now his voice was calmer, and slower. 'I'm so glad I've got through to you. I've been going mad down here, thinking about you and thinking what you must be thinking . . .'

'I thought, I thought I'd scared you off . . .'

'Not at all. I knew you'd think that. God, disastrous timing! I'm *so* sorry.'

'That doesn't matter now.'

'It's so good to hear your voice.'

'Are you coming back?'

'I can't, right now. My mum has shocked us all by going to pieces. Completely. She needs me here, for a bit longer at least.'

'Oh.'

'Can you come?'

'I'm working.'

'You could take the train. I'd meet you.'

'I've got a few days to run at this company I'm temping at.'

'And you can't wheedle out of it?'

'I need the money. I'm . . .'

Suddenly the ticket money didn't seem quite as important. Ed's voice was quiet. He sounded stung. 'God, I'm sorry. Stupid, selfish . . . I didn't mean to sound desperate.'

'I quite liked you sounding desperate.'

'I'd love to see you, Amanda.'

'I'll come.'

'Are you sure?'

'I'll tell them I've got the 'flu. Lot of it going about, I hear; time of year.' She sniffed theatrically and smiled. The woman in the line behind her raised an accusatory eyebrow. Obviously something in Human Resources. She didn't care; nosey old bag.

'You're a star, an absolute star. Thank you, thank you, thank you.' She didn't remember the last time someone sounded quite so pleased that they were going to see her. It felt nice. 'How are things, you know . . . with you . . . ?' he asked.

'That'll keep.'

*

Train stations could be terribly romantic places. Black-and-white filmmakers knew that, didn't they? Like airports, only less high tech. When people on films didn't catch the plane they were supposed to be on, it always bothered her. All that wasted money. And what about their suitcases? Planes can't take off with unclaimed suitcases in the hold, can they? All too complicated. To miss a train you were supposed to be on, you simply climbed down the steps into the waiting arms of the man you loved and the steam enveloped you as you embraced. She'd stood on platforms in Mumbai and in Paris and in South Africa, watching people part and reunite. None of those exotic settings was quite stacking up to Truro right now. The five-hour journey had taken six and a half, thanks to a lingering heavy frost, and something about rolling stock around Exeter, but she was here now, shivering on the platform with her rucksack beside her, watching Ed walk towards her, smiling, she noticed, rather shyly, and looking, she also noted, rather handsome.

After their conversation she'd finished the day at the temping job, working on her pathetic cough and pained expression, and excused herself early the next morning with a fake croak in her voice, and a sincere apology for letting people down. The guy she'd been working for had been more of the 'collect my dry cleaning and brew my tea' kind of boss than usual, and she wasn't, in truth, all that sorry, though. He'd manage. Her absence would not be a major spoke in the wheels of industry. One day she really ought to think about doing something more important. She'd caught the train straight afterwards, arriving at Paddington in her customary manner with seconds to spare and collapsing, panting, into a vacant seat. She liked long train journeys; she loved to watch the changing landscape. When you caught a plane, once you got to 35,000 feet, everything was off-white cloud, and landing somewhere where the scenery and the weather were completely different from where you embarked was a confusing experience. On a train you watched as it all changed. She loved leaving London, with its relentless urbanity, row on row of terraced cottages built too close to the line, discarded shopping trolleys clinging on to steep banks, plumes of smoke, and seeing the countryside open out, greener and wilder with each rhythmic mile. It was quiet, this mid-January, mid-week train. Eventually, the carriage had emptied of most of her travelling companions, and she was alone – her nearest fellow passengers several rows away. She slept a little, balling her *Dr Who* scarf up into a pillow, finished the Sarah Dunant plus a couple of discarded newspapers. She had texted Lisa, letting her know she would be away for a few days. It felt good, to be escaping. Wasn't that what she always did? But it felt better to be heading towards Ed. This was different.

And now here he was. It was weird. This was only the fourth or fifth time they'd ever said hello in person. She was aware, as he hugged her, that they hadn't quite figured out how their bodies would fit together, standing up. They were better at lying down, she realized. He kissed her once, on the mouth, and then pulled her back into the hug. It was strange to be reunited with someone with whom she'd been so intimate, but about whom she still knew relatively little.

'You smell different.'

'That's my country smell.'

'You look different too. Is that a Barbour you're wearing?' She stood back and looked him up and down appraisingly.

He smirked at her.

'Indeed. This is "Squire Ed", an incarnation you haven't met before. All waxed jacket and wet gun dog.'

'When's the next train back?'

He adopted a Mellors accent. 'Ah, m'lady, that'll be next Tuesday, I reckon . . .'

'Bugger! Guess I'll have to stay then.'

'You'll *have* to stay. Mum'll have a Barbour you can borrow.'

'Get lost, not in a million!'

'You say that now, m'lady, fresh from town, but give it a couple of days and you'll go native like the rest of us.'

'We'll see.'

They laughed, delighted at the smooth return of the easy banter, and Ed hoisted her rucksack onto his shoulder, taking her hand with his other arm. 'Come on, it's freezing . . .' She giggled again when he opened the door to an unlocked, ravaged old Land Rover. 'You *are* joking! The transformation's complete, you bumpkin!'

'Dad totalled his car, I'm afraid. And Mum's got hers at the hospital. It was this or horse.'

'Of course.' Then, 'You have horses?'

'No. No horses. Would horses have been a problem?'

'Can't stand them. Got thrown off, once. All my mates were into riding, when we were about, I don't know, 10. Just before boys, you know. They talked me into going with them one day. Happened first time. I thought the bloody thing was going to trample me where I lay on the ground. Possibly the scariest moment of my life.' She had climbed in. 'How far?'

'We're going straight home, if that's okay. I've been at the hospital all day. Dad's at the Royal Cornwall, here in Truro. Home's about twenty minutes in the other direction.'

'Fine. And how is your dad?'

'Talking today. Complaining, actually. Says the food's awful. Why do people always say that? He wants to come home.'

'Don't blame him. I hate hospitals. I've only been in overnight once – I had appendicitis, when I was about 14. Couldn't wait to get out.'

'I've never stayed. All my childhood accidents were of the out-patient variety.' She made a note to ask him about his childhood accidents. Check thoroughly for scars at some point, too . . .

'And how soon is that likely to be? Him coming home?'

'Another week or so at least, they say. They've got to treat the injuries as well as the heart thing. He's had to have all these tests, find out what caused the problem . . .'

'How's your mum? You said, on the phone that she wasn't coping all that well?'

'That's the strangest thing. She's this amazingly capable, strong woman, you know. She was a nurse when she met Dad. Did I tell you that? She never actually finished her training. But she was always really calm, you know. Three boys bring home a lot of bloody noses and broken limbs and black eyes. Nothing ever phased her. That's not just how I see her – that's how she is . . . was. This has really knocked her for six. She literally fell apart. When she rang me that morning, she could barely speak.'

'He's her husband.'

'I know.'

'She must have been frightened.'

'We all were. I'm not ready, you know. Not ready to let him go.'

'I don't suppose anyone ever is.'

'No.'

He took one hand off the steering wheel, and squeezed her knee.

'Thank you *so* much for coming, Amanda.'

She was very glad she had.

The Land Rover was not the most comfortable mode of transport. She felt every bump in the road. Add an unidentifiable smell, three dozen more people, some chickens, and she could have been back on the bus in Cambodia. Ed acted as tourist guide, pointing left and right at significant points – left down there was where he'd gone to junior school, right down here led to his brother's house. At one point he gestured upwards, to the high hills in front of them, where a huge white house sat majestically surveying the road and everything else. 'That's where the Duchess lives. You remember, my dad's first wife.'

'It looks like a stately home!'

'It's about as welcoming too, from what I've heard. Must have loved it when they built this road a few years back, mustn't she? Not far now – just a couple more minutes.'

'Isn't it uncomfortable for them, living so close, when they don't get on?'

'Not really. They move in totally different circles. The Duchess is in with the hunting set. Wankers!'

'I'm *so* glad you said that. I was beginning to get worried.'

'What, that my idea of a good time of a Saturday morning was dressing up like a twat and charging around the countryside, torturing foxes?'

'Yes, frankly. Let's face it, you look the part!' Finding out Ed was in the hunting fraternity would have been a deal breaker, she realized, and would have wasted the price of a (heinously expensive) single ticket from London.

'Don't lump everyone who lives outside the M25 into the same category, you urbanite.' He was smiling.

'Sorry, sir. Point taken!'

She recollected that Ed had told her his parents had downsized, leaving the bigger, family home of his childhood to his elder brother a few years ago. Which was worrying, since the house at the end of the driveway he pulled into a few minutes later looked pretty bloody big to her. It was ludicrously pretty, too – white, with big square windows. It was built into the side of the hill and overlooked a stunning estuary.

'Wow!'

'Great house, isn't it? I prefer it to their old one. They're so close to the water. You can actually get down there, to the banks – there are these steps in the garden behind the house – round there – that go all the way down. You could moor a boat there. But up here, you get this incredible view.'

It was beautiful, even in January, with a fierce wind and a grey sky. Amanda realized it would be stunning in the summer.

'Come on, I'll show you around.' Ed had retrieved her rucksack from the back and fished around in the pocket of his coat for a key. 'They're not big in interior design, the aged Ps. Don't think they've painted a wall since they moved in. Just plonked their furniture down and got on with it. It's all a bit *Country Life* for my taste, I'm afraid. Oh, and the central heating is woefully inadequate. They've got plenty of money to fix it, but they're just not bothered. We've been on at them for ages to get it upgraded, but they're odd – they like it this way. Although how you could enjoy the kind of draughts that fly around in here up your jacksy, I don't know! They've still got those archaic bar heater things in the bathrooms. Dad is the kind of bloke who'll have the windows open in mid-winter, but there are fireplaces downstairs and there's an Aga in the kitchen. It's just getting into and out of bed that requires nerves of steel!'

The kitchen did, indeed, have the mother of all Agas – a vast, four-oven cream one, with a drying rack hoisted above it and a battery of cooking equipment hung from the wall behind. In the chill air, it was giving off lovely heat and Amanda went straight to it. She'd grown cold, driving over here in the draughty Land Rover, and she wanted to warm her hands.

Ed came over and hugged her from behind, his arms snaking around her waist.

'It's bloody wonderful that you're here.'

She turned within his embrace and kissed him properly. The tip of his nose was cold. They stayed that way, kissing against the Aga, for a few minutes, just long enough for Amanda to get warm and to start to feel woozy-kneed.

She pushed him away, playfully. 'Right, enough of that! What's a girl got to do around here to get a cup of tea?'

'I've a few suggestions,' he groaned, pushing his hips into hers lasciviously, but he took the kettle from behind her and went to the sink to fill it.

'Are you sure your mum doesn't mind my being here? It's kind of a family time.'

'She's fine. I told her I wanted you here. She understood completely.'

'Really?'

'Really. Actually, she's incredibly curious about you . . .'

'Why?'

'You're the first girl I've ever brought home.'

'You're kidding me?'

'I'm not. I mean, there were girlfriends, while I was at
school and stuff – they were around. I'm not weird. But
since I left home not one. Why?' He seemed amused at
her incredulity. 'How many blokes have you taken home
to meet your parents?'

'Well, none really.'

'So – what's the difference?'

'Well, you're older than me, for a start.'

'Hardly. A couple of years, isn't it?'

'And . . . and . . . most of the boyfriends I've had have
been while I was travelling and I could hardly bring them
home, could I? They weren't that serious, not that I'm
saying you have to be serious about someone to bring
them home, or anything like that . . . and anyway, they
were thousands of miles away, most of them.'

'Longest relationship to date?' He was making the tea,
opening the fridge to look for milk.

'I don't know . . .' She wasn't going to say first. 'What
about you?'

'Five months at university; a couple of three-month
ones. That's it, the rest shorter than that. Not that there
have been dozens, you understand . . . Not several
dozens, at least . . . I'm a serial monogamist, and not a
very good one.'

'Oh.'

'What does "oh" mean?' He squeezed the teabag, took
it out and brought her a mug. 'What were you expecting?'

'I don't know. We don't know each other very well at all, do we?'

'So tell me yours. Then we'll know that, won't we? Afterwards, I'll get my inoculation records, my GCSE certificates and the small box of my milk teeth my mother has rather macabrely kept all these years in her knicker drawer . . .'

'You're laughing at me.'

'You're evading me.'

'Four months, okay? Four months. He was called Guy. He was from New Zealand, and he was my ski instructor – I did this course over there, a couple of years ago. We got together when I arrived and we split up, if that isn't overdramatizing things, which it probably is, because it wasn't all that serious, when I left. Okay?'

'You ski well?'

She slapped him on the shoulder. 'Hey, big picture, please! We were talking about exes.'

'Okay, so we've established we're both borderline dysfunctional with the opposite sex and possibly incapable of forming lasting relationships. Next. You ski well?'

'Oi! Speak for yourself. I'm not dysfunctional; I'm peripatetic.'

'Ouch! Isn't there an ointment for that? I could take a look in Mum's medicine chest . . .'

'Be serious!'

'Why?' He took her mug from her, and pulled her to him. 'Why be serious? Look, I'm glad you haven't got a closet full of skeletons. I'm glad you haven't got a "one who got away" or a "he was the love of my life" in your past. I'm glad you're here with me now. I'm glad I get to introduce you to my mother – lousy circumstances notwithstanding. And *she'll* be glad I'm not gay! I suspect she had her suspicions, after all these years of apparent inactivity on my part.'

Amanda smiled into his shoulder. 'Well, I can certainly clear that up for her.'

'Thank you! Although maybe go easy on the details of my heterosexuality . . .'

'I'll try and hold myself back. I'm sure she'd be very proud of you, though. When will she be back?'

Ed looked at his watch. 'About an hour or so, I expect . . . Why?'

It was her turn to lead with her hips. 'I thought you might give me a tour . . . show me . . . you know, where I'll be sleeping . . .'

'That would be my pleasure . . .' He took her hand and led her towards the stairs . . .

It was actually 45 minutes. By then it was completely dark outside, and Ed's mother's headlights, turning into the driveway, flashed a warning signal to them where they lay, catching their breath in the pretty guest bedroom, having once again proved Ed's credentials as a very, very straight guy.

'Jesus! Is that your mum?'

'Yep.' Ed had jumped up like a scalded cat and was pulling his boxer shorts on.

'Great, perfect. She'll think I'm a slut!'

'Not if you move your bloomin' arse.' He threw her bra at her and smirked.

Ed was dressed, but dishevelled and flushed, his shirt tails hanging, by the time his mother opened the front door and began calling him. Amanda was hastily pulling her sweater over her head and smoothing her wild and tangled hair into a low ponytail.

'Ed? Are you here, love? Why aren't there any lights on down here? You haven't started any fires . . .' She sounded tired, but not really cross.

'I'm on it, Mum. Give me five minutes . . .' There was no way down, except past her. Amanda rather wished for back stairs. 'I've just been . . . showing Amanda where she's sleeping . . .' Behind him, Amanda could see eyebrows being raised. He stood aside, and she saw the raised eyebrows topped a wide, and utterly knowing smile. She wanted the ground to open up and swallow her. 'Mum, this is Amanda. Amanda, Mum.'

'Also known as Nancy.' Ed's mum stepped forward and held out her hand.

'Nice to meet you, Amanda. Welcome.' There was no edge at all to her voice and the smile stayed broad. If she was shocked or appalled, she was hiding it well.

'Nice to meet you too.' She tucked a stray wisp of hair behind her ear and grinned sheepishly.

Ed's mum was still a very pretty woman. Her eyes were edged with crow's-feet now and her wavy auburn hair flecked with grey, but her big eyes were still a bright green, with long, sweeping eyelashes, and her skin was fantastic – her cheeks were flushed rosy with the cold. She must have been stunning when she was younger, Amanda realized. And she must be exhausted. If she looked this good after days on end spent crying and worrying at the hospital, imagine how she'd look when she was trying.

She looked kind, too. Her deep voice was softened by a slight burr and it made her sound gentle.

'Ed, now that you've . . . orientated Amanda . . . perhaps you'd like to start the fires! It's cold down here.' She said it in a way that let them know she knew exactly how warm it had been up there . . .

'Absolutely.' Ed started gratefully into the living room, leaving the two women together in the hallway.

'You . . .' and she put her arm through Amanda's, 'can come with me to the kitchen, where it's at least warm, while he gets on. Tom and Ginny will be here in a bit – Ed's brother and his wife. I left them with his dad. They've left the boys with Ginny's mum for a couple of nights, and they're picking up some fish and chips in Truro on their way over . . .'

Amanda glanced at Ed, who shrugged and smirked back conspiratorially, and went with Nancy into the kitchen.

Once there, Nancy drew a chair up to the Aga, gesturing for Amanda to sit down. 'I'm sorry Ed's mercy dash put a spanner in your works, Amanda. He explained to me . . . about the phone, and everything. I told him to go back up to London, but he wouldn't leave me, sweet boy. Then I told him if you were any kind of girl, you'd give him a chance to explain, which you clearly did . . . In case he hasn't convinced you, I can confirm that he was tearing his hair out, trying to get hold of you. He'd kill me for saying so, but I've never seen him so worked up about a girl. I'm so glad he finally did.'

'I hope it's okay that I'm here. I don't want to intrude . . .'

'Listen, we're glad of the company. I'm glad you're here! I know it's miserable for my husband, stuck in the hospital, but it's no picnic being here without him, either. Ed's been a star, and so has his brother Tom. Dan's away, of course, but he calls when he can.'

'It's nice you're so close to them all.'

'Very nice.' She nodded. 'I've been a real drip – I

surprised myself how much. Don't know what I would have done if they hadn't been around.'

Amanda didn't say anything. She was thinking about Mark and what those last few weeks with Mum must have been like for him, thinking she hadn't been around. Nancy shook herself. 'Still, we've been very lucky. He'll heal from the accident. And the heart attack, it was one of those warning jobs. He'll have to give up some of his vices, but like I say, we've been lucky.'

Supper was far jollier than Amanda might have expected under the circumstances. Ed uncorked a couple of bottles of wine while the fish and chips were reheated in the Aga. They stood, leaning against it, drinking and chatting. They all seemed to have Ed's easy, friendly manner. You could see straightaway that the boys got it from their mother and she guessed Tom had looked for the same things in a wife. She instantly liked Ginny, who was loud and earthy, and funny. Dead posh, and slightly horsey, but great. Tom looked just like Ed, except that he was about three stone heavier and wore his hair in an altogether more conservative fashion. 'Are you joking? I couldn't get a client, looking like that, not down here!' he had exclaimed, reaching for Ed's head and being deflected by a sibling blow and a fast ducking.

When they had eaten, they moved to the living room. The fire Ed had set a couple of hours earlier was still blazing in the hearth. Tom poured port for all of them, except Ginny, who was driving. They sat for a while in companionable silence, staring at the flames.

'So, Amanda,' began Tom. 'Tell us how you met my little brother, and what on earth you saw in him . . .'

'She doesn't have to do anything of the sort!' Ginny

rallied to her defence. 'No cross examinations here, Amanda.'

'I don't mind,' Amanda smiled demurely. 'It's a very sweet story, actually. I caught him staring at some model type girl's tiny arse in a Starbucks, a few weeks before Christmas. He caught me catching him, and it sort of went from there. Terribly romantic!'

Tom laughed out loud.

'This Christmas? The one we just had?' This was Ginny.

'Yes.'

'So you guys have been together, what, less than a couple of months?' Tom looked amused. Amanda wondered if she had said the wrong thing and was suddenly grateful her rucksack was at the end of the guest bed and not, as he had half suggested earlier, at the end of Ed's.

'I suppose so!' she admitted. When you put it that way . . .

Ed put his arm around her shoulder protectively.

'Mind your own business, you lot! We're together now.'

'Yes, shut up, Tom!' Nancy chimed in. 'We're not all like you.' She directed her remarks to Amanda. 'Tom has known Ginny since he was about 12 years old. Was in love with her for years from afar, so far as his dad and I could tell. In the end, she gave up waiting and asked him out. Then, if I remember it correctly, you had to ask him to marry you as well, didn't you, Gin?'

'I did. More like beg, to be perfectly honest. You've never seen a man so loath to commit. I had to withdraw privileges in the end,' laughed Ginny.

'*Ginny*!' Tom pretended to sound horrified.

'Worked, though, didn't it?' She put her hand on his thigh.

'Ed's more like me, clearly,' Nancy said. 'I knew I was going to marry your father the first time we had dinner together.'

'I didn't know that,' said Ed.

'Me neither,' Tom added.

'I probably never told you before, that's why. The testosterone-laden nature of this home when you were all growing up didn't exactly lend itself to that sort of romantic revelation. But I think I did. He was almost a quarter century older than me, divorced, and he came with plenty of baggage, but I already knew he was the one for me. Fate might have screwed up the timing a bit, made him, in the words of my mother, old enough to be my father, but that didn't change how I felt. It's never made a difference to me. I remember because I went home and told my sister, and she said it was disgusting and called me a . . . What was it? A gold-digging grave robber. Yes, that was it. A beautiful turn of phrase.'

'Auntie June called you *that*?'

'Auntie *Meg*! The one who lives in South Africa now. Married a farmer, lives on that sheep farm, hundreds of miles from other people, which is where she belongs. Fewer people to insult. Yes, she did.'

'That's really horrible!'

'I didn't care. She was jealous, as far as I was concerned. I'd had the time of my life. He'd taken me to the classiest restaurant for miles. It's been closed for years now. It was wonderfully old-fashioned – the waiters wore white coats and did silver service, you know. I felt like I was in a film. There were single red roses at every table and the menu was all in French . . .'

'That's a bit more romantic than soggy cucumber sandwiches at the cricket pavilion!' Ginny giggled, slapping Tom's thigh affectionately.

'And nearly as romantic as a venti latte and a double chocolate chunk cookie,' Ed whispered to Amanda.

Nancy's eyes had filled with tears. Ginny reached across and took her hand, but Nancy rubbed her face, impatient at her own reaction. 'Not to worry, honestly.' She pulled a handkerchief from the sleeve of her cardigan and blew her nose. 'Look what you've done to me, you toads – you've given me wine *and* port, and made me reminisce about your old man. And I'm too tired to do that without crying. What did you expect? I think it's time I took myself off to bed.'

She stood up and kissed them all goodnight, including Amanda, holding her face in her hands briefly. 'I'm happy you're here, Amanda.' The boys held her tightly, patting her shoulders, and Ginny stroked her back sympathetically.

It was later than they had realized. Soon afterwards, Ginny and Tom left with hugs and kisses, and promises that if Amanda was still here at the weekend, Ed would bring her over to meet the boys.

Ed locked the door behind them and came to sit beside her again on the sofa. The fire was dying now and she curled up against him.

'The boys are horrors.'

'Really?'

'Horrors in a good way. Naughty, full of energy and mischief; run Tom and Ginny ragged. You'll see for yourself at the weekend.' It was part question, part assertion.

So she was staying.

'It's weird.'

'What's weird?'

'This.'

'What about this?'

'All of it, really. You and me, being here.'

'Weird good or weird bad?'

'Weird lovely. I feel like . . . well, I feel more at home here with you and your family than I ever have anywhere else. In lots of ways, even more than with my own.'

He tightened his grip on her. 'I'm glad.'

'Me too.'

Ed kissed the top of her head. 'I'm knackered, but I want to go to sleep with you.'

'I want you to as well, more than anything. But won't your mum mind?'

'I hope my mum is sound asleep. She looked pretty shattered herself. But I don't think she'd mind, no, even if she wasn't. I'm an adult. I think we broke the ice in that department with the afternoon delight. Plus she really likes you, I can tell. And she's not old-fashioned, about stuff like that. But if it makes you feel better, I promise I'll creep back to my own room nice and early before she's up to preserve your reputation.'

'Sounds like a plan.'

'Come on, then. Let's go to bed. I want to take you to the hospital in the morning. I want to introduce you to my dad . . .'

It was, as promised, freezing upstairs. Amanda changed into her nightshirt, leaving her socks on, and brushed her teeth as fast as possible. Ed was already in her bed when she got back.

'Love the socks. That look really gets me going.'

'Take it or leave it. It's too sodding cold for bare feet!'

'Get in here and let me warm them up . . .'

He held back the duvet and she dived at him, grateful for his solid warmth. She put her cold feet up between his knees and they lay wrapped together. They kissed for a while, lovely lazy kisses, their faces on the pillow, but they were both tired. Anyway, just lying together was enough that night. You could hear the sea faintly, outside, she realized. They hadn't drawn the curtains and outside the clear sky, unpolluted by city lights, was studded with bright stars. Amanda felt calmer and quieter than she had for a long time. They hadn't talked about much of any significance – they'd barely had an hour alone in each other's company, and they'd spent most of that not speaking at all. It didn't matter. She snuggled up against him, and they were both asleep within five minutes.

Your Dad

Reading that bit, about when you were born, got me to thinking about your dad, so this one is about him . . . glossing over isn't really fair. I have to remember that this is for you, and not for me.

I haven't been very fair to your dad. I always say that I let you make up your own mind about your dad, and that it was your choice not to have much to do with him, but we all know that isn't quite fair, don't we? I wasn't exactly cheering for him stage right. He's dead, of course, so this is a bit late in the day but I'm going to write it anyway. I know I never exactly encouraged conversation about him either. Do you even know, or remember, how we met? I bet you don't. That isn't fair. I'm sorry, maybe he told you . . .

Actually, it isn't all that interesting. We met like a million other people our age met: at the pub. I was 21 and he was 26. Those five years felt like a lifetime to me, at first. We both still lived at home. You did, then. He was working for his dad. The family had a furniture store, a million years before MFI. They sold dining sets and three-piece suites and bedroom furniture. His mum ran an upholstery workroom at the back of the shop. You could buy things on 'lay away'. Do you lot even know what that is? The business did well, and Donald was their only child, so he knew it would be his eventually. He had that about him, you know, that certain confidence. We weren't talking rich, but comfortable, and, more to the point, secure. I was working at Lilley and Skinner, selling shoes. This was a job I hated. Other people's feet didn't do it for me. All

the time I used to talk about doing something different –
going to teacher training college, something like that.
What I really wanted was my own shop. I was obsessed
with haberdashery – ribbons and buttons and
trimmings . . . little things in little boxes, all neat and
shiny. But I never did anything about it. I got my wages
on a Friday – all cash, remember, in little brown
envelopes – paid my mum some board and lodging, and
spent the rest on clothes and cigarettes and going to the
pub. My dad despaired of me, I know he did.

So, I used to go to the pub with my mates, and he
used to go to the pub with his. First off I fancied his
friend Charlie, so I got talking to Donald just to get
closer to Charlie. In the way of things time eternal,
Charlie had a thing for my friend Mavis (Mavis –
what a name! Who could ever fancy someone called
Mavis?), but by the time I learnt this I'd taken a shine
to Donald. Fickle things, we all were. Mavis was a bit
twisted about it, actually. Said I was only interested in
Donald because of the shop, which hadn't occurred to
me. Or didn't occur to me until later . . .

Donald's mum was a tartar, but his dad was lovely.
When Donald and I started going out together, I would
go by the shop after work and wait for Donald. He was
often out doing deliveries and things, so I'd sit and talk
to his dad for ages, waiting. He was a lovely man. He'd
been in the navy during the war. He had these blue
tattoos, all up his arms. He'd married Donald's mum
before he was called up, in 1939, and came home to a
bride he didn't know all that well and a small son he
didn't know at all . . . God, what that war must have
done to families . . . I think he married in haste –
I know he repented at leisure. She was scary with an
upholstery hammer in her hand, that woman! I think I

was as much in love with his dad as I was with him, in a way. He was so different from my own dad.

Marriage to Donald represented escape. In my day, you didn't just go off and get those things for yourself, like you can now. You needed a man. It meant a home of my own, freedom. It meant his dad was my dad. Besides, it was what everyone was doing. You couldn't have sex until you got married, apart from anything else, and it was pretty much all any of us ever thought about – the normal ones at least. We were married within 18 months of meeting. Too fast. We didn't know each other well.

Which is not to say that we weren't happy. I don't want you to think that. We had a lot of fun. It was all a big adventure, having our own place. I learnt to cook. I can't tell you the laughs we had over my experiments in the kitchen. Not that this is news to you lot. Never improved much, did I? We used to have to retire to the pub for a Cornish pasty quite often. We spent a vast amount of time in bed, learning how all of that worked. That was fun too. I have to really cast my mind back because the truth is that when we split up, I didn't love your father anymore. But that doesn't mean I didn't love him then. I remember walking up the aisle to stand beside him on my wedding day and thinking I would burst with joy. He was a handsome bugger! My mum said 'handsome brute'. And there was something brutish about him. You know who he reminded me of? Marlon Brando in Cat on a Hot Tin Roof. *Without the brooding violence, of course.*

He didn't really know what to make of you two. He was better when you were older. But babies, babies left him cold. He was too big, too awkward for you when you were small. He couldn't change nappies, or do up

233

the buttons on your clothes – not that many men did in those days. But you frightened him a bit. And he was a bit jealous, to be truthful. Some men are, I think. They get knocked down in the pecking order. He loved you, I know that – he just wasn't all that interested in you. I never once saw him get down on the floor and play with you. He hadn't the patience for your games. The three of you learnt to ignore each other mostly.

I fought badly with his mother. She helped out a lot when you were very little. But there was a price and I decided early on that I wasn't willing to pay it. She wanted to interfere, to tell me where I was going wrong. All our worst arguments were about that. He used to side with her. I thought he was a spineless git when it came to her, and I used to tell him so. He would wince and shout back, then disappear off to his mother's house and not come home for his tea, and when he did come home I'd sometimes throw it at him, cold and congealed on the plate. I'd never do a thing like that now. Apart from anything else, it was me who had to clean mince and potatoes off the walls! But I was young and I got so cross. In the early days we made up easily. Had fun making up, in fact. We both had a temper and we knew it.

But gradually, the fights became more frequent and they got worse, and the making up was harder and less entertaining. It was like each time we moved a little further apart – like each argument moved us a notch away; then eventually we couldn't find our way back. I remember the first night we fell asleep without making up. I think that was the beginning of the end. Don't do that, will you? Don't fall asleep without making up.

We started fighting about money, as well, about the shop after his dad died. He had a bad heart, too. He wasn't as good as his dad had been with money. He wasn't forward thinking. I was full of ideas. My dreams of my own shop might have been shelved when I had you two girls, but I had plenty of ambition and plans. He didn't like that, I don't think. He had me in a compartment and he wanted me to stay there. Wife and mother . . . homemaker, although his jibes about that increased all the time. My not being able to cook wasn't so funny anymore and I was too tired to distract him with my skills in other directions, like I used to. He would take business problems to his mum, not me, and that drove me mad. It was like he was trying to keep me in my place and I was frustrated and thwarted.

I think the death knell sounded when his mum got sick. I so wanted to do the right thing, but even when she was really, really ill, she didn't like me and she wouldn't take help from me, and that drove such a wedge between us – me and Donald. He spent more and more time up there, and by the time she died, he was pretty much a stranger to the three of us. I couldn't get close to him. I couldn't help him, and I wasn't even sure I always wanted to. I was glad when she died, the old battleaxe – I know that's terrible, but it's true – and he knew I was, and he couldn't forgive me.

The affairs started when Lisa was about 10, I suppose. He was replacing me, and his mother. The first time he cheated, it was with a stranger – I never knew her name. Nor how they met, or when exactly it started. It didn't last long, and I honestly don't think it meant much to him. Believe me girls, details don't help. The second time it was someone I vaguely knew. The third time it was a so-called friend. Meg, she was called. We weren't really friends. We had children the same age, and so we went to the same playgrounds and sat on the same benches. That doesn't exactly make you soulmates. God, I haven't thought about her for years! She wore French knickers. I should have known. But it was never really all about the women. They weren't cheating on me, were they? It was him. It was like he made it crueller every time, brought it closer to my door, made it more about me. I stopped thinking about it after that. I don't know how many more there were. I ignored it. Which was pretty hard sometimes. Eventually his attempts to cover up his behaviour were pretty minimal. He goaded me.

When someone cheats on you, it's easy – and almost obligatory – to blame them entirely. You have the facts, don't you? You have the proof. It's their fault. It can take years for you to realize that you were in there too.

When I first found out, I was shattered. Devastated, angry and hurt; all the things you think you would be. But I was also ashamed and embarrassed. And it was that, more than anything else, that kept me in my marriage for years. Long, wasted years. Wasted for both of us.

He hit me once, just once. Please don't think that I was a battered wife. I don't want you to see me that way, or him. Your dad was many things, but he was never a violent man. He had a temper, but shouting and ranting was as far as it ever went, until this one time. God knows, I'd been violent towards him often enough over the years. I'd thrown more things at him than I can count. Punched him, too. It really was just the once, and I'd provoked him, believe me. I was totally shocked. He'd never even raised a hand to me, and seldom his voice, before then. It was a slap – straight across the face. It was hard, though. When I looked in the mirror I could still see the shape of his fingers, red and angry on my cheek. He was sorry afterwards, straight afterwards, and sorrier than he'd ever been for any of the affairs. I think he frightened himself – I don't think he ever believed he was capable of something like that. He begged me to forgive him. Almost crying, he was. I don't think he would ever ever have done it again.

But for me it was the final straw. Like the slap woke me up and made me realize what I fool I was for still being in this marriage. Or maybe, like the slap gave me the chance I'd been waiting for. I was gone within a week, just as soon as I could find somewhere to take Jennifer and Lisa. I was pregnant. I never told anyone he hit me.

Lisa

Reading her mother's journal, Lisa realized that she'd never really thought about her dad as a person. She supposed she wasn't the only child to do that, to compartmentalize a parent that way. He was just Dad, as dads everywhere were just dads. In her case he wasn't even a good one.

She hadn't lived with him since she was 14 years old. That was a pretty lousy age at which to lose a father, however rotten he might be. Actually, she corrected herself, he wasn't a rotten father, then. He was a totally crappy husband. By then, Lisa's loyalty and devotion to her mother would have been formidable. Jennifer's too, though it was less fiery and passionate than hers. Jennifer was less passionate than Lisa about everything at that age. She'd never kissed a boy and Lisa had been spending vast chunks of her lunch break behind the proverbial bikeshed for at least a couple of years by then.

The fighting was nothing new to them. Lisa remembered when Gran – Dad's mum – had been ill; that was probably the most volatile time. Mum and Gran had never been close. Mum resented the amount of time Dad was spending with her. Dad always said that if Mum would let Gran come and live with the family, he wouldn't need to be away. Mum would reply that Dad was crazy if he thought either of them would agree to live under the same roof. Dad would scream that it was Mum's fault . . . and on it would go. They never fought in front of them, but it wasn't a huge house and you could hear them. Lisa supposed that a psychiatrist would have a field day with them, imagining cowering, frightened children scarred daily by warring parents. She didn't remember it that way at all. Mum was never angry with them, so far as she could recall. What happened downstairs, late at night, with Dad somehow never came near them. Sometimes she thought the fights were funny. Afterwards, Mum would talk about herself and Dad a little strangely, in the third person – 'Mum and Dad had a silly fight about nothing. Don't you worry.' As an adult, Lisa knew Mum had been very unhappy – to herself, as a child, she never seemed it. Maybe you couldn't see it if you didn't know how to look for it. The 38-year-old Lisa recognized what an achievement that had been for Mum to keep her unhappiness from them. She never saw her cry over it. Of course, if you had been looking, and you knew enough to recognize it, you would have seen Mum come to life, like a butterfly from a chrysalis, once the three of them had left and found a new place to live. The new Mum was strong and confident, and more colourful. But, of course, she and Jennifer had then been teenagers, impervious to nuance, deeply buried in their own navels and unaware of so much.

In her journal, Mum said she was unfair to Dad. But she'd never told them about his affairs. It would have been easy to do that. Maybe they were already enough on her side. It didn't take a genius to work out that he must have been seeing Marissa before he and Mum split up, though. She moved into the house so quickly. Mum said she couldn't imagine why any woman would want to live in another woman's house, with her curtains, and her cushions, and her crockery. Of course, they hadn't done for long. Marissa wasn't that kind of woman, after all. The old family home had gone on the market within six months and was sold quickly. He hadn't told them he was selling – why should he? They'd seen it in the local paper. Mum got half the money – Dad was never bad about money, at least – and that was how they bought the house on Carlton Close. It was much nicer than the rented flat. Lisa and Jennifer had their own rooms for the first time. Mum let them paint them whatever colour they wanted. Lisa had chosen all white. Mum said it made her feel like she was in a hospital and tried in vain to introduce splashes of colour, but Lisa would only hang moody black-and-white postcards of grumpy-looking French couples on the walls that she bought at Athena. Jennifer had chosen Laura Ashley. Something pretty and prissy, with too much matching stuff.

For a long time Mum's room was full of boxes. She said there was no way she was going to leave anything personal at the house for another woman to go through and judge her on. She had old photograph albums and back issues of magazines, and maternity clothes, stuffed toys and cookbooks. She'd stripped herself from the house completely, and left nothing of her spirit behind.

Donald and Marissa moved a long way away after that. He'd told them one Sunday, between a matinée of a film they both found too childish, and a packet of crisps and a coke in the local pub garden. Marissa had family in Kent, he said, and wanted to be nearer them. Amanda was just a few weeks old then and he had only seen her once, just after she was born. Jennifer asked him why he didn't want to be near to his family, but she only did it to make him feel bad, really. Lisa couldn't remember what his reply had been.

After he'd gone a change-of-train ride away, the regular visits dwindled. This was the early 80s, and there had been no provision for visitation in their parents' divorce. It was up to all of them. Lisa remembered spending one or two strange and uncomfortable weekends in Sevenoaks with Dad and Marissa. She tried too hard. She made elaborate breakfasts and tried to plan excursions. She took them shopping, and offered to buy them things in Chelsea Girl and Dorothy Perkins. Lisa suspected that what she wanted was for the two of them to go home and rave about her to Barbara, and there was no way she was going to do that. Their house in Sevenoaks was nothing like the home he'd shared with their mother. They had a living room they never lived in. They just sat in it, like a Jane Austen parlour, when they had guests. There was no television in it, so why would you go in there any other time? Marissa kept the tissue boxes under embroidered cotton covers and there were proper fabric napkins on the table at mealtimes, and there was always dessert (and not just Walls' ice cream). Mum was never into all that then.

Fortunately, and inevitably, Marissa lost interest in them when her own daughter was born a couple of years later. She'd only ever been practising. With hindsight, Lisa suspected that persuading her father to have another baby might have been quite a task, and demonstrating her maternal qualities on them was presumably part of her charm offensive. Olivia never felt like their sister, of course. She was . . . well, she must be about 21 now. Lisa hadn't seen her since their dad died. Olivia had been 16 then. She was the spitting image of her mother. Lisa didn't know, and had rarely wondered, whether he was a better, more interested father to Olivia than he had been to them, but she hoped so.

They never had a summer holiday with their dad, after they left. Or spent a Christmas. He never came to visit them at university, and they didn't invite him to attend their graduations, although his cheques arrived regularly throughout their time there. It sounded cruel now, but it hadn't felt so at the time. It wasn't as if he was champing at the bit to come; it wasn't that he didn't love them. Lisa believed that on some level he did – at least Jennifer and her. Not Amanda, perhaps – they'd never known each other at all. He just didn't love them very much, and Mum loved them enough for two.

Jennifer had been on the horns of a dilemma, engaged to Stephen and planning a wedding eight years ago. Should her dad walk her down the aisle? Should he even be there? Mum said it was up to her. She hadn't seen him herself, at that point, for more than a decade. She promised to behave (although Lisa hadn't been convinced she was capable, especially if he brought Marissa with him). Jennifer compromised. She sent an invitation, but implicit within that was that he was to be an invited guest, not a member of the wedding party. Whether it was that demotion which made him decline, or really the previously booked summer holiday he used to legitimize his refusal, they never knew. But everyone felt relieved at his absence. In the end Mum walked Jennifer down the aisle. In that huge, beautiful hat.

When he died, neither of his older daughters had seen their father in more than six months, and Amanda hadn't seen him for years. On the day of his burial Amanda was supposed to be on a school trip to the Tower of London. Barbara said she should go ahead and make the trip with her friends, and Amanda had agreed gratefully. His funeral was completely uncomfortable. Lisa remembered feeling like a fraud. Marissa had awkwardly insisted Barbara, Jennifer and Lisa sit in the front pew with her. She'd almost pleaded with them. Lisa knew almost no one else in the church. She didn't associate the hymns with her father, didn't know any of the readings or poems selected to be read. She could tie nothing about the service to the man she had known. There were freesias on his coffin, and she supposed they must have been a personal preference.

It seemed funny – her dad had been such a big man, and freesias were such little flowers. Marissa and Olivia had worn the hollow, vacant expressions of the truly grieving. Marissa sniffed and cried quietly. Olivia had violently twisted a lace-edged handkerchief in her hands throughout the service, staring intently at the embroidered kneeling cushion at her feet. Lisa wished she hadn't come, and wondered why she didn't feel more.

Lisa watched Andy with Cee Cee as she had watched Mark with Hannah. They were fathers. She knew, with both men, that their daughters were their world; that they felt all the things that songs and literature and films said you were supposed to feel, that they lived for them, would die for them in a minute and cared about the happiness of their children above their own. Donald was nothing like that.

Amanda

Nancy asked them both to go to the supermarket while she was at the hospital – she had no food in, she said, but she couldn't concentrate on doing it herself. Ed drove them to the giant Tesco on the edge of town. When he wasn't changing gear, he kept his hand on her knee, and she liked him doing it.

It felt very grown up, doing the grocery shopping with him: it was coupley, in a nice way. He kissed her, hard, in the cereal aisle. Opening her eyes, Amanda watched a young mother watching them, leaning heavily on the double trolley she was pushing, filled with nappies and white bread and babies. Afterwards, they went to a café for something to eat before they went to see Ed's dad.

She was getting used to him sitting so close to her. She liked that too. They ate croque-monsieur and drank coffee and, when they'd finished, Ed asked: 'You haven't said anything about what was going on with you when I left.'

Amanda met his gaze.

'Is that because you don't want to talk about it?'

She shook her head and smiled gently at him.

'Afraid of returning to the subject that made me go psycho on you last time . . .'

'That's stupid.'

'Sorry.'

'I care about you, Amanda. I thought you got that.'

'I'm starting to.' She put her hand up to his cheek and he caught it there, pulled it round to his mouth, and kissed her palm.

'So what's happened? About your "dad"?'

'Nothing's "happened".'

'But you've talked about it, to someone? To your sisters?'

'To one of them. My sister Lisa.'

'That's the one you're closest to, right?'

'I'm probably closest to Hannah, but she's the youngest one, the daughter Mum had with Mark, my stepfather. She doesn't need to know. Not right now, at least. Lisa's my "cool" sister. She's the one who was closest to Mum – I thought she might know. I talked to her.'

'And did she know?'

'No, it seems Mum really had kept her little secret

completely to herself all those years. She was as shocked as I was, almost.'

'And what did she have to say about it?'

'Well, she said all the right things, I suppose. She kind of defended Mum to me, which was a bit weird. And pretty brave of her, given the mood I was in when I told her. But she said all this stuff about nobody being perfect, and all of us making mistakes and I suppose she's right . . .'

'What about your stepfather? Are you going to talk to him?'

'I don't know. The thing is, when I left your place, when it was all fresh and new information, I was so incredibly angry. I wanted to *do* something. But there's nothing I can do, is there? I mean, I can't have it out with her because she's dead. I can't talk to Donald – he's dead too. I can't find my real father, and try and figure anything out through him because I haven't got any clues about who he is or where he is . . . I can't *do* anything.'

Ed nodded.

'So, I have two choices, I think. I can either forget about it, or I can let it eat me up. Stay angry, you know? And I can't see the point in that.'

'That makes perfect sense on paper. I'm just not sure how easy it would be to do. I mean, if I try and imagine myself in the same position . . .'

'That's a quantum leap for you, my friend. You're from the original perfect family.'

Ed snorted. 'We're not so perfect.'

'You could have fooled me!' She smacked his arm playfully.

'Okay, I'm pretty lucky. I know that.'

'Well, you know what? I'm pretty lucky too. In the big scheme of things.'

'Really?'

'Really. I might wish it was different, but it wasn't so bad.'

'And that is what you really think? Not just what you're saying?'

She narrowed her eyes at him. '*What*? You think you know me well enough to say stuff like that to me, do you?'

'I think I'm starting to.'

And, of course, he was.

Ed's dad looked just like Ed. Silver-haired, but otherwise just the same, down to the twinkle in his eye. Amanda hovered near the door of his private room while Ed embraced his father, kissing him on the cheek.

'How are you, Dad?' He dropped the copy of *The Times* he'd bought at Tesco onto his father's lap. 'Thought you'd rather have a paper than a bag of grapes.'

'Absolutely. Hate grapes, love news. Thanks, son.'

'Feeling better?'

'Feeling fine. Doctors are talking about letting me out tomorrow or the day after. Bloody good thing! I've been saving these things – Christ knows I don't need them to eat the rice pudding, which is utterly inedible – and I'm going to tunnel my way out by myself if they don't sign the ruddy papers.' He held up a small collection of plastic spoons retrieved from the top pocket of his stripy pyjamas.

'Mum says you've got to behave yourself.'

'Hah!' He raised a cynical eyebrow. 'Now, enough about me. Even I'm bored to tears, and I'm an egomaniac. Who is this lovely you've brought to cheer me up? This must be Wilhemina.'

'Amanda, Dad.'

He laughed at his own joke. 'I know, I know. Amanda, of course. The girl from the coffee shop. Come here, my dear. Don't hover about over there.'

Ed must have been talking about her. She liked that he knew about the coffee shop. Amanda, enchanted, came up to the bed and held out her hand.

'Hi. It's really nice to meet you, Mr . . .'

'Call me Jeremy. Much nicer for me to meet you, I'm sure. You're ever so pretty.'

Amanda blushed at the simple compliment. 'Thank you. You're ever so kind.'

He was still holding her hand. They smiled broadly at each other. Without looking at his son, he issued instructions.

'Ed, bring the girl a chair. Then go and get her a drink, will you. There's a machine out on the ward. Tastes like hell, but it's hot. And it comes in plastic – disposable plastic. Cuts down on your MRSA risk. The place is riddled, I expect. I'm going to boil wash myself when I finally get home!' Ed obediently complied, rolling his eyes at Amanda as he backed out of the room.

'I saw that,' Jeremy said.

'No point getting old if you can't get cantankerous and eccentric, I say,' Jeremy said, when Ed had gone. 'Now, Amanda . . .' He said her name slowly and deliberately. 'I see why my son was so smitten.'

'He was, was he?'

'Instantly. He's told me everything, all about you. I hope you don't mind.'

Amanda didn't. She loved it.

'Nancy says you're a complete poppet, and she is never wrong about people.'

'I think she's lovely too.'

'She certainly is. Best thing that ever happened to me. Ed's just like me, you see. My theory is that he needs someone just like her . . .'

He let the unspoken question hang in the air.

This craziness didn't bother her, and that was the craziest part of all. She was just meeting this man, for the first time, in his pyjamas in a hospital bed. Somehow, though, she desperately wanted his approval.

Ed came back with two plastic cups of tea. 'Is he talking nonsense at you? I'd like to say it was the drugs, but he's always like this . . .'

'Bugger off, you cheeky so and so! I'm getting to know Amanda. I hope you're staying a while, love. I look much more handsome in clothes . . .'

'Look,' said Ed later, when they were walking back through the hospital car park, 'I adore him, but he's an acquired taste.'

'I think he's completely wonderful.'

'You do?'

'I absolutely do. He's warm and funny and kind.'

'I think you're completely wonderful.' Ed stopped and kissed her.

'What did he say about me, when I went to the loo?'

He picked her up and span her around. 'Oh no, I'm not telling you that! Isn't one male conquest in the family enough for you? Will you stay?'

'And do what?'

'Just stay.'

'I don't want your family to think I'm a freeloader.'

'They won't.'

'What about you? Don't you need to get back?'

'Not yet. I've spoken to them. I can defer the whole term, if I need to.'

'Do you need to?'

'I'm not sure. I want to get Dad home and settled in, make sure everything is okay. I want to spend some time with him.'

'Won't I get in the way?'

'No. I want to spend some time with you too. And, if it's not too scary, I want you to be a part of all of this. I really want that. It feels right. Is there somewhere else you need to be right now, somewhere you'd rather be?'

There wasn't.

Me and My Empty Nest

I hated it when you two — my big girls — went away. I felt bad about hating it. I had Amanda — I was better off than a lot of women I knew. My 'staggered family' was supposed to save me from loneliness. It was supposed to make it easier for me to let you go, but I still hated it. We'd been such a unit.

Do you remember Carlton Close? It was just the four of us. We had so much fun in that house. I hate it when women say their daughters are their best friends. That seems so suffocating. That's not what mothers and daughters are supposed to be to each other. I was always Mum; I was always in charge. But it didn't stop us from having fun. I sometimes wonder if you remember it as well as I do. I don't suppose that you can. Childhood distorts things, I know.

And then you left. I was so proud — prouder than you ever knew — that the two of you went to university. (And you, Amanda, and . . . you, Hannah, but only if that's what you want. I'll be proud whatever you choose to do unless, in the immortal words of Joyce Grenfell, you should choose to blow at Edgar. You probably don't even know what that means. But trust me, it's funny and I'm laughing right now while I write . . . See if you can download her onto your iPod sometime . . .) I almost couldn't believe it. It was something that had been so far beyond my grasp. It just wasn't ever a possibility for me. I even wondered if I was jealous. You had chances I didn't have. Back to that living through your kids stuff. But you wanted to go, you weren't pushed . . . Lisa first, then Jennifer. Did you know that after I dropped you off, that first day, both times I had to park around the corner, out of sight, and sob my eyes out? I told Amanda they were 'happy tears', but that was only partly true. I was thrilled for you, of course, but I felt so desolate to be going home without you.

I must have had a premonition of what was going to happen, or the common sense to realize. You were going to grow out of me. Not in a big, dramatic way. In a quiet, inevitable, growing-up sort of way. The phone calls dropped off. Both of you – yes, Lisa, even you – called every day for the first week. They were heart-wrenching calls; you sounded small and lonely and scared. And then I started to hear names and places, and the laughter crept back into your voices, and then the calls were every other day, every few days, and then – so quickly – once a week. Lisa, you were once every ten days. You didn't need me anymore, and it hurt.

I know that Mark seemed like a shock to you. I understood that you felt betrayed, that I could have formed a relationship with someone that was close enough for me to get pregnant, to agree to marry him and for that someone to be a stranger to you – I saw that that hurt you. But you left me first. Maybe life has a rhythm that we no longer have control over (this bit does, this I know for sure). Mark and Hannah came to me when you left. I always thought motherhood offered the best, most exquisite moments of my life, but I saw that every single one of them had to paid for. Your capacity to fill me with joy was matched by the same capacity to hurt me. And you hurt me when you couldn't accept me and Mark. I'm not telling you this now to make you feel bad, to torture you from the grave. It's just that it has been a part of our story, and I can't write this stuff without referring to it. I felt like I was torn, that first year. On the one hand, I was deliriously happy. I was in love, and Hannah was born. But you didn't come home, you didn't feel able to be a part of it. I missed you.

When you were little, we used to talk about how much I loved you. I once told you both that there was nothing you could do that I couldn't forgive. You must have been about 5 or 6. I don't remember exactly why we were having this conversation – you must have been naughty, or something. Oh, I remember – it was the time you glued the living-room rug to the carpet. God, I was mad at you then. So, we must have had this big scene, and we'd made it up and you were trying to get back into my good books, and I told you this thing about there being nothing you could do that I couldn't forgive you for. And I remember laughing because Lisa started testing the theory. She said, 'What about if we stole sweets?' and I explained that, although this was wrong and I'd be very cross, I could forgive you. So she asked if I could forgive you for murdering someone (what *an* imagination!), and by now I was a bit anxious, but I said that I'd be heartbroken and probably very angry, but that you would still be my child, and I would still love you and forgive you. So Lisa sat up, with great excitement, and said, what about if she murdered Jennifer? Could I forgive that and would I still love her after that? So I changed the subject – I guess we started trying to figure out how to get the rug unstuck. But the point of the story was – and it still is – there was nothing that you could say or do that I couldn't forgive, or that would stop me from loving you.

February

Jennifer

Jennifer poured herself another large glass of red wine. It almost drained the bottle, which she held out questioningly towards Mark.

'More for you?'

'I'm fine.' He still had half a glass. It was the second bottle of the night.

Mark had been pleased, earlier that morning, when Jennifer had rung and said she would like to come down and stay the night. Hannah was going to someone's Sweet Sixteen, with an afternoon of the requisite primping and squealing planned at a girlfriend's house, and he hadn't been relishing the thought of a long Saturday night alone. Jennifer said Stephen was away in Scotland, golfing with some friends, and that she thought she'd spend the day out his way, doing some shopping, and that she'd enjoy the company too. He'd said he would cook for them and asked what she'd like to eat. She'd laughed and asked him if she was that transparent . . . They'd agreed that she'd bring the ingredients and he'd cook them. A bit like *Ready Steady Cook*, except with a smaller audience and a bigger budget . . . He'd laid the table, for once, with the good linen napkins and the tall glass candlesticks. Hannah liked to eat at the breakfast bar, but the table made it more of a meal. He laid a fire and listened to Chopin as he tidied instead of Snow Patrol, Hannah's current obsession.

When Jennifer arrived, he'd just taken a shower and his hair was dripping on his collar when she put her arms around his neck and hugged him. Over his shoulder, she saw the set table, the fire already roaring in the grate, and was touched that he'd gone to so much trouble to make it nice. Last Saturday night, she and Stephen had eaten a takeaway curry on their laps in front of an ancient episode of *Inspector Morse*. She must have fallen asleep. When she'd woken at about one in the morning, cold and stiff-necked, her tray had still been on the coffee table, the vestiges of masala sauce dry and crusty on the plate, but Stephen had already gone to bed. She'd punished him with cold feet, and by yanking the duvet so that it uncovered his shoulder, but he'd been irritable and unrepentant, shrugging her off and claiming he'd tried to wake her and been given the brushoff. The next morning, padding through to boil the kettle for tea, she'd looked at the tray, still there, sniffed the stale smell of a curry not cleared away and an equally stale marriage not addressed, and felt utterly depressed.

This was much nicer.

They poured her ingredients out of the Waitrose carrier bag onto the work surface. She'd bought monkfish tails, pancetta, fresh herbs, wild rice, mascarpone and biscotti ... Also figs, and a great bottle of red, which they'd drained by the time he served dinner. He'd handed Jennifer another bottle and the screwpull corkscrew while he plated up.

And now they'd finished that one too. Chopin had given way to Joni Mitchell – Jennifer's choice. They'd moved from the dining table to the giant squashy sofas, each of them curled up on one, facing the other. He thought of Hannah, and looked up at the oversized railway clock on the wall behind Jennifer's head. 11.00pm. Hannah had promised to be home by 12.30am. She'd moaned and claimed she'd be leaving before all the real fun started (which was, of course, *exactly* his intention), called him a Victorian father and stomped a bit, but she'd promised. He'd given her cab money and issued all the usual warnings about safety in numbers and making sure her phone was switched on and fully charged. He trusted her, he just wasn't sure about any other bugger.

Jennifer watched him check the time.

'Worried about her?'

'Not really, no. She's a pretty sensible kid. And so are her friends, by and large, I think. I still can't sleep properly when she's out, though. Keep one eye and one ear open until I hear her come in, you know?'

Jennifer smiled. 'I bet. How's the studying going? When do the O-levels start?'

'*GCSE*s, my dear! Giving your age away. Mocks before Easter and the real deals in the summer term but lots of it is coursework these days. That's going on right now.'

'Poor thing.'

'Ah, she's a clever kid. Her teachers think she's going to do well despite everything . . .'

'I'm sure she will. Has she got a boyfriend at the moment?'

'Don't think so, no one special, at least. Although I'd probably be the last one to know, wouldn't I?'

'Nah – you two always seem pretty close.'

'We are, I suppose. We certainly have been since Barbara died. She's been a bit of a teenager just lately though. You know, pushing the boundaries a bit, flexing her muscles. She's probably fed up with being cooped up here with me. And I just think talking to me about boys, and what she may or may not get up to with them, might be a confidence too far, you know? She's probably more likely to confide in you lot than in me . . .'

'Amanda maybe, even Lisa. Not me, I don't think. Hannah just sees me as some old married woman, past it.'

'Come on!'

'Listen, I was 15 once! I know how it works. Well past the age and stage of sex for sex's sake, I am, as far as Hannah and her generation are concerned. Purely for procreation at this point.'

If Hannah was unlikely to confide in Jennifer, Mark thought, it was less to do with her marriage than with her personality. Of all Barbara's girls, Jennifer was the one least like her. She was always a bit proper and stiff and remote. He'd never met Donald, but he imagined she must be like him. The wine, which she'd been rather knocking back tonight, had loosened her tongue and her whole persona. This wasn't the usual conversation you had with Jennifer.

He'd actually enjoyed her company tonight, and that was a bit unusual. Lisa was a riot, a mini me of her mother, funny and earthy and warm. Amanda he found interesting; endearing and sweet. He loved to listen to her describing the places she'd been, the things she'd seen. He adored her energy and passion for life. Hannah – well, Hannah was his, wasn't she? And he adored her accordingly, more than he could ever have imagined before she came, even more than watching Barbara with her own children led him to believe was possible. But Jennifer? She could be a bit difficult. Brittle, Barbara always said, prickly, especially in recent years, when he and Barbara had known things weren't going well for her, even if she never shared with them which things they were. But not tonight. They chatted easily, about lots of things; she'd laughed more than she usually did, and now she appeared to be opening the door to a conversation he never thought he would be having with her.

Anyone could see that things with Stephen weren't all they should be. The rot seemed to have been setting in for, well, a couple of years now. It had worried Barbara, he knew that much – she'd said so often enough. But he knew that even she hadn't known what was wrong. You didn't ask Jennifer, she had once said, it was how she had always been – proud and intent on emotional independence. You hoped she would come to you, and you waited for her to come to you, to ask for advice. She said Jennifer would close up like a clam if she ever raised the subject with her, and she wanted to leave the door at least a little ajar. She'd died waiting, and Jennifer had never, so far as he knew, said a word about what was wrong but it seemed that she might be about to start now.

Mark risked a prompt, partly because he was curious and mainly because he knew it was what Barbara would have wanted him to do, although God knows what he would say if she asked him for an opinion. He wasn't always wild about Stephen himself. It was nothing specific; he just had the feeling that if he met Stephen, independent of their family connection, in the pub or somewhere, they would never be mates. Andy he'd have immediately liked anywhere, in any context; Stephen he'd always had to try to like.

'And is she right? About the procreation bit?'

When Jennifer first replied, he thought he'd blown it, which was either a shame, or a relief, only he wasn't quite sure which, because, after all, he had helped her drink two bottles of wine.

'Oh God, Mark, not you too! That was Stephen's dad's big fucking theme of Christmas, the state of play with my uterus!'

'Sorry, I really didn't mean to pry.'

Her face softened. 'I know, I'm sorry – I shouldn't lump you in with him. You have *no* idea how insulting that is, actually. I know I'm touchy about it. It's because I feel like everyone's watching us and thinking about it and wondering why we aren't getting on with it.'

'And . . .'

'And, why aren't we getting on with *it*?'

'Only if you want to talk about it.'

'I don't especially. It depresses the hell out of me but I suppose I should. You don't mind, do you?'

Tears were welling in her eyes.

He minded badly, he realized a little too late. They'd had a nice, light evening. She'd been good company, better than he'd thought she would be. The time had passed. He was a little drunk and a little sleepy. Now he wanted to go to bed and sleep off the red wine just as soon as he'd heard Hannah close the front door behind her and creep upstairs.

'Of course. What is it, Jen? What's wrong?'

He assumed this was going to be medical and took a deep breath. This was Barbara's department, very definitely.

'There's something wrong with me, at least I assume that's what it is. Stephen's had the test – he's up to the job. So it's me.'

'Have they found a problem?'

'"They", as you put it, haven't had the chance.'

'I don't understand.'

'Me neither.'

He looked at her, waiting for her to elaborate.

Jennifer rubbed her nose roughly and shook her head. 'I haven't been "tested". I've been putting it off. That's what's wrong with Stephen; he's sulking. He's been sulking for ages. He's been good and gone along and performed for the plastic cup, and passed with flying colours and he's furious with me because I haven't done the same.'

'And why haven't you?'

She shrugged, but didn't answer.

He hazarded a guess. 'Frightened? Of the tests themselves? Or of what they might reveal?'

'Neither of those. Matter of fact, I tried both of them, as excuses. They've worn thin, of course . . .'

'Then why?'

'I don't want to have a baby.' He wasn't expecting to hear that.

'At all?'

'With Stephen.'

'Oh.'

'Yes, oh.'

'Do you know why?'

'Because if I have a baby with Stephen, I'll have to stay with Stephen. And I'm not sure that staying with Stephen is what I want to do.'

'Right.'

'So, you see, this not being able to get pregnant, this thing which is supposed to be, like, absolutely the worst thing that can happen to a woman like me, is actually a gift. And I don't want to go to the doctor, and get in the stirrups, and let them poke and prod and probe me because my greatest fear is that they might actually find out what is wrong with me and they might actually be able to fix it, and then I won't have anything left to hide behind and I'll have to tell him that I don't want to have a baby with him. Because I'm not sure that I want to stay with him.'

Mark didn't speak at once, and Jennifer laughed a red wine laugh. 'So I'm the happiest infertile woman in England, you see. Except for being so unhappy, that is . . .'

'And Stephen doesn't know any of this, how you're feeling?'

'Now that's a good question, Mark. Does Stephen know any of this? I'm not sure. He knows things aren't right. Any idiot can see that. But he chooses to believe, I think, that it's all because we don't have a baby. This baby, this non-existent baby, he thinks, can fix all that ails us. Hence the sulking. I'm stopping it from happening, of course. I'm standing stubbornly in the way of all our future happiness, which lies vested in one teeny, tiny 6lb baby that isn't even born. Isn't that daft? Isn't that the craziest thing you ever heard?'

'Jen, if he loves you, of course he wants the two of you to have a baby. Like it or not, it's the next logical step for most of us. Babies are a physical manifestation of your love for one another.'

'A love I'm not at all sure I still feel.'

'That's a separate issue. I don't think you can blame him for being angry at you for not seeing the doctor, if he doesn't know how you feel . . . And even if he knows things aren't all perfect – I mean, he wouldn't be the first person to think having a baby can fix things. And I'm not sure he's all wrong, to be honest. It doesn't always work, granted. It didn't work for your mum and Donald, I know. But for some people, having something else to focus on, someone else, that can change things a lot for the better. I'm sure . . .'

'Mum and Donald?' There was a strange new look on

Jennifer's face. He seemed to have made her angry, but he didn't know why. She sat up, a little unsteadily, and leant forwards.

'Yes.' He had no choice but to go on. 'I mean, it doesn't take a genius to look at the timing of Amanda's conception and think that it was some sort of attempt, by one or both of them, to hold their marriage together . . .'

'That's what she told you?' Jennifer's tone was almost accusatory.

'She never talked about it much, to tell you the truth. We left the past where it belonged when we got together. But I think it's pretty obvious . . .'

'You do, do you?' Now it sounded a little like she was mocking him.

'What do you mean?'

'Nothing.'

'Jennifer?'

'Nothing, I mean nothing.' She shook her head and then passed the point of no return. 'I'm just saying . . . you don't know what was going on.'

'I don't, no.' He paused, feeling the great weight in her silence. 'Do you?'

If Jennifer had been sober, she would have stopped there, before it was too late. But she wasn't sober. She was drunk, and she didn't get drunk.

If Jennifer had stood up then, she would have realized how drunk she was. She might have felt nauseous, excused herself, gone to lie down and let the feeling and the moment pass. But she didn't stand up, and it was out of her mouth before she even knew she was going to say it.

'I know Amanda didn't belong to my dad.'

Mark himself was a little anaesthetized by alcohol, so his world didn't stop when she said it, rather began spinning alarmingly on a new axis.

'*What?*'

'Mum had an affair when she was married to Dad. She got pregnant with someone else's baby. I guess she was a little more fecund than me.' She laughed an ugly, humourless laugh. 'And pretty bloody careless – that must be why Dad left her.'

'How do you know?' Of all the questions, that was a bizarre one to start with. Shock was setting in.

Still, what she was saying wasn't dawning on Jennifer.

'She wrote it in her letter to Amanda. Didn't let her dirty little secret die with her.' Until she said it, she didn't even know she thought of it that way. *In vino veritas.*

'Amanda told you that?'

'She told Lisa. Lisa told me. It's just you and Hannah who don't know, who didn't know.'

Mark didn't say a word. His face made her start to back-pedal. That, along with the fact that drunken logic allowed her to return almost immediately to the point of her revelation, which actually had nothing to do with her mother. 'But that doesn't really matter, does it? It was a long time ago. I suppose she could have told you, maybe she should have told you, but she didn't. Guess we'll never know her reasons. The point is . . .' For a moment, she forgot what the point was, but then it came back to her and she nodded her head as though it had been spoken out loud to her, before resuming. 'The point is, babies don't fix things, do they?' She looked as pleased as a prosecution barrister delivering closing remarks in an open-and-shut case. He wanted to slap her mouth closed.

Mark looked at her as though suddenly he didn't recognize her and stood up. 'I think that's enough. I'm going to go to bed now. I think you should too, before Hannah gets home.' Jennifer stood up in front of him.

262

He was only a couple of inches taller than her. She was too close to him. When she spoke again, he smelt the red wine on her breath. Then, a moment of clarity. 'Oh God, Mark. I'm sorry.'

He didn't answer; he just looked at her.

'You're a good man, Mark, a really good man. I'm sorry she did it. Too good a man to be lied to. A really good man.'

'Don't do that.'

'Don't do what?'

'Don't you apologize for your mother.'

'Well, she sure as hell never did!'

'She had nothing to apologize to me for.'

'What about Amanda? What about my dad? She didn't apologize to them either.'

Jennifer knew she should let this go, but the rage and distress on Mark's face was making her defend herself.

'And you. You're so sure, are you? That she had nothing to apologize to you for? What is it they say, once a cheater, always a cheater? Isn't that it? She'd done it once, hadn't she? Fucked someone else, when she was married.' She drew out every syllable in the word, made it ugly and violent. 'How can you be sure she didn't do it to you too? She might have been sleeping with other men the whole bloody time. Are you even certain Hannah is yours?'

'Why are you saying all this?'

'Maybe because someone needs to. All these secrets, all these months of deifying her. She was the perfect bloody woman, wasn't she? No one could possibly hope to live up to her complete . . . marvellousness. The perfect wife, the perfect mother. Who could compete with that? Certainly not me. Brittle, she said I was. Bloody hell! She was always just pissed off I wasn't more like

263

her. That's why she loved Lisa more. Peas in a bloody pod!'

Mark didn't recognize her. The venom poured from her so liberally that he wanted to move physically away from her to escape it. And she wasn't finished.

'Only she wasn't perfect, was she? She was a liar, a cheat. She lied to you, she lied to her own daughter, to all of us. And she was a coward.'

Mark shook his head.

'So forgive me if I've had enough of the Barbara Forbes for Sainthood movement, if I've stopped trying to live up to something that never actually existed in the first place, if I've stopped mourning her.'

'Stop it!' He put his hands on her shoulders, held her hard and spoke through gritted teeth. 'I won't have you talk about your mother like that in my house, in her house . . .'

'I'm sorry, Mark.' Instant contrition.

'Go to bed, Jennifer.' Mark didn't want to hear it.

His voice was cold and quiet, and full of fury. He walked off quickly, anxious to be as far away from her as his house allowed. If she wasn't drunk, he'd have thrown her out. He went into the garden, without turning around, and gulped at the cold air that assaulted him.

He was beyond angry with Jennifer. How dare she come to him, and behave that way? No amount of unhappiness, or red wine could excuse her. He felt panic – how could things ever be normal again? Still under the influence of the wine he'd drunk himself, he tried hard to sort the new information he had received that night. He pulled his sweater around him and sat down on a teak chair, glad that the cold night air was doing its job on him.

He thought about Barbara. Amanda had been eight

when they met. She'd been gorgeous, too. Just like her mum. With pigtails and an overbite. A ballerina, at that point, always twirling and leaping. She'd had so much energy. Their closeness had been apparent – in the same room together, Amanda would always sit on her mother's lap, one hand behind her mother's neck, smoothing Barbara's hair between her fingers. When she was tired, Amanda would suck her thumb and rest her head against Barbara's chest, instantly relaxed. Her breathing would slow, the sucking calming and soothing her, although Barbara told her she was getting too old to do it. Mark had found Barbara the most beautiful when she was sat that way, with Amanda on her lap. She looked like some modern-day Madonna.

He hadn't lied to Jennifer – he and Barbara had agreed, early on, not to get bogged down in the detail of their pasts. That had been her idea, he now realized. She said the only thing he needed to know about the girls was that they were hers, and that they were the great loves of her life. He needed to understand that. But she no longer loved their father, so that part of her heart, the part not occupied by them, was free. For him.

He'd had a girlfriend. He'd been seeing someone for a couple of years. He was still with her when he went into the gift shop and was hit by the thunderbolt. They were both 30, and their friends were starting to get married. He had known that she wanted him to ask her, but he hadn't, some part of him always sensing that whatever he felt for her, it wasn't enough. He'd broken up with her straightaway but Barbara hadn't wanted to know about that girl either. She said it wouldn't help. They both had a past, and it didn't belong in this present, or their future. He could hear her saying it, remember her saying it, sitting across from him.

Was that why she hadn't wanted to talk about it? Because she had something to hide? Because she was afraid he'd think less of her if he knew? And would he have done?

Mark thought about the one thing he'd never told her. When he'd been 17 years old, finishing his A-levels, hoping to get good enough grades to take up a place in the Architecture and Civil Engineering department at the University of Bath, he'd gotten his girlfriend pregnant. They'd been together for a year or so. They'd met at sixth form. It had been the first serious relationship for both of them. They'd been virgins when they first had sex together, in her bedroom on Boxing Day, while her family sat downstairs eating Quality Street and watching television. She was called Kate, and he had believed himself in love with her. They'd grown careless, carried away, whatever you called it, and she'd become pregnant. She took the test while he was sitting his last A-level mathematics paper, and told him when he came out. He watched his friends whooping and laughing, and felt like the sky had fallen in on him. They told their parents, of course. What else could they have done? He still remembered, all these years later, the abject humiliation and embarrassment of sitting with them all, in Kate's living room, at a meeting called to discuss their 'situation'. His mother's disappointed face, his father's cheek muscles flexing with suppressed rage.

Kate's mother had cried throughout, silent tears mopped with a white handkerchief. Her father had done the talking for both of them, but he never once looked Mark in the eye. It was a fait accompli, the discussion more a briefing. Their futures must be safeguarded. They were too young to handle the responsibility of a baby. There was, of course, no question of them getting married. It was the 1970s, for God's sake, not the 1950s! Kate was only a few weeks pregnant, less than three months, and she would have an abortion. They would both get over it. Any relationship the two of them might have had was killed that day.

Kate, her blue eyes red and downcast, didn't say a word. He never really knew what she felt about it. He felt relieved. That summer Kate went away, while he stayed at home, working at the pick-your-own farm outside town and trying to regain some kind of footing with his father. He didn't see her before he left for Bath, and he never saw her or spoke to her again. He thought only occasionally about her and the child they never had together. That child would be almost 30 now, which seemed ridiculous. How was it your life sped up without you even noticing it happening?

Everyone had secrets, didn't they? Silly, really. Barbara would have felt desperately sorry for him, he knew. And that is how he realized he would have felt about her, if she had told him that Donald wasn't Amanda's father. She never promised him she was perfect. How could Jennifer, who had lived with her for so long, think that she thought she was? How could she have gotten it so wrong? Barbara knew her flaws better than most people. There was no pretence about her. She didn't want Jennifer to be like her; she didn't want anyone to be just like her. She wanted Jennifer to be happy, and that was all.

He hated Jennifer – in that moment – because a plague seed of doubt had been shaken free by the row. He hated the doubt, and his brain and his heart battled against the spores of it. She hadn't, she hadn't, she couldn't have done . . .

After a few minutes, he was calmer. He felt sober, out there in the fresh air, and back in control of himself. Also cold. He'd been outside for about half an hour. Long enough for Jennifer to get out of his sight, he hoped. He opened the door from the terrace and went inside just as Hannah stepped through the front door.

'Are you mounting a search party? I'm not even late yet!'

'Just getting some fresh air.'

'Fresh air? It's freezing, you nutter!' Hannah peered at him from across the room. 'Have you been smoking out there? You promised, special occasion cigars only . . .' she asked, suspicious.

'No!'

'You wouldn't lie to me, Dad, would you?'

'Of course not. I just drank too much wine, felt a bit fuzzy and went out there to sober up while I was waiting for you . . . Sergeant.'

'Where's Jennifer?'

'She went to bed already.'

'Did you guys have fun tonight?'

Hardly. Mark opened the dishwasher and began stacking it with the dirty plates and cutlery on the side.

'Just a peaceful evening. How about you?'

Hannah drew up a bar stool and put her elbows on the granite, watching her dad while he worked. 'Brilliant. Party of the year.'

'It's only February.'

'It'll be tough to top. It must have cost her parents a fortune . . .'

'Don't go getting any ideas . . .'

'What, you mean you won't be letting me have a live band, plus a disco, plus chocolate fountains? And look, goodie bags!'

She held up a small pink stiff cardboard bag.

'You haven't had one of those since you were 10! What's in it? Bubbles and a balloon for later?'

'Lipgloss, and a Starbucks card. Ruby's dad works for Starbucks. How cool is that?'

'Beyond cool. I'm overcome with how cool.'

'Shut up, Dad!'

Mark looked at his daughter. She looked so happy.

'What's the grin for?'

'I met a boy.'

'You did?'

'I did.'

Funny, he hadn't thought about his old girlfriend Kate in years and now he'd thought about her twice in one evening. Hannah was almost the age she had been. That thought process, he knew, opened the door to a whole new ball game, and one he was far too wrung out tonight to play.

He closed the dishwasher, leaving the cooking pans and utensils where they sat. They could wait until the morning. Walking around to where Hannah sat, he laid an arm across her shoulders.

'Tell me all about him tomorrow?'

'Get lost!'

'Goodnight, gorgeous.' He kissed her forehead and smelt cigarette smoke on her hair. She pulled away too quickly but he didn't have the energy to open the topic.

''Night, Dad. Love you.'

'I love you too, Hannah. Very much.'

Upstairs, behind closed doors, he kicked off his shoes and lay down across the mattress, with all his clothes still on, and closed his eyes. For a moment he thought he might cry, but he was too tired for that. He was acutely aware of Jennifer just across the hall and he didn't like the new, uncomfortable feeling. Christ, she must be unhappy! That poison must have been festering inside her for years. He felt more disconnected from her than he had ever done before. With a huge effort, he sat up and pulled his sweater and the shirt beneath over his head, dropping them to the floor next to him. He unbuckled his trousers, pulling the leather belt out in a single movement, and they, too, pooled into creases on the floor.

On the bedside table beside him was his favourite picture of Barbara. It had been taken just before Hannah was born. She was in profile, sitting ramrod straight, like Whistler's Mother. She'd had such backache latterly in the pregnancy and that had been the only way she'd been comfortable. She was watching television, her hands resting on top of her bump. He loved the curve of her belly; he loved the shape of her nose and her chin. He loved her glorious hair, normally thick, but then at its most lustrous and glossy, swinging easily across her shoulders. He loved everything about the picture, and he'd loved everything about her; always had and still did. He opened his bedside drawer and took out the letter she'd written for him before she died.

My darling Mark,
What can I write to you? We had a card once in the shop that I loved. It was meant to be from parents to their kids, I think. It said that their job – the parents – had been to give them – the children – two things: roots and wings. But I always thought of you that way. That's what you've given me: the simple things and the extraordinary ones. I don't know which one love is. I

think, when it's good, it can be both. And ours has been good, hasn't it, sweetheart? It's breaking my heart to leave you, so I guess it's breaking yours too, and I'm so, so sorry to be going too soon. Please carry my love for you with you forever but don't let that be all. Our capacity to love is vast – all of us. My daughters taught me that. There is room.

Barbara

In the morning, his head hurt. He lay in bed, willing the return of sleep, until nine, when he admitted defeat and shuffled downstairs to make tea. Jennifer must have already left. Her car wasn't in the drive. She'd been very early, or very silent. She'd left a note for him, propped up against the fruit bowl, sealed in a brown envelope she must have found in a drawer in the kitchen.

Mark,

I'm more sorry than I can say. I hate myself for what I said. I never realized I could be so cruel or so insensitive. I'm not going to ask for your forgiveness, because what I've said might well be unforgiveable. Just please know how truly sorry I am.

Jennifer

'Is something wrong with Jennifer, Dad?'

'What makes you think that?' The question caught Mark off guard. Inside, he answered with a resounding yes.

'She went so early. She didn't even bother to wait and see me, and I haven't seen her in a while. That's not like her. You've been weird all morning. And she left you a note. I saw it.'

'Hold on, Inspector Clouseau . . .'

'Is something wrong? Is it Stephen and her? Did you guys have a fight about something?'

'No, to all of the above.'

'So why did she go without seeing me? Why the note?'

Mark lost his patience. 'For God's sake, Hannah! Stop with all the questions, will you? There's nothing wrong.'

Hannah jumped off her stool like she'd been scalded. 'Fine, don't tell me! None of my business. I'm just a kid when it suits you, aren't I?'

She stomped off upstairs. A minute later, Mark heard her door slam shut.

Where had that come from? He couldn't begin to imagine telling Hannah the substance of his fight with Jennifer, if that's what it was. He just didn't want her to know, not while she still saw the world, and the people in it, in black and white, and not in shades of grey. Hannah's memory of her mother was something he desperately wanted to protect and preserve. If she wanted to be mad at him, she could be.

Upstairs, Hannah threw herself on to her bed in frustration. She knew something strange had happened and it angered her that her dad wouldn't tell her what it was. It was all well and good treating her like a grown up when it suited him – when he wanted help in the kitchen or someone to share a glass of wine – but he switched back fast enough as well, and that wasn't fair. She was 16. Her phone buzzed on the desk, next to an untouched French assignment. She reached for it. The caller ID flashed the name she had hoped it would; the name she'd programmed into it the previous evening: NATHAN.

Amanda

Life in Cornwall had fallen into a gentle rhythm. Jeremy was home now, up and about. Frailer than he had been, Ed said, but getting stronger every day. Nancy's greatest fear, that he would fall prey to the curse of the elderly and never recover fully from his injuries, appeared to be unfounded.

Nancy had washed all the sheets one day and Amanda had found herself officially moved into Ed's room. Passing the doorway, Nancy had winked at her. 'Save you all that time wandering up and down the corridors, won't it?' She and Ed had more or less taken over the shopping, and Amanda was learning the art of Aga cookery. Funny, Mum had had one for years, but she'd never been near it, except to lean against it on cold days. Nancy taught her which ovens were which temperature, how you could cook a whole breakfast in the top oven in only one pan and how to set the plastic timer stuck on the fridge because Agas had no smell, so you had no idea if anything was burning. She said Aga owners were getting it in the neck for being environmentally unfriendly but that she couldn't live without hers. 'I'd rather give up loo paper and go back to corn husks,' she said. Certainly the house would be unbearably cold without it. Amanda had learnt to wear layers – a thermal vest, long-sleeved shirt, a polo neck and one of Ed's fisherman's sweaters on top. She told Ed that the only place she was ever really warm in the house was in his bed. He said warm was all well and good, but it was *hot* he'd been going for.

They made love almost every morning, before it was completely light. That, invariably, was how Ed woke her up, and it was delicious. At night, they lay in bed and talked for hours after the rest of the house had gone to sleep. About their childhoods and their siblings, and their travels and their hopes and dreams. In just a few weeks, Amanda felt Ed knew her better than any other living person. She could talk for hours to anyone – she had the traveller's easy habit of friendship – but there were things she had only ever said to Ed. It felt like they had shorthand. He got her. He gently mocked her for the things she used to be prickly about, and she didn't feel irritated anymore. He didn't judge, he didn't push. He listened and concentrated, like she was a jigsaw puzzle he was trying to piece together. She was more herself than she could ever remember being with anyone except her mum. Mum was probably the only one who'd come close to understanding her as well. How was that possible?

It was like that with Jeremy and Nancy too. Easy and comfortable. She felt safe here. She'd fallen in love with the man and the whole family.

'So, you two delightful young creatures...' They'd finished dinner and were in the process of finishing a bottle of wine – except for Jeremy who was drinking grape juice under duress. 'I'm very thrilled that you've chosen to base your bohemian life here, and your mother and I love having the pair of you. And I may be terribly bourgeois to even consider it, but I do begin to wonder whether there are any actual plans for the immediate future...'

Ed and Amanda exchanged glances. 'Ah ha,' Jeremy exclaimed. 'I see there are...' He sat back to listen to them.

'I've spoken to the Dean and they're prepared to let

me take the rest of the year off. Start again in September.'

'I presume you laid it on with a trowel how ill and decrepit I am?' Ed blushed, which provided the answer.

'Good for you! Why be a rat in the run, I say. You never took enough time off when you had the chance, if you ask me . . .'

'Thanks, Dad.'

Jeremy raised his hand. 'Fine. I'll try to sound weak and close to death, should I answer the phone to someone I don't know.' Amanda giggled. 'So what *will* you be doing with this free time?'

'We want to travel together,' Amanda answered.

'Ah – little nomad. That's what I hoped you'd say. Where to?'

'We thought South America, Chile, Peru, Argentina and Brazil.'

'Splendid . . .'

'We'll need to get jobs here, for a while at first, if that's alright. To help pay. It isn't easy to get casual work in those places while you're travelling. You sort of have to live on what you take. I've got some saved up, from when I was temping, but . . .'

Again, Jeremy raised his hand. The gesture might seem imperious in some people, but with him, it didn't. He was always just in rather a hurry to get to his point.

'Your mother and I have put our heads together. We'll finance the tickets and bung you a wedge for living expenses. We thoroughly approve.'

'You *can't* do that!' Amanda was embarrassed. Mum had baled her out once or twice, sure, but she'd never actually funded a trip. It was always understood that, after college, Amanda had to earn what she spent, just like her sisters. They spent it on mortgages and shoes, she spent it on plane tickets.

'Yes, I can! Call it a reward for helping out. We've got lots, relatively speaking. We'll be giving HMS Revenue and Customs plenty when we're gone. There's all sorts of nonsense about trusts and so forth. You won't have to think about that until they've carried me out. This bit will just be for fun. Go and do the gallivanting we're too crumbly to do. I'm too crumbly, your mother's just too loyal . . .' Nancy laid her hand on his cheek, and he took it and kissed it. 'Go. Live. Love.'

Amanda felt tears spring to her eyes at his extraordinary generosity. She stood up and bent over him. 'You're lovely. Thank you, thank you so much . . .'

'You're welcome, sweetheart. Very, very welcome.'

She kissed Nancy, who stroked her head. 'Thanks,' she whispered.

'I can't believe they would do that for us.' They were curled into each other in Ed's bed. The wind was howling outside, and the branches on a tree near the window tapped against the glass, but their minds were already in Rio.

'I can – it's very them.'

'So you're just a spoilt rich bastard, are you?'

He pinched her bottom. 'And you're just a spoilt rich bastard's girlfriend.'

'Ouch!'

'Not really. I mean, I've had jobs since I was a teenager. They paid for college and stuff, but not for extras. I didn't get a new car or anything. They're not interested in that kind of thing. It's the travel thing that excites them, I think.'

'And me.'

'We'll go into town tomorrow, get some *Rough Guides*.

And we should check out flights.' She could hear the excitement in Ed's voice. It would be *so* lovely, travelling together. She'd always travelled alone. She might hook up with people she met along the road, and sometimes she travelled for a week or so with a group from a train, or a bar, or a boat, but eventually, she always broke away again and continued on her own path alone. It was what she did to feel free. Now she could hardly wait to be travelling *with* someone.

'I'd better go home, see my folks.' She hadn't even spoken to them for ages, she realized. Lisa texted, checking in with her. She should make the effort. 'Maybe next weekend?'

'Yeah.' He held her tightly. 'I'll miss you.'

'You soppy thing!' But she loved it.

March

Mark

It was a long time since Mark had been on a date. He'd only come on this one to keep Hannah quiet. He hadn't expected to enjoy it.

She was divorced. She and her husband had split up four years ago. He had moved 100 miles away. She'd given up work when their children were born and never gone back, even when the youngest one – Hannah's classmate Susie – was at school full time. She said that was half the problem: she should have done. By the time she realized it was too late, and the marriage was over. She didn't blame her husband. She was retraining as a teacher. She felt a bit silly, having discovered something she was so good at so late in life. She loved the teaching, loved feeling that she might be making a difference to a young life.

She told him this over a bowl of pasta and bottle of Valpolicella at the local Italian restaurant.

She was a little too thin. Ash blonde, with a modern, feathery haircut and green-grey eyes; she must have been very pretty when she was young. She was still attractive now. Well maintained and neat, but soft, too. He liked the faint lines around her eyes. She smelt nice. Her black sweater had little sequins sewn into it and they sparkled in the candlelight. He wondered why her husband had stopped loving her.

Over tiramisu, she told him she'd been on a few dates since her husband left. Mostly set up by well meaning friends, although she had, briefly, joined a dating agency.

She was funny when she talked about the application form she'd had to fill in, and the various unsuitable men she'd met – self-deprecating and honest. None of them had been worthy of a second date, apparently. One she had watched come into the pub, see her and surreptitiously turn and leave. She said the woman who ran the agency told her that her age would be an advantage. She was post menopausal and so men could relax about her biological clock – she wouldn't be desperate to entrap them into parenthood. She laughed loudly when she said that she'd wanted to hit the woman repeatedly over the head with a shovel. She had a warm laugh.

While they drank a cappuccino, she'd asked him, tentatively, about Barbara. She'd known her, just a little. Their girls weren't really friends, but they had once sat on the PTA together for a couple of terms. He answered her gentle questions briefly and steered her away from the subject, which did not belong at their table.

He drank a grappa; she had the last of the wine. It seemed to him that it was a little more than either of them was used to drinking. He went to the bathroom and felt just a fraction lighter, giddier, than he could remember feeling.

She lived within walking distance of the restaurant, in the home she had been married from, and raised her children in, and been granted in her divorce and so, without discussion, they walked, even though his car was parked right outside. It was pretty warm outside for March. When they reached the door of her small cottage – well maintained, and neat, he noted with a smile, she was talking about the council's recycling policy, but he wasn't listening.

He didn't especially see the desperation in her eyes when she asked him if he would like to come in for a moment and maybe have another drink. Her daughter wasn't there, she added. She was sleeping over at a friend's. The moment he nodded and walked through the door they launched themselves at one another. They were both surprised they'd lasted so long. He wasn't so much kissing her as consuming her, and she completely surrendered to it. They got no further than the sofa just inside the door. They began to tug at each other's clothing, but quickly realized it would be more efficient to undress themselves. Mark pulled impatiently at the buttons of his shirt and kicked himself out of his trousers. He was so hard he wasn't sure he could wait. She was as thin naked as she had looked dressed. He could see her ribs in the half light, and her stomach was totally flat and smooth. He was kissing everywhere he could reach – her neck, her nipples, her shoulders. There was no plan beyond having her.

She clawed at his back, equally fervent. He was inside her before they even lay down. She was hot and wet, and he began thrusting fast, banging relentlessly against her sharp hipbones. Her kisses made his face wet. He left one hand under her and brought another around to squeeze her tiny breast. It felt unbelievably good to be fucking her. If he cared at all how it felt to her, she seemed equally into it. In fact, she came first, fast, her legs straightening out under him as though she had cramp, her pelvis suddenly still as she concentrated on the sensation. She kept shouting, 'Oh God, oh God, oh God!' He kept moving, and then she moved again, her mind on him now, digging her nails into his buttocks, pushing him into her, kissing the side of his neck. When he came, it felt like the orgasm started from his spinal column, and it lasted forever.

Mark fell on her, so heavily that he forced a guttural

breath from her. She stroked his back languorously, but she didn't speak. Neither of them had the breath. And that wonderful, thoughtless, 'we're not so different from the other mammals' feeling lasted exactly as long as it took for his breath to slow down and return to normal.

Mark rolled off her and lay awkwardly next to her on the sofa. He had a sudden, random thought about condoms. How stupid, and ridiculous. He hadn't used one – and she hadn't asked. Suddenly exposed, embarrassed and a little chilly, she pulled a throw from behind her and covered herself. He couldn't look at her straight away, but he made himself turn and smile at her.

'That was . . .' she didn't know what to say it was.

'Sudden?' They both laughed, a brittle, sociable little laugh and fell momentarily silent.

'I haven't had sex since my husband left,' she finally volunteered. 'Nearly four years, unless it counts when it's with yourself.' And, after everything else, that was the one thing that made her cheeks pinken.

'It counts, but it's not as good.'

'Four years. That explains my . . .'

'Hey, mine too.' He believed her, but he was surprised. Surely she could have slept with any number of men. The urgency had been pretty mutual. He put a hand on hers. The chatting seemed more revealing than the sex, somehow. He realized that he wished he was one on a list.

She had made him remember the last time with Barbara. It hadn't mattered how much she'd told him that he didn't need to be gentle with her, that she wanted him to make love to her like he always had, to do all the same things, at the same pace, with the same pressure, to take his own pleasure as much as worry about her own, he couldn't. He was frightened. Of the cancer, of hurting her, of it maybe being the last time, each time until it actually was. It was that way between them for almost a year – infrequent, too gentle, apologetic, incredibly unsatisfying physically and completely overpowered by love. Once, afterwards, he felt her tears on his chest and he'd asked her, as if he needed to ask, why she was crying. Her answer surprised him. She said she was crying because the way he had touched her reminded her so much of how he made love to her when she was first pregnant with Hannah – like she had stopped being a woman, his lover, and become this fragile, delicate thing – a porcelain china model of herself. And that the irony was that then it had been all about life, the new life growing inside her, and now it was all about death, and its inexorable, ugly march through her body. And wasn't that stupid and sad?

Now he was lying with Jane in his arms, thinking about Barbara. Fighting feelings of betrayal and self-loathing; wanting to get up and run away. She felt it. She was a good woman: she knew the difference between an ex-husband and a dead wife, and she lay alone beside him, castigating herself for letting it happen. She really liked him. He was normal. He was handsome, and kind, and he had a great relationship with Hannah – you could see it when you saw them together. He appealed to her, physically and emotionally. Not just because she felt sorry for him. If she'd met him twenty years ago, she knew she would have liked the look of him. And she was so, so very bloody lonely. If she could script this next bit, they would go upstairs together, hand in hand. They would climb under her duvet, wrap themselves around each other, and fall asleep. She wanted to wake up with someone, with him, far more than she actually wanted what had just happened. But she knew it wasn't going to go that way, and if she was quiet for a moment, it was because she was struggling to find a way to make it easy for him to leave her there on the sofa without stripping her altogether of the dignity she already felt she might be quite close to losing.

She forced a light tone. 'So, thanks are in order.'

'Thanks?'

'For services to womankind.'

He wasn't self-absorbed enough to buy that, but he knew what she was trying to do.

'You're more than welcome.'

And then 'Thank you.'

'Anytime.'

'I should get going . . . Hannah . . . these mocks . . .'

She stopped him with a hand on his arm.

'That's fine, Mark. Whatever. I understand.'

'Do you?' He looked into her eyes.

'I think so.'

'I'm sorry. I know I should . . .'

'There's no "should", Mark. We're grown ups. I wanted this; I even sort of made it happen. You have nothing to apologize for.'

Again, he didn't quite believe that. He grabbed his shirt and pulled it over his head, buttoning up the three buttons he'd undone minutes before. 'This was . . .'

'This was lovely. Let's go with that.'

He nodded at her and smiled. 'Lovely.'

But it wasn't. It was distinctly unlovely and he felt bad. Bad for himself, and for Barbara and for Jane.

She made herself a toga from the blanket while he put on his boxers and trousers. Now they were both self-conscious and shy. When he was ready to go, he pulled her into a brief, awkward bear hug, but he didn't say anything and he didn't look her in the eyes again when he left. As he closed the door behind him, Jane curled up in the corner of the sofa and cried for a long time.

Mark slept badly; he'd been doing that a lot lately. When Hannah knocked on the door and came in without waiting for an answer, two mugs of tea in her hands, he felt like he'd only been asleep for twenty minutes. She still had on pyjamas and a dressing gown and, when she'd put the teas down, she jumped onto the bed, grabbing a pillow to hold across her chest and crossing her legs. She was grinning.

'So . . . how was it . . . ?'

'How was *what*?'

He wasn't ready for this conversation, which was ridiculous because he might have known he would have to have it this morning, and he'd been awake half the night to think of what to say.

'Your date, idiot!'

'It wasn't a date.'

'You had dinner with a nice-looking woman. No one else was there. That's a date.'

'If you're a teenager. If you're as old as me, it's just dinner.'

'Semantics, Dad, but okay. Question is, *was* it just dinner?'

God, Paxman eat your heart out! He realized his head hurt. He didn't want to lie to Hannah – he sort of had a policy on that.

'Do I ask you what happens on your dates?'

'So it *was* a date!' she exclaimed triumphantly. Mark groaned. 'And, since you ask, yes, you do. Not that I have that many.'

'That's different. Me parent, you child. You underage minor, to be precise.'

'Gross! Anyway, stop deflecting. I want details.'

'I ate a tricolore salade, sage gnocchi and a fabulous tiramisu . . . We had a bottle of their finest . . .'

She hit him playfully with the pillow she'd been holding. 'Daadd!'

'What do you expect, Hannah?' He drew out the syllables of her name, like she had done with his. 'She's a very nice woman, I liked her. The conversation flowed well enough. It was a pleasant evening.'

'That's more like it. Pleasant is a bit of a killer word, though. Sounds like you were at some classical music concert. I'd kill a guy who described an evening with me as "pleasant". Will you see her again?'

He realized Hannah wasn't really expecting there to have been anything else for him to confess. Of course not. She'd be shocked/disgusted/furious if she really knew, wouldn't she? It was a first date – if a date was indeed what they were calling it – and when you were in Hannah's world, nothing more than kissing would ever happen on one of those.

'I'm sorry that my vocabulary displeases you. Would you prefer rocking evening, killer evening? Sick evening?'

'Good vocab, Dad!' She giggled. He sounded ridiculous.

She lay back and put her head on his shoulder. She smelt of shampoo and the kind of sugary perfume that only young girls thought smelt good. 'Will you go out with her again?'

He sighed, suddenly serious. 'I don't know, Han.'

'But you liked her.'

'I liked her. She's a nice person. If I'm allowed to say "nice". But . . .'

'But what, Dad?'

'But I'm not sure I'm ready for all this. I'm not looking for anything . . .'

'You don't have to be "looking for anything", Dad. It doesn't have to be "going anywhere", does it?'

He squeezed her arm. 'Why are you so interested, anyway?'

'I don't want you to be sad, Dad. I want you to be happy.'

It was different for Hannah. For Hannah, Barbara had been gone now for eight, nine months; going for a couple of years before that. Her recovery time frame was different, he knew. It wasn't less or more, or better or worse – just different. Maybe he was leaning on her too much. Maybe she wanted him to find someone so she could share the burden of him with someone else. He didn't mean to be a burden, of course, but he recognized that in some ways he was. Jennifer hadn't been since . . . since what had happened last month. He hadn't been in touch, either. He was still angry with her, still embarrassed for her. Lisa came when she could, but their weekends were often taken up by Cee Cee, and they both worked all week. Amanda was all wrapped up with her new man. Maybe it was all a bit much for Hannah, being stuck here with him all the time. Maybe his head hurt and he couldn't think about it any more right now.

'You make me happy, Hannah.' He kissed the top of her head. 'Tea in bed makes me happy, Hannah.' She sat up and smiled at him. He glanced at his alarm clock. 'An extra hour of sleep followed by a bacon sandwich in bed would make me happier still . . .' She smirked. 'Then this Sunday is all yours – we'll do whatever you want . . . chick flicks excluded. I can't do a chick flick today, even for you.'

She jumped up and backed towards the door. She was growing up, for sure, but there was still plenty of the bounding puppy in her.

'Can't. I'm going out. You don't mind, do you?'

'So the tea was to butter me up?'

'No. The tea was because you're my daddy and I love you.' She was batting her eyelashes at him and it made him smile.

'Hold the sugar, please.'

'So it's okay?'

'That depends. Who, what, where, why, when?'

'God, Dad!' She was rolling her eyes at him.

'God, Hannah.' He rolled right back.

'My mates, shopping, maybe a film or a pizza, town, because, by nightfall. That thorough enough for you?'

'Don't be saracastic.'

'I'm just answering the questions.'

'Have you got your phone?'

'Yes, I've got my phone. And clean knickers and a handkerchief.'

'Again, I'm not loving the sarcasm.'

Actually, he didn't mind it. It seemed normal; normal that Hannah should want to go out with her friends. Normal that she should resent his interest.

'And it still depends.'

'On what?' Hannah's attitude was now bordering on belligerence. Her switch flicked easily these days.

'Do I still get my bacon sandwich before you go?'

She grabbed his shirt from the back of the chair, where he had thrown it the night before, and aimed it at his head. Mark mock-groaned and rolled over, pulling a pillow over his head. Not for the first time in the last few weeks, did he have the vague feeling that she was lying to him. She'd become a little closed off, a little stroppy. She'd started closing doors a lot. She was on the phone the whole time.

He'd put two and two together and made what he was sure was five: it had started when she'd met that guy at the party a few weeks ago. When he'd asked about him, she'd brushed the questions off, making a joke of it, until he persisted, when she'd gotten sulky and spent the rest of the night in her room, whispering into her phone and listening to awful music.

He realized she was a masterful manipulator. She'd just deflected him with all this Jane stuff; made him a much juicier topic for conversation than she was herself. It wasn't fair, shutting him out like this. He'd always been easygoing about stuff like that. Their house had always been full of her friends. Not like some parents. Barbara always said you kept them close and you kept them safe. He wasn't some Dickensian papa. Maybe he was worrying about nothing. Maybe she actually was out shopping and eating with her friends. Maybe his head hurt; maybe he'd go back to sleep.

Hannah

It was the first really serious lie she'd ever told her dad. Fibs, of course; half truths, exaggerations and stuff . . . But this was a big fat lie. Her chest was hot from telling it, but the feeling wasn't all bad. Like when she'd been really young, 7 or 8, and her friend Cheryl had dared her to steal a Bazooka bubble gum from the newsagent. Taking it felt really bad, but kind of good too; exciting and daring. Like she was someone else just for a moment. Of course, she'd been caught with the Bazooka and frogmarched back to the shop to hand it over and apologize, and then not allowed to have Cheryl for tea *ever* again, or to watch television for a week, which hadn't been half so bad a punishment as Mum's disappointed, sad face. But that wasn't going to happen this time. She certainly wasn't going to be caught by Mum, was she? Besides, she'd been working really hard for these stupid exams. She deserved a bit of time off. Why shouldn't it be up to her how she spent it?

She was going to Nathan's house. Not to a film or for a pizza or to shop; not out with her friends. The bit about having her phone with her was true, but Dad hadn't asked her if it was switched on.

She'd told him to pick her up a couple of streets away and he hadn't protested. He wasn't wild about parents, he said. His own were going to be out and they would have the house to themselves that afternoon. Hannah was nervous. She'd never been alone with a boy in that way before. At the cinema, sure. And she'd done her fair share of slow dancing and snogging, at parties and things. She wasn't a prude or anything but this was something different, with someone who seemed older and more serious. The boys at school were still such colossal idiots.

But he was so sweet as well; he said the nicest things to her. He had since the first time they met, at Ruby's party a couple of weeks ago. He'd been calling her and texting her ever since. On Valentine's Day he'd sent her a card and he'd signed it 'Nathan' so there was no doubt. It wasn't one of those schmaltzy, sick-making cards, either: it was a postcard of a painting of a pre-Raphaelite sort of a girl, all Rapunzel hair and dreamy expression. He'd written 'Be Mine' with a question mark and signed his name. She'd never been so thrilled with an item of post and three words.

Nathan would be 18 in September. He was doing his A-levels and he'd be going to university in September. He was very tall and skinny in a cool way, not a geeky one. He wore drainpipe jeans and kept his fringe swept forward across his eyes. Dad would almost certainly call him girly and say he should get it cut. He listened to bands she hadn't heard of before. She'd started downloading them onto her iPod. Nathan had given her playlists. He said he was her Svengali, but she didn't really know what he meant. He read loads. If Dad could see behind the haircut, he'd be impressed with how clever he was. Hannah didn't realize, or admit to herself, that she hadn't given her dad the chance, either to object to the hair or respond to the intellect. And, of course, there was the car. It might be a Ford Focus, and it might belong to his mother, but the point was it no longer needed to be driven by said mother. He could drive it himself, which was, of course, impossibly glamorous. The six long months before Hannah would be able to get her provisional licence seemed interminable. He was trendy and smart and obviously romantic, and Hannah thought everything about him was breathtaking.

Dad wouldn't have wanted her to go to his house if he'd known it was just the two of them, hence the lie. But Hannah wasn't worried. She felt confident Nathan wasn't the kind of boy (she corrected herself – man) to expect her to do things just because they were alone. It would just be so nice for it to be the two of them, to have time to talk and ... oh, it was just thrilling all round, and the real truth was that, alone with him or not, she just didn't want to talk to her dad about it yet. It would be cringy. This was private and grown up and ... private. And, actually, she might want to do *some* things ...

Nathan had the music on very loud in the car. It wasn't one of his mum's CDs. She climbed in beside him, and beamed at him.

'Hiya.'

'Hiya.'

He leant over. She had kissed him a bit, that first night, at Ruby's, right at the end. But this was different – it was broad daylight, and there was no atmosphere, and she felt self-conscious. She returned the kiss chastely. He grinned at her, switched on the ignition and drove off.

Lisa

March 5th was Andy's 41st birthday. Last year, when he'd turned 40, he'd rented a house out in Norfolk. They'd gone there with twelve of his best friends for the weekend. The weather had been unexpectedly beautiful – crisp and blue-skied and still. There had been long walks and roaring fires, and boozy, funny evenings. Lisa had given him a first edition of one of his favourite novels – a Thomas Pynchon. She and his friends had put on a show, hurriedly rehearsed in the weeks before Norfolk. They'd called it '40 Things We Love About Andy'. Someone had made an iPod mix of all the hits from the year he was born.

This year, no celebration had been planned. Cee Cee was with Karen – she had been promised birthday dinner at Pizza Express at the weekend, which compensated her for her absence on the actual day. Cee Cee thought that any birthday which came without cake and someone who could make balloon animals was a total washout.

Lisa had asked him if he wanted her to book a

restaurant and meet some friends. He'd replied that he'd rather eat at home, just with her, have a nice bottle of wine and a quiet night. She'd cooked a lamb casserole and chosen a good Barolo. She'd handed over her presents a little apologetically – a new tie, some socks, a pair of silver cufflinks. Dad presents, she called them. She hadn't found inspiration this year. He said they were great. They reminisced a little about Norfolk.

'Actually, I've got something for you,' he said, getting up from the table and fumbling in his bag.

'But it isn't my birthday.'

'I know that. Still, I have.'

He put a small box on the table, just as she had been afraid he might. She was scared of little velvet boxes.

'It isn't a ring,' he spoke quickly, watching her face intently. 'I know you'll have a view on how a ring should look. I wouldn't risk getting it wrong. Not when you're going to wear it . . . all the time.'

She held the box in one hand and gently opened the domed lid. Inside, nestled against navy-blue velvet, lay a small, uncut diamond.

'See – it's a diamond. Uncut, just the stone. You get to choose everything. The setting, the cut, what colour gold you want the band to be . . . all of that stuff. I thought yellow, but he says everyone is into white gold now. Or platinum. Whatever. That's the point – you get to go and see him and choose yourself. Impact, without risk, the guy in the shop said.'

'It's beautiful.' It was funny how seeing a diamond that way, like it came out of the mine, and not dressed up in its setting, made you realize how ridiculous it was that they cost so much money. Who decided that the little shiny stones they were digging up should be the most valuable thing on earth?

Andy sat down at the table beside her.

'Thank you. But . . .'

'Listen to me for a minute, Lisa. I've got something to say.'

This was the conversation she'd been dreading since December, when he'd proposed on that one amazing night and it had all seemed so stupidly perfect. And she still, in the end, hadn't been the one with enough balls to start it.

'I've been pretty good. You said you'd marry me in December. That's two months ago. In that time, you haven't let me tell my daughter and you haven't told anyone else. Not Mark, or your sisters. We haven't set a date.'

'I know,' she began.

He raised his hand to stop her. 'I'm not finished.' Lisa looked at her plate. 'I haven't had a lot of experience in this area, but I know this is not how happy, excited brides behave. An engagement isn't supposed to be a secret. It's supposed to be something you want to tell people. It's supposed to be leading up to a wedding. It's supposed to be a good thing.'

'Andy . . .'

'Let me finish, please, Lisa. I need to say these things to you. I love you very much. I want to marry you. I thought you wanted that too. I want to set a date. Soon. Now. But if that's not what you want, Lisa, you need to tell me now. It just isn't fair to keep going along like this.'

He was right. It was horribly, nastily, cruelly unfair. Lisa took a deep breath. She was getting good at these killer opening lines. Must be her year for them.

'I slept with someone else, Andy.'

Endless silence.

'You did *what*?' Why was that everyone's standard response to something they didn't want to hear? They made you repeat it.

'I slept with someone else.' It didn't sound any more palatable the second time around.

'When?'

'Last summer.'

'Who was it?'

'You don't know him. Just a guy – I met him through work.'

'Just once? Was it a one-off thing?'

'No.' She wished it was, but she couldn't stop being honest now. 'It lasted for about four months.'

'*Four months . . . !*'

The time frame seemed to throw him more than anything else. It had been about fifty actual times, she supposed. Fifty occasions she had told herself it was okay to cheat on him; fifty individual moments of betrayal.

'I'm sorry.'

Andy didn't speak for a minute or two. She could see the pain on his face. His eyes were moving rapidly as he went back over the last summer, looking for clues, wondering about specific days and times.

'Did you love him?'

'No.'

'Then why did you do it?'

'I don't know.'

'You don't just not know.'

'I don't know Andy, I don't know. I'm sorry. I didn't mean to hurt you.'

And then the words came. 'That's just bullshit, isn't it, though, Lisa? That's just something people say, isn't it? It's one of the great meaningless bullshit sayings.

Of course you did! You slept with someone else while we were together. You knew I loved you; you said you loved me. But you shagged somebody else anyway. You knew what you were doing. You sure as hell didn't mean *not* to hurt me.'

'I don't know what you want me to say.'

'I want you to make me understand why you would do a thing like that.'

'I can't.'

'Try. Bloody well try, Lisa.'

He didn't wait for an answer. 'Christ! Four months; four bloody months.' He stood up, his hands white-knuckled on the table. 'I don't know who you are.'

The front door slammed behind him. She heard the car start outside; reverse down the driveway, too fast. The bottle of wine was empty. He'd easily had half of it. He shouldn't be driving. Lisa felt a sudden stab of fear. Please God, let him not drive off, too fast, angry and over the limit. He could hurt himself, or someone else. But he'd gone by the time she opened the door to go after him.

For a long while, she stood on the front doorstep, paralyzed. She willed his car to turn back into the road, but it didn't. Eventually she had to go back inside. She cleared the plates from the table and washed the dishes. She rinsed the bottle and put it in the recycling. The phone rang and the panic made her feel physically sick. It was a friend, calling to wish Andy a happy birthday, and she squeezed her eyes shut, making her voice sound like everything was okay. When she'd hung up, she slid down the wall where the phone was, onto the floor, and sat there, hugging her knees.

*

He came home five hours later, at 3am. She was sitting in the living room, staring at the blank television screen. She almost cried with relief when she heard his key turn in the lock.

'I thought something must have happened to you.'

'It did.'

'I know. I thought, I thought you might be hurt.'

'I realized I should never have driven. I'd had too much to drink. I left the car a couple of miles away. Walked back.'

'I'll drive you over there in the morning to get it.' It was meaningless trivia. He shook the offer off distractedly.

He sat down on the sofa, not next to her, but as far away as possible. He wasn't looking at her.

'What was his name?'

'Chris. Does it matter?'

'I think I'm entitled to ask you anything I want, don't you?' He didn't sound like himself. She hoped he wasn't going to ask about the sex. She didn't think she could bear to say it. She remembered when she'd extracted every infinitesimal detail about Karen from him. She had thought it would help, but it hadn't.

'Andy . . .'

'You know what.' He slapped both his thighs, with open palms. It was a strange gesture. 'I thought I had lots to say to you . . . when I was sitting in the car. My mind was racing with things I wanted to say to you, in fact. But now I don't. I can't think of a single word to say to you.'

She hadn't expected that, and she had no idea how to react to it.

'I don't want to see you for a while.'

Lisa was frightened.

'I think one of us should go and stay somewhere else.'

'I'll go. This is my fault. And Cee Cee . . .' She wanted him to know that she was thinking about Cee Cee.

'Fine.' He cut her off in mid-sentence.

He stood up. 'I'll sleep in Cee Cee's room tonight.'

'Andy . . .'

'Don't, Lisa. Please don't say anything. I'm sorry if I'm cheating you out of your big dramatic scene, but I'm really not up for it.'

He paused at the door. 'I thought we were worth more than that. I thought you were better than that.'

Lisa didn't remember when she'd ever felt more worthless. The diamond, still in its open box on the table, sparkled malevolently at her.

He'd already left when she got up the next morning. She'd slept, eventually, too heavily. He must have taken the alarm when he went up last night. It was 8.15am by the time she'd opened her eyes and looked at her watch. She called work and told them something personal had come up. Her assistant agreed to let her scheduled appointments know and to hold the fort for a couple of days.

Lisa filled a couple of suitcases with a random selection of clothes, feeling slightly as if she was hovering on the ceiling watching herself do it. She didn't know how long she would be gone. Then she realized she didn't know if she'd ever be coming back. She sat on the bed and cried. What a bloody mess. She had practised telling Andy dozens of times. It hadn't come out the way she'd wanted. But she'd still expected that there would be some relief in it, that she would feel in some way better for no longer keeping the secret. She supposed she had taken his understanding for granted. He loved her, didn't he? He would be angry, of course; upset, understandably. But he'd start making excuses for her, wouldn't he, the moment he calmed down long enough to remember that he loved her? She was human. Wasn't that what she'd said about her mum? Wasn't that what she'd say about anyone? People screwed up. People screwed people they weren't supposed to. For the first time, sitting on the edge of the bed next to a suitcase full of her clothes, Lisa realized that Andy might not – ever – get past this. He might never understand, or forgive her. This might be the end. It was colossally stupid of her not to have understood that before.

Mark was working from home when the phone rang. It was Jane. Damn! He should have rung her first. He'd hoped she wouldn't ring him.

'How are you?'

'I'm fine, thanks.'

He didn't know what to say, and the silence was deafening.

'You left . . . you left your sweater here last week.'

'I hadn't realized.' He knew he had, of course. He'd realized immediately.

'I was wondering how to get it back to you.'

'Right.'

'I mean, I can't exactly send it in to school with Susie, can I?' She was trying to sound light-hearted and maybe even a little flirtatious, but he knew that wasn't how she really felt. He had the sense that this phone call had been as hard and awkward and embarrassing for her to make as it was for him to take. More so, of course. He cursed his cowardice, and wished she hadn't called.

'Oh, just forget about it, why don't you? It was old.'

It was Paul Smith. He knew it, she knew it. A Discovery Channel image of a wild animal chewing off its own foot to escape from a trap flew around in his head.

He was supposed to arrange another meeting. He was supposed to offer to come around and get it, or to fix lunch or dinner for an exchange. He wasn't ready to do that.

'It's really nice. Seems a shame. I could ... drop it round.' Why was she doing this? He didn't want her to come here.

'No ... no ... I couldn't ask you to do that.' He paused. 'Look, why don't I come and get it?'

Her relief manifested as a laugh. 'Okay, great.'

'I'm a bit tied up with work this week. Can I give you a call next week and fix a time?'

'Sure. Sorry to have disturbed you.'

'No, no. Please, you didn't. Thanks for ringing.'

'I'll talk to you soon then?'

'Yep, soon. Take care of yourself.'

'And you, Mark.'

Great. Now he felt like a pig again. He hadn't thought about whether or not he would see her again. He'd tried not to think about her at all. And he'd been doing pretty well.

The phone rang again less than five minutes later. Please God, let it not be Jane, calling back! It was Lisa. She was on her mobile phone – it sounded like she was driving. She had one of those hands-free things. Barbara had always gone on at her about it – she said just because you had your hands on the wheel and not on a phone, it didn't mean you were concentrating. She'd hated mobile phones altogether. She'd been on one of those local committees, trying to stop the phone companies from putting up a mast in the area, going door to door getting people to sign petitions about protecting local children. When she lost her hair with the chemo she said she was tempted to tell people it was phone masts that had given her cancer, but he didn't think she ever actually had.

'How are you, sweetheart?'

'I'm okay. Can I come and stay with you guys for a few days? Explain when I get there?'

''Course you can. I'm really pleased you called, actually. Amanda surfaced yesterday. She's taking a break from the country seat – she'll be here at the weekend. We'll have both of you. Hannah will love it.' He felt a brief flash of relief – he could tell them about Hannah. Get her to talk to her sisters. He wondered if Lisa would mention Jennifer. He wasn't sure he was ready to see her yet, but he didn't want Lisa to know anything was wrong. 'Shall we look for you tonight after work?'

If Lisa thought it was strange that he didn't mention Jennifer, she didn't say so. 'Can I come right now?'

He was surprised. Her voice sounded teary. 'Yes, I'm working from home . . .'

'I don't want to be any bother . . .' She was so quiet he had to strain to hear her. She had never sounded so . . . small.

'Don't be daft. Nothing that won't keep. Are you okay, Lisa?'

'I'm alright.'

Mark knew she needed to wait until she got here.

'I'll be there in half an hour or so. Okay?'

'Okay. You drive carefully.' It was what Barbara would have said.

What Mark was doing could wait, but he needed to make a few phone calls himself, so he went back to the office to work through them while he waited for Lisa, wondering what was going on. He felt exhausted before she even arrived. He felt more that they were falling apart now than he had last summer, when Barbara had died. It was like everything stopped working when she left them. Jennifer, then him, Hannah, now Lisa. It was like her going had upset the natural order. She was emotional El Niño. Everything was going to hell. He felt like a juggler whose brightly coloured balls were speeding up, veering out of control and tumbling to the ground.

Lisa had clearly been crying. A lot. Her face was pale beneath the angry red blotches of a prolonged bout of sobbing. Something really bad must have happened. Not an accident, or an illness. That she could have said on the phone. Something inside. He was glad she'd felt she could come to him, but part of him wished, like with Jennifer, that his step-daughters had had better friends. Weren't women supposed to tell all to their girlfriends, not their step-fathers?

'I'd have gone to my friend Anna's, but she's away.' That much was true. Anna was Lisa's best friend from university and she *was* away. She worked in fashion journalism and she often was. She always said it wasn't as glamorous as it sounded, but no one ever believed her. Lisa had other friends, but they were Andy's friends too. She didn't want them to feel awkward, and she certainly didn't want to tell them the truth.

'What on earth has happened?'

'I think Andy and I have broken up.'

Later that night, Mark excused himself not long after dinner and went to bed, claiming to be deeply involved with the thriller he was reading. He didn't read a page. He and Lisa had talked until Hannah came home from school, but he wasn't certain he understood everything that had happened and was even less certain that he could see how they would resolve it. Lisa had sat at the breakfast bar, and between sobs and loud sniffs, had spilled out all that had happened. The affair, the proposal, the rejection, the revelation ... Mark was shocked, though he tried hard to keep that reaction off his face. She had been really stupid, that much was true. Andy's reaction to being cuckolded was predictable, and deserved. It was asking a lot of a bloke, getting past that. And he saw now that he knew what had been going on, that she'd been stringing him along, accepting his proposal months ago, wriggling out of commitment and then dropping this complete bombshell. What did she expect him to have done?

By mutual agreement, they changed the subject when Hannah came in, refreshingly chatty for a change, full of the school play and the auditions scheduled for the following day, and she hadn't noticed anything was up. She'd assumed Lisa had come home to hang out. Kids took everything at face value. She didn't notice the puffy eyelids because she wasn't really looking. When boys went through puberty and their voices were breaking, there was that disconcerting period when you never knew whether it would come out deep and chocolatey, or smurfy and squeaky. Hannah was like that. Sometimes very much a kid, sometimes not. She and Lisa were downstairs now, watching TV. Hannah was sitting on the floor between Lisa's knees, and her sister was putting her hair in small, tight braids so that it would be curly for her audition. He could hear Hannah shouting at Sir Alan Sugar on *The Apprentice*.

As he often did, he closed his eyes and tried to imagine what his wife would say. It occurred to him that this thought process was definitely different now because he knew now that Barbara had been unfaithful once, too, even if it wasn't while she was married to him. Whatever the back story, and however he felt about it, it meant she was capable of it, once. You became a trespasser on the moral highground after a transgression like that. It had to affect the way that you judged everyone else. He realized he'd forgiven Barbara in an instant because he wanted to. He wondered if Andy wanted to forgive Lisa. It was different, of course. But also the same. You made new rules for the people you loved. They weren't subject to the same judgment criteria reserved for the rest of the world. In some ways you were way easier on them, and in others, much harder.

At 10pm the phone beside the bed rang and he picked it up on the second ring.

'Mark?' It was Andy. 'Is she there?'

'Yeah. She is.'

Andy sighed. 'Okay.'

'Do you want me to get her for you?'

'No, I don't want to talk to her. I just wanted to know . . . that she was okay.'

'She's in terrible shape.'

'Not okay like that. Okay – safe. As in not lying in a ditch.'

'She's safe.'

'Okay, then. Thanks, Mark.' His voice sounded tight. There was nothing of the warmth their relationship had had for years.

'Andy?'

Clearly he wasn't going to get into it now. 'Do me a favour – don't tell her I called. Bye.'

He hung up before Mark could say another word.

Downstairs, Lisa had finished Hannah's hair, but the two of them were still sitting in the same position. Hannah had dropped her braided head onto Lisa's lap. *The Apprentice* was over and now they were talking.

'How is life with you, little sis?' Lisa was glad of the distraction and wondered if Hannah might confess to her. Mark had told her, before Hannah came home from school, that he was having a few communication problems with her. Nothing specific, he said. He just thought she might be holding back from him. She knew he hoped Hannah might open up to her. 'You only have to tell me if it's illegal,' he'd half-joked. 'I just want to know she's not doing anything too wild.'

'Brilliant.'

'In your O-level summer? That's highly suspicious. I had hives and coldsores at this point . . . What's so brilliant?'

Hannah turned her head and her eyes sparkled. 'Promise you won't tell Dad?'

Lisa nodded.

'I'm in love.'

'You *are*?'

'I am.'

'Who with?'

Excited now that she had decided to confess, Hannah scrambled onto her knees and began . . . Five minutes later, she stopped extolling Nathan's virtues. Lisa couldn't help smiling broadly.

'Are you laughing at me? What's funny?'

Lisa shook her head. 'Nothing's funny. I'm not laughing at you; I'm smiling. It's nice, Hannah, honestly. I'm happy for you. He sounds *great*. Really.'

Hannah nodded in agreement. 'He's perfect.'

God, perfect. What a word! If nothing else gave away Hannah's age and inexperience and innocence it was the utterly absurd notion that anyone could be perfect. Life was going to slap her around the face a few times in the next few years, just as it did everyone else. Had she ever thought Andy was perfect?

'So why won't you talk to your dad about him? Have they even met?'

'God no!' Hannah sounded like she'd just suggested the earth was flat. She shrugged. 'Nathan isn't into parents.'

Lisa nodded. 'Right.' She bet he wasn't. 'Does he actually have some of his own?'

'Yeah. I mean, I haven't met them. But yeah – 'course.'

'So are you just afraid Dad will be really uncool? Is that it?'

'No, Dad's not that bad. I just, I mean, I just . . . It's all a bit new and a bit private. You get me, don't you? I mean, you didn't tell your dad stuff like that, did you?'

'My dad wasn't really around at that point.'

'What about Mum?'

'God, yes! Try not talking to her! She made the Spanish Inquisition look like casual questioners. Always wanted all the gory details, did Mum.'

'Yeah, well . . . Mum's not around to pummel me for my gory details, is she . . . ?'

And wouldn't she love to be, thought Lisa.

'So . . .' Lisa did some gentle physical pummelling to emphasize her point. 'Are there gory details you need to share with your big sister? Are there?'

Hannah laughed, and pushed Lisa's hands away. 'One or two,' she said, archly.

'Do we need to have THE TALK?'

'Eugh! No, we do not.' Hannah looked like she'd been sucking lemons.

'Are you sure? We don't need to talk about the special cuddle?'

Hannah giggled. 'No!! We all know you don't have the special cuddle until you're married – Cee Cee told us.'

Cee Cee had indeed, announcing this scintillating piece of information to the whole table over Sunday lunch, the first time Lisa had brought her to meet them. Barbara had reached over and patted her hand. 'Quite right, Cee Cee,' she'd said, winking at the others. 'You listening, you lot?'

Later, in bed, Hannah hugged herself delightedly. Lying here, thinking about him, her heart was still racing. She didn't feel at all sleepy. She felt . . . alive. She couldn't think about anything much except Nathan. She would lie in bed at night, like this, and go over every word, and every kiss and every touch. Last time, she let him take off her bra, under her shirt. There'd been a lot of fumbling. Not to see her, just to touch. It had felt amazing. She felt like a woman. He'd groaned, and she'd felt powerful and sexy. It had been almost shocking to her. She'd been right about him – he wasn't pushing her into anything she wasn't ready for. He was patient and tender. And anyway, she really did think she might be ready soon. Maybe she'd make an appointment to see a doctor about going on the pill. She'd use a condom too, of course. She wasn't an idiot. She was 16, wasn't she?

That was old enough. And she loved him. That made it different. It changed everything . . .

She didn't like lying to Dad. Okay, that wasn't quite true. It got easier each time. She wasn't doing anything wrong. She had the right to make her own decisions, didn't she? It felt, to Hannah, like she was finally living her life. Mum being ill, Mum dying . . . that had all taken so long. And she'd put everything on hold. To be with Mum, to be with Dad, afterwards. Now it was her time.

She hoped Dad might start something with Jane and take the heat off her.

Amanda

'Blimey, it's sweltering in here!' Amanda peeled off two of what appeared to be several layers of clothing. Mark looked at the thermostat. Sixty-six degrees. She looked . . . bundled up, but lovely. She'd arrived by train and Mark had just picked her up at the station. Lisa and Hannah were at Waitrose.

'Hannah can't wait to see you!'

'How is she?'

Mark shrugged. 'Typical teenager.'

Amanda grimaced. 'The lesser-spotted typical teenager! They're pretty horrid. And I should know . . .'

'You weren't so bad.'

'I was just breaking you in for Hannah . . .'

Mark put a mug of coffee down in front of her.

'So . . . how are you? You look great.'

'I am great.' She did look great. By the look of her, she'd put on a bit of weight unless it was all thermal vest. She looked fresh-faced.

'I guess it worked out after all, with the mixed-tape guy?'

Amanda smiled shyly. 'It worked out.'

'I'm *so* glad. Tell me about him?'

'You'd love him – least I think you would. He's gorgeous and smart and kind. And *so* nice to me. He's going to be an architect. He's got, like, a couple of years to go. He's taking the rest of this year out because his dad had this accident. Memento mori, and all that. His parents are *amazing*. His dad – Jeremy – he used to be a lawyer. Nancy, his mum, she was a nurse, but she stopped work to have her family. He's got two brothers – I've only met one. He's got a wife and two boys – great boys – a complete handful, but lots of fun. They're incredibly close, and they live in this amazing, amazing house by the sea. It's freezing, because they don't believe in central heating, but it's beautiful. They're just this completely amazing family. I feel like I just fit in there so well.'

Mark was surprised to find that he was jealous. Sitting here, watching her so animated, enthusing about another family, he didn't like it. Suddenly he felt inadequate.

'Don't you fit in here?' He didn't even know why he said it. It was a bit cruel. Amanda's face fell.

'I didn't mean that, Mark.' See, that was it. He wasn't Dad; he was Mark. He didn't think he'd ever minded quite so much as he did at that moment.

'I'm sorry. I was being stupid.'

'Why would you say that to me?' She looked crestfallen and mystified, and he wished he hadn't said anything. His conversation with Jennifer was an enormous elephant in the corner.

'I'm sorry – I'm a bit jealous, I suppose.' Then, before he could stop himself, 'I know, though, Amanda. I know about your dad.'

'*What?*' Now she looked astonished. 'Mum told you?'

'No, no. She never said a word!'

'Lisa told you?'

'No, Jennifer told me.'

'Lisa told Jennifer?'

'Yeah.'

'I asked her not to; I specifically asked her not to.'

Mark looked down at the counter. He felt as though he'd stepped off solid ground into conversational quicksand.

'I don't think anyone told anyone anything in malice.'

That wasn't true. Malice was the perfect word for Jennifer that night. She'd wanted to spoil something. A memory, a feeling . . .

'But you've all been talking about me.'

'Hannah doesn't know.'

'Oh no, that wouldn't do. We have to protect Hannah, don't we? The baby.'

'That's uncalled for.'

'Everyone talking about me behind my back, *that's* what's uncalled for.'

'Why are you getting so angry? We're your family.'

Amanda made a noise of triumph. 'Sort of. I'm mad because they had no right. I didn't want to hurt you.'

'Hey . . .' Mark reached for her. If that was the problem, he could fix it. 'It didn't hurt me. I admit, to begin with, I was shocked. But I'm okay. It really wasn't anything to do with me. It's you we've all been worried about.'

A car pulled up. Hannah came running in, Lisa followed with her arms full of shopping. Mark moved to take the bags from her while Hannah hugged Amanda.

'Hey stranger! It's *so* nice to see you . . . !'

*

309

If Lisa wondered why Amanda's greeting to her was a little frosty, she was stopped from asking by Mark's frantic eye signals. While Hannah was downstairs, they made small talk. Eventually, she said she needed to send some texts and get back to studying and went upstairs.

'What's up?' Lisa asked her sister. 'You seem cross.'

'I *am* cross. You told Jennifer about Dad.'

'How do you know that?'

'Because she told Mark.'

'She told *you*?' Lisa turned to Mark.

'You didn't know?'

'No, you didn't tell me.' Lisa looked accusingly at her step-father.

'Blimey! I see only some of the lines of communication are running well round here – the ones that aren't supposed to be.'

'Mand . . .'

'You shouldn't have told her, Lisa. I asked you not to.'

'I didn't think she'd betray the confidence.'

'What – like you did?' Amanda laughed. 'Right!'

'I was concerned for you.'

'And how exactly was that going to help?'

'I don't know.' Lisa looked a little shamefaced.

'And Jen told you, Mark. Why? Out of concern for me?'

She told me to hurt me, Mark thought, but didn't dare say it out loud.

Lisa perched on a bar stool next to Amanda and spoke to her as gently as she could. 'I don't understand why you're so upset. If you want to be upset about what happened with Mum, then that's fine, but I don't understand why you're making such a big deal about who knows. I really don't.'

'I'm upset about the whole bloody thing! Don't you see?' Lisa could see that her sister was close to tears. Amanda turned away, and went upstairs without saying another word.

And Lisa felt like crying herself.

Lisa

Lisa couldn't bear to call him on the phone. She was afraid of hearing the coldness in his voice, terrified of long, awkward pauses. At home, Cee Cee might answer. At work, it could be his secretary, or a colleague. Who might know, or might not know. What she'd done, what had happened, how things were between them now. She couldn't call him. But she needed to see him. Everything was going wrong. Nothing could be right without him. She felt like she was failing all the people she loved.

She waited for him to come out of the office. She sat on a bench opposite the entrance to his office and waited. She arrived at 4.30pm and sat there, hardly moving, not reading, just watching the faces of the people leaving the building until 6pm, when he came out and saw her sitting there. She stood up and hovered, and for a moment he hovered too, as though he was deciding whether or not to walk away. After a long pause – and she was sure she could see the rise and fall of his chest as he breathed deeply – he took a slow step towards her and she sank down onto the bench again.

He sat down, but he left a big space between them and barricaded himself with his briefcase, and he didn't look at her.

'How are you?'

'I'm rubbish.' He didn't ask how she was.

He didn't look good. His eyes were baggy.

'Andy, I . . .'

He turned to look at her directly and she almost wished he hadn't. It was quite a shock when someone you were used to seeing look at you with love and fun and fondness in their eyes now fixed you with a stare of hostility and rage. However much you believed you deserved it, and however much you expected it, it was still a shock, like jumping into water you knew was going to be really, really cold.

'I'm sorry.'

A small snort of derision; a narrowing of the eyes. Everything about his reaction demanded to know, is that it? Is that the best you can come up with?

'Look, Andy. I know it's a stupid, small word; I know it can't fix things. I know it doesn't make things go away. But don't you see? It's the only thing I can say. I can't make it not have happened. I would; I would if I could. But I can't. I'm not sorry I told you – I had to do that. I'm sorry I ever did it. I'm sorry I was so stupid and so thoughtless, and so selfish and so . . . so wrong. I'm sorry. I love you.'

'I don't understand.'

'What?'

'I don't understand how the two things can exist alongside each other.'

'What do you mean?'

'I don't understand how a person who loves me could have done it.'

He didn't look angry anymore, and he wasn't looking at her anymore. He looked confused and he was looking at the floor between his feet.

'I mean, I'm sure it makes me sound naïve and probably like an idiot, but you don't do that to people you love. Maybe you do that if you don't love someone, or you've fallen out of love with them, or you never loved them in the first place, or you say you love them, but you don't really know what it means, or really mean it. I mean, I'm a grown man. I'm a divorced grown man – I get some of that. But if you really do love someone – like you're still in it, still in love, want to be with them, want to stay with them – if you love someone like that, I don't understand why you would do a thing like that. It makes no sense to me.'

'It makes no sense to me either.'

'But it *must* have done! You did it, Lisa. You had sex with him, with this man, and then you got out of his bed, or his car, or wherever the hell you two were, and you came home to me. And you let me tell you I loved you, and you let me make love to you, and you said you'd marry me.'

'And I wish more than anything I've ever wished that I hadn't done that.'

He smiled. 'I don't doubt that. But don't you see? It isn't about that; it isn't what you did. It's what that means about how you feel about me. *That*'s what I can't get past; that's what I can't get out of my head when I lay down at night. It isn't an image of the two of you together. It isn't all dark, possessive sexual jealousy like it is in films. That's what you think it is – it's probably what I'd have expected, but that isn't what it is. It's an image of the two of *us* together. You saying it, and not meaning it. Not you lying. You not really, really meaning it.'

She didn't speak for a minute. Then she shrugged. Tears were welling up in both their eyes now.

'I don't know how to fix it.'

'I don't think you can.'

'Oh.'

He sniffed, and pushed his thumbs into the corners of his eyes.

'This can't be it.' She felt a sense of panic.

'I think this *has* to be it.' He stood up.

'I don't want it to be.'

'Nor do I, Lisa.'

'Then don't let it be.' She had to fight the urge to grab his legs, to physically stop him from walking away from her. For a second she thought she might scream.

He didn't say another word.

She watched him walk away until the crowd of commuters absorbed him and she couldn't see him anymore. She didn't care where she was, or who might see her. She sat for a long, long time and cried.

Mark

For the last ten years Mark had been meeting his brother for lunch every few weeks, ever since Vince had moved into the area. It was the first time they'd lived in the same town since they'd been kids. Vince had gone to Durham to read Veterinary Sciences the year after Mark had gone to Bath. They hadn't been especially close as kids, or as young men, but after Mark had married Barbara and Vince had married Sophie, and Hannah and her cousin Bethany had been born, their relationship had had a renaissance. The safe, common ground of their families created the foundation for a new friendship, which they both valued. With both of their parents dead, this family bond meant more than ever.

Vince had been brilliant when Barbara was ill. He and Sophie had taken Hannah to their house on many occasions. Sophie had delivered casseroles and disappeared with baskets of ironing. Vince had been great at those awkward silences people have when they are grieving. He hadn't tried to fill them; he'd sat through them, just been there. And, more than once, he had held his brother in an awkward, masculine embrace when Mark cried, again not tempted to speak over the strangled, apologetic sobs.

Now, Mark sat across from him in the pub, nursing his second pint of the evening, and told him about Lisa moving back in. Then he told him about Jane. He had to tell someone; it had been weighing heavily on his mind for the last few weeks. Vince listened without interrupting, sipping now and then, at his beer.

'I feel like a bastard,' Mark concluded.

'Why? It sounds like she wanted it as much as you did.'

'She wanted something – just not sure it was the same thing *I* wanted.'

'Which was?'

'Truthfully? Okay, I just wanted to have sex with someone other than myself. You've no idea how long it's been. Actually, you probably *know* how long it's been. Too bloody long! I'm sorry if that makes me some kind of animal, but I just wanted to have quick, good, silent sex and then get the hell out of there.'

'And you think that just because she's a woman, she wanted a "relationship"? I'm no Germaine Greer, but isn't that a bit of a sweeping generalization?'

'Not just because she's a woman. Because she's *that* kind of a woman. I spent the whole evening with her. She's a . . . a *nice* woman . . .'

'And you're not a nice bloke?'

'I thought I was, yeah. Until then.'

'For God's sake, Mark! You *are* a nice bloke. Will you stop beating yourself up. As far as I can see, you two had dinner, you both fancied each other, you did "it". End of story. You're both free, you're both adults. You both did what you wanted to do. You're going on about it like you slipped her a Rohypnol, or whatever it is, and date-raped the woman.'

'So you think it's okay?'

'Well, I'm not your mother! I'm not your moral compass. It shouldn't matter what I think. But, yes, since you ask, I think it's okay. I think it's good, actually. And so does Soph . . .'

'What do you mean, so does Soph,' Mark asked incredulously. 'You *told* Soph?'

''Course I did. Needed the woman's perspective, didn't I? After what you said on the phone the other night.'

'And she thinks it's okay too?' Irritation gave way to curiosity. Vince was right – the female perspective was all in this case. He'd have told Lisa, if he'd been brave enough. He had a nagging suspicion he knew what Barbara would have had to say about it, and it went something like – 'about bloody time, you mopey git'.

Vince nodded, and drained his pint.

'Have another?'

'Please.' Vince raised his hand at the barman, who came over and refilled their glasses.

'She told me to ask you whether you were going to see her again. She said, if you said no, I was to say "If not, why not?"'

'Does she tell you everything to say?'

Vince nodded. 'Pretty much, about this kind of thing. I need an official interpreter at home. Bethany's so bloody touchy lately I have to have permission in triplicate to speak to her at all – I'm seriously thinking of putting a woodburner and an air mattress into my shed and moving in there. Until all the hormones have finished surging, or whatever it is hormones do.'

Bethany was only a few months older than Hannah. She looked like Britney Spears. Mark had always been vaguely scared of her – even as a young child. As a teenager, she was positively terrifying. Hannah hadn't had the chance to be a horrible adolescent. She'd been going through all that stuff while Barbara was ill. Barbara had made it to the first period and training bra stuff, thank God. Bethany had apparently jumped right over training bra into full-on vamp, with breasts that were hard to ignore. If Hannah had wanted to strop and throw fits, and argue and rebel, she'd suppressed it very well. There'd been one or two during that time and not much since, until just lately. She certainly wasn't Pollyanna, but it sounded nothing compared to the ordeal Bethany was putting Vince and Sophie through.

He felt huge relief – talking to Vince about what happened had helped already. He hadn't mentioned the Jennifer stuff to him; what she'd told him that night. He didn't ever want anyone else to know. It was bad enough there was now this situation with Amanda and Lisa and her. What a bloody mess! He wished Barbara had let the secret die with her. He just didn't see that anything good could come from Amanda knowing the truth. Certainly none had so far . . . But this was different. This was his present, not the past.

'So – are you going to see her again?'

'I'll have to – I left a sodding shirt there.' Vince sniggered. 'Shut up! And anyway, the girls are at school together. We're bound to run into each other from time to time.'

He'd been avoiding her, of course. It wasn't that difficult. He hadn't made the call about the shirt yet, and she hadn't chased him. He'd seen her car, at school, the day before. They'd both been picking up late. He'd been slightly ashamed of himself for driving past without stopping and parking in the next street. He hadn't seen her, so maybe she hadn't seen him. Still, it was cowardly. Like he said, they'd be bound to see each other – best to get the initial awkwardness over and done with . . .

'I don't mean that. I mean, are you going out again?'

'I don't know.'

'Listen, if you like the woman, if she makes you feel good, what the hell's wrong with it?'

'It feels disloyal.'

'That's bollocks, mate, and you know it! I'm sorry, but it is. And that's not Sophie talking, that's all me. You can't stay at home on your own forever. You can't expect Hannah to be your surrogate wife. She'll be gone before you know it.'

'I don't treat her that way!' Mark was indignant.

'You don't think you do, but you *do*. Look, it's great that you two are so close, but she's got to have her own life. God knows, the poor kid had a tough enough ride when Barbara was alive. You don't want her sitting at home with you for the next three years, do you, keeping you company? You shouldn't want that for either of you. You've got to have your own life too, Mark. You've got to get up from this at some point.'

'I *have* a life.'

'A life of mourning.'

'There's no right or wrong time to stop mourning.'

He felt cornered, ambushed. His tone was harsher than he'd expected it to be.

'No, there isn't. And don't get mad at me, I'm trying to talk to you. Of course there isn't. Christ knows, I'd be lost without Sophie. I'd rather cut off my right arm. We both know how much you loved Barbara, how much you miss her. Maybe you aren't ready. Maybe you won't be ready for another year, two years. I don't know, I'm not an expert at this stuff. And that's fair enough. But this rubbish about being disloyal is just that – rubbish. You don't need me to tell you what Barbara would have to say about that, do you?'

'No.'

'So, all I'm saying to you is, don't hide behind words like that. You like this woman, you have fun with her? Then you see her, enjoy that for what it is. No one's going to think anything about it, except, if they're bothering at all, that you deserve a bit of happiness. No one's saying you have to marry her, hey?'

He sounded just like Hannah.

Amanda

The three sisters (I'm only their *half*-sister, Amanda realized – it was a strange thought) sat at Jennifer's kitchen table in tense, awkward silence, waiting to see who would speak first. There was a big pot of tea, milk, sugar and a plate of cakes on the table. It looks like some WI coffee morning, Lisa thought. It was never like this, Amanda realized. It was usually noisy, full of the cut and thrust of family life, the jibes, the inside jokes . . . This wasn't funny, though.

Two phone conversations had brought them to this

point. Amanda had called Ed and told him what had happened.

'I'm coming home.' Was it 'home' already? She'd already packed – she was great at packing.

'No, you're not.' Ed was quiet for a moment.

'What do you mean?' She'd expected him to tell her to catch the next train, that he'd be her refuge.

'You need to sort this out before we go away.'

'No, I don't.'

'Yes, you do!' Ed took a deep breath. 'Listen, Amanda, I love you.' It wasn't how she'd imagined he'd say it and she'd hear it, although she had known for a while that he did. 'I *really* love you.' It was the first time he'd said it. She wished she could see his face. 'And I want to go travelling with you. I don't want to run away with you.'

'I don't know what you mean.'

'I think you do, if you're honest with yourself. You run away when it gets tough – it's your thing. In some ways, I think you've been running away all your life. Maybe this is what you're running from. Stop doing it! Change the habit. Face it, deal with it and then we'll go wherever you want.' Then, again, 'I love you.'

Wow!

Lisa had called Jennifer.

'You told Mark about Amanda's letter!'

'How do you know?'

'I know because for some unknown bloody reason Mark blurted it out to Amanda – she's home, by the way.'

'Oh God! Why would he do that?'

'I don't know. I suppose he wanted her to talk to him about it, but I ended up getting it in the neck. Thanks a bloody lot!'

'I'm sorry.'

'You're an idiot. Why would you tell him?'

'I know I'm an idiot. I didn't mean to – it just . . . it just came out.'

'Yes. Well, I'm not going to be the only villain of the piece. I'm going to bring Amanda round and the three of us are going to talk it out . . .'

'Okay.'

'And Jen, don't you dare start on your Heywoods theory! Do you hear me?'

After she'd hung up, Jennifer sat by the phone chewing her thumbnail. It was obvious that Lisa didn't know about the row, just about the revelation. Mark had at least kept the shameful secret to himself. She still felt awful about it. She wanted to cry every time she thought about it. But then she wanted to cry a great deal these days. She hated the distance between them. Several times she had picked up the phone to talk to him, to try again and apologize for what she'd said. But it seemed so huge to her, and it got bigger each time she thought about it. She didn't even know where it had come from, but it was obvious, even to her, that *in vino veritas* she had some real issues. She didn't remember everything, but she knew she'd said vile, unkind things. She read Mark's silence as disgust and she was afraid she might have severed things between them permanently, but she was too frightened to find out.

And now she had to face Amanda . . .

'I'll start,' Amanda said, once Jennifer had played hostess with the tea. 'I suppose this seems like an OTT reaction to you two. It probably is. I guess it doesn't really matter who knows. I would have liked to be the person who made the decisions about who knew, and I felt like you – Lisa – betrayed my trust, and you –

Jennifer – were just interfering. But you're right, Lisa. It's not that much of a deal.

'I think the reason I'm so mad is that I can't do anything with this information. I have nowhere to take it. Mum's dead, Dad's dead – Mark didn't know anything about it. I've got all these questions I can't answer. That festers, you know.'

They nodded.

'It played on something that's always bugged me a bit. I always felt like I fell in the gap between two families. The one you two had with Mum and Dad, and the new one she had with Mark and Hannah. Like I had middle child syndrome, with a twist.' She smiled faintly. 'It probably sounds bollocks to you two.'

'No, it doesn't,' Jennifer replied.

'And also, it shook the way I see Mum, and I hated that. She'd been it, for me. My "real" dad was pretty much crap. My great dad wasn't actually my dad. There was just Mum. I was really, really pissed off with her when she turned out not to be perfect. I was much happier blaming Dad for what happened between them and for what happened to us as a family. And it wasn't his fault, not all his fault, anyway.'

'She fell off her pedestal.'

'Exactly.'

'So where is she now?'

'Just on the ground, like the rest of us.'

'Actually, she's *under* it . . .'

'God, you're sick!'

'Not as sick as she was.'

'Lisa, stop it!'

'Come on you lot, lighten up for God's sake! Think about it. So bloody what? Mum was a real person, not a saint. I'm more interested in what's going on with the living; in what's wrong with all of us, not what was wrong with her. I'm too independent to let someone love me, Jennifer's too flipping proud to admit she and Stephen have a problem – or problems. Who the hell would know? Amanda runs away from problems. We're all screw-ups, aren't we, in our own way? If we ever wanted to see what was wrong with Mum, we just had to look at the flaws and weaknesses we inherited. There you go. Haven't had a chance to figure out what Hannah's Achilles heel is yet, but she'll have one. Mum's inability to walk past a fresh cream cake, probably. Or her insistence you can't carry a brown handbag with a black outfit.'

Amanda burst out laughing. 'You silly mare!'

'Takes one to know one.'

'She'd bang our heads together.'

'I'd like to bang *her* head!'

'Fine, I'll drive you down to that wretched field. You can swear your head off and kick the sod. The earth sod, I meant, obviously. Will that help, do you think?'

'No!'

'Do you want to kick Jennifer?'

'Lisa!' Jennifer interjected, shocked.

'No!'

'Me?'

'Probably not.'

'Fine. Well then, enough! What is it Hannah says? Build a bridge and get over it! I can live with the person she was and the things she did. I love her just the same. I always will.'

When Amanda called Ed that night, she couldn't make him understand how a council of war that had started so tensely had ended with three sisters (half or not) crying with laughter and sadness and relief and anger, bemoaning and celebrating their mother, and eating fresh cream cakes.

Mark

Mark made his way back through the crowded pub with two pints of Old Peculiar in his hands. Andy had chosen to sit near the back, far from the after-work Jack the Lads and the trivia machine. It was quieter here, although you could still hear the Motown soundtrack playing through the loudspeakers. He put the drinks down, one spilling a little onto the cardboard coaster on the table, and pulled a couple of packets of ready salted crisps out of his jacket pocket.

'Thought you might be hungry.'

Andy picked up his glass and drank deeply, totally without salutation, and almost without eye contact.

Mark hadn't told Lisa he'd called Andy. She thought he was meeting Vince tonight. She'd gone out with Amanda, anyway. He hoped they'd sort things out. The atmosphere at home had been tense, to say the least. He couldn't remember a time when Amanda had been so angry. She and Lisa were determined to keep Hannah out of it, so they switched on and off depending on where their sister was. It was exhausting.

He'd been a little surprised when Andy accepted his invitation to meet. It all sounded a bit hopeless. Still, he had, and now they were here. Mark took a deep breath and dove straight in.

'Listen, Andy, you can tell me to mind my own business if you want to . . .'

'If I wanted you to do that, I'd never have agreed to meet you, would I?' Andy smiled weakly.

'I suppose not.' He'd thought they were friends, the two of them, but the truth was, if Andy and Lisa didn't get back together, Mark knew they probably wouldn't see each other again. They were strange relationships, the ones you had with your children's partners. More intimate than the ones you had with most of your own friends, but more fragile, too. He'd always liked Andy a lot. He liked his quiet, dry sense of humour and his gentle manner. He liked how Andy didn't always need to fill silences, how Andy was with Lisa.

Barbara had always said he was the one for her daughter. She hadn't necessarily had that sense with Stephen and Jennifer. The night before their wedding, she said she had her fingers crossed for the two of them. She'd always thought she needn't have kept them crossed for Andy and Lisa – it was an obvious fit. Andy had reminded her of him, a little, and maybe that was why, since Lisa reminded her so very much of herself. And now he wanted to see if he could help.

'I suppose not.'

'How is she?'

Mark shrugged. 'She looks about as good as you do.' Andy's hair had grown over his collar. He looked dishevelled and a little unkempt. His suit needed pressing and his shoes were unpolished. He looked thin, too.

'Thanks!'

Mark leant forward on his elbows now. 'She's dreadful. I've never seen her like this, Andy. And I'm not telling you this to make you feel sorry for her. I just need you to know. She isn't sleeping, she's barely eating. She's weepy, she's . . . she's heartbroken.'

Andy rubbed one hand across his eyes. 'I suppose you know everything?'

Mark didn't want to talk in code. 'I know about the . . . affair she had, yes. I hope you don't mind?'

'*Mind*?' Andy looked like this was mildly amusing.

'Mind her talking to me?'

'No, I don't mind that. No machismo at play here, I assure you.'

'I see that. So, yes, I know what happened.'

'And?'

'And what?'

'What do you think?'

'About what she did?'

Andy nodded.

'Well . . .' The question blindsided Mark a little. Wasn't it obvious? 'I think she was a bloody idiot! I honestly don't know what she was playing at, stupid girl, and I don't think she does either.'

Andy nodded again.

'I'm not making excuses for her at all, Andy, so please don't think I am. I don't think there are any excuses for that sort of behaviour. It's stupid and cruel, and destructive and dishonest – it's all of those things. But God knows, I'm no expert. I don't know whether she did it to keep you at arm's-length, or to test you, or . . . or whether she was just . . . mad for a bit. I don't know why. And if I was you, I'd feel just like you feel, or like I imagine you feel. But for what it's worth, I'll tell you the one thing I *do* know, what I absolutely and completely believe is that she loves you.'

'What makes you so sure of that?'

'She wouldn't be in the state she is now if she didn't.'

Andy didn't say anything, so Mark asked the question he really wanted an answer to.

'How do you feel?' He got the answer he had hoped for, the one that meant there was still hope.

'I love her.'

'I know you do.'

They both drank, and sat. The silence was sad, but not awkward. Eventually, Andy put his glass down.

'I'm not trying to punish her.'

'No.'

'I just don't know if we can recover from this, you know? If *I* can. It's a cliché, isn't it? Forgive and forget, either or both. Don't know which one is more important.'

'I think there has to be both.'

'I know.'

'And I think both have to be real.'

'What do you mean?'

'I mean, I don't think you can make yourself feel those things. If you forgive her, you have to forgive her 100 per cent. And if you forget, you have to forget forever. As in it never, ever gets mentioned again. Not brought up in an argument, not used as a weapon or a bargaining tool, or an excuse. It just goes away.'

'That sounds impossible.'

'Only you can know whether or not it is.'

'Do you think my ability to do that or not depends on how much I love her?'

Mark thought for a moment. 'Entirely.'

'So if I love her enough, I can do that?'

'I think so, yes.'

'Could you have done it, if it had been Barbara?'

'By those criteria . . . too right! I loved her more than anything. The worst thing would have been losing her.'

He stared at his beer as the irony washed over them both. Then, still looking down, and more quietly, he almost whispered, 'Don't lose her, Andy.'

Jennifer

The words 'skiing' and 'holiday' were not, for Jennifer, words that could ever be used in the same sentence. She arranged countless holidays for people every year, people for whom a weekend in Grindelwald, or Easter in Val d'Isère, or a week's heliskiing in Canada was heaven on earth. For her, skiing was an ordeal. A holiday was something that relaxed you, that allowed you to recharge your batteries, that took you away from stress and worry. Skiing did not do that.

Bob Newhart wrote a very funny sketch about Sir Walter Raleigh introducing tobacco to England in which he explained how you took a leaf from a plant, rolled it up, stuck it in your mouth, and yes, Walt, yes, you set fire to it! Her dad had had it on vinyl when she was young. He would play it and laugh until tears rolled from his eyes, even though he'd heard the punchline a hundred times. Skiing was exactly like smoking. It made absolutely no sense when you explained it. You put these narrow little planks of wood on your feet – and ps, you are freezing your backside off as you do so – and then you get dragged to the top of the mountain, where you throw yourself off and try to get to the bottom as fast as possible. It made no sense whatsoever. Oh, and it costs you thousands of pounds to be scared for your life and give yourself muscle ache like you couldn't get anywhere else, doing anything else.

Jennifer stood in line for the chair lift, and looked at the people around her. The mountain was alive with skiers. Were they all honestly having a good time? It seemed so alien to her. When the queue in front was still three or four people deep she started to worry about the chairlift. She shuffled forward on her skis, desperate to stay in the tracks of the man in front of her. You could never let your guard down, you had to concentrate at all times. It was when you got distracted that you fell, and then you had to get up. With dignity. And speed.

The encroaching throng had no time for fallers. Nothing could be allowed to interfere with their passage to the top of the mountain. It was like *Lord of the Flies* out here. She felt every muscle in her body tense as the lift swung around behind her, then caught her sharply mid-thigh, and set off. You had to make sure you had your poles in the right place before the overhead safety bar came down and trapped you in, otherwise you wouldn't be able to get off at the top. This manoeuvre successfully completed, Jennifer looked at the travelling companions to her left. Three young guys, with peculiar facial hair, in trendy voluminous jackets, on snowboards. Well, that was another thing entirely. They ignored her completely, chatting loudly and raucously in what she thought was German. They made it look so simple, damn them, with their arms flailing about in expansive gestures and their easy laughter. Her own hands were firmly gripping the bar, white-knuckled beneath her gloves. That was another thing. This was a sartorial challenge like no other – even eight-stone women looked like yetis in this get-up.

She turned to her right. It was so beautiful up there. Just like a round of golf spoilt a good walk, skiing ruined perfectly lovely scenery for her. If she could sit in a troika (she had no idea what a troika was, but it sounded impossibly romantic), covered in furs and blankets, and be driven around here, she'd be in heaven. The snow was so white, the trees so pretty – their evergreen branches dusted with powder. The air was pure – you could really taste the nothingness in it. Beyond, the sky was that particular shade of blue you so seldom saw at home. Lovely. Snowshoes, even a walk – that would be wonderful too. It was this incessant need for speed and the fear it induced in her that spoilt everything.

This was her seventh year. She'd been shocked to realize it. The first time they came, not long after they were married, they'd both been novices. Skiing hadn't been a feature of either of their childhoods – it was a modern pursuit for the middle classes. Stephen had some mates at work who were putting together a chalet, and they'd both been excited. Jennifer was fit, an effortless long distance runner with a couple of half marathons under her belt, and she enjoyed lots of the sports they'd tried together, especially in their earlier years. Stephen had been good at everything. He had that natural sporting ability thing. He'd been a scout at school and had done the Duke of Edinburgh awards scheme, and he'd taken to almost everything he'd tried. He had persuaded her to have a go at windsurfing and then, when that had been a hit, kite surfing and paragliding and, while she knew she wasn't particularly good at any of them, she loved trying; loved being with him, too. She knew she had no problem with speed, nor heights . . . Just with speed, heights and snow. The feeling she got – standing at the top of a run that was anything beyond green with the snow falling away at an angle its bright whiteness made it almost impossible to calculate, but which she knew for sure was too bloody steep – was like nothing she'd experienced before.

Maybe she was too old when she started. Amanda

could ski, having been taken by a boyfriend's family when she was 18, and although she'd never actually seen her do it, she knew she was of a reasonable standard. She'd even done an instructor's course in New Zealand, a few years ago when she was travelling, so she had to be pretty good. Hannah had been going with the school since she was 12, and was obviously excellent. She always said she'd rather be on the beach, but she was nevertheless a competent skier. Even Mark could do it. Jennifer had started in her 30s. Maybe it was just asking too much of an old dog in the way of new tricks.

Not that Stephen had felt the same way, predictably enough. Duck to water. He'd only stayed in ski school for a couple of days that first time and then he'd been off with his mates – leaving after breakfast, and returning, full of stories of daring, late in the afternoon. He loved it from the first day when, incidentally, he had not fallen once. The end of that first week, she'd watched him, from the haven of a café on the piste, swoosh down the run, legs tight together, knees bent at the perfect angle, turning effortlessly, a huge wide grin on his face, and she'd known she was in trouble.

Every year the conversation went more or less the same way. They were careful-ish with their money – they had plans and schemes, and they put away a larger chunk of their salaries than most of their peers into pensions and savings plans. They allowed themselves one 'grand' holiday each year. When they'd started, after a luxurious, beyond-their-means honeymoon in the Maldives, they'd agreed they should do what they could before children came because afterwards, it was Devon and Cornwall for them – the self-catering cottages of their childhoods – for the foreseeable future. They didn't say that anymore, obviously – mustn't mention the 'C' word – but the principle remained. Jennifer would collect brochures – for Hawaii and the Seychelles; for Capri and South Africa. And Stephen would get the Snowline brochure his mates were passing around at work, and figure out which part of the three valleys he wanted to conquer next. She had never pushed – she knew how much he adored skiing. She just wondered, annually, why he hadn't quite worked out how much she hated it . . .

The other people in the chalet were okay. Every year there were changes – a couple would drop out, or be somewhere else – but a caucus of four or five couples remained faithful. They were quite nice, actually. The evenings were always fun. Someone else was cooking, a ludicrously old-fashioned three-course meal with sparkling wine and canapés, and peach schnapps flowed. It was the only place in the world, apart from at home with Hannah, where Jennifer played – and enjoyed – games. She was even pretty good at charades. The trouble was that after the big meal and the copious quantities of alcohol, and the late night, you were expected to get up before eight, shrug yourself into four layers of restrictive, unflattering clothing in a too-hot chalet and go skiing.

She'd abandoned formal tuition herself, after the second year. Not for the same reasons as Stephen, but rather because she decided that she preferred her humiliation to be less regimented. The Ecole du Ski Français was not renowned for its sympathy and gentleness. At 33, she reasoned that she didn't need to take unreasonable orders barked out impatiently at her by some suntanned kid smoking a Gauloise and planning a night out with his mates on a mobile phone. She skied alone, poring over the piste maps to find the longest, widest green runs available – the ones with the fewest lift-hazards, as she had come to think of them – and the most opportunities to stop for hot chocolate. Occasionally one of the other 'wives or girlfriends' would tag along with her, but they usually got bored and peeled away after the first three or four times around, and that suited Jennifer. She would rather fall down in front of total strangers than people she would be sharing raclette with later that evening.

She was rescued by the baby years. In the fourth year, she had been, suddenly, the only 'wife or girlfriend' not chalet-bound by a small infant or a large bump. She had skied the first two days that year, but then realized that a decision to stay home and help could be entirely 'blamed' on the babies and how adorable they were, and how maternal she must be, and she could easily enough have nothing whatsoever to do with skiing. In years five and six she hadn't even bothered to rent skis and boots. (That was the stage in the skiing holiday when you really remembered how much you hated it – the never-ending, winding route through the Alps from Geneva could be slept through, the chalets were hospitable enough, but the sensation of pushing your socked foot into a hard ski boot in a crowded and sweaty ski shop on the first night brought it all flooding back.)

This year, there were ten adults and seven babies. The oldest were three or four now, old enough to be indoctrinated, careering down the nursery slopes with no discernible skill or fear and wearing helmets that practically outweighed them. It was the second round of children, the youngest of whom was six weeks, who held court in the chalet the whole day. They were all getting more affluent, and the chalets had increased in comfort and grandeur over the years. Now there were ruddy-faced, perpetually smiling nannies bussed in at 8am to free the women up for a morning's sport.

They had no business being there, really, she and Stephen. It was in the company of these perfect nuclear families that Jennifer most felt a failure. She just wasn't performing as she should. These people were not good enough friends to ask the inevitable questions. She assumed they assumed there was a problem, and they were too polite or frightened to ask. Without being unkind, they had their heads down in the task of obsessive motherhood. She could help out, and she could make the right noises about their babies, but she couldn't really belong.

It spoilt the fun, too. Late nights of screaming drunken hilarity were out completely. Now, it was two glasses of wine with dinner and an early night because the nannies did not sleep in and the babies did not sleep through. At nights, not too tired from a hard day's skiing to lapse into the coma that seemed to creep up on everyone else, Jennifer lay listening to the traffic of young parents. Babies being fed, and burped and comforted. Toddlers being lifted for the toilet, and calmed down after nightmares, or, more spectacularly, falls from bed.

They'd driven her out of the chalet, these babies and their sunny caregivers, back onto the mountain. Talk about Hobson's choice. So, in a last-ditch attempt to conquer her fear, she'd booked a course of private lessons with an English company, who promised her an English instructor. She was to share with one other – a woman, her own age, who had never skied before. That sounded alright. She was on the chairlift to meet him for her first lesson. Stephen had been a bit sneery, she thought, when she'd told him, making some reference to the amount of money spent on lessons thus far, but she'd looked at him reproachfully and he'd apologized, briefly squeezing her shoulders on his way out early that morning and wishing her well.

She wondered fleetingly whether one of the things Stephen loved about these skiing holidays was the opportunity afforded him to escape from her. If they'd been side by side on sun loungers on a deserted beach he would have to talk to her. Here they were never alone, except for the five minutes he was in bed before her while she washed her face and brushed her teeth, and he was always apparently deeply asleep by the time she climbed in beside him.

If you didn't talk much, you didn't have to acknowledge that there was anything wrong. If neither one of you drew attention to the widening gap between you, you could pretend it didn't exist.

The skiing instructor was just where he was supposed to be, standing beside a flag bearing the company's name, a little way from where the chairlift disgorged its passengers. She tried to come to a graceful stop in front of him, but ended up planting her pole at an unnatural angle to her body, too far away, and jamming herself into an ungainly skid, barely managing to stay on her feet. He was short and slight, with dark wavy hair that was too long, and very dark brown eyes. He was deeply tanned, but the hollow of his neck was very white. When he spoke, it was with an incongruous Newcastle accent. He was on his phone when she arrived at the appointed meeting place and her heart sank, but he raised his hand in apology and continued to talk in Geordie French. Her translation and his tone told her that he was begging his landlady for an extension on his overdue rent. He had mastered 'louer' – to rent, and 'Vendredi', which she knew was Friday, and clearly several days later than it should have been, but not 'pay' or 'promise', both of which he said, with emphasis, and increased volume, in English. She smiled sympathetically, and turned to look for her fellow instructee. At that moment, a woman with a comedy hat and a startled expression, her poles raised in a defensive gesture, slid into view.

'I'm Wendy,' she said, her voice full of surprise and laughter, as though she wasn't entirely sure she was.

'I'm Jennifer.' They daren't shake hands, but nodded emphatically to each other in greeting.

'I feel like I'm at one of those anonymous meetings!' Wendy continued. 'Skiers Anonymous. I'm Wendy and I'm an absolute beginner. Actually, I've been taught by amateurs for the first part of the week, but they've given up on me . . .'

Jennifer found her giggle contagious. 'I'm Jennifer and don't I wish I was a novice! I've been coming for seven years, and I'm still this bad.' Wendy laughed out loud and Jennifer found herself laughing along. For the first time in ages, she realized how ludicrous it was.

'Great – we'll have a ball together then!'

Jennifer thought they just might.

'I'm Justin, and I'm going to change all that!' the little guy said, clearly warming to their theme, and clearly, now, off the phone. 'Sorry about that. Bit of a problem with the rent.'

'Bet it's expensive out here, if the cost of my chalet is anything to go by,' said Wendy, rolling her big eyes. When she spoke, the bobbles on her hat bounced.

'Not that bad where we are. No chalet maids, you see. Unless one of the boys gets lucky, of course. We just drink it all, to be honest!' Justin cheerfully replied. By now he'd stowed his phone and put his gloves back on. 'Right, ladies, let's get out of here and find somewhere a bit quieter and flatter, shall we? Follow me, bend zee knees . . .'

And he tried. He really tried. Wendy was unlike most women Jennifer had ever seen on the slopes. Clearly she didn't give a fig how she looked. When she started going faster than she wanted to go, or when her knees refused to cooperate in letting her make the required turn, and she was careering towards the drifts at the edge of the piste, she simply turned into the mountain and fell. And every time she did, she laughed. She was physically incapable of getting up again, so Justin had to ski to her and pull her up by her pole, every time. This had the combined effect of making Jennifer feel just a bit better about her own technique, and making her laugh so much with Wendy that her stomach ached more than her legs were ever going to.

After two hours, they begged in unison for a mulled wine stop. 'You're the customers, ladies,' Justin declared, unperturbed. He agreed to meet them in thirty minutes and they planted themselves in a quietish corner of the nearest mountainside restaurant and ordered two large glüweins.

Jennifer had forgotten the way you could be anyone you wanted to be in a holiday friendship. It wasn't about lying. It was just that the person you were making friends with had no former preconceptions about you. She was happy to take Wendy's lead, and be funny and self-deprecating and jolly. It felt good.

Although Jennifer would have guessed her new friend's age to be similar to her own, Wendy was a newlywed. She'd married into a long line of skiers late the previous autumn after a courtship so whirlwind and so summery that no mention of skiing had been made. The skiing husband and his skiing family made this pilgrimage annually, and non-participation was not an option so Wendy was fulfilling her wifely duties, with gusto.

By day two, they had mastered turning to some degree. Although Justin said he thought they held the new resort record for the number of turns taken to get down a green run, he agreed that they had all been beautifully executed. Wendy's fall rate had fallen away dramatically. They took a two-hour lunch, dismissing a willing Justin, who made eagerly for the nearest black run. Jennifer told Wendy about her mum, surprised even as she started speaking that she should be sharing such intimacies with a virtual stranger. Wendy was a great listener: her face flooded with sympathy and Jennifer didn't feel she had to be polite. She talked for a while. Wendy's own mum was the domineering matriarch of a large chaotic family in Cheshire, she said, and she squeezed her hand when she spoke and said that she couldn't imagine losing her mum, and how awful.

On the third day, their muscles were really rebelling. The blue sky of previous days had given way to something much greyer and less inviting. 'I'm a fair-weather skier, me!' Wendy declared. Despite Justin's half-hearted protests that the best way to deal with the pain and the weather was to ski through it, they stopped at lunchtime and descended back to the village in the cable car to share a fondue lunch. Wendy told Jennifer she didn't want children. Funny how, even when neither of you had them, two women their age couldn't be friends for more than three days without talking about kids. Like men and cars.

'Never have, really. I kept waiting, you know, for my biological clock to start ticking, but it never has. Thought I heard it, a few times. Realized it was my mates' — getting louder and louder! Never heard my own, and I don't think I ever will.'

'What about your husband?'

'He knows, of course. It wouldn't be fair to a bloke, would it, to marry him without having that conversation first? We had it very early on, to tell you the truth. When you're our age, you can't afford to muck about, can you? After 35, the whole world is one massive speed date, isn't it?'

'You're not *that* old!'

'I'm 39. Dangerous number, that. Just about "too late".'

'Too late for what?'

'Babies. It's all downhill, isn't it, after the age of 40? Nature remains unmoved by women's lib. We're supposed to have our babies when we're in our teens, aren't we – body wise? Not wait until we've got a degree, broken through the glass ceiling at work and slept with a load of toads while looking for Prince Charming, like I did. So a woman who's 39 usually has a neon sign on her forehead, flashing BABY MACHINE at blokes. Which, strange to tell, they do not find all that alluring . . .'

'But not you.'

'Nope.'

'Why not, do you think?'

Wendy shrugged. 'No especially complex reasons, I don't think. I had a perfectly normal childhood. Great parents, lots of kids around. I'm not "damaged" or anything like that, I don't think. I don't not like babies, don't get me wrong. Or children. In fact, I prefer children to babies – you can talk to them. Babies always frightened me a bit, to be honest. I once asked a friend of mine, who had a couple of kids, why she'd done it, and when I got her to stop going on about how wonderful it is, and how precious, and all that bollocks, she shrugged and said: "What about when you're old – aren't you worried you'll be lonely?" That didn't strike me as the best reason in the world to do it. I'm sure it's not true for everyone, but it really made me think. I wonder why people *do* do it? Change everything, I mean. It's just . . . well, I suppose I think that my life is pretty great without them. I've always loved my freedom, not being tied down. I love to please myself – selfish bugger, probably. I've no desire to spend my life exaggerating about my kids' achievements, covered in stains, with a handbag full of Wet Ones and tiny boxes of raisins.' She'd obviously thought about this.

'But you've got married.'

'Yes, true – but to someone who, it turns out, thinks just like me.'

'You're lucky.'

Wendy narrowed her eyes and stared intently at Jennifer.

'And you? You've had the world according to me, whether you wanted it or not. What about you and your fella?'

'I'm not sure my husband thinks just like me. I used to think he did, but now . . .'

'You're not so sure?'

'I'm not.'

'About babies?'

'About everything.'

Wendy waited to see if she was going to continue.

'And about babies – he really wants them.'

'And you don't?'

'I'm not sure.'

'How old are you?'

'37.'

'See, the danger years. Told you.'

Jennifer laughed. 'That's no answer.'

'No. Don't think I can come up with an answer, my

love. I'm not a card-carrying member of the Anti-baby Club. That's just me. And my fella, lucky for me. Seems to me, you've got to think whether you don't want babies at all, or you don't want babies with him. And I don't mean to sound like the Time Police, and you'd be entitled to tell me it's none of my bloody business – and you wouldn't be the first – but I've never thought much of small talk. I'd rather have big talk. But you've got to do it soon. If it's yes to babies but no to babies with him, you've got to give both of you a chance, haven't you?'

Jennifer had a sudden image of Stephen with someone else's children. It was a new thought for her, and a very peculiar one.

'You're too clever for your own good.'

'Ah, see! Babies haven't sucked my brain out through my boobs, that's why!' Jennifer winced, but Wendy looked unrepentant. 'Can't ski for toffee though, can I?' She laughed.

She'd never had a conversation like this with anyone else, not about Stephen. Not with Lisa, nor with Barbara, though she had sensed, a few times, that her mother was trying to lead her that way, and she'd panicked and drawn the conversation elsewhere. She'd never really understood why she hadn't wanted to admit these things to her mum, to admit failure. It wasn't as if Barbara's life had been perfect. Bloody hell, who knew, until Amanda's letter, how imperfect a person she'd been! She didn't know where the foolish pride came from. She was surprised that Wendy didn't offend her, to be honest. But maybe it was the ephemeral quality of their relationship that made it okay – the fact that she'd probably never see her again. Or maybe she was just that desperate . . .

*

341

The next day was their last lesson together. Wendy was leaving that night, on the snow train. They got down a blue run with a red patch halfway down without falling once, yelling with triumph, and hugged a startled Justin at the bottom. As they parted, exchanging email addresses neither of them really believed they would ever use, Wendy held her close for a minute and wished her luck.

'Think about it this way,' she said, 'and see if it helps . . . Imagine he's not here any more. Be as melodramatic or as low key as you want. He's left you for someone else, or you've moved away for some reason, or he's dead, or in a coma or something – whatever. Then think about how that makes you feel. That'll tell you, if you're really honest with yourself, whether there's something to save.'

Jennifer watched the retreating back of the temporary friend she had granted more access than people she had known her whole life, skis and poles balanced on her shoulders like a pro, and realized that the admiration of their early acquaintance had become more like envy. This woman knew exactly what she wanted, and she'd got it. How was it possible that she could still be so mired in indecision? One thing she was sure of was that she couldn't keep blaming Stephen, and she couldn't keep ignoring it.

She spent the rest of the afternoon in her room, thinking, and pretending to read. That evening was the chalet maid's night off, and they were all to fend for themselves in the wild hinterland of the village. Emboldened, perhaps by Wendy's words, or that last blue run, Jennifer determined to separate Stephen from the others, for this one night at least. They would go somewhere nice, just the two of them, and talk, really talk. She took a long, hot bath, full of Molton Brown bubbles, dried her hair and applied the kind of make-up that looks bare-faced, and waited for Stephen on their bed, naked under a dry towel.

Sex had become, for her, leverage. She still enjoyed it, and knew herself to be quite good at it, at least so far as Stephen was concerned – she hadn't had a lot of practice on other people. Well, no one, except for John, and she didn't remember that part of their lives as being particularly fulfilling. She was a late developer, but she knew what worked for her and Stephen. Mostly, these days, it was a means to an end. It softened Stephen up, mellowed him out.

She heard everyone come in. It was already dark outside, and it had started to snow again. Boots were stamped against the ceramic tile floor, the whistling kettle was boiled for tea. Everyone was laughing and exuberant. Children ran up and down in the room above her head, screaming wildly. She put her head back against the wall behind the bed, closed her eyes and tried to think sexy thoughts amid the ensuing chaos. There was this one time, really early on, when she and Stephen had made love . . . she supposed she remembered it so well, and as being so perfect, because it marked the real beginning of them. It was all new and raw. She'd been someone she didn't recognize, and she'd liked being her. There'd been a mirror, across from the bed, in the place where they were staying and they'd watched themselves. She'd never done anything like that before; it was the first time she'd seen herself naked in such a position, and she'd surprised herself by being totally into it, watching herself climb on top of Stephen, watching them move together, their faces, their straining. She thought about that, her hand moving gently under the towel, and waited for him, with increasing, delicious impatience.

He knew from the look on her face, when he closed the door behind him and saw her lying there, what she was doing, what she wanted. And his response was gratifyingly instantaneous, despite the long day of black runs. He smiled, and locked the door. Of all the things he might have expected at the end of his day, this was not one of them and he had no desire to deconstruct her urge. Coming over, slowly, he knelt beside the bed, pulling the towel to one side and planted a trail of little kisses around her navel. She peeled his thermals over his head, wanting to get to his skin, and he took his ski trousers down to around his knees, his growing erection clearly visible through his long johns.

'I stink like a racehorse.' He spoke against her stomach.

'I don't care.'

'I should take a shower.' His voice was muffled. She wasn't sure she could wait that long. He raised his face, and grinned sexily at her. 'Come with me?'

'I dried my hair.'

It was his turn. 'I saw, I don't care.' He pulled her to her feet.

In the bathroom, he turned the water on to hot and pulled off the rest of his clothes, leaving them in a heap on the floor. Turning back to her, he put both arms around her and drew her close, so their bodies were touching all the way down. She watched herself again in the mirror, watched the angle of her long neck as he gently kissed and nuzzled at it, until the steam covered it, and them. In the shower, he reached for the soap.

She took it from him without speaking and lathered it between her hands, then ran them under his arms, across his shoulders and down his stomach. He was in good shape, and she could feel the hard muscles running under the surface. His belly had a pelt of dark hair, and she ran her fingers through it possessively. He gasped when she took hold of him. The water was running on both their faces as they kissed. He pushed her hand off him, then, and for a moment she was worried, but he held her close, his hands resting in the small of her back.

'I just want to hold you, Jen. Just let me hold you for a moment.' She let him. It felt good.

Then, at last, they both wanted more. Wrapping themselves in towels, their hair dripping, they went back to the bed and lay down together. Either the ambient noise in the chalet had stopped, or they just weren't listening anymore. They didn't make a sound either. The sex was slow, and almost silent. When the headboard started banging against the wall, Stephen grabbed a pillow and shoved it roughly down between the wood and the plaster, silencing it, without ever breaking his rhythm. It had been a while, and they had both been turned on by the shower; it didn't take long. Stephen came with his face pushed into the pillow next to hers, his fingernails digging into her buttocks.

Doors opened and closed as they lay recovering their breath. People yelled goodbye, shouted the name of a bar to anyone listening, and then it was quiet again. The room was dark, lit only by the bathroom, and Stephen went to sleep beside her, one hand still on her belly. She looked at his familiar face, then gently slid out from under his heavy arm and went to the bathroom. Her carefully applied mascara had run and she wiped it away with a cotton ball and some remover. Her chest was flushed with sex, and she wrapped the dressing gown tightly around her before tiptoeing into the hall, ready with a quick excuse. She didn't bump into anyone – it seemed they were the last people left in the chalet. In the kitchen she found a half-drunk bottle of Cava, two Duralit water glasses and a tube of Pringles. She gathered her booty and went back to their room. Stephen had shifted slightly. He woke up when he heard her close the door and rubbed his damp hair sheepishly.

She smiled, and poured two glasses. The very reason for the seduction – the need for serious conversation – had passed for the moment. She felt suffused with the same calm she had been seeking for Stephen. She kissed him, briefly, on the lips, then they clinked glasses and drank.

Jennifer put her glass down and jumped onto the bed beside him.

'Are you hungry?'

'Not really. Had an enormous piece of fruit cake before, with my tea. You?'

'Nope.'

'What do you want to do, then?'

She grinned. 'What are you smiling for?'

'Do you know what I want to do?'

'No, tell me.'

'I want to stay here, in this room, all night.'

'And do what, play scrabble?'

'Play . . . but not scrabble . . .' She leaned across him and grabbed her Cava. Filling her mouth, she kissed him again, opening her lips so that some of the fizz tingled against his. Stephen groaned.

'What's brought this on?'

'Do I need a reason?' Please, she thought. Please don't analyse this. Please.

346

'Nope. Never. Just asking.'

'So can we?'

'Can we what?'

'Stay here and play . . .'

'Too bloody right we can . . .' Stephen rolled on top of her and laughed. 'In fact, you ask any of the other blokes here, what they'd think of that suggestion, and they'd all chew your arm off.'

'I hope you're not steering the conversation around to swinging?!'

'Not with you, you vain mare! With their own wives . . .'

'What would they do with the babies?' The second it was out of her mouth, Jennifer wished it was left unsaid. That was the high octane subject. But Stephen let it go. His mind was on other things. 'If these are the perks of being childless, I say bring it on . . .'

After the second time, it was Jennifer who fell asleep, sated and content in a way she didn't remember feeling for a while. Her mind felt empty. When she woke, an hour or so later, Stephen was smiling at her, his fingers in her hair.

'I don't know, you promise a guy a night of lust and then you fall asleep on him.' But he was smiling. She poked him gently in the stomach with her index finger. 'Be careful what you wish for, stud.'

Stephen clucked quietly, and pulled her gently, so that her head was on his chest. She couldn't see his face, but she could hear his heart beating.

'Why can't it always be like this?' he asked, with a sigh that might have been happy or sad. He wasn't talking about the sex.

'I don't know.'

'I love you, Jen.'

She took a deep breath, feeling him holding his own breath, and his chest tighten beneath her face, and then told him the truth.

'And I love you.'

He paused long enough for her to know that he hadn't necessarily expected her to respond that way.

'So why do we let all the other crap get in the way, then?' His voice was small. 'Why are we making each other so unhappy?'

It was the first time he had said out loud that either one of them was unhappy. Jennifer stayed where she was – she didn't want to see him.

'I think . . . I think we've let things get bigger and bigger, and not sorted them out. We've been . . . I've been a coward.'

'Well, if you have, then so have I. It isn't all your fault.'

'Can we talk . . . now?'

She thought of a song she'd once loved. The words – words she'd never forgotten – said something about love having a voice of its own, but there only being a limited time when two people could both hear it. Something like that. Maybe this was their time. Maybe now they were both listening. She sat up, pulling her dressing gown over her shoulders. Reaching for the bedside light, she turned it on and they both squinted against the sudden brightness. Stephen looked right at her, and his eyes filled with tears that she hadn't heard or felt coming. She couldn't remember the last time she'd seen him cry. If she ever had . . .

'You don't want to have a baby with me, do you?'

Another first. That hadn't been said out loud. She didn't answer.

'I should have asked you straight out, ages ago. I've been an idiot. I didn't want to ask because I was afraid of what the answer would be. But you'd have to be an idiot not to realize what was going on, when you wouldn't go for the tests last year. It wasn't anything to do with the doctors, or being afraid you might not be able to have kids, or anything else you told me, or I told myself. That was all a smokescreen. I've known for a while. You don't want to have a baby with me.'

'Stephen.'

'Don't you love me anymore?' One tear had rolled down his cheek. Jennifer found it unbearably sad and shocking. 'I know I've been a pig – I know I have. I don't know what came first. I've been a pig because I've been frightened. I know that sounds like the biggest excuse ever, and I know that doesn't make it okay, but I think . . .' He struggled to put his feelings into words. 'I think I've been afraid, for ages and ages, that you don't really love me, and that you've been getting ready to leave me. For a while I wondered if there was someone else.' She shook her head vigorously. 'I almost wished there was – that would have been something I understood, a tangible problem, something I could try and fix. The baby thing is a red herring, really, isn't it? I mean, whether we have a baby together or not isn't the point. I mean, I want one. I always thought we'd have one . . . more maybe. But it isn't really about that, is it?'

He was right. It wasn't. She wasn't Wendy: it wasn't cut and dried for her.

'We don't even know if I can.'

'That doesn't matter. I don't care – that's not what matters to me. What matters is whether you're going to stay with me, Jen. Not whether we have a baby. You not trying to find out why we can't ... that's what that means.'

She didn't know he'd figured that out. She didn't know he'd been thinking in shades like that. He had seemed so black and white, so cruelly simplistic. That's why she hadn't attempted this conversation before. She'd expected an ultimatum, threats. She hadn't expected he would have thought this through, and had been able to see what was going on in her head. She didn't know he still knew her that well.

He was still speaking. 'I don't know what's gone wrong, Jen. When we're ... like that ... like we were just now, it seems the unlikeliest thing in the world that we're falling apart. Then, other times, I feel we have no chance.'

'When do you feel that?' She didn't know he did.

'I don't know. Times like when your mum died last year. You shut me out. You made me feel like I'm not important, that I couldn't help and you didn't want my help anyway.'

'I didn't mean to do that.'

'But you did. You did make me feel like that – you're always so strong.'

'I'm not strong at all.'

'You are. You don't see what I see.'

'I'm sorry, Stephen. I'm sorry.'

'Don't say you're sorry.'

'What do you want me to say?'

'I want you to say that we are worth saving.' She thought of Wendy, and her words of earlier. 'That's the only thing that matters now.'

The snow was falling thickly now. Through the gap in the thin cotton curtains she could see it on the window ledge, almost an inch thick now. Jennifer watched it for a moment, swirling and dancing outside. This was it; this was crunch time. Whatever she said now, however she answered his question, it had to be true. She had to mean it.

Her mind swam with a dozen images. Wendy, on the piste, Mum's journals and her letter, Kathleen laughing about Brian in the garden, their wedding day, just now in the mirror, his face running with tears . . . She turned back to look at him and felt her own tears starting now. Suddenly she was very tired. She was tired of this, of being unhappy, of making herself unhappy. She didn't even understand it. She'd maybe never be able to explain it to him, or to anyone else. Or to herself.

'I want us to stay together, Stephen. That's what I want. I want us to stay together and be happy, and be good to each other . . .'

And that was the truth.

'Do you think we can?'

He stroked her shoulder. 'I think, if we want to, we can do anything.'

They woke up late, the next morning, and only then when someone banged on their door, giving Stephen a five-minute warning for the shuttle bus.

'You lot go. I'll see you later,' he answered sleepily, one arm clamped around her waist under the duvet. 'I'm skiing with Jen today.'

She groaned. But she was delighted.

The rest of the week was like a honeymoon. It seemed so straightforward. During the conversation, they'd both committed to this new start and it seemed so easy now to enjoy each other, to be together. Jennifer knew this was a holiday, that they had to carry on when they got back home, that it wouldn't really count until they did. But it was such a relief. They skied, they had long lunches, holding hands under the table. They took longer siestas, making love quietly in the chalet, while the young parents swopped envious glances. They both slept like babes, mountain air, physical exertion and a profound sense of newness acting like a sleeping pill for them both. It was the best time she could remember them having together. For years. Maybe ever.

Mark

Amanda had called collect long distance, far too early. She and Ed were about to get on a flight, she said. Next stop Peru. She didn't know what the internet café situation would be like, or how often they'd be able to charge their mobile phones or get to a call box. They were going to do some trek thing. She wanted to let him know – let *all* of them know – that they were fine. Well. Solvent. Safe. Happy. And at the end she'd told him she loved him. She hadn't said that for a long, long time. He'd lain in bed, after she rang off, and imagined her – where she was, what she was doing. He wished he'd had the chance to meet Ed, but he instinctively trusted him. He still missed her, even though it had been years since she'd lived with him. He loved her too.

For years Mark had been a smoker. Who hadn't? Not a serious one – more the ubiquitous 'social smoker'. He'd given up when he'd met Barbara. She didn't want him to smoke around the children, and he wanted to be around the children . . . Thing was, it had been much easier than he had thought. All except for the first ciga-rette of the day. The one that went with Radio 4, a cup of coffee and *The Times*. He went cold turkey on every other fag of the day, and it was fine. It took six months to give up that one.

And now, most other times of the day – on the average, good day – were okay. And this was the time he most missed Barbara. In the morning. His first Barbara of the day – the one that went with Radio 4, a cup of coffee and *The Times*. The one who smelt of shampoo and toothpaste and Fracas, and sat next to him at the breakfast bar, and listened when he talked about the day ahead. Maybe he should take up smoking again.

Wandering aimlessly into the kitchen in search of one of his daughters, he picked up the local paper from the kitchen counter and saw the 'flats to let' section, dotted with red circles and question marks. He was reading a few, and being profoundly grateful he owned his own home, when Lisa came into the kitchen. 'What's all this? Either things with Hannah are worse than I thought, or you're making plans . . . ?'

Her face was full of mock reproach. 'You and Hannah will be fine! It's me, preparing to fly the nest, again. I can't stay here forever, can I?'

He supposed not.

'Can't go back to where I was . . .'

'Are you sure about that?' He hadn't heard from Andy since they'd been to the pub. Now it seemed apparent that Lisa hadn't either. He'd come home hopeful. And sheepish. Desperate to tell her he'd seen Andy, that he believed he still loved her, that he hoped there was a way through the mess. Afraid she'd go nuts if she knew he'd interfered.

'Andy can't forgive me, Mark. He's made that pretty clear.'

'Are you sure he doesn't just need more time?'

'I don't think time will make any difference at all. Truly . . . I don't think this is one of those "time heals all" situations. I think I have to accept that it's over.' Her voice broke. 'And if I accept that I have to get on with my life. "Move on" – isn't that what they call it?' She sounded sarcastic and harder than normal.

'But this is move *out*, not on.'

'They're the same thing, Mark.' She smiled right at him for the first time and put her arm up, round his shoulder. 'You'll live. It's not like I've been doing your laundry.'

'I meant to mention that, actually. Why not?'

'Dream on! I've never done a man's laundry in my life, and I'm not starting now.'

'God save me from feminism.'

'Huh!'

'I'll miss you.' Mark's tone was suddenly serious. He sounded wistful.

'I'll miss you too. But we can't keep playing Derby and Joan, you and me. Watching crap TV and going to bed early; waggling our fingers at Hannah.' She waggled, didactically, to emphasize her point. 'We're both hiding out here a bit, aren't we?'

Mark leant his head on her arm. 'Where did they teach you to do that?'

'Do what?'

'Take a conversation about you and make it into one about me?'

'Classic deflection?!'

'Exactly! You know who.'

'Mum.'

He was right. She had been a master at it – it was how she had tackled every one of the issues she and Lisa ever had.

'So . . . back to you, my evasive one. Where are you going to go?'

'Local, I hope. Somewhere I can afford, obviously. I've been spoilt, I'm afraid, by the whole double income thing. Andy paid the mortgage, I did the bills. Doing both will be a stretch.'

Mark hated the idea of her struggling, but he knew her well enough to know that she would rather eat baked beans in a freezing hovel than take money from him to help out. He didn't think it would come to that. He wondered whether he should raise the trust. He and Barbara had matching wills, but Barbara had had her own plans for the money she'd made with the shop. The girls knew Barbara had put money in trust for them after they'd sold it. There'd been a difficult, sad meeting at the lawyer's office when it had all been explained to them, last summer, after the funeral. Mark was a trustee – so was the lawyer. It wasn't a fortune, but it was probably the deposit on a flat. At least she knew it was there if she needed it . . .

Lisa picked up the paper.

'There are a few possibilities in here. I'll make a couple of calls later. Go and see some places, maybe.' She sounded half-hearted, even to herself.

'I'll come with you, if you want. Second pair of eyes.'

She squeezed his forearm. 'Thanks, Mark. I know.' It was neither an acceptance nor a refusal. 'You've been a bloody star, letting me stay, listening to all my bleating.'

'I think the bleating has been fairly mutual.'

'Maybe. See – we're Manic Depressives Anonymous. Got to shake it off!'

'You'll be alright, you know.'

'I know I will. Eventually.'

He pulled her into a sudden, fierce hug. Lisa let herself be held for a while. He felt her relax into him.

'I miss my mum.' She sounded muffled and instantaneously tearful in his sweater, like she was 5 years old again.

'I miss her too.'

They felt themselves teetering on the edge of an abyss they had both fallen into too many times in the last few months. Both smelt the self-pity in the fibres of each other's clothes and the air around them. Lisa moved first. She pushed herself back from her step-father, open palms on his chest. 'Right,' she said, her tone no-nonsense. 'Come on, enough of this wallowing.'

He aped her tone. 'Okay. What's on your agenda today, Gidget?'

'Well, I'll be procrastinating a little bit on phoning the estate agents so, I'm going to meet Jen for lunch. She just got back from skiing, so there'll be venting to do! You?'

'Not a lot. Thought I'd try and engineer some "quality time" with Kevin.' He grimaced. He and Lisa had recently started calling Hannah 'Kevin' behind her back, after Harry Enfield's belligerent, monosyllabic teenage character. Having your own Kevin wasn't quite so funny as watching one on television. 'A bit of gardening, maybe. It's all about to go crazy out there.' It had been raining for what felt like weeks. Spring was about to spring in a big way.

'Do you want to come with me? We're going Chinese, in town – the one next to Tesco. You haven't seen Jen for a while, have you?'

'No, no. You go – girls' lunch.'

If Lisa noticed a tightening in his tone, she didn't say anything.

As he watched her drive away, he wondered whether he should have gone and faced Jennifer. It had to be done at some point. Otherwise there would continue to be a rift, and that rift would have to stop being a secret, and then it would have to be explained to Hannah. Everyone else had sorted themselves out. He knew it was up to him to offer Jennifer absolution. He sighed. Speaking of Hannah – he glanced at his watch. 11.30am, and, so far as he knew, she was still snoring upstairs. It seemed to be all she wanted to do these days – stay out, sleep late, watch Channel 4 in her pyjamas all afternoon and go out again. He put the kettle on. Perhaps she would respond to a cup of tea . . .

Jennifer arrived first and chose a table in the window of the restaurant. She sat, watching the world go by from behind a red-and-white gingham café curtain, and sipping a Diet Coke. While she waited, she thought about her sister. Sentences she wanted to speak formed in her mind, and she rehearsed them quietly. She supposed she must get this urge to want to fix things from their mother. It was her big theme, this year. She'd fixed herself, or at least she believed she was on the way. Now she wanted to fix Lisa. She'd never realized how alike they were. Both, in their way, commitment phobes, non-believers. She hadn't recognized it in herself as readily as she had seen it in Lisa. You could see Lisa holding herself back from Andy. She might blame all sorts of things. Andy had been married before. Weren't the statistics for second marriages always lousy? Andy had a child. All of that. But that wasn't it. She wasn't prepared, never had been, to commit.

Jennifer had told herself she'd bought into the whole commitment thing. She'd married Stephen, hadn't she? She'd put on the dress and walked down the aisle and said the vows in front of everyone. But that just made her more of a fraud than Lisa. More self-delusional too. It was the baby – that represented the real commitment to Stephen. That was where she'd fallen down. So they had more in common than either of them thought.

They'd been nothing alike, as kids. Jennifer liked dolls and dressing up; Lisa had Matchbox cars, and an encyclopaedic knowledge of tractors. Jennifer had liked to play with girls while Lisa preferred the company of boys – years before she knew what she really wanted to do with them. If they had homework, Jennifer did hers on Saturday morning; Lisa was a Sunday night girl, if not a Monday morning on the bus one. When they were both at university, they'd visited each other – once. Jennifer had come to Lisa first and been dragged to a smoky party where the music was too loud for conversation, and friendships were forged through the passing around of a joint. Gone home alone to a messy room in a damp shared house, full of unironed laundry and cups of half-finished tea while Lisa stayed behind to work on a guy she was interested in.

When Lisa visited Jennifer, her room – in a civilized hall of residence, with an ensuite shower room, no less – smelt of washing powder and Anaïs Anaïs. Jennifer's friends all seemed to be girls. They existed in a girly, giggling gaggle completely alien to Lisa. They did a yoga class, and ate at a vegetarian café. Jennifer introduced her to John, a man Lisa found so anodyne that she barely addressed a remark to him through two rounds in the student union. He had rounded shoulders, Lennon glasses and a shaving rash. Lisa believed she knew the type, and she just wasn't interested. Jennifer was cross with her, she knew – she said she hadn't given him a chance. Lisa retorted that Jennifer had been going out with him for almost the entire year, which was surely chance enough for any guy. Jennifer didn't come to the station, at the end of the weekend, to say goodbye. The whole thing had been a disaster.

By tacit agreement, neither visited the other again. They had no interest, at that point, in anything to do with the other's lives. They were sisters, of course, but it seemed they were not destined to be friends. What common ground the shared experience of their child-hood had given them ebbed away as soon as they moved away from that home. It might have been more of a wedge, if it hadn't been for Mum. Mum and Mark. That gave them, finally, a reason to come together again: shared, indignant disapproval.

There were some conversations in your life that you remembered vividly, forever. Mum telling them she was pregnant, that she was going to marry Mark – that was one of *those* conversations. The three of them had been in the garden at Carlton Close. It was June – the start of the long summer break from university. For both of them the significance of home had shifted inexorably in recent months. It had taken its place as a stop on their journey, no longer the destination. They loved their mum, and their kid sister, Amanda, whose delight at their return almost compensated for her irritating tend-encies to climb on their beds, chattering inanely, at six in the morning. They were fond of their familiar rooms, the Spaghetti Bolognaise and the fact that their laundry disappeared and then reappeared, miraculously folded and ironed. But now they were just passing through – it wasn't really where they wanted to be.

Jennifer was going inter-railing with John in a few weeks – a trip they had meticulously planned and dreamt of. Lisa was in far too much debt to consider something like that. She'd spent what money she had by the sixth week of term, raced through her overdraft limit with similar alacrity and seriously needed to earn some extra cash. She was going to Weston super Mare, where her friend Emma lived, to chambermaid with her in a 3* hotel as soon as the season started. Long hours, but good pay. And all the bars and nightclubs of an English seaside town to explore after the evening turn down . . . Characteristically, both sisters thought they were the most likely to have fun . . .

They'd known Mum was going out with someone. She would never have kept something like that a secret. She'd never have had the nerve, after she'd extracted every nugget of information from Lisa about every boy she'd been out with. She'd told them, on the phone, that a guy had come into the shop and that they'd got talking, and that he'd asked her to lunch. They knew she liked him. Beyond that, neither of them had thought about it much – Jennifer busy trying to read train timetables in six different European languages, and Lisa's days and weeks and terms passing in a fog, literally and metaphysically. So it was a bit of a conversation stopper, when the news came.

'I thought you should know, it's getting serious.' She'd mixed them all a white wine spritzer, laughing, as she had done before because she was so glad they were both finally old enough to drink with her.

'*How* serious?' Jennifer had asked.

'*Very* serious, actually . . .'

'How serious is "very serious"?' Lisa echoed, taking in the inane grin spreading across their mother's face. 'Are you in love with him?'

'Oh, yes. Very much in love with him.'

Jennifer had squirmed a little. This was far more Lisa's territory. She wasn't sure she wanted to think about Mum being in love.

'I suppose I'd better meet him, then, hadn't I?'

It hadn't happened, so far. Now Lisa couldn't remember whether that was by her design, or her mother's. It hadn't seemed important.

'I've met him,' Jennifer added, unnecessarily. She was pleased, for once, to have something to lord it about over Lisa. Lisa always made her feel so . . . gauche and immature. No one else did that.

'Good for you!' Lisa's tone told her that her remark had hit home. Of course, reprisal was swift. 'But forgive me if I don't think you're the ultimate judge of men.'

'That's a horrible thing to say – pot calling the kettle black! Do any of your blokes stick around long enough for you to get to know them?'

'Girls, don't fight.' Mum's tone was light. Like she wasn't really listening to the squabble.

'Did you hear what she said, Mum?'

'I heard what you *both* said. This isn't about you, believe it or not! I'm trying to tell you both something.'

'What?'

'Mark's asked me to marry him. And I've said yes.'

Jennifer spat a mouthful of spritzer back into her glass. 'Bloody hell, Mum!'

'Yes, well, I'm sorry to shock you. Seemed to be the only way I could get your attention.'

It had worked.

'And while you're busy catching flies and looking stupefied, I'd better tell you the rest.'

'There's more?'

'There's a lot more. I'm having a baby.'

'You're what?'

'I'm having a baby, with Mark.'

'What do you mean, having a baby? You mean you want to have a baby, with Mark? Mum, you're 45! You're . . . like . . . well, you're way too old to have a baby.'

'I don't mean I *want* to have a baby. Well, that's not true – of course I want to! You're making me nervous . . .' For the first time, they heard a slight tremor in her voice. 'I mean, I AM HAVING ONE! I hate to defy medical science and burst your bubble, Lisa, but I'm pregnant. I'm three months pregnant.'

Neither of them had a single word to say, and Barbara had said everything she had to say for now. For long, long seconds, the three of them sat there, staring at each other. Jennifer looking like she might cry, Lisa with an expression of pure revulsion, and Barbara, defiant and, in every sense of the word, expectant.

Lisa broke the silence. She burst out laughing.

'Why are you laughing? I'm not joking. You realize I'm serious?'

'But I've never met him.'

'I know – you haven't been home. You'll meet him now. You can meet him tonight, if you want to.'

'Does Amanda know him?' Amanda was at school.

'Yes, of course. She lives here! This isn't some flash-in-the-pan, girls. I know it's a shock . . .'

*

On reflection, that year was probably the time the two sisters had been closest. It all went very fast after that. Mark was introduced, and inspected. Then the house was put on the market. Boxes marked 'Lisa's stuff' and 'Jennifer's stuff' were filled and put into store. That had particularly horrified Jennifer. 'What if I need things from it?' The dismantling of the home the four of them had shared since Amanda's birth was painful, and felt cruel. It was 'their home' suddenly.

'For God's sake, you two!' Barbara had exclaimed in exasperation. 'You haven't lived here since you both went off to university. You've been using it as a doss house for the last I don't know how long. I don't understand what all this sentimentalist rubbish is all about. You'll always be welcome in the new house. You're acting like you've been suddenly turned into Brazilian street children.'

They weren't welcome in the caravan. At least, however welcome they may have been, there was no room for them. Lisa christened it the 'Passion Wagon', a name Jennifer loathed and never used. She and Jennifer tutted together, and rolled their eyes together, and tried not to look at Barbara's swelling form too much together. It made them closer.

The détente didn't really come until Hannah was born. It was hard to stay disgusted when something so small and perfect and sweet-smelling entered the fray.

Lisa had arrived. She looked tired. She bent over and kissed Jennifer and then slid into the chair beside her, shucking her jacket off her shoulders to the back of the seat. 'Hiya, snow bunny!' Lisa peered at Jennifer, who looked tanned, except for startling white panda eyes, and relaxed. 'You look good, by the way. Must have been sunny.'

'It was. It was fantastic!'

'Wow! Fantastic? You hate skiing. Have you finally got the hang of it?'

Jennifer smiled to herself.

'Something like that! How are things with you?'

'I'm okay.'

'How is life with Mark and Hannah?'

'Tense. Hannah's turned into a teenager. A teenager with exams coming up. Grumpy? Just a bit. She's making up for lost time, I think. Slamming doors, four-hour phone calls, monosyllabic conversation . . . Too much eyeliner, not enough manners. She's driving Mark nuts, I think.'

'Poor him.' Jennifer wondered if her cheeks were red underneath the tan. She hadn't spoken to him in ages. Not since she'd been such a bitch.

'Poor Hannah, too. I feel sorry for her. She's had the shitty end of the stick for ages now, hasn't she? I think it's probably just normal, a bit of rebellion. Normal for anyone, actually, but when you've had a couple of years like the ones Hannah's just had, it's no wonder, is it?'

'I guess not . . .'

'Have you heard from Amanda?'

'Not much – you?'

'You know Amanda.'

Lisa wasn't sure either of them did, particularly. 'I had a postcard from Rio. Pert bottoms in neon thongs.'

'Me too.'

'Do you think that represents forgiveness?!'

'Or is she just saying "up yer bum"?'

'Room for one more?'

364

It was Mark. Jennifer's heart began to race when she saw him, and she wondered if her cheeks reddened. Lisa didn't seem to notice anything.

'You came!'

'Couldn't rouse Hannah from her pit, and I didn't fancy eating lunch alone, so I thought I would . . . unless I'm interrupting.'

'No, not at all. Sit down.' Lisa pulled out a chair.

Mark bent and kissed Jennifer on the cheek. 'How are you? You look well.'

Jennifer touched her face, where his lips had been. 'Thanks. I'm good.'

'I'm going to the loo. Get the waiter to bring me another glass when he comes to take your order, will you?' Lisa grabbed her bag from the back of the chair and wandered to the back of the restaurant in search of the ladies.

Jennifer fiddled self-consciously with her fork.

'Mark . . .'

He put a hand on hers, making her leave the fork alone.

'Listen, Jennifer. I'm glad we've got a minute.'

'Me too. I still want to, *need* to say how sorry . . .'

'I know. I know you are.'

'I was *so* unhappy. I know it's no excuse . . .'

'No excuse, maybe. But it's an explanation. It's always unhappy people who make all the trouble . . .'

'*Have* I made trouble? For you, I mean. I think me and Lisa and Amanda sorted things out before she left. What about you? Have I made trouble for you?'

'No, I don't think you really meant to, and you didn't. I can't say I wasn't surprised by what you told me. I was. But not really shocked somehow. And it's okay. It had nothing to do with me, what happened.'

'I know.'

'That was how her first marriage worked, I guess. It wasn't how ours did.'

'I know. But I upset you.'

'Do you know what really upset me?'

Jennifer shook her head, still not entirely comfortable with meeting his eyes.

'The thought that she might have believed I would have thought less of her. The fact that there were things I never told her for the same reason. The wastefulness of that worry. You know?'

Jennifer nodded.

'None of that matters, you see. It's all so very simple, when you love someone, *really* love someone.'

She had tears in her eyes now.

'Your unhappiness – that's the worst part. She would want me to help you. *She* wanted to help you; she was waiting for you for talk to her. You know that?'

He held Jennifer's hand. Now she looked at him and smiled.

'What?'

'I'm not unhappy anymore, Mark.'

'What do you mean?'

'I'm not unhappy. Me and Stephen, we're fixing things. We've both been making each other so bloody miserable, and we both thought we knew what the other one thought, and never bothered asking, and that's why things were so bad, why they weren't getting any better.'

'And?'

'And we talked. Skiing. We actually, finally, sat down and really, really talked about whether we wanted to be in this marriage. And we do, we both do – baby or no baby. For each other.'

'That's great. That's really great!'

She held his hand. 'It *is* great. All this time I've been letting my stupid foolish pride and my oh-so arrogant assumption that I understood everyone and everything stop myself from admitting the problem.'

Mark smiled shyly, and nodded a little.

'And I made it so bloody complicated. And it isn't, is it? Loving someone. You could have told me that a long time ago, couldn't you, if I'd just asked you? Or Mum could. You two understood it better than anyone else all along.'

'Understood *what*?'

Lisa was back, looking for her replenished glass. 'Understood *what*?' she repeated.

'Love, and how simple it is.' Jennifer replied. 'I was just saying, that Stephen and I have turned things around. Sorted things out for the better.'

'Bloody hell! How long was I in there? You two have gone all deep and meaningful on me, haven't you?'

'Sorry.'

'And it isn't, by the way – simple. At all. That's just some hokey Hallmark thing you've got going on.'

'It is. Like you and Andy. I know what's happened, but it doesn't matter. If you love each other you've just got to make him see it too.'

Lisa was gesturing to the waitress.

'Pardon my cynicism. I'm glad you've unravelled the deepest secrets of the universe – doesn't mean we all have.'

'Either you and Andy love each other, or you don't. The rest is all crap.'

'I love him. Think I managed to cure him completely of loving me. When I shagged someone else – someone, incidentally, who I absolutely didn't love. Smart move, hey? So that's my problem, isn't it? End of story. I don't think a Pollyanna approach is going to be of much use to me in this situation. Can we talk about something else now, please. Otherwise I'll be forced to sound really bitter – and no one likes their Singapore noodles with a side order of bitter and twisted, and then I'll get drunk, and it's only lunchtime . . .' She busied herself with the menu, but angry tears brimmed in her eyes and made the words hard to read.

It was horrible to see her so low. Mark felt it, and Jennifer felt it even more, since it stood in such sharp contrast to how she was feeling. Lisa sniffed hard and tried to make them smile. 'Tell us about your parallel turns, hey Jen?'

It was almost four when they left the restaurant. Mark offered to drive Lisa home – saying they could come back and get her car tomorrow, but she maintained she couldn't park it overnight where it was, and said she wanted to get some shopping done first, and that she'd meet him at home later. He figured she just wanted to be left alone for a while. Jennifer hugged her. 'Call me,' she said. 'I'll come looking at flats with you.'

Mark walked Jennifer to her car.

'Daughters, who'd have 'em,' she joked. 'First me, now Lisa.'

'Don't forget Hannah. She'll be waiting to bite my head off when I get home. And then there's Amanda . . .' He smiled ruefully. 'I sometimes feel like the guy in that cartoon, the one who plugs the hole in the dam and then another one springs, and he has to stick a finger in that one, and then another, and so on, until he's got all his fingers, and toes in holes, trying to hold it all back. And I'm only the bloody step-father!'

'Left all on your own to take care of us all.'

'Exactly. It's like you all held yourselves together for your mum, and the minute she was gone, you all fell apart . . .'

'I think some of us had been falling apart before that – we just couldn't let it show.'

'I know. I don't mean it. It's just that sometimes, I feel . . . tired.'

'Hey, I'm not surprised. I'm sorry I was part of the problem. I'm sorry I was such a colossal bitch. I'm better – I promise. Take me off the critical list.'

'Thank God! I'm really pleased, Jen. Really.'

'That means a lot to me. Now' – she kissed his cheek – 'go home and talk some sense into my little sis, will you?'

His two elder step-daughters had given him conflicting advice about Hannah, over lunch. Lisa advocated a softly softly approach, while Jennifer was more for coming down on her like a ton of bricks. Lisa thought he should be her friend, Jennifer said he needed to assert himself as her father. If Barbara had been alive . . . if she'd been well . . . he *knew* how they would have played it. Tough cop, soft cop with Barbara being the tough one. He was happy with soft cop; he could handle soft cop – that's what he was used to. That was how it had been with Amanda when she was growing up (how could he have been anything else – the new, young stepfather?) and with Hannah when she was younger and the issues seemed more manageable. He'd never sided with either one of them against their mother – not outright, but he'd provided the shoulder to cry on. And the occasional £10 note.

When she was about 15, Amanda borrowed a pair of Barbara's dangly, sparkling earrings, without asking, to wear to a party. She'd lost one, walking home. Creeping upstairs, she'd come round to his side of the bed, tugging gently on his T-shirt until he woke up, motioning for him to come out so she could talk to him. Instantly alert and alarmed, he'd done so, and then spent the next 45 minutes, at 2 o'clock in the morning, in his dressing gown, retracing her steps outside with a flashlight, looking for that bloody earring! He was that dad.

He didn't know what to do with Hannah. He remembered Barbara's mantra: keep them close, keep the lines of communication open and then you won't lose her. The trouble was, that mantra didn't apply. He blamed himself for this new display of independence and rebellion in his daughter. He'd told Lisa and Jennifer he thought it was all his fault. 'I've relied on her too much,' he said. 'I've made her my confidante, my companion, my emotional crutch, even. No wonder she's desperate to get away.'

'Nonsense.' This was Jennifer. 'She's just being a teenager. That's all! It's got nothing to do with what's happened. She'd be like this whatever. Your guilt is her biggest ally.'

'Hang on,' Lisa had retorted. 'You can't just sweep the last couple of years under the carpet. Hannah's had a hellish time.'

'I'm not saying she hasn't. I'm just saying that doesn't make it an excuse. Anyway, it isn't relevant why she's being like this, is it? It's what Mark does about it now. He has to stay in charge.'

'I'm running a home, not a detention centre for young offenders.' Jennifer was sounding a little draconian for Mark's tastes. Not for the first time . . .

'And you're making it sound like she's sleeping around and shooting up. Honestly, Jen – it's not that bad! A bit of attitude, a bit of backchat. She's hardly a candidate for rehab.'

'She's lying. Mark's just said so.'

'I said I *thought* she might be.'

'She can't be allowed to do that. Then you really have lost control.'

He was sitting in an armchair contemplating his control, or lack thereof, when Hannah appeared. Her entrance had been heralded by 45 minutes of toing and froing from bathroom to bedroom, and back, and by the buzz of the hairdryer, followed, blissfully, by the Red Hot Chili Peppers being turned off. Every song sounded the same, to him and they all made him want to put cushions over his head. Or polythene.

He swung round in the chair as she came down the stairs, trying not to look too much like a Bond villain. Then trying not to appear too shocked. Your child's phases of development never seemed to happen gradually – they were always, somehow, shocking. Long hair. Second front teeth – the ones that are always a little too big for their mouth. The ability to stand on two feet. And now, breasts and hips. It seemed to him that Hannah had gone skipping upstairs to bed five minutes ago, in a floral sprigged nightdress and pigtails, and had come down now transformed into a white Beyonce. All curvy. It was utterly disconcerting. Hannah was wearing long skinny jeans that buttoned at least four inches below her navel and a tight stripy top four inches above. The mid-section, a very slight layer of flesh on top of obviously strong muscle, drew your eye immediately. Until you noticed the eyeliner, applied in the Bardot method (if Bardot had been drinking meths and no longer had a very steady hand). The effect could have been comic, if it hadn't been so scary.

Barbara might have tried to send her straight back upstairs to wash her eyes; might have suggested a thermal vest to bridge the gap. Might have threatened to lock the front door and send the ride away. He'd seen her do it with Amanda. He didn't know what to say. Hannah's eyes – what little he could read of their expression – challenged him. 'Am I allowed to know where you're going?'

The other night, they'd fallen out about something relatively insignificant. Hannah had told him she was old enough to move out and live on her own. Over 16 – 'practically 17'. Which meant driving a heavy goods vehicle was out, but almost everything else was acceptable, apparently. He'd managed to bite back any comment about what she might live on, and he'd won that little argument, whatever it was – he couldn't remember. There seemed so many of them these days, but the 'old enough' argument felt like it was getting harder to win. Still, he hadn't meant to start so aggressively.

'Out!'

He sighed. 'Hannah, don't be so bloody rude! I asked a perfectly civilized question. Don't I deserve a proper answer?'

'Sorry. Yeah, you do.' Flashes of the daughter he recognized. 'I'm going out with Alice and Phoebe.'

He knew both girls. They were nice girls. They didn't, so far as he knew, wear eyeliner that looked as if it had been applied with a wax crayon.

'Really?'

'*Really*! If you don't believe me, you can call either one of their mothers and ask them.' He hated the defensive, aggressive tone – and his own anger. This wasn't how he wanted to talk with his little girl.

If she was calling his bluff, she was doing it well.

'And where are you going?'

'I'm taxi-ing it to Phoebe's – we're all meeting up there. Then there's a sixth-form party down her road, so no one's driving. And I'll get dropped back – probably by Alice's dad.'

'By when?'

'By one?'

'Those two are allowed to stay out then, are they?'

She looked at him as though he had suggested something absurd.

'Doh! Of course.'

Mark wasn't happy about it, but before he had the chance to say anything else, the taxi driver pulled up in the drive, honked impatiently and Hannah was gone, giving him a quick peck on the cheek, and responding to his request that she take a coat with a giggle (not a coat). For about a nanosecond he thought about calling Phoebe's mum. He didn't know these people, not well. He didn't want them to know he didn't trust his own daughter, even if that was true. Christ, life moved fast! At Christmas she'd been helping him bake and pick out a tree. Now she didn't seem to want to be with him at all.

Hannah sat back in the taxi and tried to calm herself. Her heart was beating so fast. He hadn't called her bluff, thank God. Her mates knew exactly what was happening – they'd spent the previous afternoon working on this evening's ensemble together. But their parents would be more than mystified by a call from Mark. The only part of what she had just told her dad that was actually true was the bit about the party. There *was* a party, but she wasn't going to it with her girlfriends, and it wasn't just down the road from Phoebe's house, and she wasn't going to be dropped off by Alice's dad. She told herself, and almost believed it, that she was protecting him, that it was for his own good – what he didn't know couldn't worry him. She knew what she was doing – it wasn't like she was taking risks. He should trust her more. She didn't like being asked questions all the time. If he trusted her, she wouldn't have to lie.

She was going with Nathan, of course. It was his friends having the party. He'd told her they'd be a bit older and cool. She'd decoded his explanation, hence the crisis wardrobe talks with Alice and Phoebe, and the eyeliner. She wanted to look older, to look right. Tonight was important. This was the first time she was properly meeting his friends, and she didn't want to be perceived as some silly schoolgirl.

He'd asked her to stay with him all night. His parents were away for the weekend, he said. They didn't have to have sex, he said. He'd said that straightaway, knowing it would be the first thing she thought of. He just wanted to be with her, to hold her all night, to wake up with her . . . It did sound wonderful. He'd said she could say she was with one of her mates.

She wasn't ready for that – in all sorts of ways. That was too big a lie. The consequences of being caught out frightened her. Mark would be furious, and his rage, while seldom seen and almost never before directed at her, was pretty scary. She'd be lucky to be allowed out on her own again before her 18th. And worse, he'd be really, *really* upset. She didn't want to do that to him. And then there was Nathan. He was still saying all the right things, about waiting until she was ready, and not wanting to pressure her, but he was doing things that made her think otherwise. His erection, strange and hard beneath his jeans, was omnipresent when they were alone together, and his hands were becoming more insistent, moving frustratedly beneath clothing she wasn't yet ready to remove. Things were getting hot and heavy – which thrilled and discomfited her – and she wasn't sure either of them actually believed it would be possible to sleep all night together in a bed without something 'significant' happening.

She'd said she couldn't make it. Made up a story about having to go somewhere with her dad early on Sunday morning. More lies. Sometimes she didn't recognize herself, and it had nothing to do with the eyeliner. He'd seemed pissed off. All the more important that the party was a success . . .

When Lisa finally let herself in as quietly as she could, it was after one in the morning. She expected the whole house to be asleep. Mark, sitting statue still in the armchair, scared her to death.

'What the hell are you doing, sat there in the dark? You made me jump!'

'Sorry. Waiting for Hannah.'

'She isn't home yet?'

'She said she'd be back by one. She promised.'

Lisa flicked on the light switch in the foyer and looked at her watch. 'It's twenty-five past. That's only a few minutes. Has she ever done this before?'

'No, she hasn't. But I'm still going to kill her. I only agreed to one o'clock under duress. In fact, I didn't even completely agree to one.'

Lisa peered at him, half-amused. He hadn't even asked her where she'd been all evening. 'You look knackered. You go up, she'll be back in a minute – I'll wait for her. I want a cup of tea anyway.'

'And miss the chance for another showdown? Are you kidding? This one's been brewing for hours. Jen would be proud of some of the lines I've been rehearsing in my head. Stick the kettle on – make two mugs . . .'

Hannah

She might have looked 18, but Hannah felt distinctly 13. She felt like she was still *Blue Peter* and that this was a very MTV crowd. The kid whose house it was, his parents were away too. Nathan said they'd given permission for the party, but Hannah suddenly doubted it. She'd been to loads of parties where people were drinking. She'd drunk her fair share of the bizarre cocktail that was teenage contraband – everything from cider to campari, and once, memorably (but for all the wrong reasons), anisette. But she'd never been somewhere where there were drugs. People were smoking joints here and passing them to her. The first time she'd said no, thanks, and raised her plastic glass of nasty wine in unsolicited explanation. The second time, she'd watched Nathan watch her say no, and she didn't like the look he gave her, so the third time she nodded, and took the shortest drag possible, letting the herbally smoke seep from the side of her mouth before it got past her teeth, and resisting the urge to splutter. She'd tried smoking, but hated the taste and the sensation of dirty smokiness in her throat and lungs. This tasted the same, with a sweet, flowery sort of add-on. She waited to feel dizzy or strange, but nothing happened. She supposed she hadn't inhaled much.

Girls were dancing. The music was loud, and thumpy. Even people not dancing – i.e. the guys – were moving their heads back and forth to its insistent rhythm. The girls looked much older to Hannah. Their eyes were closed, their arms above their heads. They looked sort of dreamy. A couple of hours ago, it had all seemed thrilling. Now it was disconcerting. The joint kept coming back round. She kept puffing on it, hoping it would be okay.

The atmosphere had deepened, somehow. The party had grown more volatile and unpredictable; the dancing more trance-like; the air foggier. People were coupling up, sloping off. Hannah didn't know what she was doing, not really. She didn't belong here. She felt a bit sick. When she looked at her watch and was able to focus, she was almost relieved to see it was 12.30am. Nathan had promised he'd have her home in time. He'd drop her off on the corner.

Nathan had been drinking and smoking. She'd seen him. He wasn't falling down drunk or anything; he was still coherent. She couldn't see him at the moment. He must be in another room. She wasn't sure which one.

Pushing her way through two huge guys in the door-frame, she went through the kitchen. He wasn't there. It was still too noisy to hear, so she moved further away, into the small utility room at the back of the house. She wondered, briefly, as she passed about the family who lived there, who must have gone leaving the white Formica surfaces clear and clean. Now there were empty bottles and piles of ash and spilt bags of crisps everywhere. It was a complete mess. Her head was starting to throb in time to the music and it was a relief to be in the cool silence of this tiny room, which smelt only of legal things, like fabric softener and furniture polish.

She dialled the number of a taxi firm. The guy who

answered told her he didn't have any cabs for an hour. Busiest time, he said. She should have booked. She tried another one, where the woman said the same thing. Her drivers were all out on jobs, and there were more booked. When Hannah expressed dismay, the woman sounded suddenly maternal. 'Are you somewhere safe, love?' she asked. It shocked Hannah to realize that she didn't actually know where she was. She knew roughly, but she couldn't give a house number. What an idiot. 'I'll try and switch a few fellas around, get someone there in 40 minutes or so . . .' She looked at her watch. 12.45. She was already late. She began to panic. Bloody hell . . . She thanked the woman, and said she was fine, and that she'd try someone else. But she couldn't remember any more taxi numbers.

She knew she should ring Dad. She knew he'd still be half awake, waiting to hear her. But she'd have to admit that she had been lying. And it was a big lie. She didn't want him to be mad at her, and she didn't want him to be disappointed in her. Leaning against the chest freezer, she realized she was disappointed with herself. She knew better than this, didn't she? She didn't know anymore.

Things were faster and slower when she came back out into the party. The dancing was more frenetic, but her own movements felt like she was wading through treacle. Her hands looked like they were someone else's, taking the joint and raising it to her lips. She didn't want to do it, but she was doing it anyway. And Nathan, when she found him in the front room, loved it. And that was good, right? He laughed, and pulled her possessively towards him by the belt loops on her jeans, knocking their pelvic bones together through the denim. 'I've got to go home, Nathan.'

'Stop worrying, babe. We'll go soon. I said I'd take you, didn't I?'

'I think I'm going to be sick.'

'Don't be sick in here, for Christ's sake!' Someone – was it Nathan? – was pushing her towards the front door. The fresh air that had been so welcome in the kitchen a minute (an hour? A week? A lifetime?) ago hit her like a train, and made her so dizzy she tried to sit down on the front step. Someone wouldn't let her, and now she knew it wasn't Nathan, because Nathan was swaying in front of her. She vaguely understood that she was being ejected.

She wanted to, needed to lean on Nathan, but she couldn't, otherwise she knew they'd both fall down. She kept thinking about the infant Bambi, learning to stand up, in the film. That was how her legs felt. It made her giggle, but she didn't sound like herself. When they got to his mum's car, he pushed her hard against the door and kissed her hungrily. He tasted of smoke and beer. She was horribly, lucidly afraid for a moment that his tongue was going to make her vomit. And there was the erection, poking at her.

'Nathan,' she protested, her palms against his insistent chest. 'I'm late. We can't . . .'

He stood back, hands raised in a gesture of surrender. 'Okay, okay.' Then opened her door and gave a flourish. 'Your chariot, madam . . .'

Hannah climbed in, leaning her head gratefully against the back of the seat and closing her eyes in the vain hope that it might make the ride slow down so she could get off.

Mark

'So where were you?' Mark fed Lisa the question, hoping Hannah would interrupt the answer.

'I met a friend in town. I ended up going back to her place. Actually, she hadn't heard about me and Andy, so I poured out the whole sorry story, and had a good cry then had fish and chips and watched DVDs. A rocking single girl's Saturday night.'

Lisa looked at Mark for a response, but he wasn't really listening. It was nearly 2 o'clock now. He'd tried her mobile, twice, but it was switched off. Anger had long since given way to fear.

When the phone rang, Lisa exhaled. At last, bloody Hannah! Mark picked up on the second ring.

'Hannah?'

Lisa watched his face.

'Yes, I'm Mark Forbes. Hannah, yes. That's my daughter.'

His face drained of colour instantaneously.

'My God!'

'What?'

He put his hand over the receiver.

'There's been an accident.' Went back to the call.

'Yes.' A long pause. 'Right. Okay. I'll be there as soon as I can. Thank you.'

He hung up, and leant his head against the wall.

'Mark? Talk to me. What's happened?'

'Hannah's been in a car accident. She's in casualty.'

'Jesus! Is she okay?'

'She's okay.'

'Thank God!'

'I'm going down there . . .'

'I'm coming with you . . .'

Already she had her jacket on. Mark grabbed his car keys from the hook by the door, and they almost ran to the car.

Hannah

Casualty departments at 2.30am Sunday morning told a very sorry story about society. Mark couldn't believe he was walking into the narrative. He gave his name – and Hannah's – at the desk. The harassed receptionist didn't look up at him as she told him to take a seat; that someone would be through to talk to him in a moment.

Lisa took his hand, and squeezed. 'It's good that we have to wait. The longer the wait, the more trivial the injury. It's being whisked straight through you don't want.'

She'd been there for three hours with Cee Cee last summer. Cee Cee had pushed an orange tic tac into her left ear. She wanted to see if it would come out the other side. Some boy at school had said it would, if she tipped her head over. It hadn't. It had been a really hot day in May – the kind that surprised and overexcited people, and resulted in a casualty waiting area full of sunstroke and barbeque burns victims.

Mark was insistently tapping one toe against the linoleum floor. Lisa put her hand out on his knee to stop him. He looked at her and smiled weakly.

The young casualty doctor approaching them from be- hind the ominous swinging doors was, according to the hospital badge pinned to her white coat, called Quincy York. A slender blonde, with piercing blue-green eyes behind flattering round glasses, and a soft American accent, she smiled encouragingly at them as Mark jumped to his feet at the mention of Hannah's name. 'Don't worry. Your daughter is okay.'

Relief flooded through him, and for a moment Mark felt weak on his feet.

'Sit down here,' she said, not unkindly, steering him towards a quieter bench at the side. 'I'll take you through to see her in a moment.'

Mark sat down next to her, his face white and pinched. Lisa was still holding his hand. The doctor looked at her questioningly. 'I'm her sister,' she offered. Dr York nodded.

She looked down at her notes. 'Hannah is fine. The good news is that she was wearing a seatbelt, which protected her a great deal from the impact. She'll have some nasty bruises from where it restrained her, and she's got a few small lacerations on her face from the windscreen, but nothing that will need stitching. We've steristripped a couple of the larger ones, but they should all heal without scarring.'

'Thank God!'

'She was lucky.'

'What about the driver?'

'His injuries were more serious, but not life-threatening. His parents are here with him . . .'

'*His* injuries?'

Dr York was confused by the question, and looked down again. 'Yes, Nathan Spring – the driver of the car.'

'She said she was out with her girlfriends . . .' His voice trailed off. Nathan Spring. The boy from the party.

'I see.' Clearly she did. She paused before speaking

again. 'Look, I don't know what happened earlier in the evening, but Hannah has had a drink or two, Mr Forbes. I don't suppose there's anything particularly unusual about that, although she is below the legal drinking age, as you know. She wouldn't be the first teenager we've seen here on a Saturday night who's been drinking when she shouldn't have been. She isn't "drunk" – we were all teenagers once. The problem was that she got into a car with someone who'd also been drinking. The driver had a substantially higher blood-alcohol level. It would have been pretty obvious that he shouldn't have been driving . . .'

'Oh my God!' Mark couldn't believe it. He rubbed his jaw. Hannah? 'Stupid girl!'

Dr York put her hand on Mark's forearm. 'Listen, I understand your reaction, but they've both had a lucky escape. It could have been a lot worse. I've spoken to Hannah and she seems like a sweet kid. She was obviously scared stiff. I think she realizes fully what happened. My guess is she's given herself enough of a fright to make sure she never does anything like that again.' She smiled at him kindly. 'Take her home, let her rest, talk to her . . .'

'Okay, thank you.'

'You're welcome.' She stood up, and spread her arm toward the ward. 'Let's go and find her.'

Hannah was sitting up on the high hospital bed, behind the green curtain. Dr York excused herself, saying she'd be back with Hannah's discharge sheet in a moment or two, and pulled the curtain closed so the three of them were alone. Hannah was pale and dishevelled; she'd obviously been crying. She had cuts and grazes on her cheeks, some held together with small white strips, and an angry blue-black bruise on her collarbone, exposed by the neckline of her shirt.

The big, high bed made her look like a small, frightened child. She didn't say anything, but her wide eyes looked imploringly at her father.

'You stupid girl!' He sounded loud to himself in the hushed ward. 'You *stupid*, stupid girl!' Hannah shrank back against the pillows as though each word was a physical blow. Her face contorted with fresh tears.

'Mark,' Lisa put her hand on Mark's arm. 'Take it easy.' Mark's shoulders dropped. Like the rage had blown, tornado-like, through him, and left him deflated and broken.

'Doesn't she realize? Don't you understand? Don't you get it, Hannah?'

Hannah was sobbing now.

'I can't lose you; I can't lose you too – I can't!'

Lisa's heart broke for him. Her relief at seeing for herself that Hannah was okay was instantly displaced.

'I'm *so* sorry, Dad. I'm *so*, so sorry.'

'What the hell were you thinking? You know better than that.'

'Not now, Mark.'

Lisa realized she needed to take charge. Mark was in no state, hysterical with relief. 'This isn't the place. Let's just take Hannah home, okay?'

Mark nodded and turned towards the curtain. Stopped, turned back and, moving back to the bed, pulled Hannah into his arms.

She put one arm around him, grateful for the embrace and the forgiveness it implied, but the pressure of his hug hurt the bruise.

'Ouch.'

Now his voice was gentle and soft. 'I'm sorry, sweetheart. Does it hurt?'

Ten days later, the cuts had all scabbed over and the bruise had turned from aubergine to black to purple and was now a livid, almost acid yellow. The rest of Hannah was pale golden. Turns out they both knew how to apply Factor 30 after all.

At first, Mark had been afraid of the holiday – the one Amanda had bullied him into booking earlier in the year. He'd been dreading it for weeks before the accident, actually. Without the closeness he and Hannah seemed to have lost, and without the distraction of life's minutiae and routine, he feared long silences and reproachful faces. In the aftermath of that Saturday night, he was even more anxious.

Thank God Lisa had been there that night! She'd taken over. It was Lisa who'd tucked Hannah into bed, held her while she cried, listened to the ridiculous, desperate story of how a 16-year-old with more sense than she'd shown would take the decision to get into a car with a boy she knew was drunk, just because she thought she loved him, and just to avoid getting into trouble with her dad. Mark had glowered and paced downstairs, drinking neat whisky.

He hadn't cried until much later, when he'd gone up to bed. There was almost no point. It was after 5 in the morning, and he thought he was too wired to sleep. But eventually exhaustion broke over him like a wave, and he climbed the stairs. Hannah's door was wide open, and since it was almost daylight outside, he could clearly see the cuts and scrapes on her beautiful, precious young face. This had been too close, too lucky.

Hannah had more or less come straight out of hospital into her exams. The mocks, thank God. She hadn't said much about how they'd gone. They wouldn't get the results until they got home.

It wasn't until their third night in Antigua that they'd really talked. That first night they'd both been exhausted by the flight. At dinner on the second – with their noses turned red by the hot sun – they'd made small talk. On the third, after they'd eaten, they'd sunk into the white lounge furniture on the terrace, with tall glasses of coffee, and Hannah had talked to him, properly. She told him, with the grave, nervous tone of the confessional, about Nathan, and the lies and the events leading up to the accident. He knew most of it – Lisa had told him, that Sunday morning, while Hannah slept soundly – but he listened without interrupting, and without judging. There were a lot of tears. Hannah's shame touched him. Poor kid.

And then he talked. He told her he was sorry; sorry for how he'd been. That he could see, now, that he'd leant on her too much. She shook her head, wanting to refute it, but he'd smiled gently, and told her it was true.

'I thought you were okay. I let myself believe it was easier for you than me; that you'd recovered more quickly.'

'Maybe just differently?'

He had raised her hand to his lips and kissed it. 'Differently.'

'I thought I was okay,' she said, tears rolling down her cheeks. 'But I was so angry with her, Dad. I was so angry with her for leaving me. The journal goes on and on about how *she* wasn't ready – but what about me? I felt like she gave up and let it happen. And I felt so jealous of the others because they were grown up already, and they'd had her for all of their childhood, and I wasn't going to get that. And I felt all of that, almost all the time. I didn't know where to put any of it; how to get rid of any of it. I kept waiting for it to go away on its own. But I was so worried about you that I could never tell you.'

Mark was crying too now. 'I wish you had.'

'Me too.' They held hands across the wicker chairs. 'And Nathan – Nathan was . . .'

'Sssh. I know.'

Hannah got up, and moved to sit beside her dad. He put an arm round her shoulder and she lay her head against him. He stroked her hair, and said words he'd never used, words he'd heard Barbara use a hundred times. 'I've got you.' And they stayed that way for a long time. They'd agreed, made a pact: to talk to each other, and to listen.

But Mark didn't suppose that was the end of it. There were still difficult years ahead; Hannah wasn't going to be grown up overnight. She would make more bad decisions, and wrong choices. And he would lose his temper again; treat her too much like a child. Or too much like an adult. He hoped there would never again be anything so potentially catastrophic. His stomach still knotted with the knowledge of how he might easily have lost her that night. But, for now, there was an understanding, and there was peace.

They swam, and snorkelled and rode the banana boat that the young guys pulled around the bay on the back of a speedboat. They went parasailing, Hannah screaming with delight as they were pulled along on 12 hundred feet of rope above the resort. The sea was an extraordinary colour and the white sugar beach stretched for miles. He read Ian McEwan and Nelson de Mille; she read *Elle* and *Hello!*, ignoring the fat copy of *Middlemarch* she'd brought to study. They both slept like corpses. For both of them it felt like a convalescence.

They didn't talk about Nathan. He didn't know what Hannah intended, and he didn't want to push her. He hoped she would never see him again, but he stopped short of forbidding it. Mark knew he'd stayed for almost a week in the hospital, being treated for a badly broken arm and a couple of broken ribs. A couple of days after the accident he'd had a surreal conversation with his dad. He'd felt he had to ring, though he didn't know what to say, and Hannah had given him the number, anxious for news.

Nathan's father hadn't known any more about Hannah than he'd known about Nathan. He sounded mortified and upset, and kept saying he couldn't believe how stupid Nathan had been, how sure he'd been that Nathan knew better than that . . . a horribly familiar note sounding in Mark's brain. Gordon Spring sounded just like him. He probably ought to be angrier with Nathan than he was. The night it happened, he could have wrung his neck with his bare hands. Might have done, if he'd seen him. But what was the point now? The kid had probably been punished enough.

May

Lisa

It was the kind of evening when she and Andy might ordinarily have met up after work, gone for a drink that turned into a few drinks, and supper. Somewhere outside. With friends or on their own. The kind of evening she'd loved. It was warm – the temperature had reached the mid-60s and stayed there, and the sun was still warm as Lisa came out of her office building, even though it was 5.45.

It was not the kind of evening for flat hunting. Lisa had two appointments, but she was tempted to cancel them both. She'd seen a couple of places earlier in the week, and they'd depressed the hell out of her. It wasn't that they were horrid. Okay – one was horrid. She should have known that somewhere that cheap would have been dodgy. It actually had one of the last avocado bathroom suites in the city. More fool her for hoping to get away with paying that much. The agent had said that avocado bathroom suites were having a renaissance. Lisa almost snorted her lungs out through her nostrils. The second place was fine – she knew the agent was right when she said that it probably represented the best she could hope for within her price range. Lisa had hated the agent. Some impossibly young girl called Felicity with perfect teeth and hair, who wore 4" heels and a 1" cushion-cut Tiffany diamond engagement ring. Everything about her expression when she'd looked at Lisa screamed 'I know your story. You've blown it with a bloke, and you're on your own again, and you're climbing back down the property ladder and it's killing you!' At least that's how it felt. Paranoia was a new and desperately unattractive habit, she knew.

She could have lived there, in the second place. It had a newish bathroom – which was white, meaning the current owners had let their subscription to *25 Beautiful Homes* lapse and clearly had not heard about the avocado renaissance – and an okay kitchen, so long as you weren't into swinging small domestic pets, and built-in shelves. It wasn't painted in a palate of ever more hideous colours, like the first place, which progressed from a navy blue dining room through a forest green living room into a dark red bedroom which said agent managed to describe as 'womb like' without a hint of irony.

The second place was beige. 'Slipper satin', according to Felicity, but then she was an idiot. And it was so . . . empty. So much a house and not a home. Not easily fixed with a sectional sofa and a few framed canvases from Ikea. She missed the mess of Andy, and Cee Cee. Even Mark and Hannah's was too tidy for her, and this place made theirs look like Pete Doherty's hotel room. She wanted DVDs strewn around with no hope of being reunited with their boxes, and red wine stains on rugs, muddy footprints in the hallway and grubby fingerprints on the door frames. Anyway – and she knew this was churlish – she hadn't wanted to be a part of engaged girl's success story. She didn't want her to get a bonus for meeting sales targets which she'd use buying lingerie from Janet Reger for her honeymoon at the Ritz in Paris. Oh no. She'd said no. It was too far from the tube. She'd said she'd look again at the budget, which was a joke only she got and not even she found amusing. She was already at her maximum, and probably a little bit beyond it.

She didn't want to go out there again. She wanted a huge gin and tonic in a pub garden and a good laugh.

Andy was waiting for her this time. It felt like ages since she'd seen him. Her heart lurched. He looked so absurdly handsome and the thought surprised her because she wasn't used to thinking of him in that way. He'd cut his hair differently, and his glasses looked new. They'd only been apart a couple of months. Maybe he'd washed her right out of his hair and developed 20/20 vision so he could see her clearly. She hoped not.

Forcing herself to walk slowly, refusing to let herself get excited, she went over to him. His expression betrayed nothing of his motives. He might just have come over to ask for her share of the council tax, or to return the Georg Jensen silver earring she was pretty sure she'd left on the bedside table.

Again, a bench. This was all getting very *Forrest Gump*. Except that if life was a box of chocolates right now, she thought she knew what she was going to get: the marzipan one no one else ever wanted. Maybe it was more CIA classic movie. They were both wearing raincoats. He didn't look at her as he spoke.

'Your sister came to see me.'

'Which one?'

'Jennifer.'

She would have guessed Amanda or Hannah. Jennifer surprised her a little.

'I'm sorry. She shouldn't have interfered.'

'She was trying to help. It was pretty nice of her.'

'I know, but you made yourself abundantly clear and I'd told her that. She shouldn't have come. She's got things back on track with Stephen and she's gone evangelical about love all of a sudden.'

'Is there something wrong with that?'

'No. But we're different, aren't we?'

Andy didn't say anything. Lisa couldn't bear it.

'What did she say?'

'She showed me something your mum wrote before she died – something in her journal. Pretty powerful tactic.'

'I'm sorry.' She wasn't quite sure why she was apologizing for Jennifer's actions. She'd kill her later.

'Don't be. I always liked your mum.'

'And she liked you.' Lisa remembered Barbara's letter – 'Ask Andy sometime . . .'

'And she was right.'

'About what?'

'About what a waste of time it is, holding onto the bad stuff. I suppose when you know your time is limited, you find it easier to cut through the crap.'

'I suppose.'

'So . . . the point is this . . . I'm letting go of the bad stuff, Lisa.'

'Am I the bad stuff in this scenario?' She couldn't tell from his voice and he still wasn't looking at her.

'No, what happened was the bad stuff.'

This was all too cryptic. She wished he would get on and say why he was here. She felt as if she could barely breathe.

'I don't understand what you're saying, Andy.'

He turned so quickly she jumped. Now he was looking right at her. She met his gaze and waited, like the accused waits for the foreman of the jury to speak.

'I'm saying I want to forget all about the last couple of months. I'm saying it's not worth ruining everything for. It really isn't. I believe you, after all, and I believe that. I'm saying I want you back.'

'Just like that?'

Andy whistled and shook his head. For a moment she thought she'd made him angry.

'Nothing "just like that" about it. I wanted to take you back that first night, after you'd told me. I never wanted you to leave, not really. I was angry and I was hurt, really hurt. But I never stopped loving you. I was just really, really afraid you didn't love me. That you couldn't love me and do that.'

'Andy . . . I said all along . . .'

He put up a hand to stop her. 'I know, I know. I get it, I think. You're a bloody complicated woman, Lisa. I still don't think I really understand why it happened. I don't need to, so long as it never happens again.' She shook her head with vehemence. 'Like I say, you're a bloody complicated woman. But you're *my* bloody complicated woman.'

'I'm so sorry, Andy . . .'

He gripped her shoulders tightly and brought his face close to hers.

'No more apologies, no more explanations. If I'm going to let it go, forever, then you have to, too. It just has to go away.'

'And you can do that?'

'If it means I can have you, then yes. I can, I have – I wouldn't be here if I hadn't. I'm fed up with playing games, Lisa. If you come back, I have to have all of you back. You have to mean it. Forever. Till death do us part, all of that stuff. No more messing around.'

'Does that mean the proposal still stands?'

'Of course it does, you daft cow! Don't you get it? What's the point in coming back if I'm not coming back for all of it? I *love* you. You're not getting the down-on-one-knee stuff this time, mind you. The moonlight and roses. You had that – it didn't work, did it?' He was almost laughing now, and she felt that same laughter bubbling within her chest. Relief, delight, gratitude, joy ... All at once. 'This is the no-frills version.'

'Don't I get the diamond back?'

'As a 10th wedding anniversary present, maybe!'

She put her arms round his neck and pulled him close, taking in his familiar smell, her hands in his hair, her lips on his neck. 'I might be nuts, Lisa. But marry me.'

She couldn't see his face, but she could hear the tears in his voice. 'Thank you, thank you, thank you. I will. I love you so much.'

They stayed that way, on the bench, until it got uncomfortable and chilly. No more talking. They just hugged and kissed. In a funny way, Lisa felt almost as if nothing had ever happened. He really was an amazing man. And she felt she'd gotten herself back, as well as him.

Later, they wandered, hand in hand, in search of that gin and tonic.

'How's Cee Cee?'

'She wants her ears pierced and she wants her bedtime changed. She misses you, too.'

'What did you tell her?'

'Never told her anything – didn't need to. You know Cee Cee. She has the attention span of a squid! Told her you were working, or shopping, or away with a friend. She was back to *Charlie and Lola* without a second thought. Kids are like goldfish. The next weekend, same routine. She won't turn a hair when you're there, the next time she comes over from Karen's.'

'I'm glad you didn't tell her.'

'I suppose it meant something – the fact that I didn't. I never let go, I suppose.'

'Thank God you didn't.' She stopped him, and pulled his face down to kiss him hungrily, months of frustrated longing poured into the one gesture.

'Lisa?' He murmured in her ear, familiarly sexy.

'Mmm?'

'Do you really want that drink?'

'What did you have in mind?'

'I want to take you home . . .'

'Get a cab . . .'

Maybe she'd been afraid that, if ever they were to reunite, there'd be the ghost of a third person in the bed with them. If Andy felt it, he covered it well. It was as good and close and honest as it had ever been between them – better, because it had been so long, and because she had begun to believe it might never happen again. Andy kissed her all over, reclaiming every inch of her, and then watched her as she came, straddling him, the heels of her hands digging into his shoulders. In turn she watched him, her eyes wide with love and pleasure, as he climaxed inside her and then brought her head down to his chest. A few long forgotten words of poetry formed in her mind, and she spoke them quietly, almost to herself as she lay there.

For no other reason than I love him wholly
I am here; for this one night at least
The world has shrunk to a boyish breast

On which my head, brilliant and exhausted, rests,
And can know of nothing more complete.

. . .

I am as far beyond doubt as the sun
I am as far beyond doubt as is possible.

    'Come again, Lise . . . ?'
    She smiled. He knew exactly what she meant. She was
home. She pulled his chest hair, gently.
    'Yes, please, but give me a minute . . .'

And it was as simple as that, after all. It was over. The
worst had happened, and the storm had come, and Oz
had stunk, and she was bloody glad to be back in Kansas.
Maybe Jennifer was right. Lisa called her, a couple of
days later.
    'Andy told me you went to see him.'
    'Are you going to call me an interfering old some-
thing?'
    'No. I'm going to say thank you. It worked.'
    'You're welcome – I thought it might. He didn't need
much persuading. For some bizarre reason, sis, you're it,
so far as he's concerned.'
    'And aren't I glad? You know how much Mum used
to hate us fighting?'
    'Yeah?'
    'She'd have *loved* this!'

Mark

The post-it with Jane's telephone number written on it was still on the noticeboard in the kitchen, between the number of Betty, who had come to take the ironing away every Wednesday morning for as long as Mark could remember, and a flyer for a new curry house and its 50 per cent off grand opening announcement. Mark took it down, went to the phone, changed his mind and put the number in his shirt pocket. Took the recycling out to the garage, came back and stood by the phone for a while, read about the curry house's specials, and then metaphorically slapped himself around the face and picked up the receiver. Vince was right, damn it!

She answered on the seventh ring, just after he'd exhaled and begun composing his ansaphone message. 'Jane?'

'Hello?' For a moment, when there was no recognition in her voice, Mark almost hung up.

'It's me, Mark.' Should he say his surname?

'Oh. Hi.' Did she sound offhand, or just wary?

'Sorry – sorry it's taken me so long to get back to you . . . about the sweater . . .'

'That's okay.' It didn't really sound like it was.

'Have you given it away to Oxfam yet?!'

'No, it's still here.' She didn't laugh, though, and it had been a joke.

'I wondered if I might come and get it.'

'Okay.'

So she wasn't going to make this easy for him. Fair enough. He probably deserved it.

'I wondered if you were around tomorrow, midday?'

Tomorrow was Saturday. She hesitated for a second or two. Oh God, she had plans. She probably had some other bloke. Who was listening, right now, to the dickhead who'd had his chance and blown it big time.

'I mean, if you're not, then some other time . . .'

Mark felt like the gawky teenager he had never been.

'No . . . no . . . tomorrow's fine. Midday, you say?'

'Yeah, around 12.'

'I'll be here.' At least she hadn't said she'd leave it in the front porch.

'I wondered . . . if you weren't doing anything . . . if you wanted to, I mean . . .' Spit it out, for God's sake, you moron! Ask her. 'If you would like to have lunch. It's supposed to be nice. We could go for a drive – find a country pub, with a garden. Something like that, if you wanted to.'

Again, Jane hesitated.

'I don't know, Mark. I'm not sure it's such a good idea, you know?' So she had no plans, but no plans and a ham sandwich in the kitchen alone was better than lunch with him.

He felt his cheeks burn. 'No problem. Thought it was worth asking . . .'

The silence was practically solid. He had no idea how to end this conversation.

'Lunch, you say?'

'Yes, just lunch. I just thought it might be nice . . .'

'Okay.' She sounded more decisive than he did. 'Lunch. Thank you.'

'Thank you, Jane.'

By the time he hung up Mark had beads of sweat in his hairline. Cool, he told himself, very cool.

*

The next day, at 12.05pm, she opened the door ready to leave, almost as soon as he knocked, with a handbag over her arm and his abandoned sweater in her hand. She seemed much more nervous than she had on their first date and she pulled the door closed quickly behind her.

He bent to kiss her on the cheek. The kiss missed its mark and landed awkwardly near her ear.

'It's nice to see you.'

'Nice to see you too.'

He'd really done a number on her, hadn't he? Mark felt guiltier than ever and wondered if this had been such a good idea – calling her again. It wasn't like he had a plan of action. Maybe it wasn't fair.

He opened her door for her and Jane climbed into the car. She looked pretty again. She was one of those women who could dress young without looking daft. She was wearing a white dress with a high waist line, trimmed with broderie anglaise, and a short pale yellow cardigan.

They talked about the weather for a couple of minutes. About the girls and their exams. Jane kept her handbag in her lap, gripping it more tightly than was necessary. Mark concentrated on the road, although there was little traffic. Then they stopped talking, and Mark wondered whether he should put the radio on.

'Why did you call me again?'

'I'm sorry?'

'I was just wondering. Why you called me again? After all this time. I mean, it seemed to be such a disaster last time, I just wondered why you would want to see me again?'

'A disaster?'

'Well, not for me, no. It was the way you left. The

way you sounded when I called you about the sweater. I just thought you wished . . .'

'That it hadn't happened?'

'Yes – that it hadn't happened. And then, at school, I just had the feeling you were avoiding me. And so I didn't expect to hear from you again . . .'

They'd pulled into the pub's gravelled car park now. Mark parked in one of the empty bays and turned the ignition off. Then he shifted around in his seat to look at Jane. Her chest was red and blotchy with the effort of speaking about it.

'I'm sorry. What a prat!'

'You're not a prat, Mark. You just went too fast, I think . . . *We* went too fast.'

'I think so too. I felt like crap, afterwards. Like I'd taken advantage of you.'

'Hardly.'

'That's how I felt. It's like that evening was in two parts. The dinner part – that I was ready for. I enjoyed being with you, talking to you. I felt better than I had done in ages.'

'Me too.'

'But what happened back at the house, I wasn't ready for that. It wasn't fair.'

'I know.'

'So I skulked off. I'm so sorry if you thought it was something to do with you. It truly wasn't. It was me. I know that sounds like the biggest line in the book, but it really was.'

She smiled faintly.

'You were lovely. You were beautiful and sexy and great. Honestly. You were. I just wasn't ready . . . to be with someone in that way. I felt like I used you.'

She nodded understanding.

'And afterwards, I realized you were vulnerable too. That you were probably a bit damaged too, and then I felt like a shit, and then I just made it worse . . . I know . . . by being weird. Ostrich behaviour, I'm afraid. I really am sorry.'

'Apology accepted.'

'Thank you. I'm not sure I deserve it, but thank you.'

'So . . . why did you call me again?'

'I wanted to apologize. To make it up to you. And . . .' Mark ran his hand around the leather of the steering wheel.

'And . . . I wondered if you might give me another chance. Let me backpedal and start again. Have lunch with me, have dinner with me. Take it slowly. Give us a chance to see if there's something there?'

Jane didn't answer straight away.

'If, however, you want to take your apology and your Stilton Ploughman's and give the fucked-up widower a very wide berth from now on, I'll understand completely . . .'

She laughed.

'You're a very lovely woman, Jane. You deserve to be happy.'

'We all deserve that.'

'Mmm.' Was that an answer?

'So, you're suggesting we date? No sex. Friends. See where that goes?'

'How does that sound?'

'Can I think about it?'

Jennifer

Jennifer sat back on her heels and wiped the sheen of sweat from her brow. It was hot out here today. She surveyed her work critically, and nodded with approval. She'd almost finished this bed. She'd started with this one because it was the biggest, and it faced the terrace most directly. Here, her efforts would have the greatest result. Glancing at her watch, she saw that she'd been at it for almost an hour, listening to Wimbledon on a small Roberts radio she'd borrowed from the kitchen.

Gardening was one of those things you really had to grow into. Like eating olives, listening to opera and voting Conversative – it was not the natural preserve of the young. She had a clear recollection of Mum falling for gardening. They'd moved a couple of times, after Mum and Dad split up – first to a rented house, in which the small garden had been entirely paved for the convenience of tenants. She and Lisa had cycled for hours in tight circles around a single terracotta pot, containing a rose of indeterminate colour and very dubious strength. The tiles had been murder on Amanda's hands and knees when she'd started crawling.

Before their baby sister was a year old, they'd moved to Carlton Close. It was a 70s box, on a cul de sac full of 70s boxes, a fact which had been of less interest, of course, than the size of their bedrooms – bigger – and the potential for new friendships on the close. The front had had a lawn, with a low brick wall at the front, and a tarmac drive to the side. Mum had never done much with that. The front was where Jennifer and Lisa and their friends congregated. But the back – that became something really rather lovely. It seemed like they'd gone down the path one day, after money for the ice cream van, or begging for an extension on bedtime, and found it transformed from a wilderness to a paradise. Mum gardened at the weekends, all through the spring and summer, in a bikini, a sunhat and a giant pair of Jackie O sunglasses, while Amanda rode her trike and held tea parties for her dollies on the small patio.

In the autumn she built bonfires. Jennifer remembered their smell and their noise. They invited the kids from the street, and their parents, and Mum cooked baked potatoes with sausages and beans. Everyone loved Mum. She had this energy – it was hard to describe. She made everyone feel interesting, like she had time for them. People enjoyed being around her.

Lisa used to say she should get married again. Jennifer couldn't imagine it, then.

When Mark was building the house, and he and Mum were living in the caravan, Jennifer had only visited once or twice. She found it so uncomfortable – this new, younger man. Her mum living . . . like that. And most of all, being pregnant with Hannah. But the first time she'd gone, they'd shown her the plans, excited about their new home. Mark had unrolled the blueprints of the floorplan – technical and detailed, slightly unfathomable to the untrained eye. But Mum had filled an A4 blank notebook with garden plans – drawn in pencil and coloured in meticulously – each item labelled in the margin in her loopy round handwriting. She had talked about this new garden with her eyes sparkling. A grassy area for the new baby to play in, a fruit and vegetable patch, with asparagus and raspberries, a place to sit that caught the last rays of the day . . . she'd been so happy.

Why hadn't Jennifer seen it then for what it was? Why had she worried so much, about how it looked, how it affected her? It was, for Mum, the perfect thing . . .

Mum wanted to grow and nurture, and make the world prettier. Jennifer had always seen it, before, as something different. A perfect garden for her perfect life. That had changed too. Doing Barbara's garden now made her feel closer to her mother.

It was a beautiful day. June was her favourite month. It seemed the whole garden was in bloom. Foxgloves and mallows; fat, creamy English roses and Sweet Williams, their blooms proliferated everywhere. Mum's lavender bed, planted the summer after Hannah was born, was a riot of purple fragrance. The whole thing was so fecund it was verging on the wild. April and May had been wet, but now it was dry, and warm. She'd found Barbara's old gardening gloves in the shed, and a pad to kneel on. Earlier, she'd felt her neck beginning to burn in the sun, so she'd returned to the shed, and come out with a straw hat. Not at all glamorous, but very effective. There was a lot to do.

Hannah came out with a plastic jug of iced water. All the physical evidence of her accident had gone, except for one small scar, about an inch long, low on her left cheek. She seemed almost back to her old self.

'Blimey – you look just like Mum!'

'Got all her gear on, that's why. Hope you don't mind.'

'Why would I mind?' Hannah shrugged happily. 'Listen, if you weren't out here doing this weeding and whatever . . . Dad would have roped me in at some point, so you won't hear any complaints from me. I hate gardening.'

'You know, that's so weird. You spent all your time out here when you were a baby. Mum used to park your pram,' she turned and pointed to a tree near the side of the house, 'there, and you'd lie there contentedly all day, with your fat little legs pumping away mid-air while she gardened.'

'I didn't say I didn't like *gardens*. I said I didn't like garden*ing*! I don't know a euphorbia from an aruncula, me.' She winked. 'I'm a teenager. I don't, by definition, like anything that involves physical or mental work. I expect I'll grow into it.'

Jennifer laughed. 'When you're my age, you mean?'

'Listen, if the cap fits . . . !' She was laughing. 'You're making me hot, for God's sake, and I'm not doing anything . . . Come and have a glass of water, will you . . .'

Jennifer stood up, and rubbed the small of her back with a gloved hand. 'Okay, you win. Bring any biscuits?'

Hannah was wearing a vest with narrow spaghetti straps. She pushed them down her shoulders and leaned back in the garden chair, pulling her long denim skirt up to her thighs, and sticking her long legs out in front of her to catch the sun. Jennifer peered at her sister's exposed skin. 'Have you got cream on?'

'Shut up, Mum!' Hannah scowled at her. 'Just ten minutes. Did you know, none of us get enough sun, these days. People plaster themselves in Factor 500 before they step outside their door, and they're just not getting enough Vitamin D . . .'

'Is that right, doctor?'

'That's right. I read it in the newspaper.' Hannah poked her tongue out at her sister, who poked back.

'I'm going the Nicole Kidman route myself.' Jennifer spread out her milky arms. 'I give up with the tanning. Stripes and sunburns and flaky skin, who needs it?'

'You haven't got a prom coming up in a couple of weeks, then, I guess.'

405

'What's going on? What the hell's a prom? Are we in an American movie or something?'

'Get with the programme, Gran! We have one every year now.'

Jennifer shook her head.

'I know, I know,' Hannah smirked. 'It wasn't like that in your day.'

Jennifer flicked her with a glove. 'No, it bloody wasn't! Not so much of the "your day", thanks! I didn't go to school in the last century. We had discos, not proms, that's all. What do you wear to one of these proms?'

'A prom dress. Mine's strapless and black, and Dad says it terrifies him so I know I must look foxy. Guys wear black tie.'

'See, completely different. I remember Lisa once got in terrible trouble with Mum. She wasn't around – I can't remember why – and Lisa needed something to wear to the disco, so she got this kilt – which some relative had sent, and which turned out to be a proper one, dead expensive – and cut, like, 15 inches off the hem – so it was a mini – really, *really* mini. All sort of jagged on purpose, stuck it up with Wundaweb, and wore that. She went nuts.'

'Sounds hideous.'

'It was trendy then, at least I'm sure it must have been or else she wouldn't have done it. She was always much more into that stuff than I was.'

'Yeah, weren't you all listening to the Bay City Rollers then? In the Tartan Army?' She was giggling.

'How old do you think I am?'

'I don't know – about middle-aged?'

'Cheeky monkey! It was a long time after that. This was more an Ant Warrior, Culture Club thing.'

'Equally sad.'

'Fine. Just ten years later. At least give me credit for that.'

'What happened to the kilt?'

'Mum threw it away. She was pretty cross. Not even really because she'd cut the kilt up, more because she'd made such a bad job of it, I think!'

'Sounds like Mum. She'd have probably hemmed it with the machine, if Lisa'd just brought it to her.'

'Probably. Anyway, it was almost certainly all Lisa's fault. She was always the wild one – I was just trying to keep up with her . . .'

'So who are you going with, then, to this prom?' Jennifer knew Hannah wasn't seeing this Nathan guy anymore. Not that he'd sounded much like a prom date. He'd written to Mark – a short, formal note, clearly written with his father standing over him, apologizing for his irresponsible actions. The note said the police were pressing charges. He had to be seen to be doing penance. He'd certainly lose his licence, he said, probably for five years, maybe even get a suspended sentence. What an idiot.

'Just Alice and Phoebe – I'm off blokes.'

'Indefinitely?'

'At least for now . . . Made a right balls-up back there, didn't I?'

Jennifer reached over and patted Hannah's shoulder. 'Didn't we all, at some point, Hannah?' More recently than you might think, young Hannah, she said to herself, draining her glass.

'How's the studying going?'

'Crap!'

'But it's soon, isn't it?'

'A couple of weeks 'til the first one.'

'Are you ready?'

'Not according to my mocks results, I'm not.'

'Ah, but they were special circumstances . . .'

'Hope so.'

'You'll be fine – you've got clever genes.'

'Easy for you to say. Won't be you sitting them.'

'I've sat them.'

'In the olden days . . . !'

'Exactly! When they were actually difficult. Before they invented A*s, whatever the hell they are.'

'Shouldn't worry about what they are. I don't think there'll be any of those on my list.'

'Stop it, Hannah. You're going to do great . . .'

'We'll see . . .'

Hannah was saved by the bell. Her phone rang, its ringtone a tune Jennifer recognized vaguely as the hit of the summer, and she turned her back to answer it. Then she got up and lolloped to another part of the garden so that Jennifer couldn't hear who it was and what she was saying. Jennifer smiled to herself at the secrecy. Still a teenager, then.

When she rang off, Hannah came and sat down again. The interruption hung briefly in the air. 'I miss her.' Hannah didn't say that often.

'I miss her too.'

'I'm lucky, though. I know that. I've got Dad, and you and Lisa, and Amanda. I know I don't always act like I know that's lucky. But I do, really.'

'We always said you had four mums. To love you and to nag you.'

'Could do without the nagging.'

'Can't have one without the other. Did our mum teach you nothing?'

'You weren't around much, when I was little.'

'You don't know, you were little. Little people have notoriously unreliable memories.'

'I know, I don't remember, because Mum always said so. She said that she and Mark had tried to make you and Lisa feel like a part of the family, but she was afraid you didn't, not really. She said you were too old when she and Dad got together to ever really accept it and want to belong to it.'

'She did?'

'She did. I think it made her sad.'

'I'm sorry.'

Hannah shrugged again. The universal gesture of adolescence.

'Don't get me wrong. She wasn't, like, very sad, very often. She was a pretty fun person.'

'She was, wasn't she?'

'That's what I miss most. Dad's fun too, I know that. But the funny they made together, the funny only the two of them could make – that's gone, and I miss it.'

Jennifer put her arm around Hannah, and hugged her.

'You're a wise old head on young brown shoulders, aren't you Hannah?' she said softly.

'I am. With the odd fuck-up in between . . .' This Hannah seemed much more like the old one. 'Get that from my mum! The wisdom part. I *know* things.'

And there are things you will never know, thought Jennifer, but she didn't say.

'What things do you know?'

'I know that you seem much happier, lately.'

Jennifer smiled. 'I am actually.'

'That's good.'

'Yeah.'

She sat for another moment or two, feeling a giant

grin spread across her face, not wanting, or needing, to conceal her joy for a minute longer.

'I do know one little thing you don't know, missy.'

'What?' Hannah sat forward. The grin was contagious, before she even knew why she was grinning.

'That I'm pregnant.'

So, the thing was, that when you'd tried to get pregnant and it hadn't worked, and hadn't worked for long enough that it was time to get it investigated, you forgot about birth control. Obviously. There'd been a while, back there, when it was redundant anyway; they'd made love so infrequently. But, since the ski trip, before Easter . . . well, that was no longer the case.

A missed period was nothing new for Jennifer. She'd never been especially regular. That had been noted, written down on the charts. Sometimes she was so late she wasn't sure whether the period was the last one or the next one. She'd been tired. Dead tired. The kind of heavy, sudden tiredness that makes sleeping face down on your desk, or standing up in the Underground seem a suddenly attractive proposition. She'd wondered whether she might be anaemic, and started buying dark green leafy vegetables, which was unlikely to help since she hated the taste of them and, although they got steamed and served up, they were seldom eaten in any great quantity. Sore boobs should have been a sign – indeed they might have been, if she'd been looking for one. But babies, and all things baby, had been so definitely shelved, so removed from the agenda of this relationship she and Stephen were rebuilding from the ground up. Quite honestly, it never occurred to her that she might be pregnant.

Until she started to throw up. Blessed with the constitution of an ox, inherited by all four of them from their mother, this almost never happened. Amanda hadn't been sick once in India, for exactly the same reason, even after eating watermelon sold at the roadside and taking ice in her Coke. They were all roller-coaster, choppy sea, stop-start traffic proof. But one morning, she woke feeling as unfamiliarly sick as the proverbial parrot. As she sat, legs akimbo, pyjamas awry, on the cool tiles of the bathroom floor, clutching at the toilet pedestal for dear life, a new and awe-inspiring thought slowly dawned.

Stephen had been away at a two-day sales conference in Manchester. Jennifer resisted the strong impulse to phone him and tell him. She wanted to see his face. She'd gone to the chemist and bought four tests, and done them, one after the other, until she'd perfected what she judged to be mid-stream urine. Even then, she had the sense of entering a new and alien world. She'd never considered the length or time span of a stream of her urine before.

Each obliged with an affirmative blue line. Peering from test to box and back again, Jennifer thought pregnancy tests would be better if they just said 'yes' or 'no'. Better still, if they came with the kind of computer chip which would just announce, in a Stephen Hawkings voice, whether you were, or you weren't. Some of the four lines were fainter than others. But they were all there.

The GP, who she called immediately, fingers shaking as she dialled, exclaimed with joy. She didn't think doctors were supposed to do that – register an emotional reaction to an outcome. But this was the GP they'd seen, ages ago, and who'd referred them for tests ... Of course she assumed the news was good. Four lines, she'd laughed, almost certainly meant she was pregnant. It wasn't that unusual, she said. Unexplained infertility sometimes resolved itself without intervention or explanation. It was just one of those things. Had they been on holiday? Sometimes a change of scene or a distraction was all that was needed. Couples had been known to become too focused on getting pregnant. Sometimes, when they took a step back, it just fixed itself, and it worked. She was thrilled for them, she said, and suggested that Jennifer should come and see her in a couple of weeks, and they'd work out some dates and fix a scan.

And that was it. She was pregnant. *They* were pregnant. One part of Jennifer's brain wondered whether it was too soon. The other registered it was extraordinary to have gone so quickly from questions about if, to questions about when. The bigger part just went yippee.

The world was full of babies. It was full of babies when you wanted to get pregnant, and it wasn't happening. It was full of babies when you weren't sure you wanted to get pregnant, and everyone else wanted it to happen. And it was still full of babies when you were pregnant at last. The babies all looked the same, but you looked at them completely differently. Jennifer didn't think she could have gotten pregnant in France. Maybe April. She'd missed two periods. Maybe earlier. If she was already about two months pregnant, then her baby would be born around Christmas time. Noëlle. Holly. Christopher. Wenceslas. She remembered Jake, the Christmas baby, and hugged herself. This time it was her turn.

She meant to tell Stephen in a special way. Make a story that could be told and retold. She bought sea bass.

412

Decided that cooking sea bass was definitely going to make her sick. Put the sea bass in the freezer, in the hope and belief that morning sickness could not last for the whole nine months. She took a bottle of champagne out of the coat cupboard in the hall where they kept the bottle rack, then remembered she wouldn't be able to drink any and put it back. She rehearsed ways to say it.

He was late. Traffic was terrible on the M1. He called on the mobile from the car and told her he wasn't sure when he'd be back. She tried to watch television, but there was nothing interesting enough on to hold her attention. She tidied the apartment, remembering what she had once heard about women nesting. For ages she stood on the threshold of their second bedroom, imagining where they might put a cot, a changing table. What colour they might paint it. She felt, standing there, as if she'd instantly changed, in the very moment she'd found out. She remembered something Mum had written in the journal and wished she knew. She'd be so pleased. She couldn't imagine Stephen granting her admittance to the labour ward, like the diary had said, but she'd have been pleased enough, maybe, to wait outside.

She'd been almost asleep, feet up on the sofa, when he'd finally come home. All her grandiose schemes for breaking the news evaporated when she saw him. The burden of carrying the news alone for two days was too much. All he said, smiling at her from the doorway, and starting to come towards her, was 'How are you?'

'Pregnant.'

'You're *what*?'

'I'm pregnant, Stephen. I'm pregnant!'

That was a few weeks ago. The scan had confirmed it last week. She'd lain there, jelly-bellied, and he'd sat behind her, holding her hand raised over her head just like the films and on TV. And when the coffee bean baby hoved into view, grey and grainy, but definitely pulsing with life, she felt absolutely as she knew she should. She was twelve weeks pregnant. Labelled an elderly *prima gravida*, just as Barbara had complained, but pronounced at least a healthy and perfectly normal one, carrying a foetus about X long, who would be born not at Christmas – maths had never been her strong point – but at the end of January the following year. The radiographer said she thought the baby was a girl, although she made no promises.

Hannah jumped up and punched the air triumphantly. 'You're pregnant! That's fantastic!'

Jennifer laughed.

'It *is* fantastic, isn't it?'

'It's fantastic.' Good word.

'I'm going to be an aunt.' With teenagers, in the nicest possible way and however wise the head on their young brown shoulders, it was always just a little bit about them. 'Auntie Hannah.'

'I can expect plenty of free babysitting, then, I assume.'

'Too right! As long as it's not prom night . . . Or Saturday nights. Or Fridays . . .' But she was grinning. She hugged her big sister.

'I'm so, so happy for you!'

'Thanks, Hannah.'

'And how does Stephen feel about it?'

Stephen was quietly ecstatic. All his lines, in the ski chalet, about babies not mattering . . . she'd known what he meant, but she hadn't bought it. This was what he'd wanted all along. That was fine. He'd just been more sure. There was nothing wrong with that. They hadn't told anyone yet. At some point, there would be a trip to his parents. She looked forward to telling Kathleen, but part of her resented giving Brian what he said he wanted. She'd get over it. This wasn't about any of them, anyhow. It was about herself and Stephen, and this baby.

'When are you going to tell Dad?'

'Tell me what?'

Neither of them had seen Mark come into the garden. Hannah looked at her watch. 'You're home early.'

'No law against that, is there? It's such a gorgeous afternoon. I came home to observe this delightful bucolic scene. I knew Jennifer would be out here toiling in the heat. I assumed she'd be getting precious little help from you, so I thought I'd come and give her a hand . . .'

Jennifer winked at Hannah. The wink granted permission.

'Quite right. She shouldn't be working so hard . . . in her condition . . .'

Hannah had never been able to keep secrets. Amanda complained bitterly about this trait for years. She hadn't had a surprise gift for a childhood birthday since Hannah learnt to talk.

'Very subtle, Hannah. Highly cryptic.' Jennifer laughed so her sister knew she didn't mind.

'You're . . . pregnant?!' Mark put down his case, and laid the jacket that had been on his arm over the back of the chair that Hannah had been sitting in.

'Three months. So I suppose it's official.'

'That's the best news I've heard in I don't know how long!' He came to her and caught her in an easy, close embrace. 'That's brilliant, Jen. I'm made up for you.'

He pulled back and smiled at her. 'And so would your mum have been.'

415

She nodded, not wanting to cry. 'I know. I know she would.'

Later, when Jennifer had gone home and the newly self-styled Auntie Hannah was doing her homework upstairs (or at least *said* she was, though Jennifer noticed she took both her iPod and her phone upstairs with her), Mark, who'd changed into shorts and an old T-shirt, poured himself a beer, and went out onto the terrace. Jen had done a great job, but there was still a lot to do before July. He pondered his work schedule in his head, and wondered about taking some time off in the next couple of weeks. It was dusk, so he turned the hosepipe on at the wall and positioned the sprinkler so that droplets arced across a section of the lawn and the bed that Jennifer had been working on. Thank God there was no watering ban yet, though if the weather continued as it had been these last few weeks, doubtless there would be. He remembered Barbara, barefoot and wrapped in her robe, carrying bowlfuls of dirty bathwater across the terrace to pour onto the thirsty, cracked earth in previous summers.

He lay back in his Adirondack chair, and took a long drink, enjoying the sounds and scents of his garden. The evening primroses were all open, like a yellow choir. God, she'd be pleased about the baby. A first grandchild. She'd have loved it. She'd be so fed up she was missing it, wherever she was . . .

Lying there, Mark realized he was relaxed. Really relaxed. For the first time in ages he had nothing pressing on his mind. Nothing to worry him. Everyone was okay.

D Day

I was reading what I'd written before – back at the beginning of all this. I said it would be sporadic, didn't I, and I was right. I've no staying power. There's not a lot to show, not a lot left behind. I hope some of it is helpful, or makes you smile or brings me back for a second.

Because I'm going. I know that now. As of today. Don't know when, don't know how soon, although, truthfully, now that I know it will happen, I want it to happen soon. I'm afraid. I know you're not supposed to be, and I know it doesn't help, but I am. I'm afraid of being in pain, and I'm afraid of being helpless, and I'm afraid of lingering on and making everyone miserable. Since I'm going to die, I might as well get on with it. You can't start to get better until I'm gone. And I'm your mum, so I want you to get better. I guess motherhood is the ultimate selflessness. You want to die quicker so your children can get over you.

No more treatment. No amazing hospitals in the States doing experimental medicine that might save me – eleventh hour. No miracles, no nothing. It's ridiculous, but it's almost a relief. The treatment is so disgusting, and I've had enough. When she said so, today – the oncologist – when she started talking about palliative care and hospices, I almost exhaled. I think I knew it was coming. My body didn't feel better. I don't want to go into a hospice. I'm selfish about that. I want to be at home; I want to die at home. I was watching Deal or No Deal *today. Won't miss daytime television*

417

much, but I like that one. It's like this: when you start that game, there are 26 suitcases to open, and all the possibilities exist, and you feel strong, and full of optimism and expectation. I was like that, at the beginning. I thought I could win the million. I won't say beat the odds. The odds beat me. More people recover from my cancer than die from it. It's a 'good' cancer to get. Then the cases start opening, and the big numbers start disappearing, and ten minutes later you'd settle for 100,000. I've had a horrid feeling since halfway through that my case contains the penny, and bugger me, it does. Does that make any sense? Or does comparing my relationship with this illness to a game show just prove my morphine dosage needs looking at? I know what I mean, anyway.

Now I don't have to worry about me any more. I'm a foregone conclusion. I don't have to wonder, like I was doing, whether there was any point booking a summer holiday for this year (there isn't) or whether I'll be around when Hannah starts driving (I won't – not all bad, then!), or whether I'll have another birthday (probably not one I could enjoy), or another Christmas, or stuff like that. Because I won't.

I just have to worry about all of you, and how you'll be when I'm not here. Not just how you'll feel about me dying. About how you'll live your lives, about the decisions and directions and choices you'll make. My beautiful girls. If you've read this, you'll know it contains some – not all, but some – of the things I want my daughters to know.

And the greatest of these is love.

Please know that you had mine, unconditional, and powerful and awesome. So strong that I can't believe it will die with me. I want to imagine it as a living thing *that goes on beyond my body and my death, as a vine that has grown and wound its way through the very core of you all, and cannot be uprooted or destroyed, but rather will hold you erect when everything else is crumbling and withering inside you.*

June

Lisa

The wedding was simple. Lisa had always assumed she'd be a bit of a Bridezilla. Designer dress, architectural flowers, cake with four different flavoured layers, that sort of thing. Turned out, when it counted, she wasn't at all. They'd left it too late, of course, to find a hotel that could take them. The nicest places around almost sniggered at her when she mentioned her date, and suggested, that if it were that date two years hence it still might pose a problem. ('Christ,' Lisa had exclaimed to Andy, 'who the hell are all these terrifying people who know what they want two years before they do it?' His retort, of course, was that *he* had known what he wanted two years before he was finally going to get to do it. That earned him rolling eyes and a playful punch on the arm.) It was Mark who suggested the garden. Initially Lisa hadn't been sure – it was so much work for him. And maybe a little weird and folksy? But the more she thought about it, the more appropriate it seemed. Simple was exactly the way it ought to be. Because, hadn't she learnt, love was simple. Pure and good and wonderful, and all of those other things, of course. But, above all, love was simple. Just like Mum said it was.

And this morning, in the calm before the storm, circling the marquee, open-sided and flooded with warm sunshine, in curlers and a cotton robe, Lisa was more than glad. The notoriously unreliable summer weather was as it had been twelve months ago – perfect – only now, that felt right, and not an affront. She stopped in front of her chair, running a pink manicured fingernail along her new name in calligraphy on the place card, a shy smile crossing her face.

Mum always said someone should get married in this garden. She would have done, if it had existed. She and Mark had married in a register office, in front of only a dozen or so witnesses, and had lunch at the pub. Lisa knew she and Jennifer had made it awkward, sucked some of the joy out of it, and she was sorry. Now it was Mum's turn to take away some of hers – not deliberately, of course – she could never have done that. But by not being there. At least they were in her garden. Jennifer had been coming out here a lot lately, working in the garden. She said it made her feel closer to Mum. Lisa felt a sudden, strong surge of joy that she was going to be here, today.

Everyone congregated at the house the night before. Amanda and Ed had arrived at about six, exhilarated by some complicated tale of a missed connection and a cancelled flight and the possibility, up until 12 hours earlier, that they might not make it back for the wedding. ('We were petrified – I said Jennifer would KILL US!!') Amanda was glowing so much that both the bride-to-be and the expectant mum felt the smallest flicker of envy. Deeply tanned, as slim as only a restricted budget can make you ('Blimey,' Lisa had exclaimed. 'I hope your dress fits!') and lit from within by something new that both her sisters recognized as pure happiness – and probably, Lisa whispered to Jen, quite a lot of acrobatic, unmarried sex – she looked fantastic.

'Don't knock married sex until you've tried it, you!'

Jennifer had nudged Lisa in the ribs. In return, Lisa had rubbed Jennifer's belly. 'Works, anyway, right?!'

They had eaten lasagne and drunk Prosecco and stayed up too late, despite Lisa's half-hearted protestations that she needed some beauty sleep, and Andy's vociferous declarations that she didn't require a wink.

At some point Mark stopped at the top of the stairs, looking down at them all: Jennifer and Stephen, Amanda and Ed, Lisa and Andy, Hannah – ecstatic to have her exams behind her, and a long empty summer ahead of her – and Cee Cee. He felt his throat constrict and his heart ache with longing for her, Barbara. She would have loved this so. She might have stood there beside him and squeezed his hand, and said something about having got some things right after all, or about how lucky they were, and they would have had a moment, the two of them, of shared happiness, the kind he would never have with her again, but which he could, standing here now, have *for* her. This year, without her, had seen her daughters cross bridges and build them, discover secrets and learn from them. She had been as much a part of this, absent, as if she had never left. The letters and the stories had seen to that. She would have loved tonight, and tomorrow.

He knew, too, that his grief was changing shape. Tears still came easily, and nights were often interminable. His pain was still real, sometimes very physical. But there was a future now that perhaps hadn't been there a year ago. Now he could see years ahead of him, and looking at them, imagining them, was not so painful as it had been. It would never go away, but it would get better, and keep on getting better, until it was something he had in just one part of himself, instead of all through him, a part he could put away when needed and access again just as easily. But not the greater part of him, which was, he was surprised to learn, intact. He had her children, and he would have *their* children. And she would never not be with him, because they would be with him.

Satisfied everything downstairs was as it should be, Lisa went upstairs in search of her sisters. Following the commotion, she opened the door to Hannah's room just in time to see Amanda and Hannah executing a Diana Ross and the Supremes-esque dance move, hairbrush mikes in their hands, to 'Today I Met The Boy I'm Gonna Marry'. Jennifer was sitting on the edge of the bed watching them and smiling. She rolled her eyes at Lisa when she saw her.

'What *are* we listening to?!'

'Ed made it for some cousin of his, for his wedding. It's a wedding mixed tape. It's got the best stuff on it. He said we should play it while we got ready.'

'Another mixed tape – that boy is a real 80s throwback, you know.'

'I know.' Now Amanda was handing her a glass of champagne from the open bottle on Hannah's dressing table. 'But it's great, isn't it?'

Lisa laughed. It was. The music and the bubbles in the champagne and the walk around the garden – everything was fizzing up in her stomach, and the feeling was exhilarating and warm and . . . lovely. This was a childhood Christmas Eve magnified about a million times. She hadn't expected to be so uncynical and so jittery and so . . . excited.

'Let me take those curlers out – you must be suitably pre-Raphaelite by now. Come here and sit down.'

Jennifer stood behind her and started to pull out

pins, gently unrolling the foam cylinders. Big round curls bounced around Lisa's face as she stared at herself in the mirror.

'You okay?' Jennifer dropped her hands to gently squeeze her sister's shoulders.

'I can't wait.' They shared a knowing glance.

Amanda tapped Jennifer's bottom with the hairbrush. 'Oi! Stop that.'

'What?'

'You know what. The knowing glance thing. We hate it, don't we, Hannah?'

'What do we hate?' Hannah was fiddling with her unfamiliar stockings now, feeling very *Moulin Rouge*.

'The whole "we're the big sisters, we know it all thing". They've done it to us our whole lives . . .'

'Huh?'

'Well, no more. I'm now, officially, in a serious relationship. So you've either got to stop with the knowing glances, or start including me . . .'

'No way! That's only one of out three, Mand. You've got to have a proper job and a mortgage before you're really included . . .' Lisa winked at Jennifer in the mirror.

'That right?'

'Right.'

Amanda stuck her tongue out at them both.

'Where are the serious relationships, by the way? And the answer had better not be at the pub.'

'At the pub.'

'Really?'

'Really. Actually, the excuse for leaving was that they've gone to pick up the buttonholes. Since the florist is two shops down from The Lamb, I imagine a little Dutch courage might be on the agenda . . .'

'And they've taken Cee Cee on this little jaunt . . .'

'No, Cee Cee is watching *Charlie and Lola* on a loop downstairs.'

'So it's just the four of them? And no chaperone?!'

'Uncle Vince is with them.'

'Blimey, we've got no chance!'

'Chill out! The wedding's not for another hour and a half. They'll be back.'

'I'm sure they'll be back – well, pretty sure they'll be back. It's the state of them when they get back that worries me.'

'Don't be daft! They're not a bunch of kids.'

'They're men, though.'

'Basically big hairy kids allowed to purchase and consume alcohol.'

'Drink your champagne and stop worrying.'

Lisa wasn't worrying. They'd be back. Andy would be back. And in about ninety minutes she'd be walking towards him in the weirdly slow, stilted gait the church and organist apparently required, on Mark's arm and dressed in the prettiest, palest dress she'd ever owned, ready to say the most serious, permanent things she'd ever said out loud.

'Do my legs look orange to you?' Hannah was staring at herself in the full-length mirror on the back of the door, suddenly worrying the fake tan treatment she'd given herself two days ago hadn't quite worked out.

'Dunno. They just look long and thin to me,' muttered Jennifer.

'Don't know why you bother with that fake stuff, Hannah. Never looks real.'

'It's alright for you, Mand. You're always bloody brown.' The insinuation, and the subject of Amanda's parentage hung in the air for a nanosecond before they all ignored it. Not a subject for today. Today was too happy.

Lisa turned round and looked at Hannah. 'You don't look orange at all! Don't listen to them – you look fabulously sunkissed.' She did, in fact, have a distinctly Tangoed hue, and her ankles and knees really didn't bear close examination, but this was clearly an unhelpful observation that late in the day. Besides, it was a long dress she'd be wearing . . . so long as the colour didn't run in the heat . . .

They were all – believers and devout atheists – grateful for the cool, still interior of the church. Outside, it was already in the high 80s by the time the enthusiastic organist began pounding on his keys, and guests were mopping their brows as they came in and sat down. Men ran their fingers inside their collars, and women wondered whether their make-up was streaking on their sugared almond coloured dresses. The strapless dress had been a good choice: Lisa congratulated herself as she stood and waited for her cue. The dress was long and lean, ivory silk, with an overlay of fine, old lace. Not so weddingy she felt ridiculous, nor so unweddingy you could wear it again to parties. She'd eschewed a veil, chortling that veils were for virgins, until Jennifer and Hannah, ignoring her protestations, pushed the comb of a short one into her French pleat in the changing room of the bridal salon and made her cry sudden, unexpected tears. 'I look like . . . a bride!' she had exclaimed, amazed.

So there was a veil – filmy and long, and trimmed with crystals and seed pearls. Even Hannah had given her sartorial seal of approval. Jennifer had checked for the somethings old, new, borrowed and blue. (Mum's drop pearl earrings, which they knew to be a present from her parents on her first wedding day, almost 40

426

years ago. These were a resolutely unemotional choice since none of them could ever remember seeing their mother wearing them, her taste veering latterly towards the far more showy; the dress, which had been the first one she tried on in the shop; the Christian Louboutin – one concession to designer fashion – sale shoes beneath, borrowed from Jennifer, who had bought them half a size too small, for £150.00, in the red mist of one shopping jag because they were so very beautiful, and, presumably, because she believed it possible her feet might one day shrink to the point where the shoes fitted; and the ubiquitous baby blue polyester lace garter, purchased by Jennifer and Hannah in a pink-cheeked and giggling foray into Ann Summers one afternoon.) Amanda had been less anarchic and more sentimental than one might have expected. Seemed she was changing her views on quite a lot of things lately . . .

She could see her sisters now, at the front of the church. Thank God the new vicar was progressive and had agreed to marry divorcees. A register office wouldn't have felt the same and a blessing would have felt hypocritical to her. She wanted to be here, for the whole thing. Not because of God, of course. The last time they had all been in here, she had sat with them and none of them had wanted to turn around, afraid of what they might see in the faces of those behind them, but now it was different. She was standing here, waiting to take Mark's arm, and they were up there, straining and turning, waving and smiling.

Now that she knew about Jennifer, she convinced herself she might have guessed. She was, not rounder, but somehow softer at the edges. The colour in her cheeks was clearly natural. And, now that she really scrutinized, her boobs were enormous. Already. Blimey! They were going to play havoc with her sister's penchant for Jackie O shift dresses . . . Cee Cee – the unwilling bridesmaid, dressed the part but not planning to walk the aisle – had taken up proprietary residence between Jennifer and Stephen, thrilled with the baby news, and desperate, as she had pronounced last night, for a brother or sister of her own.

'Whoah, Neddy!' her dad had laughed. 'Don't scare the horses.'

'Am I "the horses" in this scenario?' she spluttered in mock incredulity.

'Damn right you are! It's taken me long enough to get you here. Don't want you thinking about babies now – you'll bolt.'

'I won't, you know,' she muttered into his mouth, kissing him in front of Cee Cee and everyone else. 'Think she might be on to something, as a matter of fact . . .'

Still, with Cee Cee holding court between them, Stephen had his arm along the back of the pew, resting gently on Jennifer's shoulder. Jennifer had sounded tentative, alone with her in the bedroom. 'I don't know,' she had confessed. 'It's all a bit of a shock.'

'But you're happy?'

'I don't think I realized how happy until I saw his face when he first knew,' she answered. 'It was like, I'd forgotten how good it felt to see him happy, to make him happy, you know?'

'I know, more than you know,' Lisa had laughed.

'So, we're all grown up, then, are we? Finally mature, finally sussed?'

'Mum would be proud of us!'

'She was anyway.'

'I know. But now she'd be proud and relieved.'

'Anyway, I wouldn't say all grown up. Or all sussed, for that matter. Like I said, I'm bloody terrified.'

'Proves you're alive, or something like that, doesn't it?'

'Something like that. Maybe we're supposed to be terrified.'

'Maybe we're supposed to take risks.'

'Yeah.'

Lisa had put one hand on Jennifer's tummy then.

'It's way too soon to feel anything.'

'Who's the expert, all of a sudden?'

'Stephen's bought a book.' She rolled her eyes affectionately. 'He read it out loud to me. We'll feel the baby move in a couple of months.' She hesitated. 'If everything's alright.'

'Everything's going to be alright.'

Lisa wondered if anyone else remembered 'Be Thou My Vision' from Mum's funeral a year earlier. Mark made himself concentrate on keeping time with the notes. He needed, very badly, to keep himself in this moment, in this place, at this ceremony. Of course he recognized the song. He just couldn't think about it now.

Amanda was sitting with Ed, tucked into the crook of his arm. Alarming hairstyle aside, Ed had that rare gift of being able to fit in straightaway. Last night had been the first time he'd met most of them. A pretty intimidating crowd, on a fairly high pressure occasion. With jet lag. But it had felt like he'd always been there. He was easy company. Lisa had watched him, standing between Stephen and Andy, drinking beer from a bottle and chatting easily, talking iPods with Hannah, stacking plates in the dishwasher after dinner; his eyes followed Amanda wherever she was in the room, just like he was

going to follow her, once the wedding was over, wherever she decided to go next. Until September. In September he was going back to college, and he'd confessed
to Lisa, he intended to make her stay put with him.

And Hannah was behind her. The bridesmaid, again.
Dressed, this time, to please herself. She'd confessed
to Jennifer, the previous night, how much she hated
the primrose yellow Thai silk dress she'd worn for
Jennifer's wedding a few years earlier.

'But you looked so beautiful, Hannah! Everyone said
so.'

'I felt like a dork!'

'You did not! You spent the whole day lisping to
everyone how much you felt like a princess!'

'Okay then, I *looked* like a dork.'

'You looked like an angel. Mum's favourite picture of
you – the one she had as a screensaver on her computer
– that was taken on my wedding day!'

'I know. Talk about embarrassing!'

'Oh shut up! At least this time it's one of your cool
sisters getting married . . .'

'Too right!'

Hannah was indeed delighted. She'd chosen her own
dress, from a proper shop, and not some poncey bridal
salon, and her own shoes, with a 2" heel, and she hadn't
had to have her hair painfully teased into King Charles
Spaniel ringlets. And today, there was definitely mascara.
Three whole coats.

At the back of the church, Dad had pretty much
stared at her, and when he finally spoke, he had said,
'Blimey, Hannah, you look about 21 years old!'

'In a good way?'

'There *is* no good way for a man's 16-year-old daughter to look like a 21-year-old!'

She'd stuck out her tongue at him, in a reassuringly childish way.

'But you look gorgeous!'

'Thanks, Dad.'

Dad had looked from one to the other of them, and for a horrible moment, Hannah thought he might start to cry, and that set them both off. But he didn't. He looked all proud, and coughed a bit. Shook himself a little, and started to concentrate hard on the music.

So, Lisa thought, as she neared the end of her journey towards Andy, here we all are. And here I am. I never thought I'd be here, but here I am. And thank God I am!

Mark saved his first glass of wine for after his speech. He held it in his hand, to help keep himself steady, as he stood up to deliver his toast. He'd jotted a few things down – even googled 'father of the bride speeches' on his computer, but he'd decided to be brief and off-the-cuff. Now he wasn't so sure that had been the sane approach and rather longed for some cue cards. He didn't do this often, and when he did he had a model or some drawings in front of him as prompts, and never had to say anything that might at any moment make him cry, so this was new territory. He felt his neck redden, as he began to speak, the first few words sounding, to him, shaky and uncertain.

'It's always a bit of a relief to be the first speaker. I daresay I should be funny, but I think I'm going to go with sincere, and I hope firstly that you'll indulge me in that, and secondly, that the groom and his best man have a lot of jokes up their sleeves to make up for me and my sobriety.

'Step-father of the Bride is a rather special position to

be in. Step-father to a teenage girl was another story altogether, and perhaps not one for this speech! We've had our moments, me and Lisa. You don't love your step-children, when you get them. You want to, because you love their mother and she loves them, but you can't, of course. In fact, they rather get in the way, in some situations you might imagine . . . !' Everyone laughed. 'You sort of *have* to fall in love with them – you grow on each other, gradually. Sometimes like roses, sometimes like mould. And then one day, whoof, you find you love them and that you're a part of this weird, wonderful blended family – isn't that what they're calling us these days?! And I wouldn't change it. Nor would Lisa want to change hers, her new one, I know. I might not normally have expected to get to walk my step-daughter down the aisle, but I did today, and I want to thank her for that privilege. She couldn't have looked more beautiful and radiant, and she did a far better job than me of keeping step with the music. That was a little jaunty for me – I'd practised doing it to the "Wedding March" – altogether more sedate! Nor might I ordinarily have expected to get to speak. That, I also do by default, and that, I have to tell you, I wish were otherwise. Your mum would have given anything she had to be here with all of us today, with *you* today, Lisa. I hope she sort of is, somehow. She would have been making this speech, if she had been, and she would have been a thousand times more eloquent than me, because she always was. She'd have been funnier, too, of course. She was always that too. I see so much of her in you, Lisa. And in all of your sisters.'

Mark's voice broke on that last sentence and he paused, looking down at the tablecloth. Hannah saw her dad's knuckles whiten, his fists clenched by his side, and

felt a shiver of pure pain pass through her. But he recovered, and raised his gaze again to the crowd.

'So . . . this is what I think she would have said, if she'd been here. I think she would have said that she adored you. That you'd made her proud every day of your life. That she had a million memories of you stored away, and that the pair of you were laughing in nearly every one of them. I think she would have said that she was so, so glad you were marrying Andy. Some of you,' and he glanced from Jennifer to Lisa, 'know the part – even though she isn't with us anymore – that she played in getting the pair of you here today. She thought he was perfect for you, you know. I remember what she said about you, Andy, the first time we met you. We were washing up, after Sunday lunch, I think, and watching the two of you in the garden, and you were laughing at something Andy had said. She said he was what you needed. She said you were the sort of bloke who'd make her laugh and understand her cry. I said that she was ridiculous, of course. No offence, Andy, but we'd only just met you. Turns out I agree with her. I think she knew you so well because the two of you were so much alike. And so, if I'm right, Andy, mate, and she turns out to be like her mum, my beautiful wife, then you're in for a magical, enchanted, marvellously happy rollercoaster of a life together. So let's drink to that.'

He held aloft the glass of wine.

'To a magical, enchanted, marvellously happy life together. To Lisa and Andy.' Everyone stood and repeated. 'To Lisa and Andy!'

Andy was funny and warm, both together. He couldn't keep his hands off his bride and kept squeezing her

shoulder as he spoke. She would lie her head against his hand, gazing up at him. His best man was funnier, not so warm, and had brought along visual aids documenting the chequered history the two of them had shared since primary school. He told a hilarious joke involving keys and women planted in the audience which might have got lesser men into hot water, but in his hands had the whole marquee falling about. And then the music started.

'Nice one, Dad,' was Hannah's verdict. She was the first of the sisters to get to him, planting a quick kiss on his cheek on her way to the dancefloor, determined to show the dress off to best effect. 'Not too sad, not too sentimental. Just right. You did good.'

He blew her retreating frame a kiss. 'Thanks, kid.'

Amanda threw him a double thumbs-up. She was already dancing with Ed, auburn hair flying. Mark watched Ed kiss Amanda, open-mouthed. Heard Hannah, swinging past them with Vince, entreat them to 'get a room!'

Jennifer came up to the table. Stephen veered off to the left, to the bar, it seemed. She hugged him.

'I loved the speech, Mark,' she said, smiling directly at him. 'Mum would have loved it too, and I know Lisa did. You made her cry. You made us both cry.'

'Thanks, Jen.'

'You've been a brilliant step-father,' she suddenly said. 'I feel like an idiot when I think of how I didn't appreciate it, when I should have done. You loved my Mum, and, even when you two had Hannah, you never once made us feel we weren't important to you. Never once.'

He didn't know what to say to that.

'Just wanted you to know. And you'll be the greatest granddad.' She lay her cheek against his, very briefly, and

then walked off towards Stephen. Mark caught her hand as she passed, and squeezed it tightly.

'Do you remember our wedding day?' Stephen asked her.

'Of course I do. Every wonderful second of it. Don't you?'

'God, no – not every second! I couldn't tell you what my mother was wearing, or what we ate, or what colour the flowers were. I don't even remember what time we got married. I'm a man – we just don't have the right software for that sort of thing.'

'But you remember some of it. Tell me you remember some of it!' They were dancing – the music was slower now.

'I remember the bride. She was bloody gorgeous! She came down that aisle with a smile wider than I'd ever seen. I think she was wearing white . . .'

Jennifer pinched him on the forearm. 'Off white. Ivory really. It's in Mum's attic somewhere – shall I get it out later, remind you?'

'Wouldn't do that – don't think it would fit, and I don't want you getting all depressed about this middle-age spread . . .' He moved the hand he had placed in the small of her back round to the front, stroking her baby belly gently.

'Watch it!' She laughed.

'Oh, I'm watching it, darling. I'm watching it!'

They went off on their own, just the four of them. The speeches were over, and the band had started. The improbable dance couplings of old and young, friend and stranger only found at weddings had begun taking to the floor. As pre-arranged, and with unspoken agree-

ment, they had scooped up their flowing dresses, jammed themselves into Jennifer's car, grateful for her enforced sobriety, and driven the short distance to the field. There were a thousand things to talk about, a thousand things to say. But they were almost silent.

But not sad silent, Hannah thought. She liked being here, with her sisters. She liked belonging to them, being a part of this.

It was almost dusky by the time they arrived, but still warm – like a Mediterranean evening. The sun was setting behind the trees.

Barbara's maple sapling was thriving: strong and healthy. Soon, they'd plant daffodil bulbs all around the base. Wild flowers were growing everywhere now: evening primrose saluted the sunset among the asters, rose mallow and scarlet flax. As she did every time she came here, Amanda thought how right her mum had been, choosing this. No granite headstone or 'walkway of remembrance' at the crematorium could be so much like her. A small brass plaque, no matter what it said, could never summon her up, somehow bring her once again to life, the way this place did. This tree, with its sweet sap, would grow stronger, thicker and taller: its roots thriving in the good soil. It would be here forever – or at least for as long as she could imagine. Its leaves would be always moving, catching the light, and rustling in the breezes. In the autumn, they would flash auburn. It was a good place; it was a good tree.

Jennifer was imagining a round pink baby, legs brace-leted with pudge, lying on a rug, shaded by branches, fascinated by the play of the light through the leaves. She took a deep, deep breath, and held it there for a moment, staunching the tears that, just for the moment, threatened. This wasn't a day for tears.

Lisa looked down at the bouquet in her hands. She opened her mouth to speak, then closed it again, realizing there was no need. It wasn't that there was nothing to say, or that it had all already been said. It was just that they all knew already.

She untied the wide ivory grosgrain ribbon that had tied the stems and the flowers fell softly into her hand. She handed a few to each of her three sisters. Then the four of them bent down in turn, each placing the red, pink and orange gerberas they held on the earth, under the tree. They laid them in a circle around the simple white stick bearing their mother's initials, and stood again, eyes downcast for a few minutes, each in their own world with their mother, just for a moment.

Then Amanda held out both hands to Jennifer and Hannah. Hannah grabbed onto Lisa, and Lisa gave her other hand to Amanda. They walked that way slowly back to the car, their arms swinging.

'Right, come on, you lot!'

'Enough of this maudlin stuff.'

'She'd be ever so cross.'

'She'd *be* at the party.'

'Drinking champagne!'

'Dancing!'

'Flirting with Ed! Who does look, by the way, totally flirt-worthy.'

'I've ruined these heels! Look at them. How can it be muddy? It hasn't rained for weeks . . .'

'Stop moaning! It's not like you paid for them yourself. You can take them off when we get back. They're no good for dancing anyway.'

'You dancing?'

'You asking?'

Want My

sit the website

rstoknow.com

dom and see what

l future generations —

by their own mothers.

sites of interest, free

litional material about

d this novel.